THIS BOOK CONTAINS SCENES OF
EXPLICIT VIOLENCE AND GORE

The Blood of Before

Scott Hale

This is a work of fiction. Names, characters, places, and incidents either are the product of the author's imagination or are used fictitiously, and any relevance to any person, living or dead, business establishments, events, or locales are entirely coincidental.

THE BLOOD OF BEFORE

ISBN-13: 978-0-9964489-4-9

BOOKS BY SCOTT HALE

The Bones of the Earth series

The Bones of the Earth (Book 1)

The Three Heretics (Book 2)

The Blood of Before (Book .1)

The Cults of the Worm (Book 3)

The Agony of After (Book .2)

The Eight Apostates (Book 4)

Novels

In Sheep's Skin

The Body Is a Cruel Mistress (Coming Soon)

CONTENTS

SHE WALKS IN VERMILLION

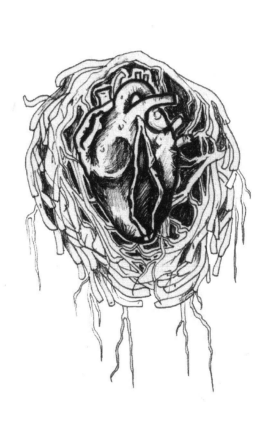

The letter arrived at the exact moment in Amelia Ashcroft's life when she would be most susceptible to its contents. It was 1888, the money she had inherited from her mother and father was diminishing rapidly, and a steady job was but a rumor told in a whisper from a source she could never locate. In her uncle Amon's emaciated scrawl, Amelia was given an apology, a plea for her to return to the family estate, and a promise to be rid of the disappointment she had felt all her life with life itself. The rest was very vague, and by the blots of ink and streaks of black across the parchment, Amelia knew that something was very wrong with her estranged uncle.

She read the letter twelve times before setting it aside.

Unlike some, Amelia had been fortunate as a young girl in that she had not only a mother but also a father; her misfortune was that neither seemed capable of loving her, her siblings, or one another. They were not unpleasant individuals. They did not view their children as burdens unworthy of their fortunes. Every ailment was attended to, and every provision provided. But each action taken by her mother and father was one made cold by indifference and distance. Never did they allow those who craved their attention and affections anywhere closer than arm's length.

Amelia began to take notice of her uncle at the age of ten. She used to sit at his feet, dampening his pant leg with her tears, her body starved for that very thing which her parents seemed so reluctant to give and that he seemed to have in great abundance: Love. Of course, being her elder by seventeen years, Amon was quick to suggest that Amelia spend more time with her older brothers and sister. But what Amon did not realize, and what Amelia knew all too well, was that her siblings, either through observation or inheritance, were without consistent, predictable emotions. They were eager enough to play with Amelia in the forest and in the fields surrounding the estate, but too often did they oscillate between kindness and cruelty.

The thirteenth time Amelia had read the letter she decided to be honest with herself and accept that, despite her uncle's sudden disappearance from the world, from her world, she still missed him and could forgive him for abandoning her.

The fourteenth time Amelia had read the letter her thoughts returned to those moments spent with her uncle traveling the countryside and the unknown paths of the forest, where they weaved with words worlds fitted with wonders from their imaginations.

The fifteenth time Amelia read the letter she regressed to the adolescent girl, who was then expected to engage in dull conversations at even duller parties with those who envied her family's wealth and acted as though they did not.

"Careful now," she remembered Amon whispering to her at a party as he passed, nodding at the obese man who'd been speaking to her for the better part of an hour, "when the hors d'oeuvres run out, you're next."

The sixteenth time Amelia read the letter, which was entirely unnecessary as she had long since memorized its message, she came to the conclusion that she needed to come to a conclusion.

It had been two weeks since her uncle had brought to life the memories laid to rest in the graveyard of her mind. Now, she was enjoying the silence of the city with her children, Ruth and Edmund. Neither child shared the same father, nor had they been old enough to get to know the men, for both bastards had departed years ago for some undisclosed location of Hell. Amelia, with several broken bones, a bloodied nose, and busted lip, had been kind enough to show them the way, first with a butcher's knife and then a well-placed kick down the stairs.

"Mother?" Ruth asked, wide-eyed. "Why don't we go to church like everybody else?"

"Because we are not like everybody else," she said as she ran her fingers through her "godless" child's hair.

Most individuals in the city were not afforded the opportunity to refuse an audience with god at the appointed hour, and yet Amelia had done so every week since her previous husband's passing. Murder, too, generally provoked a response from the local precinct or the victim's family, and yet after each killing she went about her days unscathed. This, she reasoned, was compensation for sitting so diligently all of her life on the edge of despair and knowing there was no other place that would have her. She knew that this was illogical, improbable, but what other explanation existed?

"Someone's coming, Mummy," Edmund cried from the living room. "Someone weird!"

Amelia shushed her children—they had begun to squeal and concoct elaborate tales amongst themselves—made her way to and through the front door, and waited. A carriage led by two large, black horses pulled up beside her squat house, their hooves clapping against the hard earth. At the front of the vehicle sat a gaunt man clad from head to toe in raggedy black clothes too large for his person. Looking closely, Amelia saw that his skin was soft and pink, like a newborn's.

Intrigued, Edmund and Ruth burst through the doorway, glanced at the man, and then hid behind their mother's dress. Here and there, they peeked out around her. Each time, without fail, when their eyes met his, they went stiff, as though the sight of the driver's horribly blue eyes were paralyzing.

"Can I help you, sir?" Amelia asked, disturbed by the man's behavior.

The man offered no response. Behind him, the horses grunted and snorted, steam rising from their wet noses and dispersing into the brisk autumn air.

"If there's nothing, then I must ask you to leave. I'm not one for games and I will show you if needs be."

"Mother is ferocious today," Edmund whispered to his sister, fingers clinging tightly to the fabric of Amelia's dress.

"Quiet you," Ruth hissed back.

Suddenly, without any visible provocation, the man's vacant eyes stirred to life. "My apologies, ma'am," the driver said as he bowed repeatedly. "I've a condition. I don't truly understand it, but I've had it all my life, or so I'm told."

Upon hearing the driver's voice, Edmund and Ruth emerged from behind Amelia to properly introduce themselves. They looked like diminutive adults in their suit and dress. Ruth curtseyed as Edmund outstretched his arm like a proper gentleman.

"Lovely children, ma'am," the driver said, tipping his head in their direction.

"What is it then?" Amelia snapped, placing one hand atop each child's head.

The horses sneered behind the driver as though they were insulting her for being so daft. "I was sent by your uncle Amon, ma'am. I was told to pick you up at this hour, on this day. I was told that you would be awaiting my arrival."

The driver watched as confusion spread first across Amelia's face and then the children's.

"Did the letter not arrive, ma'am?"

"It did."

"Oh, I see. Well, I should be going then, to inform your uncle of your decision. Farewell, ma'am, and I apologize once more for the fright I gave you."

Amelia went to turn away, and then didn't.

The carriage crossed the drowned land, throwing mud upon mud and leaving deep tracks and hoof prints in the road. Amelia looked through the window, at the field of green beside her and sea of gray above, and sighed. Ruth and Edmund sat opposite her, asleep upon one another, their bodies heavy with exhaustion. Occasionally, the carriage would dip into a hole, and in response the children would mumble incoherently as they threw their limbs about in sleepy agitation. This made Amelia laugh—something which she had not done in quite some time. She wanted to join them in their sleep, to hold and see them through troubling dreams, but the driver had warned of violence on the roadway, so she sat as a sentinel at the window, not trusting a man to see dangers only a mother's eyes could.

Amelia found herself thinking of the family estate, but she knew that what she remembered would no longer be when they crossed over onto the property. For a moment her heart fluttered at the idea of being reunited with her mother, father, sister, and brothers, but even this would be impossible. Through disease, brutality, and unexplainable circumstance, each member of the Ashcroft family had been taken from this world. Death had begun with her mother, who had succumbed to an infection and an irrational fear of doctors. After that, once having tasted Amelia's bloodline and finding it favorable, Death became a glutton of it, and one by one, her siblings and relatives fell to Its hunger.

It had grown dark when Ruth and Edmund came to, drool still wet upon their lips. It took them a moment to recognize their surroundings and to remember their departure. The sound of wood bending rose from the floor of the carriage as they crossed a bridge over a surging stream.

"Mummy," Edmund mumbled as he wiped his eyes, "Mummy, I'm so very hungry."

"We'll eat soon, Edmund. Ruth, are you hungry?"

"I can wait," Ruth responded proudly, even as her stomach rumbled.

"Of course you can."

In what remained of the failing light, Amelia saw the outline of a small house atop a small hill. All about it were sticks and branches protruding from the earth, like makeshift headstones or bits of shrapnel from some long forgotten trauma. There were no roads to the house, and the land it sat on was fallow. Amelia thought about who might have lived there and if they lived there still, if they were happy or if they had been shunned there. She wondered if whether they, too, had sat at the edge of despair and, worn by the sights beyond, fell from its ledge.

Amelia searched the dark of the carriage for stowed-away food. Finding it, she broke the bread into three pieces and poured the soup into three bowls. Together, the Ashcrofts ate their late meal ravenously and then slept into the morning hours.

When they reached the outskirts of an upcoming town, the driver stopped the carriage so that they could stretch their legs and relieve themselves in the overgrowth that had sprung up around the road. Despite her upbringing, Amelia had no qualms about squatting in the bushes beside her daughter, nor would she mind shoving the driver's nose into his skull if he had wandered over to watch. She had been accused many times of not being a lady, but Amelia saw nothing ladylike in silence and willful stupidity.

"How far now, sir?" Amelia asked the driver later as they both stood staring out at the town in the distance. A thick fog clung to it, so much so that, had the driver not warned of it, Amelia would have never known the town was there until they were right upon it.

"A day or so. Maybe more, ma'am. The land is strange here and seems to have a mind of its own." The driver scratched at the white stubble that had formed on his tender skin.

Amelia gasped. "Is this Parish?" She knew the town from her youth; her family had acquired many properties here. "Will we have any trouble passing through?"

The driver smiled as he patted one of the great black horses on its rear. "No, I expect not."

Eager to show the awful things it hid, the fog began to part as the carriage drew closer to Parish. At first, Amelia covered Edmund's and Ruth's eyes, but the town had more road than she had patience to keep her children restrained. It seemed as though a pestilence had passed through, a pestilence that had affected not only the people there, but their creations as well. The buildings themselves looked diseased and decayed, their collapsed roofs host to countless weeping sores. Stone walls ran through Parish like dividers between the districts. Each one was mottled, encrusted like they had scabbed over. But what Amelia found most disturbing were the strange vermillion veins that ran between each of the houses. The pulsating, root-like structures were everywhere, and the lattice they formed over the ground had choked out any life that had once dared to rise out of the land.

Edmund and Ruth coughed and gagged as they surveyed the blight. Even the air smelled and tasted of wet, sour decay. Amelia went to her children; worried about airborne infection, she pounded her fist on the wall of the carriage until the driver got the hint and sped up the horses.

"We'll be through this soon enough," he yelled back.

"I don't like it here at all," Ruth said, crossing her arms tight against her chest.

"Sissy! I like it here very much," Edmund teased.

"No you don't!" Ruth paused and looked at her mother. "Does he?"

"Of course he does, he's a boy."

"No I'm not!"

"You're not a boy? Edmund, there are many things I don't know in this life but of that I am certain." Amelia laughed nervously, hoping that a bit of humor would distract them.

Amelia's words, however, washed over Edmund with no effect whatsoever. Ruth jabbed her brother's side. The two began to quarrel over how much they annoyed one another and who their mother loved best. Amelia moved to silence them as the carriage came to a sharp halt, jerking its passengers forward.

After calming Edmund and Ruth, Amelia stepped out of the carriage to confront the driver. Before she could find the man or the words to throw at him, however, she was stunned. Beside the road, where the mist was thin and pink, a cemetery sat, each of its graves gutted. Towards the center of the cemetery, amongst a circle of chipped headstones, a silhouette stood, ragged and bent, plunging its crooked shovel into the sweating earth.

"Why have we stopped?" Amelia asked aloud, unable to take her eyes off the figure.

When the driver did not respond, Amelia marched around to the front of the carriage and found that he was missing. The horses stood there indifferently, their jaws clamping down hard and chewing on the veins tangled around their hooves.

Ruth called out from inside the carriage, "Mummy, what's happening?"

"The horses are tired, Ruth, and want to rest a bit," Amelia lied.

From out of the fog the driver came, hobbling onto the road.

Amelia noted the bright red stain on his lips. "What the hell are you doing?" she yelled.

"Relieving myself, ma'am. The horses tire quickly here, like you said to the children. We will be off soon enough."

Amelia glared at the withered man. "What... has happened here? Where is everyone? I've seen Parish and this is not how I remember it." She exhaled and gathered herself. "What is that man doing to the graves?"

"He's searching for the bodies of his wife and daughter," the driver said nonchalantly. "The rest, as you can see, have been carried off."

It was true: The graveyard had been upturned, hollowed out; each casket broken, busted open, and left to rot beside the hole it was meant to occupy.

"How do you know this?" Amelia inched towards her compartment, her children waiting on its edge like hounds to be set upon the digger. "What happened here?"

"He does not think," the driver continued, ignoring her, "he digs. And when he stops, he will die. That was his command."

From inside the carriage Edmund shouted, "Mummy, I'm scared now."

"It's fine, darling," Amelia assured her son.

She felt herself almost fall backward as her heel became caught in a

11

bundle of veins.

"You didn't answer my question," she said through her teeth to the driver.

"It'll be dark soon. Master Amon will explain all. Please, for your children's sake, let us be on our way while the sun still holds the sky."

Amelia moved to argue with the man, but she was willing to abstain from demanding his explanation if it meant leaving this place sooner. She nodded, repulsed and enraged, and climbed into the carriage to be with her children. What was she doing? How could she let herself be brought into this situation? She felt no true danger, but her senses, all five of them, were poor barometers in a place so senseless.

In seconds, hours passed, and when all the light left the world, Amelia finally succumbed to the rhythmic rocking of the carriage and slept. A dream overcame her, as though it had been lying in wait. In a matter of moments, she shed her years until she was nine again. Amelia, with a candle in one hand and the side of her nightgown in the other, was now no longer in the carriage, but in the Ashcroft estate. She moved through the house quickly, quietly, her presence no more than a shadow upon the curtains, a creak upon the stairs—a whisper of life in the dead of night.

Amelia found the basement easily enough, but what she could not understand was why she needed to find it at all. Her parents had forbidden entry into it, and that had always been enough, as the only promise the basement held for Amelia was one of spider bites and cobwebs. But that night had been a restless night. As she lay in her bed, bored and burning up, she began to think, to consider things she hadn't before, as though some invisible entity were by her bedside, whispering details into her mind she had otherwise missed.

The candle was of little help to Amelia in the basement. Somehow, it seemed the darkness had taken on the properties of light, leaving her tiny, flickering flame all but useless in that stygian place. It was strange, and it made her feel uncomfortable, so naturally she turned on her heels to go. But before she could, she felt it, the air rushing past her legs, like something was breathing it in at the center of the room. Shivering with anxious curiosity, Amelia swallowed hard and padded across the basement, until she reached the center and the source.

She went to her knees to see it more clearly, the gaping hole in the floor that was taking up all the air in the room. Her arms started to itch. She felt a tickle on the soles of her feet. She set the candle down beside the hole and leaned forward, the sweaty strands of her hair sliding past her face. Beyond, in the darker darkness there, Amelia heard a rustling of cloth and what sounded like metal grinding against stone. She leaned in closer, felt her knees slide forward, as though the air had become the ocean and she was caught in its current. Her ears pricked; there was another sound, further down—were they words?—and when she went to answer their summons, something wrapped itself around her.

Amelia screamed. In defiance, not thinking, she threw herself toward the hole. She gasped as the grip tightened around her stomach.

"Stop, stop," she heard a man say.

Amelia looked over her shoulder, and through her tears she saw her father. He shook his head, picked her up, and held her across his arms. Amelia muttered a half-hearted apology. Her father smiled back. It felt good to be held by him, so she put her head to his chest and didn't say anything, not even when she felt his hot tears falling down between her braids.

Amelia's father carried her back to bed. Between the two an unspoken promise was made.

Amelia woke up, her face wet and mouth dry, the dream still fresh in her mind. Thinking back, she realized that had been the only moment her father had held her. How had she forgotten it? What else had she forgotten? What other silent signals and strained exchanges had she misinterpreted in her ignorant youth and selfish adolescence? The basement—what secrets did the basement hold, and why, with one uneventful night, had her curiosity been suddenly satisfied?

Cracks of morning split the dawning sky. Amelia's eyes fluttered open and she looked through the window to find they'd finally reached the end of Parish.

How is that possible? Slowly, she opened the door and leaned out to have a look back at the way they had come. Parish, the town that had taken them an entire day to cross, stood behind her, the entrance in sight, no more than a kilometer away.

Between the carriage, the Ashcroft estate, and the hill it sat upon, was the swath of marshy land that Amelia and her siblings had spent so much time playing on. The Ashcroft estate itself was located at the hill's summit, which was now crowned with the very same trees Amelia's father had worked so hard to keep at bay. With no ax to stifle their growth, the trees had flourished and reclaimed the point as their own.

Unfortunately, the same could not be said for Amelia's family; their time had come and gone. This meeting, this strange and unexpected meeting with Amon would be nothing more than one ghost acknowledging the other and feeling all the worse for doing so. There would be no growth, no reclamation; just climbing into graves that had long been dug.

"Are you happy to be going home, Mummy?" Ruth asked dreamily as she stared at the soft blue sky.

"I am happy, because I am with you, Ruth, and your sneaky brother," Amelia said as she reached over and pinched Edmund's already reddening cheeks. It seemed they had forgotten about Parish, so for their sake, she would, too.

"Will he like us?" Ruth's voice shook.

"Without a doubt. I am certain of it." Amelia watched a small smile form upon her daughter's face. "Are you excited to meet your great-uncle, Edmund?"

Edmund shrugged. "Why should I be?"

Amelia thought of their fathers, of every cruel and callous individual in their lives, and felt her innards twist and constrict at their memories. In that moment, she saw her son not as he was but as he would be, a man grown and sculpted from his experiences, and knew that her efforts alone would not be enough. Ruth, too, would prove problematic, but those days of raggedy dresses and loveless nights would come much later to the girl who kept close to her mother's side. Could Amon, surely still a man of means, offset this future or delay it entirely? Is that why she let herself be whisked away by the driver with violent blue eyes and translucent flesh to this nightmarish part of the country? Perhaps these ghosts could mend the damages done after all and salvage what life was left for those still living.

They were still far enough away from the estate that the forest and the hill it sat upon fit comfortably between Amelia's thumb and index finger. One by one, worn down by the rays of the sun, the carriage's passengers answered the summons of sleep.

When Amelia, Ruth, and Edmund awoke, they found that the open countryside had been replaced by a corridor of trees. They had reached the hill, which was the only piece of the world Amelia could truly say was her own. Looking out, she found the forest path aglow with the golden shafts of light cutting through the canopy. Entranced, Amelia

THE BLOOD OF BEFORE

rapped her fist upon the wall of the carriage until the driver brought it to a halt.

"The forest is beautiful, ma'am, but you of all should know that the creatures that live within it have no fear of man," the driver said as he helped them out of the carriage.

While Amelia and her children stretched their legs and backs, she said, "Well, then we are fortunate in that I am a woman, Ruth a girl, and Edmund a boy."

"Am I not a man?" the driver asked with genuine concern as he watched them move towards the opening in the trees.

"Of course," Amelia said. "You've brought us through hell unscathed. You're an odd man, a good man, I think, but a man nonetheless."

The driver nodded at this, pleased. He bowed and turned to tend to the horses.

On the other side of the opening, Amelia and her children found a field brimming with life; it was one of those rare, impossible places that somehow had been left untouched by man's machines and machinations. The grass came up to Amelia's knees. Its warm, gentle touch was a welcome change from the cold countryside air and the rigid seats of the carriage. Flowers of all kinds and colors speckled the area through which they moved, and they minded each one like it were the last of its species. Above, from their leafy perches, small birds—blue, white, and yellow—whistled and sang, their voices intertwining, complimenting each other, as though each were telling their own part of a story.

"Can we stay?" Ruth asked, going silent as she watched a rabbit hop through the field.

"Can we?" Edmund echoed, much to Amelia's surprise.

The city's palette was limited, uninspired. Amelia was surprised that her children spoke of their intoxication with their surroundings, but there was no denying that she, too, felt dizzied by it all.

They spent a half an hour in the field. Amon had made Amelia wait years before contacting her; as far as she was concerned, he was on her time now. She regained her senses, her smarts, gathered her children up, and headed for the opening. In her time in the clearing, she became determined to not let Amon's inevitable invitation to return to the estate sway her as soon as it passed his lips.

"They're here, too?" Edmund had lagged behind. He was staring at something in the grass.

"What's that?" Amelia, with Ruth in her shadow, went to her son. "Who?"

She twisted her mouth as she saw what Edmund was pointing to. Beyond the overgrowth, where the land slanted, a tree stump sat with an ax buried in it. The stump and the ax were surely a century old—undoubtedly, the scene had been her father's work—but somehow, for some reason, the soil around the stump was ruddy and wet, and the ax head glistened, as though recently used. Amelia crouched down and then jumped to her feet. Around the base of the stump, feeding in and out of what was now clearly a puddle of blood, were the vermillion veins from Parish. What were they? Why were they here? Amelia said nothing, took Edmund's hand, and marched back to the carriage.

The trees were at their thickest surrounding the house, so as they approached, Amelia was only able to catch glimpses of her childhood home. First, she saw the gate, which was now broken and unmanned—anything could enter the property, and probably already had. Then, she saw flashes of the house's white pillars, ivy-wreathed and sun-dulled. As the carriage went around natural roadblocks, she saw windows glinting through the foliage, too dirty to do much else but bounce the light off them.

"Is it close?" Edmund squeaked.

Amelia nodded and then, as the carriage cleared the last line of trees, took a deep breath as the house came fully into view. The Ashcroft home looked awful. Time had not been kind to it. The white paint had grayed, and the foundation had cracked and sunk into the ground. The porch and the balconies appeared as though they would collapse at any moment. Even inside the carriage, she could hear the house rattling, moaning—complaining about the cruel human creatures that had forced it to go on for so long.

But despite its state, Amelia could not help but be moved to tears. She wept, and she wept hard. She balled her fists and bit her lip and sucked back the hot saliva in her mouth as she cried and failed to keep her composure. She had never been fond of the house when she lived there; often times, she had dreamt of destroying it, setting fire to it, and yet here it was, as ruined as she would have liked it to be, and she was crying.

The carriage came to a stop beside the twelve lichen- and weed-choked steps that led up to the house. As Amelia wiped her eyes, Edmund and Ruth burst out of the compartment and started up the stairs, their excitement surmounting what little good sense they had. Amelia didn't say anything—in fact, she was tempted to do the same—and took the driver's hand when he came around to help her out.

"Thank you," she said, his clammy grip making the hairs stand up on her arm.

She watched as he unloaded their belongings and left them on the ground at the foot of the stairs. She felt a flare of anger and then hated herself for how quickly her lost sense of entitlement had returned.

"I can go no farther," he said, his violent blue eyes downcast.

Amelia nodded, gathered everything up, and beckoned for her children, who had become almost animalistic in their excitement, to do the same.

"Thank you, sir," Ruth said, smiling as she skipped up the stairs with her bags.

"Thank you, sir," Edmund said, copying his sister in word and action.

"You're a good man," Amelia said, her arms weighed down at her sides by her belongings. "I couldn't have asked for a better driver. I hope to see you again?"

The driver grinned; his teeth looked too small, too closely packed, as though he still had all his baby teeth. "It was a pleasure, ma'am."

Amelia bowed slightly and, with her children waiting on the porch, disappeared into the dark of the house.

The driver stayed where he stood. His waxy lips began to quiver, to tremble. He cracked his neck and a bone broke through. His muscles started to spasm. His pink flesh became cloudy and muddled, and lost its consistency. A viscous fluid like bloody milk leaked from his pores; his shoes filled up with the substance until they overflowed. In a freezing instant, his skin became as hard as bark and by the wind was peeled away like paint chips.

Behind the driver, or what was currently left of him, the great, black horses, still bound to the carriage, gave out one final whine and then began their reversion. Together, the man and his two beasts decayed in the shadow of the Ashcroft house. They had been born at the same time, so it seemed fitting they should die at the same time as well. Their lives had been simple lives; no more than a summation of commands in the dark. They had done well as forms, but now it was time for them to return, to be whispers amongst whispers, mouths amongst mouths, in the black chambers of their vermillion heaven.

Amon was waiting for them in the foyer. Amelia's heart rioted in her chest as her eyes fell upon him. Ruth and Edmund had gone silent as well, their energy sapped by the sight of the fabled uncle who was finally before them.

Before Amelia realized what was happening, two maids closed in on her and her children and reached out to take their belongings. Amelia relinquished the bags, but not before getting a good look at the women. Their outfits were traditional enough, but covering the lower halves of their faces was a piece of cloth, like a doctor's mask. Were they sick? Infectious? Were they afflicted with what had run its course through Parish?

"It's fine," Amon said, his voice soft and deep like a practiced storyteller's. "You are home now."

He approached Amelia, smiling behind the loose strands of graying black hair that had fallen across his face. He took her hand and kissed her forehead. She meant to turn away, but he had been quick, and she had wanted it more than she realized.

Amon led Amelia and her children to the dining room, where they found their meals already prepared and waiting. The dinner table was covered in candles, and the ornate walls that surrounded the room were covered in the wild shadows they cast onto them. Each member of the Ashcroft family took a seat, and not one spoke to another until their plates were clean.

Amelia set down her silverware, wiped her mouth. She smoothed out her dress and, looking at her uncle, who hadn't taken his eyes off her, said harshly, "Where have you been?"

"Everywhere," Amon said, nodding. "China, India, and parts of Africa, and other places I'd rather forget."

"Why?" Edmund asked, bits of food pasted to his face.

Amon smiled warmly. "I was looking for something."

"Did you just now return?" Amelia asked, already hanging on his every word like she had when she was younger. She fought away the childish, girlish feelings she felt, but she knew they would be back soon enough.

"No." Amon looked into his lap, ashamed. "I've been here for eleven years. I'm sorry, Amelia."

Amelia put her hand to her mouth. The pain that she felt from his words was greater than any inflicted upon her by the dead and damnable. Eleven years, he had been back for eleven god damn years.

Sensing her mother's hurt, Ruth took Amelia's arm and pressed her head against it.

Anger left Amelia's face contorted, ugly. Her cheeks twitched while she held back every curse and insult. "Why did you write me? Why now? After all… after all this time? You could have let me be."

"Tonight, when the children are asleep, or tomorrow, if you are too weary, I'll tell you." He looked at Edmund and Ruth with his kind, tired eyes. "It's a tale too frightening for you two."

"Not for me!" Edmund said. He stood up to assert his manliness, but tripped over his feet instead.

"All the same, Edmund, I think your mother would agree."

"Edmund?" Amelia looked at Amon, confused. "How did you know his name is Edmund?"

Amon opened his mouth to answer but stopped as the two maids from earlier entered and began clearing the table. They made no noise as they worked. When the one with brown hair leaned forward to take a plate, Amelia leaned in close, listening for breaths she was sure the maid wasn't taking, because it seemed like she wasn't breathing. The maid grunted, reared up, and quickly walked way. But Amelia had noticed another curiosity: The maid's facial structure seemed peculiar, deformed; the way the mask hung and clung to the curves of her bones… it was as though the maid had no mouth at all.

"I'm sorry," Amon said after the maids left the dining room. "I've let most of the old ways and customs go over the years. No need when you're the only one." He looked at his niece and sighed. "Amelia, we have not spoken nor seen each other for years… years. I can't believe it's been… But I did not forget about you. In fact, most of my days were concerned with your wellbeing. Your fortune, you see, was squandered by your siblings. Your father, for reasons I promise to you I'll reveal later, gave me a share of the wealth much larger than I could have ever expected. So I took it upon myself to help you when I could, from a distance, like a hypocrite, like… like the kind of person you and I swore never to be so many… so many years ago."

"What's a hypocrite?" Ruth asked.

"Someone who says something is wrong but does that thing anyway," Amelia said, jaw clenched. "What have you really done, Amon?"

"Only what I could to see that you were safe. There were some things that I could not stop, but now that I see them before me, I know that it was worth it."

Amon looked at Edmund and Ruth. Amelia knew immediately he was referring to their fathers.

"I made sure to pay those who needed to be paid, but I did not want to control your life entirely. I knew you would have none of that. I wanted you to live, to forget me and this house."

Amelia leaned in closer to her uncle. She wanted to stay angry with him, but she couldn't; however, he didn't need to know that, not yet. The candles before them were failing fast—it seemed they were good for this night only—and Ruth and Edmund were too tired to sit upright. Like her children, Amelia needed a bed, a place of rest where she could lie and make sense of the madness Amon had brought to her life.

"Why am I here, Amon?" she whispered. "Why did you bring me back?"

Amon cleared his throat and brought his lips to her ear and said, "Because I desperately need your help."

Twenty minutes later and they were on the second floor, Amon taking the lead, carving away the darkness of the Ashcroft house with the lantern swinging from his arm. His mood had improved after the first wave of confessions. After his plea to Amelia for aid, he changed the topic and shared stories with her children about their mother. Amelia went along with the act; her uncle was a man who had spent the majority of his life in solitude, in the forgotten corners of the world, so she expected some eccentricities. But what did he want of her? As she had watched him laugh and tell jokes, she searched for signs of weakness, for hints of his plight, but there was nothing. If he had told the truth, if he had truly been watching her all these years from his wooded seclusion, then why did he need her at all? That kind of power, Amelia thought, was the kind that could solve just about any problem. Then again, if it wasn't, and if he had truly saved her, who was she to refuse him?

"I know a lot has happened today," Amon said, stopping at Amelia's old room. "I've hurt you, and my reasons for bringing you here are selfish, I know."

"Amon," Amelia interrupted, "did you... have something to do with the buying of my house in the city?"

"I did."

"And the menial tasks my neighbors, my neighbors who otherwise despise me, offered when I was running out of money?"

"I only asked of them that they would give you a chance. I know how proud you are." Amon went a few feet down the hall and planted himself before the guest bedroom. "Edmund, Ruth, you'll sleep here tonight. We should like for your mother to get some good, good rest."

"My husbands?" Amelia added.

Amon looked at her and ushered Ruth and Edmund into the guest bedroom.

Amelia expected Ruth and Edmund to run out of the room screaming the moment they saw a skeletal tree outside the window, but they didn't. Much to her surprise, they scoured every corner and crevice. They tested their bed for comfort and the floorboards for creaks that would give away potential late night excursions. In seconds, they had settled in. If she took them away, back to the dreary city, where nothing was good and no one was good to them, what would they think of her?

"Can you stay in here without bothering your mother?" Amon asked as Ruth and Edmund staked out their sides of the bed. "She needs a good night's sleep."

"After everything, that might be too much to hope for, Uncle, but I am exhausted." She smiled at her children. "Goodnight, my lovelies."

Amelia was asleep as soon as her head hit the pillow. The dream began immediately; perhaps, like its sister, it had been waiting all this time to show itself. In the dream, Amelia was running—no, gliding—down the hallways of the Ashcroft house. Vision blurred and doubled, she floated towards some unknown, unalterable location. In rapid succession, the walls changed from plaster, to wood, to wet cobblestone, and then earth. Farther on, she spotted torches flaring in their sconces, threatening to set fire to whatever they touched.

When the deep, raspy breaths started, she tried to steer off-course, but it was impossible: Her body was no longer her own. She panicked, and as she panicked, the darkness itself took form; it thickened, began to contract and expand like a black heart beating fast. She tried to speak, tried to call out for help, but before anyone could answer, if there was anyone that could answer, the darkness surged forward and engulfed her completely.

For a moment, she stood disoriented in black nothingness, her senses dampened to the point of almost non-existence. They came back to her slowly, but as they did, it may have been better had they not come back at all. Touch returned and suddenly she felt a great weight upon her chest that made it difficult to breathe. Then came hearing, but all she heard was a persistent droning, a thick chord of unending noise that made her teeth hurt. Next was taste. With it a flood of foulness—rotted food with notes of excrement—that made her retch. At that point, she begged the blackness to leave it at that, but vision arrived regardless, and oh how she wished it had not.

Amelia found herself standing in a large and overwhelmingly beautiful ballroom. All along the walls of this room sat men, women, and children, one hundred in all, in various states of death and decay. The fresher corpses, the ones that still possessed a bit of flesh, appeared familiar to Amelia, though she didn't know why. By the clothing the dead wore, it was obvious they were from different periods of time, but what were they doing here together?

A whimper of fright escaped Amelia's lips as her eyes followed the chains that stretched from their feet across the tiled floor, to the gaping hole in its center. She went to it, leaned over it; found within it a staircase that spiraled downward into untold depths.

The weight across Amelia's chest shifted and she struggled to breathe. A scratching sound stole her from her moment of discomfort. She looked up to the ceiling—*That's not the ceiling*, she realized. *The room is upside down*—and found Ruth and Edmund above her, over her, on their hands and knees, carving their names into the floor with shards of glass. Blood dripped from their jagged signatures, dotting her arms, getting in her eyes. She reached for her children, then froze. Something moved beneath her skin and started scratching on her bones.

And then she woke up.

Her eyes fluttered open. She waited for them to adjust to the dark. And when they didn't, she realized why. A small, black creature sat on her chest, its mouth agape, staring at Amelia with its infected yellow eyes. Its pointed chin moved up and down as though it were laughing.

Amelia struggled to be free, but it was no use—her arms would not move, and her ankles were held down by something at the end of the bed. She tried to scream, but the creature shifted its weight until she was silenced. It moved closer, its acrid breath rolling off its sore-marked mouth and into Amelia's. She threw up all over herself.

The bed dipped down beside her and she closed her eyes, too afraid to acknowledge the additional horror that had come to torture her. Broken teeth clamped down on her wrist, while leathery lips sucked on the tips of her fingers. Amelia whimpered as a fat, coarse tongue made circles on her thigh and then slowly worked its way up.

"No!" she wheezed.

She thought of her children—lovely Ruth, handsome Edmund—and the promises she had made them, the promises she had made to herself. She had to live, if only long enough to get them out of here.

"No! No! No!"

She thrashed and bucked her body. All at once, she regained complete control of her arms. Her hands shot out and grabbed the creature on her chest by its bristly throat and squeezed. The scaly exterior ruptured; bloody mucus seeped in between her fingers.

She only caught a glimpse of the serpentine thing gnawing on her fingers before it slid away, disappearing into the cracks in the floor.

Amelia kicked her feet back and forth until she shook free of the root-like fingers that bound them. Her head snapped to the sound of the door opening, where the creature that had sat down beside her—a hairy, four-armed bi-pedal—was slipping into the hall.

Amelia crawled out of bed, staggered to her feet, and ran out of the room, hoping to get to her children before anything else did.

The ground coughed up clouds of dust as Amelia's feet pounded against it. The hallway was dark, but she didn't need a light to know where she was going. She cupped the doorknob to the guest bedroom and hurried inside.

"Ruth? Edmund?" she called out, her voice cracking under the strain. "Wake up, right now. Please, we have to go."

She went to the bed and found they were not there. She grabbed the sheets, which were still tangled, still warm from their tiny bodies. She pressed her nose to the pillows, smelled them in the indentations where they had lain their heads. Her stomach sank. All the blood in her body rushed to her head. *Where are they? Oh god, where are they?*

The little courage she had managed to muster minutes ago had already fled. Like wax beneath a flame, she felt herself melt under the heat of mounting madness. She strained her ears for sounds she desperately needed to hear—footsteps on floorboards, giddy whispers from shadowy places—but there was nothing.

"Ruth! Edmund!" Amelia cried as she hurried out of the room, past her own.

She made for the stairs, shouting every step of the way. She knew she should stay quiet, stay vigilant, as the horrors that had attacked her were undoubtedly nearby, but her children were missing, which meant that her logic and common sense were as well.

"Ruth! Edmund!"

The house swayed as Amelia prowled its corridor, the bitter wind that moved it whistling through all the cracks and crevices. She held her head tightly as the condemning voices inside it gnawed at her sanity. Her feet moved independently. She retreated into thought, as the path she followed now was one she had walked countless times over, when she had been young and lonely.

She found the small stairwell at the second floor's end and descended it. Fighting back the urge to find her children on her own, because she couldn't do this on her own, not this time, she hurried towards the library.

At the furthest end of the library, the fireplace cackled and sneered, mocking the man that fed it. Amon looked over his shoulder while he threw a book into the flames. Seeing Amelia in the library, he wept. The uncle she had sat down with at dinner was no more; his confidence and his kindness had been eroded away by the secret his face now told her he held.

Amon gestured for Amelia to have a seat in one of the two chairs beside the fire. When she wouldn't, he did so himself, sinking into the cushions as though they were made of quicksand.

"Where are they?" Amelia spat out the words, her skin turning red from the heat of blaze. "Where. Are. They?"

"With the house," he said. "Please, sit. This will take a moment, Amelia."

"I don't have a moment, Amon," she said, balling her hands. Her nightgown clung to her sweating body. "What have you done? Where are they?!"

"I know where they are, and they are safe," Amon assured. "Listen to my story, as you've done so many times before, and when I'm finished, we will get them. Together."

The Ashcroft house was massive, its hiding places many, and the creatures that inhabited it beyond comprehension. Her children could be anywhere, and she could search for years and never find their bodies.

Amelia took a seat in the chair opposite Amon, dug her nails in the fabric, and said, "Get on with it."

Amon struggled to find his words. "I wanted so much for things to be different, Amelia, and I tried so very hard to see that they were. I hoped that we would never meet again, and that you would forget me, and that the world would forget us, and that it would be as though none of this had ever existed."

"No, stop. Say what needs to be said." Amelia gritted her teeth.

"Our family wasn't always wealthy or relevant," Amon began, his eyes glinting. "Our predecessors were poor and even poorer human beings. They lied and cheated their way through life and prospered from others' misfortunes. Eventually, their prosperity brought them to this part of the countryside, and in its untamed wilds, they saw potential."

"I've no time for this," Amelia said, standing.

Amon jumped to his feet. With eyes just as dark as the beating blackness in her dream, he pointed at her chair until she sat.

"Here, on this hill, where they fancied themselves kings and queens, they found something beneath the earth, something ancient. And they woke It up.

"It spoke to them, made promises only things such as Itself could fulfill. Our predecessors did not hesitate, did not question Its motives. They accepted Its offerings and Its terms and set out to leave their blighted mark on the world."

"Those creatures…" Amelia's flesh crawled as she recalled the monstrosities that had straddled her body.

Amon nodded and said, "Smaller parts of a greater whole. Forms of whispers and mouths." He cleared his throat, threw another novel into the fire, and continued. "It wanted our predecessors' children, and so they fed It their children. The house grew larger, our family's influence greater. With it, they carved a place for themselves in the countryside, erected Parish and Cairn, and other settlements now fallen. Businesses bore the Ashcroft name and backing, and the elite and the powerful suddenly found themselves vying for our family's good graces.

"The sacrifices continued, for Its hunger was ceaseless. The sacrifices became formal in who was involved and how it was carried out.

The marked children suffered the sins of their fathers, as all children do, and through this controlled killing, our family strengthened and It continued to secure Its dark place in our world."

"W-what is It?" Amelia stuttered. For a moment, she had forgotten about her children. She felt awful for it.

"A parasite eternal," Amon whispered, looking over his shoulder as the floor creaked outside the library. "I know this, all of this, because your father told me. Your mother knew as well and distanced herself from you and your siblings to minimize the pain that would come with your deaths. It was their responsibility to see the horror fed Its fair share of misery. They tried to circumvent the contract; they took townsfolk and travelers into the forest and fed It their heads. But in the end, you see, It would only have what It was promised. Your mother and father... they couldn't do it. They tried to remain unattached, tried not to love you and your siblings, but they couldn't do it. Your father, he trusted me and told me everything, and then he sent me away to find something, anything, to put an end to all of this."

Amelia sat in silence for a moment, numbed and bewildered. She recounted her memories as a girl and doubted their veracity. Thoughts of her mother and father, whom she'd had such disdain towards for so many years, moved her to tears. She felt betrayed and manipulated, hopeless and helpless.

"Your mother's and father's and siblings' early deaths were not the work of that beast but unfortunate circumstances. When I returned to this house and found the family line all but severed, I begged It to become heir to this awful burden so that you may live a life of normalcy, of ignorance. It accepted begrudgingly, for It had little choice, and you were gone. But when I learned I could not have children, It became enraged, flooding my mind with temptations, telling me anything to bring you back onto the grounds.

"After all my scheming to keep you safe, and all the love I had for you ... I couldn't do it, Amelia. I could not do it.

"So I made another deal, the most ambitious to date, or so It told me. It had driven me insane in Its lust for you. I am a terrible person and I expect no mercy in death. I..."

Amon paused, ashamed. He looked at Amelia pleadingly. "I did as your father and mother. I resorted to murdering strangers. And when suspicions arose, I invited the town, I invited all of Parish, to the house. Almost everyone came, for I promised gifts, and who would not want to be in our great and old family's favor?

"I let them in, and when everyone had arrived, I locked the doors. You, see." Amon paused and started to laugh. "You see, ha, I thought... you understand, right? I mean, so many people... Parish wasn't a good place to begin with. If I gave It so many people..." Amon shuddered and licked his lips. "In fifteen minutes, It had killed hundreds. The room where It took them... if anyone should find it..."

Amon pressed his hands against his face. "I didn't expect It to, I didn't want It to, but It must've felt my guilt, because It gave me the tools to make everything better.

"I don't think It really needs the bodies. Or maybe It does. I don't know. But It gave me something, a piece of Its power. And It worked, because I was ready to end it there, kill myself. I couldn't do it any-more."

"What did It give you, Uncle?" Amelia whispered.

"The power to create." Amon smiled at the absurdity of the state-ment. "It can create—you've seen Its creations—and It lent that power to me. So I did. I took a piece of It with me and went to Parish. I didn't think about the ramifications of taking It off the estate. I just wanted to save myself, make myself feel better for what I had let happen.

"I spread the roots there, those vermillion veins, and with the hell-ish tools It gave me, I repopulated Parish the best that I could. My imitations, they had their limitations; they were thoughtless, direction-less, and dependent upon those damned veins. I fed them, clothed them. I gave them personalities and purpose. It's funny; me, the mon-ster, teaching monsters how to be human. But it didn't matter. They weren't real people. They couldn't act like real people. So I abandoned them. I'm sure they've all gone or died now. It's for the best."

"You let It out, didn't you?" Amelia said accusingly.

Amon nodded. "I did," he said. "I did. It's a simple thing, this hor-ror, but now, after so many centuries, I think It finally wants more. Something more than bodies. I did, Amelia, I did let It out. And now It's spreading from the very wound I tried so desperately to heal.

"So here we are now. The family tradition continued. It aims to persuade you, Amelia, and will let you in closer than It ever has me. My life is nearly over, and It needs a successor. If you refuse, It need only seek out Edmund or Ruth. I have the means. Will you kill It?"

Amelia stood in Amon's room, staring at the maid uniforms laid out neatly across the bed. A thin layer of dust atop a milky puddle coated the floor around the frame.

"Where are they?" she asked as Amon entered the room, a black dagger with a wicked blade and red engravings in his hand. "Ruth and Edmund. I will not do this until I've seen them."

Amon ignored her and said, "So many years lost in finding this. I was married once, you know. You would've been good friends. She was so…" He cleared his throat as his eyes dimmed and looked inward. "I found the dagger in Africa, in a village built over a swamp. The elder there was happy to be rid of it. I assume It would have destroyed the dagger if It could, but It hasn't. That gives me some hope."

"Where are they?" Amelia persisted.

Amon cocked his head and mouthed words of protest. He looked at Amelia longingly as the hand that held the dagger twitched. "The house wants you. It thinks It can use your being a mother against you to get what It wants."

Amon went to where the wallpaper was torn and pulled it down. It looked like flesh, because it was flesh. It fell to the floor and bunched up over his feet. Behind where it had been, there was a hole, and beyond it, wrapped in throbbing, black muscles and taut, red tendons, Ruth and Edmund hung, alive but unmoving.

Amelia screamed and rushed past Amon. "Get off me!"

He pulled her back from the writhing prison. "They are safe, Amelia."

Amelia spun around and buried her face in her uncle's shoulder. In between sobs, she said, "They're all I have left."

"It won't kill them because It doesn't want this to end, the arrangement." Amon placed his hand on the back of Amelia's head. "It wants things to go back to the way they were before I took over."

"Why?" Amelia pulled away from her uncle and ripped the dagger out of his hand. "How can you be so certain?" She looked at her children's contorted bodies in the house's bloody chest and felt sick.

"Time means nothing to It. The horror wants the world to suffer slowly. I've heard Its whispers and seen Its dreams. It is bound by rules and laws just as everything else is. It cannot kill our family entirely because It is not yet strong enough, cognizant enough to act on Its own. It has spread to Parish, but It doesn't know what to do there. But It's close, though, so very close to becoming more than whispers and promises. And if we are to be free, truly free, now is the time to strike

It down, before It becomes too aware, too wanting."

"What if you're wrong?" Amelia asked, unable to tear her eyes from her children suspended in gore.

"Then I'm wrong," Amon said, shaking his head. "The outcome is the same regardless."

Their destination needn't be said—Amelia knew it already. Dagger in one hand, lantern in the other, she marched the length of the Ashcroft house with her uncle to the basement.

"You couldn't find anything else?" Amelia looked over the weapon. "I may as well just go in empty-handed. Who brings a knife to a fight like this?"

Amon paused for a moment, lifting the lantern up to light Amelia's face. "Those red engravings are from Death itself. If it's good enough for him, it's good enough for you."

Amelia batted the lantern away. "What makes you think Death is a man? If you're wrong, you think it's going to be a man that kills you tonight?" She shouldered past him. "Come on."

When they reached the basement and the gasping hole at its center, Amon stopped and said, "This is as far as It will let me go."

Amelia cringed. She had stepped into a pool of viscid liquid. As she pulled her foot back, she found part of a shirt came with it. "Is this one of your imitations?" she asked, dragging her foot across the ground, shaking off the sticky remnants of life.

Amon nodded. "She was to be a gardener."

The basement hole took a deep breath and exhaled; the air blew through the room, sending unseen shelves to the floor.

"You're coming with me." Amelia took her uncle by the front of his shirt. "Get in there."

"I can't! I would, but I can't." He held onto her hands until she released him. "It won't let me. It knows what I'll try to do. But you... It's grown proud enough to think It can sway you."

Amelia looked at the dagger and the eldritch engraving in its handle and blade and imagined plunging it into her uncle's heart. It was the first truly terrible thing she had ever imagined doing to him.

"When It realizes that I won't be stopped, It'll choke the life out of Edmund and Ruth."

"No," Amon said, shaking his head, "It won't. The family would be finished, and when It comes back, because It'll surely come back, if none of us are left, It will have to start over."

"If It's so damn powerful, then It shouldn't need us at all."

Amon shrugged and looked pathetic. "What do you want me to say? I don't know what I'm doing. This is the only thing, Amelia, the only thing that I thought may work. Why does god do as he does? No one knows, not truly."

"Are you saying this thing is a god?" Amelia posed the question, but wished she hadn't; the implications were too great. If she was going to get through this, her thoughts would have to be clear, unclouded by self-doubt and otherworldly concerns.

Amon shook his head. "I don't know. I hope not. I can't imagine loving such a god."

While she stared at her uncle, Amelia retreated inward, to the isolation chamber in her mind her ex-husbands had forced her to create so long ago. Here, she could be safe and do what needed to be done. Her children needed her, and she needed them; no story, or the creatures that gave credence to it, was going to stop her.

Amelia lowered herself into the hole, the lantern dangling from her fingertips. When she was waist-deep, her feet finally found the top of the staircase within. She looked back at her uncle—pathetic and disgusting were the words that came to mind—and then began her spiraling descent into the dark.

When her footsteps began to echo around her, Amelia knew to stop. Going to her knees, she waved the lantern in front of her and found the staircase's end. A humid haze pressed itself against Amelia; like the clammy hands of an unwanted lover, it pushed itself under her clothes and through her hair, leaving her skin glistening and red. She took a deep breath, came to her feet, and stepped off the stairs and into the abandoned ruin of her dream.

The ballroom was empty now—the corpses and the chains that had bound them gone. She had entered through the staircase in the ceiling, so she turned the lantern on the ground. Blowing and brushing away the centuries of dust there, she searched the hardwood floor for scratches and carvings, for promises writ in a child's blood. Dirtied up to her elbows and knees, Amelia rooted through the skins of her ancestors until the center was cleared and she was certain Ruth and Edmund hadn't been here.

Amelia went to the room's end and pushed past the place where the door should have been. Beyond, a hallway twisted crookedly through the earth, as though it had been screwed into place. Thick roots and strange plants grew out of every crack and crevice here, and more often than not, Amelia found herself clinging to them, for the slanted floor made walking a difficult feat.

Was this some unfinished part of the house? Numerous doorways lined the hallway. When she looked inside, she found bedrooms covered in skittering insects and great pits filled with pools of black water. *Or is this the corpse of the old estate buried beneath the foundations of the new one?*

Reaching the place where the hallway peeled back, Amelia covered her mouth. Malignant, pulsating veins, the very same she had seen all across Parish, snaked through naked earth and into the library ahead. She marched forward, the dagger in hand, ready to cut down anything that stood before her.

As her eyes followed the vermillion veins into the library, she noted how illogical the architecture of the room appeared. The ceiling was lopsided and the walls inconsistent in length; the floor buckled upward and downward, not from wear but design. And the books, of which there were many, were unreachable; they sat in shelves on the second floor, for which there was no staircase, ladder, or even a balcony to stand on to reach them.

A madman built this place, she thought, slowly making her way across the library. *And by his madness, it was warped beyond repair.*

Where the veins grew thicker, more tightly packed, Amelia went, for she was certain they would lead her to their source. After several storerooms and a garden, she stumbled into a kitchen whose floor was covered in thousands of small, gnawed-on bones. Her stomach plummeted as she waded through the ocean of the dead. Noticing a glint, she raised her lantern and then gasped. At the center of the kitchen, an old bathtub sat, and someone was sprawled out inside it, their back to her, running the rust-brown water over their pallid skin.

Amelia pushed into a dining room. Incomprehensible words rained down upon her. Looking through the busted ceiling, holding the lantern as far out as she could, she noticed dark shapes pacing back and forth in the rafters. Now was not the time to show fear, so she held the black dagger high for her tormentors to see. All at once, they were quieted. With that small victory, some of Amelia's confidence was restored.

"I need to know," she said aloud, wood shavings snowing around her.

"Did Amon lie to me?" She was speaking to the creatures now, to look stronger than she was.

She knelt down beside an engorged vermillion vein that wreathed the doorway. "Did It lie to him?"

She bit her lip and swung the dagger; the blade passed through with ease. Like a severed artery, the vein sputtered its wretched fluid at Amelia, drenching her gown in its unholy blood.

"Good enough," she said, and thinking of Ruth and Edmund, pressed on.

The house stopped Amelia, for the house had nothing left to show her. She had reached the front. Beyond the threshold, a yawning chasm stretched, its rocky walls teeming with dense, impenetrable webs of the vermillion veins. Above the front door, just before the porch that mimicked the porch in the new house above, a large, black shape hung suspended in the air. To Amelia, it looked like a hardened heart or a malformed chrysalis. Stepping closer, she saw that it was held up by a membranous structure, much like an infected umbilical cord. She followed the swollen tube as it ran down the wall and across the floor, to the wall and the painting of a distant ancestor from which it had burst.

"What are you?" Amelia whispered, feeling the house breathe in and exhale, the chasm sucking in the air, creating a vacuum. She held the lantern up to the heart and set aglow its innards.

"Amelia," a coarse voice called out.

Amelia spun around. An annihilating shadow swept over, eating reality. A million fractured images stabbed into her mind, sending her to her knees. In gut-wrenching flashes, she watched Ruth and Edmund be cut into pieces and ripped apart.

"No!" she cried, as the images coalesced into a crowd of people eager to eat the remains of her disemboweled children.

Reduced to a whimpering child, she cried out for Amon.

And then there he was, in her mind's eye—gutted and gored, stripped of his clothes and his flesh.

Amelia covered her eyes and beat the dagger against her head. She saw her ex-husbands ripping through the mouths of her children. They shed Ruth's and Edmund's flesh. Then, with clubs made of teeth and muscle, they came after Amelia. Once they had her, they beat her until there was nothing left but red water.

She yelled and struggled to her feet. Across her mind, she saw great, metal buildings rise and fall into massive clouds of dust. Surrounding the destruction were a congregation of cloaked followers. She glanced to her side and saw that she was sitting upon a vermillion throne. The congregation swarmed her; they bowed and spat coins at her feet, and offered their infants up for her services.

Amelia staggered across the front of the house, doubling back towards the heart. Again, in the images, she saw the congregation, but this time one stood out amongst the crowd: a man, elevated on broken hands and flayed shoulders, making his way towards her. And when he found her, she took him every which way she liked. In their bloody bliss, they smiled and spoke of their love; for each other, for Ruth and Edmund, and for all the others that had yet to be born from her blighted womb.

"Ruth… Edmund," Amelia begged. She twisted the tip of the dagger into her temple, drawing blood, drawing pain. "Ruth…"

"We will take care of you," the house whispered, its words wrapping around Amelia like warm sheets. "Let us take of care you. You deserve it."

Amelia shook her head, shook beads of blood all over the floor from the small hole in her head.

"What else have you?" The house rumbled, took a deep breath; the chasm glowed red and something shifted in the shadows. "We've never wanted much, and you've never had enough."

Amelia struggled to her feet; blood dribbling down her cheek, with all the anger the horror had given her, she drove the dagger into the umbilical cord and sliced outward. The appendage whipped back and forth, spewing glowing red fluid into the air. Without its support, the hardened heart a few feet above fell away, collapsing onto the ground. On its underside, there was a large hole, as though something had already broken through hours earlier.

Dizzy and nauseous, Amelia struggled to stay standing as the entryway swayed. Patch by patch, the vermillion veins turned black and brittle. And that's when she realized they were the very bricks and mortar that kept the dead house together. Wiping the blood out of her eyes, she turned on her heels and retraced her steps. She had to escape before the estate plummeted into the void, into the very horror that had once elevated it so.

Fresh patches of wriggling veins were waiting for Amelia in the halls leading to the ballroom. They must have spawned sometime after she made her first pass through. *It doesn't matter*, she told herself, their presence making her skin crawl. *It's over. I'm done.*

Amelia tore through the dining room, where the beasts in the rafters above howled and yelped. She ignored them, and for some reason, they ignored her. She tightened her grip on the dagger until her hand started to go numb. She had killed the master; she would not be undone by its minions.

Amelia made her way to the kitchen and waded through the ocean of bones therein. Splintered femurs and ribs poked and broke through her skin, but she didn't stop, or care. Feeling water on her feet, she looked to the center, where the bathtub was now tipped over, with whatever had been inside gone from it. *Almost there*, she told herself, thinking of Ruth and Edmund. *This never happened. This never happened. This never happened.*

Amelia burst into the twisted hallway. It heaved upward, and the floor snapped in half. She dropped the lantern and jumped from where she stood as the tiles fell away. She scrambled and cursed as she ran, crawled, and ran once more through the undulating hall. Her fingernails cracked and broke off as she struggled for purchase on the shivering walls. The upturned floor caught the toe of her foot. She flailed for something to hold onto. Her ankle twisted until it broke. Amelia screamed, but she did not stop, for ahead, in the swirling, deepening dark, she saw the ballroom and the dim light within it.

"Amon!" Amelia shouted. She dragged herself into the ballroom, making out her uncle's features further on by the candle he held.

Without thinking, she lurched into him, dagger out, and then quickly pulled away. "I'm sorry. I didn't hurt you did I?"

Amon lowered the candle to his stomach. He was bleeding, but more importantly, he was naked. His body looked wet as though he'd recently bathed. He smelled like an infant, soft and sweet. He moved his hand to the hole in his side and covered it.

"Uncle…"

As Amelia stepped backward, she noticed the patch of wriggling veins in which he was standing. They were attached to his feet and throbbed as though they were passing something into him.

"Get away from me." She raised the dagger, Amon's imitation's blood already coagulated on its tip. "Get the hell away from me."

"We've no need for your line any longer," the imitation said, stepping closer to Amelia. "It took a very long time, but I was able to give us the confidence to move forward."

Amelia stabbed forwards, almost catching the imitation in the neck. "Move. Where's Ruth? Where's Edmund?"

The imitation smiled—teeth were still breaking through its gums. "With the house. I hope you don't mind me taking your uncle's appearance. I promise you won't even know the difference after a while. I knew him very well."

The dead house continued to shake from its death rattle. In another few minutes, if they didn't go topside, they would be buried down here amongst the corpses of her ancestors and the spoils of the atrocities they had committed.

"We've been waiting a long time, Amelia. We've been growing a long time."

In a flash, the imitation had the arm that held the dagger. It twisted her arm until she dropped the weapon. The dagger fell into the patch of veins. Immediately, they turned to ash.

"You deserve so much more than life has given you. Help us, and you and your children will never want again. No contract, commitment. We are not cruel, Amelia. We only wish to make this world a better place."

Amelia spat in the imitation's face. She contorted her body, trying to break free of its grip. Her defiance, though it had not been her intention, had given the house her decision.

"So be it," the imitation said. It broke her arm and pushed her down to the ground. "Death tends to make most things more agreeable, so close your eyes if you'd like, because I'm going to kill you now. Then we'll talk."

THAT WHICH WALKS BEHIND THE GRAVES

"Envious am I of those who do not wake to screaming. It has been three days since I've had a full night's sleep. The townspeople have agreed to send the children away, and for this I am grateful.

"It will take years to wash the blood from the headstones."

IN THE YEAR OF THEIR LORD 189X

Entry One

I, Herbert North, should have realized that something was amiss the moment Seth offered me a drink. The longest we'd ever been away from one another were those nine months spent in the wombs of our respective mothers, so you must believe me when I say that Seth is a penny-pinching bastard.

"England or the United States?" Seth asked as we quickly claimed two seats that had opened up at the back of the bar.

I eyed him like a harlot hoping to find a home for the night. Thinking I'd figured my friend out, I said the opposite of what I thought he wanted to hear. "Europe," I slurred, the alcohol on my breath killing two flies mid-flight.

"Then I'll take the States job," Seth concluded.

"What are you talking about?" I set down my cup and rubbed at my eyes. "What did you say?"

"Try to keep up, Herbert," he said smugly. "There are two villages, one in Europe and one here, which are having some difficulty with our friends."

"I wouldn't exactly call them friends," I said, staring down my drink in the same way the judged stare down the guillotine. "Oh," I said, nodding my head like a psychiatric patient, "I see what you mean."

Seth gave me the thumbs up, leaned over the table, patted me on the back, and then whispered into my ear, "There's a woman reportedly stealing children in the States and drowning them in lakes. I'll see to her."

"What am I to do then?" I asked. I noted the faint presence of my favorite cologne upon his person.

"You're to go to Europe and find out who keeps putting all the freshly dead atop the village graves." Seth smiled and fell back into his seat. A chair leg flew past his head as a brawl broke out at the center of the bar. "How's that sound?"

I remember shrugging, finishing my drink, and remarking to myself how comfortable the surface of the table looked.

An hour later, I peeled my face from the sticky hardwood finish and moaned like the dead for a glass of water. Seth had been conversing with the bartender about, presumably, business—we'd recently rid the fat man of a bone-eating pest—and was paying no attention to my pleas for the substance of life. Defeated by dehydration and feeling histrionic, I smoothed out my hair, straightened my collar, and slid my hands into my coat pocket, convinced that if these were my final moments on this lonely sphere, then at least I should die looking damn good.

"What the hell?" I remembered myself saying as my fingers closed around what felt like a piece of paper. I removed the ragged square of folded parchment from my pocket and held it in my shaking hands. It felt strange to the touch and pricked my flesh as I ran my fingertips over its yellowy surface. I thought for a moment I'd seen a glimmer deep within its fibers, but then it occurred to me I was still drunk, and I would probably see a unicorn in a horse if one were to gallop through the front door.

"Don't open that," Seth said, leaning away from the bar, hand anchored to a glass of whiskey.

"It might be a love letter," I said, holding it up above the cloud of smoke that had coiled around our table.

Seth groaned as he relinquished his grip on the amber drink and stumbled toward me. "It's a curse. If you read it, you'll be cursed," he said plainly.

"Now, that's no way to look at love," I said, suppressing a hiccup and setting the piece of paper on the table. "Did you catch the culprit?"

Seth nodded. He took with one hand the note and produced with the other his pocket watch and said, "It's getting late, and you've a boat to catch."

Entry Two

The bowels of the ship smelled as you might've expected when you give them a name like that. Because of Seth's frugal nature, I suppose I was fortunate in that the space provided to me seemed only mildly infested with spiders. I saw a particularly large one trying to carry off my hat during supper, but after some coaxing, the fellow returned it promptly.

I'm surrounded by people I do not care to converse with, but who seem to be doing their damndest to ensure that I do. There is a man in a brown trench coat who trails me wherever I go, with a beard that seems to suggest he thinks himself to be a certain desert-dwelling deity. Unfortunately, if he does believe this, then he keeps it to himself, for the conversations he brings to me are drier than the desert he thinks he hails from.

"Where are you headed?" the man finally asked, cornering me at the bow.

I gritted my teeth as the man spoke, the cold wind gnawing at the back of my neck. "England," I said, "the countryside."

The man in the brown trench coat nodded, reached into a pocket, and produced a flask. He choked down the drink and offered to let me have a taste. "It'll keep you warm."

Tempted, I refused out of fear that I may wake the following morning in his quarters with a few parts of my person missing. "I'll manage," I said, watching as he drained the flask and dropped it back into its well-worn home.

"Are you on holiday?" The man stifled a belch with his arm; he backed away as the sea threw itself against the side of the ship. "What's the countryside hold for you?"

"I'm an investigator, and I've something to investigate there." I looked at the man in the brown trench coat and wondered childishly what he would do if I were to suddenly shave off his precious beard.

The man took a step back and scratched his nose. His eyes widened with excitement. "You're not going to the Ashcroft estate are you?"

It took me a moment to answer the man's question, for the time between the bar and the boat had been a bit of a blur. I shook my head and said, "Cairn—that's where I'm headed. Now, if you don't mind…"

The man in the brown trench coat stroked his beard. He followed me as I retreated into the ship, the sound of my chattering teeth echoing around us. Annoyed, with my patience frozen by the cold, I wondered how hard I would have to hit the man to ensure he didn't wake until we reached our destination.

"The Ashcroft estate and Cairn sit upon the same marsh, a day's journey from one another. I'm no investigator, but I cannot help but notice a connection when I see one."

"Nor can I," I snapped, "but since I have absolutely no idea what you're going on about…" I paused and took a breath. "Get on with it."

The man in the brown trench coat's eyes began to water, as though I'd offended him. He shoved his veiny hands into his pockets, spun in place. He seemed uncertain as to whether he wanted to make a scene or excuse himself quietly. He sniffled and wiped his nose, looking like an overgrown infant that had crawled into its father's hand-me-downs. At this point, I would've hit him just to see what he'd do with the pain.

"You are very rude," he said bluntly. He turned and pushed open the door to the bow, where the wind howled loudly with the secret song of the drowned dead. "A day's journey from the Ashcroft estate is Parish," the bearded baby said reluctantly. "People seldom travel to that part of the country, and talk of it even less."

"What happened?" I asked, trying, and failing, to suppress my interest.

The man shrugged and stepped outside, and as he pushed the door shut, he said quietly, "They're all gone."

Entry Three

I never saw the man in the brown trench coat again. Like all curious characters that pass through our lives and stir things up, he disappeared as soon as his presence became appreciated. I expect I embarrassed him, and his embarrassment made of him a hermit in his cramped compartment somewhere on the ship. But there was no denying that his story had resonated with me, that it had stirred my indifference from its slumber by lighting the bed afire.

So I scoured the ship for those who looked or sounded as though they were on their way home to England.

"I'm sorry," a posh old woman said, her small head poking out of the massive dress she wore. "I do not know of the family or of the place," she added, the tea cup on her lap rattling on its saucer.

"Are you sure about that?" I asked, crossing my legs and doing my best to look sophisticated. I could feel years of perfectly honed passive-aggressiveness oozing out of her royal pores. "You seem like an affluent woman. I'm surprised you've never heard of the Ashcrofts."

The old woman's eyes darkened, like she'd suddenly become possessed by some demonic entity (she hadn't, trust me; I would've known). "I am Judith Myers," she said. "Does that name mean anything to you?"

I shifted in my seat, raised my coffee in a toast, and said with a smile, "It means about as much to me as Ashcroft means to you."

"The Ashcrofts," she began with a tremble in her voice, "were a very old family. There's nothing to be said on the matter." Judith cleared her throat, set down her tea. With all of her strength, the crone pushed herself out of the seat. "They're gone, taken by the same disease that took Parish."

"What of Cairn?" I asked.

She started to hobble away, her left leg having dozed off at some point during our conversation.

"What of it? It's an unremarkable village."

"I don't know," I said, standing up. "I find it rather remarkable that every few days someone dies there and nothing is done about it."

Judith Myers laughed and turned away. "How is that any different from the rest of the world?"

I let Judith leave under the impression that she'd bested me in our dialogue. There was no doubt in my mind that she was an educated woman, but even the most intelligent in this world can be ignorant to those unseen forces of nightmare and shadow.

I've yet to decide if I envy those who believe horror's form to be confined to the atrocities committed by man. Mine and Seth's lives would be simpler, yes, but would they be better? And what of those who, by our efforts, were saved? When they were backed into a corner, blood pouring from their wounds, sanity pouring from their minds, who would have intervened if we had not?

Entry Four

We've arrived in England, or so I'm told. A thick fog clings to London and seems to have no intention of letting go. The rain is relentless, making of the city a bloated corpse that has escaped the ocean's undertow. In the swirling mist, the silhouettes of buildings float and sway and appear as though they belong to another world entirely. Down the streets and across the roadways, black figures shamble in and out of pockets of light, carrying in their wallets hope and in their hearts defeat. The street lights do their best to burn through the haze, but like those who live here, their lives are short and their efforts trivial.

By carriage I will cross this country to the fated village of Cairn, a small settlement of six hundred in the northernmost region of Blackwood Moor. By moonlight I will stalk the alleys and open windows and put my ear to cracked doorways, and discern for myself the nature of the crimes said to have been committed. According to Seth, and I apologize to you, my readers, for only now disclosing this information, Cairn has endured thirty deaths in ninety days in this cruel year of 1889. The bodies of men, women, and children have been found dismembered and desecrated, eaten away at and put on garish display in the cemetery. Two men by the names of John Gallows and Richard Dark were initially arrested and charged with the crimes by the local constabulary, but they were quickly acquitted when the deaths did not stop. How Seth had learned of these events, I do not know, and what role this Ashcroft estate plays in the mystery is beyond me as well.

I am but one man, and one man is no match for conspiracy; therefore, I will do what I do best: find the culprit, beat them until they are bloody and raw, and be on my way.

Entry Five

The inn at which I stayed in London smelled of refuse and debauchery, so when my driver finally arrived, I nearly blew the doors off the place trying to escape it. The driver was a large man with a wild beard and head full of curly black hair. His hands were massive, perfect for crushing skulls, and his face scarred, probably from trying to crush skulls.

"Grunt," he grunted, "that's what they call me."

I opened the carriage door myself, because I could tell the man had no intention of moving from his perch, and threw my baggage inside.

"What should I call you?" I strolled up beside the driver and placed my hand on the steed whose reins he held.

"Grunt is fine," he said, a grin emerging from the black jungle that had grown out of his face. "We're going to Cairn, are we?"

"Yes, we are," I said, pulling my hand away from the horse as it looked back in annoyance.

"You're from America?" He turned his head towards a child that was pointing in his direction from afar, laughing at him.

"If you'd like," I said, leaning into the man and nodding at the child, "I'll hold him down while you go to work on him. He shouldn't put up much of a fight."

Grunt made a sound that must've been a laugh and said, "Get inside before the rain starts again."

Given my previous arrangements, I couldn't complain about the cramped confines of the carriage. It was warm, and except for Grunt, whom I had taken a liking to, secluded as well. I slept for most of our trip though the city, waking only as we passed the abattoir. The air was thick around the massive complex, as though the blood from processing had coagulated on the wind. At the front of it, the workers in their white shirts and gray aprons milled about, grazing on gossip while they waited for the din of the killing bell.

"All that goes in," Grunt said through the window between us, looking at the abattoir, "does not come out as it was."

When I awoke to a new day, I found the ghostly structures of London had vanished; cement and cobblestones were replaced by endless fields of grass and gently rolling hills. Small streams had become rivers overnight, the water spilling from their banks and flooding the roadway. Farmhouses rose out of the folds of the land, their battered crops ripped from their husks and vines and left to roll about in muddy puddles and ditches.

We passed several carriages on the highway, each carting the privileged to their hidden homes far from the poor populace off which they prospered. Occasionally, we would come across groups of people moving on foot, belongings slung over their shoulders or the backs of the beasts they would inevitably slaughter for sustenance.

"Where are they going?" I asked Grunt, knocking on the window behind him.

"Why don't you stick your head out there and ask them?" he retorted.

I considered his suggestion, but out of fear we may be run off the road and killed, I decided against it. "What do you know about the Ashcroft estate?"

"I thought I was taking you to Cairn." Grunt looked over his shoulder, the sky behind him ablaze with the morning sun. "The Ashcroft family died out years ago, and most of their properties and investments were bought up." Grunt sneezed into his hand. "I have a brother who used to pass through Parish when he was a trader; said the only Ashcroft still alive was Amon, and nobody saw him unless he willed it."

I rummaged through my bags for a hunk of hardened bread and sank my teeth into it. "I heard Parish is empty now, its people vanished without a trace," I said, crumb and saliva leaping from my mouth.

"You heard wrong, like the lot of them," Grunt said. He clicked his tongue to hasten the horse. "A disease came to Parish and its people fled. I've seen them with my own eyes in the city." He shut the window through which we had been speaking and said, "You shouldn't believe everything you hear in these parts."

I shoved another piece of bread into my mouth and directed my attention outside, where a man in a ragged suit was picking the threads from his collar on the side of the road. He was covered in mud, and straw clung to his clothes. If I hadn't known any better, I would have thought him a scarecrow that had abandoned its post.

"He's from Parish," Grunt said, opening the window, letting the biting wind into my compartment. "Like I said, they're all headed for the city."

I made eye contact with the man as we passed and felt as though I had looked straight through him, for there was no life in his eyes. He continued to work at the tears in his suit, his movements rigid and awkward, like he was learning to use his limbs for the very first time.

"I've been to Cairn, you know," Grunt revealed later, the white vapors of his breath dispersing into the black night.

Half-asleep and wholly exhausted, I opened my mouth to call the man a son of a bitch for withholding this information, but what came out was more akin to a death rattle.

"Night comes early in Cairn," the driver continued, his voice an eerie reminder of the countryside silence, "and with it the wolves. Until your partner contacted me, I thought it were those beasts responsible for all the deaths."

I sat up in my seat and wiped the sleep from my eyes, the conversation having developed the potential to take an interesting turn. "What did my partner tell you?"

"Nothing," Grunt said, turning his head towards the sound of something splashing in a nearby pond, "but someone doesn't come from America all the way to Blackwood Marsh for the sights."

"Who do you think I am, Grunt?"

I pressed my face to the window beside me, fogging the glass with my breath, and felt an intense dread at the impenetrable darkness that surrounded us. It seemed as though we were no longer of this world, and the path which we followed was one reserved for the lost and the damned.

"I know you didn't cross the ocean to hunt wolves," Grunt said. He shushed the horse as it started to whine and jerk from the carriage. "That's what I thought it was when I first heard of the deaths in Cairn." He paused for a moment to swat a gnat. "Also, I know you should watch Father Clark and watch him close. For someone who lives in the church, on the edge of the graveyard, he is doing a piss poor job catching the killer when it comes time for them to deposit the bodies."

"More importantly," I said, leaning forward, "who are you? Seth didn't need to hire a specific driver to get me out here."

"My brother and I are from Cairn," Grunt said. "Our family left when the Ashcrofts found Parish to be more profitable." He looked over his shoulder to enjoy with me my moment of clarity. "My brother went back to see how the village had fared over the years, and when he told me what he saw, we knew who to ask. Your partner's name was mentioned many times." Grunt scratched his beard and pulled a twig from its depths. "Don't let that go to your head, though. You two are hardly popular."

"So it seems," I said, now wishing I had stayed in London for a few more days to learn the extent of our influence and infamy. "What did your brother see when he went to Cairn?"

"Rows of flesh," Grunt said, his voice a whisper, "and that which walks behind the graves."

Entry Six

I could tell by the crowd that had gathered at the gates of Cairn that my arrival was not unexpected. Thirty men, women, and children were waiting in the muddy streets and on the muddy walls, watching as the carriage passed into their seldom seen domain. Grunt paid them no mind as we went down the central road, in and out of the long shadows of the structures that fell across it.

"Tell me: in what state did you leave your humble little village?" I said softly.

Grunt turned his head slightly and said, "You're in good company, Mr. North. The only man you've to look out for is Benjamin Boyce."

I sunk down in my seat, avoiding the penetrating eyes of a gaunt grandmother on the street. "Why's that?" I lifted myself up slightly and saw that the grandmother had vanished, a tornado of dead leaves where she had once been.

"I took his little brother out hunting once," Grunt said, nodding at someone out of my sight, "and the wolves saw that he did not come back. It comforts Benjamin knowing he has someone to blame."

As we pressed further into Cairn, I began to see a place that had been robbed of its potential. Squinting and wiping the fog from the carriage window, I saw the skeleton of a sawmill in the distance, left to die amongst the very trees it had taken. Through the alleys, I caught glimpses of farmhouses with fields too large to tend. Over Grunt's shoulder, I spied amongst the gray hills the mouths of sealed caves, the allure of the treasure they held muted.

"The Ashcrofts came and made promises, and what they built up, they let fall down," Grunt said, turning the carriage onto another street.

"How long ago was this?" I asked. The distinct form of a church began to push through the fog ahead.

"About ten years," the driver said before grunting at the horse to slow its pace. "About the time Amon accepted inheritance of the estate," he added, looking back at me, as though he doubted I'd be able to make the connection.

I drummed my fingers on my knee. "Let me see if I understand this, Grunt: the Ashcrofts, with all their entrepreneurial prowess, ventured to this part of Blackwood Marsh to make of this village a profitable place. They realized, for whatever reason, they were mistaken, and instead set their sights on Parish. Ten years pass, and this Amon fellow is given the reins and at some point sells off the family's claims. Parish is forgotten, and while it is forgotten, a disease sweeps through and sends its citizens for the city. How am I doing so far?"

"Fairly well," Grunt said as we circled a surprisingly modest fountain outside the church. "What about Cairn and the murders? You left that part out, sir."

"Yes, what of Cairn?" I said, my agitation growing as I realized the bearded bastard was intending to stop at the church. "Thirty deaths in ninety days and all I seem to hear and think about is Ashcroft. Why is that?"

"Ask Father Clark," Grunt said. He stood up and dismounted from his perch, the whole of the carriage sighing in relief from the loss of his weight. "He's the one said to have seen Amon a week before the killings began."

Now thoroughly enraged, I sprung out of the box I'd called home these last few days and hobbled over to the large man, who was patting the horse on the head and whispering sweetly into the beast's ear. I reached for his collar to strike him, then all of a sudden I had a vision of Grunt crushing my skull with his massive hands.

"Why," I said, brushing a bit of hair off his collar instead and smiling, "why did you not tell me this earlier?"

Grunt looked at my hand like he was considering feeding it to his horse. As I retreated, he said, "I told your partner. I assumed he would fill you in on the details."

Unlike Grunt, I don't assume when it comes to Seth, for I know from experience that my friend has a predilection for withholding information. Though it pains me to admit it, I am partly responsible for this, because I find that I work more efficiently when I'm not burdened by vagaries and bias. Make no mistake, I am a heretic through and through, but I've often entertained the possibility that I was once a dog in a previous life, blindly obeying his master because of the comfort in doing so.

Note to self: Do not allow Seth to read this entry, otherwise his head will swell to encephalitic levels. The last thing I want is that fool to think himself my retainer.

"Grunt," I said, rocking back and forth on my heels, "I've a confession to make. I'm terribly afraid of churches."

"Tell it to Father Clark."

Grunt led me to the low, run-down wall that surrounded the church, and together we passed through a gate whose lock had long since broken away.

"Start here and then sleep."

"I think you have your priorities confused," I said, secretly thankful for the driver's guidance. "Will you be…?"

I intended to ask Grunt if he would wait for me while I interviewed Cairn's priest, but found that the words were lost to me, for my eyes had set upon the graveyard lurking behind the weathered church. It was fairly large given the size of the village, and would grow larger still once the recently murdered were laid to rest. There did not appear to be any particular order in which the headstones were placed, so the plots were scattered about haphazardly. The ground itself was uneven, overturned; thick roots twisted out of the soil, tired of the taste of decay. Weeds and lichen covered most of the markers, the only source of color in Death's dreary realm.

At the furthest end of the cemetery, a crypt sat shrouded under the branches of a weeping willow, quietly watching over the yard for the restless dead. Immediately, I knew I had to open its doors and descend into its depths, for there was no doubt in my mind that entry into that building was forbidden, and where do horrors come from if not forbidden places?

Interview One

Father Clark was a sinewy man whose diet likely consisted of host, wine, and holy water. He held a battered bible in his right hand and a long strand of yellow ribbon in his left. He looked tired, and the dried lines of blood on his wrist and cuff told me he'd spent the better part of the night engaged in murder or self-flagellation. Unlike his parishioners, Father Clark was not eager to greet me, which was expected, because the last time Seth and I were welcomed warmly by a priest, he had tried to let his deformed daughter burrow into our chests.

"Will you do god's work?" he asked as he beckoned me to take a seat at the end of a pew.

"I'm going to do the best I can," I said, knowing that no amount of god's work would save me from hell.

Father Clark sat opposite me, his eyes fixed on the morbid crucifix suspended at the furthest end of the church. "What do you know?"

"Less than I would like," I said. I picked up a book of psalms and flipped through its pages. "Tell me what's happened here, Father."

The priest crossed his legs, uncrossed them, and then crossed them once more. "Garrett and Geoffrey took one look at their hometown and were sickened by what they saw," he started, Garrett being Grunt and Geoffrey his brother. "How is it they'd heard of you and your partner?"

I set the book down and shook my head. "I wasn't aware our names were known in Europe, but I suppose word travels quickly amongst circles concerned with these matters." I paused for a moment. "How is it the police are not involved?"

"They were, for a time," Father Clark said, "but we are too far from civilization for London to pay us any attention." He stifled a yawn. "What are your qualifications?" he asked, as though he meant to send me away if I did not answer satisfactorily.

"Thirty have died here," I said, sounding offended, "and yet I've come all the same."

"That makes you a fool, not an expert," Father Clark said humorlessly, "and it is thirty-three that have died here. Maud Wilkerson's ten-year-old girl was found three nights ago in a burlap sack, dangling from one of the willows."

"Do you live here, Father?" I asked, incensed by the man's incompetence.

Sensing my anger, the priest stood up, closed the gap between us, and sat beside me, forcing me further down the pew.

"You've been in this town for no more than ten minutes and you're already making accusations?" His eyes shone with the light of the flickering candles atop the church's tabernacle. "This church is my home, and I've gone without sleep more times than I can remember watching that graveyard, waiting for the sinner who has shaken my flock's faith. It is only when my back is turned, when my eyes have closed, that they carry out their cruel intentions." He took a deep breath. "God was testing me, and I failed, and for my failure he now punishes me."

I wanted to tell Father Clark that he was a selfish coward, and maybe even slap the man around some since his god wasn't doing the job properly, but I held my tongue. "This will not be my first encounter with the macabre. My last assignment had me in the bayous, where the fetid water birthed fetid children longing for companions."

Father Clark leaned in and asked, "What did you do?"

"We found the source," I said, cringing, the scent of the swamp having never left my memory, "and severed its hold on our world. A husband had killed his wife when he found out that she could bear him no kids and dumped her body in the backwoods. Afterward..." I paused for dramatic effect, "she bore him all the children he could ever want and more."

"How did you find this poor soul?" Father Clark asked, enraptured. "How did you put her to rest?"

"The offspring had a habit of carting off parts of the dead back to their mother as offerings and proof, so we followed them." I rested against the pew and propped my elbow atop it to hold my weary head. "She'd taken up residence in a seldom seen part of the swamp. When we found her, she was still dressed in the white gown she'd worn the night she'd been murdered, except it had grown, having stretched across the ground and up the trees."

"How did you put her to rest?" the Father repeated, close enough that I could have given him a peck on the forehead and gotten away with it given his state.

"Well," I slipped my hands into my pockets, "we discovered she was living off the land from the fabric of her dress, so Seth cut it up the best that he could. And then we burned her body and her babies and buried her deep in the ground."

"She was a demon," Father Clark said, finally exhaling.

"She was something else, that's for sure," I said, wondering if I could convince him to let me have a sip of his savior's sweet blood to quench my thirst.

"It seems you were meant to be here then."

At that moment, I knew the priest was mine. "Half of the agreed payment now, half when it's over."

Father Clark nodded, licking his chapped lips. "It's been three months since Death took interest in our town. Dying is natural, inevitable; a reward for those who have lived piously by the teachings of the lord. But there is nothing natural about what has happened here."

"You'd be surprised how quickly your definition of the word 'natural' changes once you've seen the things that I have."

"Mary Davies was the first to die." Father Clark stood up and turned sideways to exit the pew. "You should speak with her mother first. After that, see Lee Warren."

"As of right now, I'm more interested in what you have to tell me, Father," I said, noting the old man's evasive maneuvering.

He shook his head. "I can only tell you of the bodies, that's all I know."

"That interests me as well." I took another look at the church, searching the darkness for suspicious doorways and eldritch gateways. "What of Richard Dark and John Gallows? I'm sure they've something to say on the matter, being wrongly accused and all."

"I'm sure they did," Father Clark said, moving towards the altar, the rustle of his robes sounding like the beating wings of a bat. "Thirty-three have died here. Maud Wilkerson's child was the thirty-third, and they the thirty-first and thirty-second."

"You sound suspicious."

The priest laughed. He faded into the shadows gathered in the church's center and said from the darkness, "I feel a motive is forming, but I'm too close to see it. That's why we need you."

I hate people like Father Clark. He's one of those lonely and tortured souls constantly searching for a place and purpose in a world that no longer exists. He ambles about annoyingly in the margins and the folds, and whispers words that promise enlightenment and intrigue. The man knows well enough that he cannot make good on his commitments, but that doesn't stop him from preaching them all the same. He is a glutton, and it is only through self-inflicted martyrdom that he will be filled. I doubt he's the killer, though I'm certain he's killed before and will do so again when he grows weary of waiting for the bloodstained gates of heaven.

Entry Seven

Grunt had me rent a room at Hodge's Lodge, a two story building of creaking wood and crumbling stone one minute from the death yard. In there, privacy was a commodity unattainable to even the wealthiest of residents: footsteps rang through the halls like thunder and voices carried through cracks like shrill invitations. Each room seemed fitted with ill-conceived peepholes, as though the driller had more interest in the motions of the fetish itself than the flesh and blood on the other side. The proprietor, Hrothgar Hodge, promised to be at my disposal at any hour, and the grin upon his face when he told me this suggested he would be nearby whether I called upon him or not.

I set my belongings on the floor, noted the draft creeping across the ground from its dark hideaway, and brought out the knives and daggers. They glinted in the silver light of the clouded sun. I knew they would protect me well enough when the time came. With a splintered quill and smattering of ink, I then sat at the desk, set upon it a piece of parchment, and drew from memory the layout of the village. There was little to illustrate, for I had seen little of Cairn, but it ensured that I would explore the place properly before relying on the local map.

"Settling in?" Hrothgar Hodge asked, leaning into the room.

I spun around, startled. I had not heard the man approach, and this troubled me. "What do you know of the murders?"

Hrothgar tapped his fingers on the molding of the doorway. "Not as much as I would like, to help you, I mean."

"Sure," I mumbled, nodding at the imp of a man who was far too unsettling in both parlance and appearance to have retained his innocence.

"You might find talking to the doctor enlightening," Hrothgar teased.

I spun around, knife in hand, and pointed the sacred blade in his direction. "You might find talking to me enlightening, too," I threatened.

"He's got the bodies, is all I'm saying." Hrothgar retreated into the motes of dust congregating in the hall. "He never put them back. We got two graveyards now."

Entry Eight

The first night is always the hardest. Every shadow becomes a horror, every conversation a conspiracy. The darkness seems thicker and gathers like a malignancy in the corners and the closets, under the beds and under the stairs, breeding terror and promises of death. Safety becomes a scarcity, and those ordinary objects which we once looked upon with indifference now stand sinister and cruel. No longer does a candle promise warmth but the arrival of some shambling cannibal from its dusty cellar. No longer does a clock tell the passage of time but the moments that remain until the cult comes for their inquisitive claim.

Without fail, it began at midnight. I was half-asleep, half-drunk on a bottle of stolen wine when I heard metal chipping at stone. Sobriety found me just as quickly as it had left me and brought me to the window. The streets were empty and the houses still, and the wind blew softly, clear and chilled. The trees swayed rigidly, their boney branches shedding curled leaves to the ground. If not for the thirty-three deaths that had brought me here, I dare say I might've enjoyed the moment.

I spun around as the floorboards groaned outside my door. I waited for words that I knew would never come, then went to my knives; they were meant for monsters, but they would bleed men all the same. I could hear the entity breathing on the other side, a shallow and lustful breathing rolling over wet, pursed lips. Beads of sweat slid down my forehead and into my eyes as the door knob turned slowly, carefully.

Filled with courageous stupidity, I vaulted across the room and, with the knife raised high, pulled the door open. Hoping to find Hrothgar with his pants around his ankles, I found nothing instead. The hall was empty, the only evidence of anything having been there being the faint smell of rain. Looking to Grunt's room and the two others the innkeeper had stated were occupied, I saw that the doors were shut, rumbling snores wandering out of them.

Pattering feet on loose tile sent me skirting down the stairs, my watcher still on the premises. I hit the landing and then the first floor. The front doors stood wide open before me. I snatched a lantern from the front desk and brought it to life. Shadows recoiled around me as I stumbled onto the street. No sign or shape of the stranger remained. But, through the gloom, I heard the call of a shovel cutting through earth. And so I foolishly I followed.

Like all places, the dark made of Cairn an endless catacomb of stone, wood, and soil. I wandered aimlessly, helplessly, through the night, in search of the graveyard which should have been nearby, yet seemed to have disappeared entirely. The woods that surrounded the town swayed loudly, a tide of leaves washing against the shore of the sky. Grunt had warned of wolves, and now I heard them, howling and yelping and reveling in their carnage.

"Get inside," a voice whispered.

"Who said that?" I whipped around to find the pale face of an old man floating in the doorway beside me.

"Don't be an asshole," he said, disappearing into his home. "Get inside."

Interview Two

It was the doctor who found me, and his name was Frederickson. He was the mad scientist type and seemed to enjoy playing the part. His house smelled of chemicals, of sour anxiety. After glancing nervously at my knife, he directed me into the living room and sat me down on a chair that had seen its fair share of use.

"You're the investigator, yes?" He disappeared and returned with a cup of tea.

The chair creaked as I leaned forward, scrutinized the tea for poisons, and then sipped it. "I heard something skulking about outside my room," I explained. "I followed after it."

"I've heard that's how it starts." The doctor picked at his neck. "It drags you out, makes you lose your way."

"You say 'it' as though you're certain it's not human."

"Well, if it was, why would you be here?" The doctor took a seat and lit a candle. "I know man is capable of a great many terrible things, but I have to hold out hope that no such man lives here in Cairn."

"You've lived here all your life?" I finished off the tea and searched the room for shadowed conspirators.

Frederickson nodded.

"What do you think is happening?"

Frederickson let out a heavy sigh and stood up. "Come with me."

I remembered what Hodge had told me about the doctor and the bodies and asked accusingly, "Where are we going?"

The basement, that's where we went, and that's where I found them, all of them; all of the men and the women and the children, all wrapped in sheets, all torn apart; all thirty-three corpses webbed in blood and wracked by rot, decaying in splintered coffins, their souls growing impatient and hateful as they waited for the calming rest of the grave.

"You need to bury these bodies." I shoved my nose in the crook of my elbow to escape the smell of putrefaction. "Put them where they belong."

Frederickson shook his head. "We tried that." He walked over to a child's coffin, pulled back the lid, and said, "But they kept digging them up, as though killing them wasn't enough."

The skull of a little girl peered out from the box, the rest of her bones and partially decomposed flesh surrounding it like a wreath. "Mary Davies," I muttered, realizing she was the first to have died.

"They dug her up four times before we moved her here." The doctor closed the coffin and muttered, "Her poor mother." He turned to me. "You asked what I think is happening here."

"I did."

The doctor surveyed the room, twitching at the patter of water off the sweating stones. "Something evil has wandered out of the woods and made its home here. And not just in Cairn, but the whole countryside. I went to diseased Parish to offer my services to friends and acquaintances and found only strangers. The sickness had taken their memory of me, or so I thought. I wouldn't tell this to anyone else, but you understand, you accept things others won't allow themselves to believe.

"The people of Parish were not human, had never been human. My friends, my acquaintances, everyone—they were gone, replaced by these things that looked the part, but hadn't a clue how to act it. I tried to treat them regardless, but they refused, and when I confronted them about their consumption of the strange veins that'd begun to grow there—for surely that was the source of their maladies—they turned violent. It sounds like madness, I know, but it is the truth."

"If they were imitations, then where did everyone else go?" I whispered.

The doctor shook his head. "I do not know. I can only guess."

"Grunt and I witnessed several travelers from Parish on the road heading toward the city."

Frederickson sighed and said as he stared at his feet, "I've heard, and it won't be long until the disease spreads further, I expect."

"You think something has followed you back," I said, having heard the notes of guilt in his confession.

A rogue tear streaked down the man's quivering cheek. "Yes."

"But this is different from Parish. There is no disease, no mockeries of man."

"Only bloody slaughter for the sake of amusement." Frederickson paused, took a deep breath, and said, "Mary Davies, six; John Williams, twenty-two; Alice Hall, thirteen; Colin Walker, five; Charles Bell, thirty; Eric Bell, thirty-one; Abigail Green, ten; John Ward, forty-four; Hugh Hill, thirty-seven; Ann Hill, twenty-nine; Ian Hill, eleven; Lesley Hill, four; Malcolm Wood, thirty-five; Elizabeth Baker, thirty-five; Francesca Baudin, forty-three; Alfred Axel, fifty-seven; Agnes Axel, forty-nine; Aleid Boeckman, seven; Katie Warren, thirty-two; Benjamin Ash, sixty; Christopher Babcock, nineteen; Graham Cross, two; Emily Cross, six months; Sarah Bertrand, fifty-eight; Ella Delacroix, eighty; Orphan Boy, age unknown; Gregory Haywood, twenty-seven; Orphan Girl, age unknown; Michael Hopkins, thirty-eight; Michael Norton, four; Richard Dark, twenty-six; John Gallows, twenty-four; and Maud Wilkerson, eight.

"The names of the dead and the order in which they died. I will never forget them, or what I may have done to them."

I looked over the thirty-three coffins stacked and crammed in the doctor's basement. "Orphan Boy and Orphan Girl?" I asked, the names having stood out to me.

"Yes." The doctor held his light up to the two small coffins which had small ribbons dangling from each of their cracks. "We could not identify them as our own. We'll hold the children here until someone comes looking for them."

"Doctor," I said, backing away towards the stairs, "why are the bodies being held in your house? I'm sure there are safer, more secure places."

"It's my burden to bear, and my responsibility to bring them back when this is all over."

Because the madman had me in his lair, I nodded and smiled and backed up to the first floor, where the light of the rising sun shone on new horrors yet to be seen.

Entry Nine

What I'd heard and tried to find throughout the night was the sound of murder. Lee and deceased Katie Warren's daughter, Eliza, had been butchered, her arms and legs, head and torso, and organs strung up in one of the graveyard's willows. Her tongue had been bitten in half, likely eaten, and there were bits of stone in her eye sockets. A small hole sat before the grisly spectacle, as though the killer meant to taunt the town to bury her. Those nearby reported she had been a bright girl, a beautiful girl, with a wide smile and a charming sense of humor.

Eliza Warren had been ten years old when the world was through with her.

"It's not always the graveyard," Grunt said to me as we sat down at a table in Hodge's Lodge to drink the piss he called ale.

"Where else have bodies been found?" I asked, watching Hrothgar as he watched us while he pretended to dust.

"Around the well, on the streets." He belched. "One in the woods, one all over a shallow cave." He sighed. "But mostly the graveyard."

"Do you think Father Clark is the killer?"

Grunt shook his head. "I wish Father Clark were the killer, but that would be too obvious. You'd have seen his head on the front gate if it were him."

"There's a crypt, isn't there?"

"Aye, there is. Everyone goes down it when they're young, sees how long they can last."

"Has anyone been down there lately?" I asked excitedly.

Grunt finished off his ale. "Collapsed, nothing to go down there and see."

"When?"

"Few years ago." The burly, smirking bastard clamped his sweaty hand down on my shoulder. "Don't feel bad, I wondered the same thing."

Interview Three

Seeing that Lee Warren was now without a wife and daughter, it seemed cruel of me to speak to him so soon on the matter. I went to Clara Davies instead, the first to have suffered the murderer's wrath and the woman to whom the priest had referred me. She was a large lady, but pretty; middle-aged with curly blonde hair and wide, blue eyes. She had no husband—her daughter, Mary, had been born out of wedlock. Surprisingly, the backwoods town of Cairn did not stone her for this, and by that courtesy I found I respected the place a little more for it.

"I miss her so very much," Clara Davies whispered as she led me out back.

We took a seat opposite one another.

"I can't even begin to imagine how it must feel," I said, a phrase which I've repeated so many times it has lost all meaning.

"Most can, at least here in Cairn." She offered me food from a plate. I accepted. "It's morbid, but it makes it easier knowing that I'm not the only one to suffer."

"I want for this suffering to end, Ms. Davies," I said, "that's why I've come."

"What are you exactly?" she asked, looking at me like a specimen she'd captured to study.

"An investigator, for when the crimes make no sense and no culprit can be found."

"John Dark and Richard Gallows. They promised me they were the culprits," Clara said, still craving closure.

"Who promised?"

Clara shrugged. "Everyone, but Father Clark mostly." She took a sip from her cup. "They were bad people, John Dark and Richard Gallows, and they deserved to die."

Ms. Davies's words were soaked in vitriol and she said them without regret. Her body stiffened and her fingers worried at the fabric of her dress. For a moment, I caught her wide and blue eyes looking inward, at a memory often visited but, unfortunately, not easily forgotten; and in that moment, though I didn't know what she truly looked like, I saw her daughter Mary.

"Was it John or Richard that fathered Mary?" I asked boldly.

Surprised by my discovery, Clara Davies covered her mouth and flirted for a moment with rage. "I don't know," she said, lowering her defenses, "I couldn't tell in the dark, and I wouldn't let myself believe it in the light."

"Of all the others murdered, did anyone else deserve to die?"

Clara's eyes filled with tears that refused to fall. "No, they were mostly all so young and sweet."

"It will be hard, Ms. Davies, but I need to know what happened that day, and anything that happened days before that may help me find who is responsible."

Ms. Clara Davies began that morning much like she began any morning: cold, tired, and with a migraine that would bring even the strongest of men to their knees. Rain drummed on the roof of the house as she staggered out of bed and found Mary on the living room floor, drawing.

"What's that?" Clara asked her daughter.

Mary turned over, her clothes drenched from playing in the rain. "The house where my friends live."

Clara smiled at her daughter and thought nothing of the statement.

"Here it is."

Ms. Davies brought me the drawing, handling it carefully, as though it were a holy relic. I gently took the picture and saw that her daughter had drawn a small, circular stone house; it had several windows, but no front door and no neighbors.

"Always had such a wonderful imagination."

The day went on as most rainy days did: slowly, drearily, and for Clara Davies, painfully. Much needed to be achieved, but the migraine she had felt otherwise. Bedridden, Clara waved off Mary, watched as her daughter disappeared into the hazy lull of the storm, and then slept. When she woke, the clouds had parted to the afternoon sun, the migraine had vanished, and Mary had yet to return.

"I did what needed to be done, cleaned up, and made a meal. I could hear the children playing down the street and I assumed Mary was with them," Clara said, shifting in her seat.

"Was she?" The woods swayed before us, a flurry of dried leaves blowing through their wooden alleys.

Clara nodded and wiped a tear from her cheek. "Yes. We ate together, and... and then she was off again, with her friends."

"Did she act differently when she came back home?"

"No, she didn't, but she said she saw someone while she was out, a strange man near the gate." Clara lowered her head.

"Who was it?"

"Geoffrey," Clara looked up, "Grunt's brother."

I disguised my concern as Clara continued with her tale of woe. Geoffrey, Grunt's brother, had arrived in Cairn the same day the murders began, and this same man had been the one to seek out mine and Seth's services upon commencement of the slaughter. A smarter, more diligent investigator would've jumped at the coincidence and followed it through to its disappointing end, but I knew better.

Mary Davies didn't finish her lunch that day, and she didn't return for supper. Clara was sifting through the mess of artwork on her daughter's floor when she heard the screaming, the shouting. Being a mother, Clara possessed that uncanny ability all mothers seem to possess that allows them to know when harm has come to their child.

"I felt it in my stomach, in my heart," she said, standing up before me. She disappeared inside the house and returned with another drawing, which she held as though it burned her hands. "I feel empty, Mr. North, and I don't expect I'll ever be whole again."

"What's this?" I took the drawing from Ms. Davies' shaking hands.

"One of her imaginary friends," she said, turning away, "or so it wanted her to believe."

A smarter, more diligent investigator would've disregarded the drawing and focused on the tangible, logical, and otherwise earthly evidence before him, but, again, I knew better. On the piece of crumpled paper a weeping willow stood, its bark carved to the outline of a man, his feet the roots, his arms the branches. He smiled invitingly, as all creatures of temptation do, and his face seemed to promise adventures thought only to be found in dreams.

"How long had she had this friend?" I asked, noting the bloody mouth-like hole in the grass.

Clara shook her head. "I don't know. I found this just a few days ago. I saw it through the floorboards in her room."

"Have you shown this to anyone else?"

"No, no I haven't." Her eyes widened. "I thought it would be best if you were the first to look at it."

"Your town," I stopped, noticing that the willow's leaves were not leaves at all, but eyes. "Your town has shown me more hospitality than most."

Clara nodded. "We're not like Parish. Cairn has seen its fair share of strangeness. And I think Father Clark—" her voice became a whisper, "—has lost his faith and does what must be done to see that this ends."

"The faithless do have a knack for finding us," I muttered. Returning to the drawing, I said, "This willow, there is one just like it in the graveyard."

"Yes, but they are common around these parts."

"But the graveyard is where most…"

"Yes," Clara interrupted, refusing to hear the words, "do you think that's where we will find it?"

"Seems so." I handed back the drawing. "But if that's the case, it's not doing very a good job covering its tracks." And then I remembered something, something which I had forgotten for no reason in particular. "What do you know about Lord Ashcroft?"

Clara's eyebrows furrowed. "His name is not a popular one in these parts."

"I heard that he came to speak with Father Clark."

Clara shrugged, looked over her shoulder. "Someone said they saw him talking to Nathan Moore, our agriculturist."

"Why is that?"

"The sickness in Parish… I think, I hope, he was trying to stop it from coming here. There's a plant it's all coming from, I heard, and it covers Parish."

"That's awfully thoughtful of the same man who left Cairn to die in the wilds," I said pointedly.

"You're right," she said, smiling for the first time since we sat down. "It's wrong to hope."

Entry Ten

Eliza Warren's funeral came just a few hours after the discovery of her body. Very few tears were shed. Hers had been the thirty-fourth death, and Cairn was becoming accustomed to tragedy. Father Clark spoke kindly as the town marched through the muddy streets, the coffin held high above the procession by the men at its center. Doctor Frederickson received everyone warmly, taking little Eliza Warren to be stored with the others when the moment presented itself.

I knew this needed to end quickly; the creature that hunted Cairn did so greedily, without fear of myself or the repercussions of its actions. Never had I encountered something afflicted by such a ceaseless bloodlust. *Was it the town's indifference that kept them rooted to this tainted soil?* I wondered as I excused myself from the doctor's house. *No, not indifference,* I decided as I maneuvered puddles in the street. *This is all they have, and like the pauper, they will hold onto it until their own blood slickens their hands and they lose their grip on it forever.*

I returned to Hodge's Lodge and found it just as empty as I'd hoped it would be. I went to my room and laid out my tools—the knives, powders, and potions—and consulted my journal, which detailed all previous investigations. While searching for clues in its worn pages, I remembered that the Lodge was not only occupied by Grunt and myself, but two others.

"Hello?" I called as I rapped upon the first occupant's door.

To Seth and I, no answer meant there's no reason not to let yourself in, and so I did just that. The room on the other side was unoccupied, as bare as it had likely been the day the final nail had been hammered into its wall. Quiet as the man who pressed his eyes to the tiny holes in the wall, I searched the space and found only dust and a puddle of… spilt milk?

"I beg your pardon," I began as I knocked on the chipped wood of the second occupant's door, "but I have a favor to ask."

Again, no answer; I accepted the invitation without complaint. The second room was unoccupied as well, but only in that moment, for the bed hadn't been made and a woman's garments still lay strewn across the floor. They, too, were covered in dust, yet a heavy and recently applied perfume sat within the folds of the fabrics.

"Oh Hodge," I mumbled, lifting up a red corset and holding it before me in front of a mirror, "you may be the strangest creature here."

With weapons to slay, powders to detect, and potions to neutralize, I slinked down the stairs and scoured the first floor until I found Hodge's register. Very few names were written on the stained scraps of parchment, with the most recent being Grunt and myself. The names that preceded ours were non-descript initials that read "A.A." and "R.E."; no check-in or check-out was noted.

"Either you really did have guests before us," I said, cramming the register under the front counter, "or you've got one hell of a fantasy life."

The grass parted at my approach as I moved through the graveyard and read the faded names on the headstones. I made for Eliza Warren's willow first, minding the hole that had been dug beside it. Blood dribbled onto my shoulders and the tops of my hands as the branches wept what little was left of the girl. Remembering Eliza's drawing of the tree and the man within it, I felt around the bark and the roots and dusted them with red Bite and purple Snare. The willow did not respond, did not bare its teeth and wrap itself around me, and so I left disappointed, my hopes that the culprit had been a carnivorous tree dashed.

As I marched towards the crypt, I could feel the piercing gaze of the townsfolk returning from the doctor's residence. *Let them say what they will*, I thought, *but this is why they've hired me.* I ascended the lichen-laced steps and pushed the double doors open. The stink of decay washed over me and settled into me; stumbling backward, I struggled to keep the morning's breakfast in its place.

"Jesus Christ!" I shouted in the most inappropriate of places.

Grunt had told me no lie: The crypt had collapsed some time ago, and in its failing, it took with it all the corpses to the chambers below. The large slabs of fallen stone appeared undisturbed; no gaps existed between them wide enough to allow for anything but a mouse or rat to pass through. A creature of great strength could move the rubble, but the noise it would produce in doing so would defeat the purpose of using such a place for its lair.

"That's the only way in," a voice spoke to me.

"Father Clark," I said, facing the priest, "are you sure?"

He nodded and shivered. "Yes, I'm sure."

I bit my lip and picked at a callus on my palm. I turned away from him, uncorked a bottle of Black Fey, and splattered the stygian liquid across the crypt's steps.

"What is that?" the priest asked, his neck tensing, his mind searching for words to string together a rant on desecration and blasphemy. "What are you doing?"

"Searching for ghouls," I said matter-of-factly. "Eaters of the dead," I added, seeing his confusion.

His face paled. "Do you think that's what's come to Cairn?"

"Something like that," I muttered. The Black Fey bubbled, but did not smoke. I hurried past the priest, lashing the concoction at headstones and Eliza Warren's willow. "The reaction is weak." The same results manifested at every doused location. "But it's enough, and if it isn't a ghoul, it's something very similar."

Father Clark covered his mouth and rubbed his rosary furiously. "Where did it come from? How do we stop it?"

"Sometimes, when a man or woman dies, an evil being works its way into their bodies and into their hearts," I explained, noticing that the prying townsfolk had dispersed. "It chews on their dead hearts, and from its venom the heart beats, lives, once more. Ghouls are territorial gluttons; the cemetery in which they wake becomes their home and the graves their pantries. They will attack trespassers, but, and this is where things get confusing for us, they seldom draw attention to themselves, for they prefer solitude."

"So it's not a ghoul, is it, Mr. North?"

"It's a start, Father Clark, that's what it is." I looked at the man, wondering how his faith would reconcile those things which his god should not have allowed to be. "Tell me about your meeting with Amon Ashcroft. Why's he so interested in these parts all of a sudden?"

A lie formed upon the priest's lips, but knowing better he said, "Come inside."

Father Clark led me to the church's basement. We stood in torchlight, staring at the four coffins encaged in iron mortsafes.

"Does everyone keep the dead in their basements and cellars here?"

Father Clark ignored my remark.

"Who's resting in these coffins?"

"Emily Cross, Ella Delacroix," he said, moving the torch from left to right as he spoke. "Richard Dark, John Gallows."

A child, a woman, and two rapists. They were in the doctor's basement hours ago... weren't they?

"And what are they doing below the ground instead of being in it?"

"Their bodies were afflicted by the same disease that consumed Parish." He held the light against the coffin in which Ella Delacroix lay. "Lord Ashcroft came to Cairn to see if the disease had spread to our lands, and after many late nights, we saw that it had." Father Clark let out a heavy sigh. "We quarantined the bodies as soon as doctor Frederickson found the infectious roots in their veins and arteries."

I laughed and shook my head. "The mortsafes are meant to keep people out, keep them from selling parts and pieces to hospitals and universities." My hand found the knife at my side and rested on its hilt. "You're keeping something in the coffins, making sure it doesn't escape. All the dead are stored at Frederickson's to avoid contamination."

Father Clark nodded; the torch hissed as sweat from his brow fell into its smoldering center. "Yes, that's right."

"If we were to open up one of those coffins, what would we find,

Father? An imposter? Like the doctor found when he visited Parish?"

The priest shook his head. "I don't know."

"This creature, or ghoul, is a carrier."

"It seems so." Father Clark shuddered. "Yes, it seems so."

"Where's Lord Ashcroft?"

"His estate, I'm sure."

"When did he arrive in Cairn? Who died when he strolled through your gates, all kind and considerate?"

"Eric, no, Abigail Green," he answered. "She was the seventh."

"Stayed in Hodge's Lodge, didn't he?" I asked, remembering the initials "A.A." in the register.

"Yes—" Father Clark turned, as though he meant for the conversation to end, "—but in secret, so I don't know why he would sign his name at all. I'm sure it was Hrothgar who added it. It is something he would do to amuse himself."

"And "R.E."?" I asked. "That was in the register as well, below Amon Ashcroft's name."

"I couldn't say, Mr. North." He looked at me pleadingly, looked at the knife at my side nervously. "He came alone."

I cocked my head at the priest who had once been so unwelcoming towards me. "I frighten you, Father."

"Everything frightens me," he said, starting up the steps. "If I had the strength, if I did not care for my flock, I would leave."

"What did you see in the coffins?" I asked, nodding at the four against the wall. "You looked, and what you saw convinced you that you needed someone like myself to come here to put an end to all this."

Father Clark continued up the steps, the torch throwing his shadow wildly across the room. "A newborn wrapped in red roots, sleeping in John Dark's chest, suckling from the man's slowly beating heart."

Entry Eleven

Ghouls are decrepit creatures suspended in decay, segregated by shame. It's not unheard of for a ghoul to shed its shape and take on the form of an animal. Grunt warned me of wolves in the woods, and now that I know that it has killed outside of the graveyard, it seems I've discovered its type and method of movement. If the ghoul is infected by this disease, of which I understand frustratingly little, then its behavior is expected to change as well.

Father Clark had seen a newborn cradled in bones, swathed in rot. Has the disease changed the ghoul? Has it given the creature a way by which to reproduce, to alleviate its insufferable loneliness?

I fucking hope not.

I hate ghouls, always have and always will. Seth and I have killed six ghouls between us, and each encounter has been disgustingly memorable. The smell of their bodies and the bodies they've consumed lingers in your mind for weeks after, and the ferocity with which they defend themselves almost always guarantees a scar or trip to the hospital. If one does not possess the means to exploit the creature's weakness, then one will find themselves dismembering and disemboweling the ghoul until only a bloody, chunky pulp remains, for they are surprisingly resilient.

Fortunately for Seth and myself, we happened upon several daggers crafted from the bones of a saint, with red Death engravings carved permanently into their hilts and blades. One slash or stab from the weapon and the ghoul is finished, reduced to decomposed sludge. I don't know how the process works exactly, but I can't say that I've ever been disappointed with the results.

So glad, then, that I brought two daggers with me.

Entry Twelve

As I made my way to Doctor Frederickson's residence, I began to understand how the killer was able to go undetected with such ease. No one was working, no one was socializing; the streets were empty, the windows curtained. No one was watching and no one was listening. I wondered if Eliza Warren's death had been the death to break their resolve, for, just a few days ago, the entirety of Cairn was there to meet me at the gates.

No, I said to myself, *a stranger has come to their town and made their struggles his own, and with their burden on my shoulders, they will rest, and breathe, and love what loved ones they have left to love.* I could not blame them for it. In their position, I'd have done the same.

"I want to see Orphan Boy and Orphan Girl," I said as the doctor let me into his house.

"What's that?" the doctor asked, obviously having heard me.

"Why's that?"

"Father Clark showed me the four infected corpses in the church's basement," I told him. "A plant or root is responsible for the illness, right?"

"Yes, I believe so," the doctor said, fidgeting.

"If you've found no evidence of it growing here, then it must've been brought on someone's person. The children you could not identify may have been from Parish."

Frederickson scooped up a cup and drained it down his throat. He coughed, and I smelled alcohol. "We looked them over already and found nothing."

Give me a reason, madman, I thought to myself, touching the bone dagger hidden in my coat. "Well, it's always good to double-check your work, isn't that right, Doctor?"

Frederickson laid the two small coffins on the ground and placed the ribbons that marked them atop their lids. His eyes lingered on the boxes and then his brow furrowed. He brought his crowbar down on the first coffin and worked at its edges, motivated by what appeared to be anger and disappointment.

"What is it?" I asked

"Too light," he wheezed, "they're too light."

The coffin lid splintered and cracked. Frederickson glanced at me, the coffin, and then turned his attention to the second box, red faced and speechless.

"Empty," I mumbled, going to my knees for a better look. "Where is the body?"

"Son of a bitch!" the doctor yelled, prying open the second coffin, sending the lid across the room and under the stairs. "Both are gone. Someone—" Frederickson dropped the crowbar; his hands turned into fists, "—someone took them and sealed the coffins back up!"

You won't be resurrecting them after all, I thought to myself. "Why would someone do that?"

Doctor Frederickson shook his head.

"You spend a lot of time down here, don't you?"

The doctor, sweaty and heated, studied the crowbar.

"Otherwise they wouldn't have made the effort to hide the theft." I revealed the bone dagger and my intent to use it.

The doctor kicked the crowbar away. He dropped down onto the floor, ripped the ribbons from the coffins, curled them up, and shoved them into his pockets.

"I know you've been over each body a thousand times." I took a step forward and put the tip of the dagger beneath his chin. "So tell me: were they infected?"

"Through and through," he said, removing the ribbons, both of which were yellow, and smelling them, "through and through."

Entry Thirteen

Something terrible has happened to me, and I will do terrible things because of it.

I was sitting at my desk, considering what I'd learned and preparing myself for what needed to be done last night, when three knocks rattled my door.

"Hello?" I called out, but no response followed. The ghoul of Cairn had demonstrated a disregard for tradition, so I brought the bone knife with me as I crossed the room.

"Who's there?" I asked loudly, hoping that if it wasn't Grunt, then he would hear my voice and come to my rescue.

"I said 'who's there?'" I repeated as I bent over, put my eye to one of the many holes in the wall, and peered out into the hallway.

Rain, I smelled rain, and a shape, I saw a shape just at the edge of the peephole—a small shape outside my room. I looked to my side and saw pale fingers like wriggling worms under the door. They moved up the space between the molding and the door, towards the lock, and began to pick away at the wall.

Tapping, I then heard a tapping at my window, and a shape, again I saw a shape, as it scurried over the glass onto the roof. I went to the desk and grabbed the second dagger and the remainder of the Black Fey. A hand slammed against the window, cracking, but not shattering it, and snapped away. I stumbled backward, onto the bed and, laying there, listened to the laughter that sounded in the dark.

"Thanks for stopping by," I said, sitting up and getting to my feet. I grabbed several vials from the desk and pocketed them. I went to the door. "Makes finding you freaks a hell of a lot easier."

The window blew out as I unlocked the door and kicked it open. The shape went down on all fours and crawled quickly to the first floor. I followed, because I knew if I stopped I would die. My feet pounded down the stairs as my heart pounded in my chest, with the second pursuer nipping at my heels. I shouted for help that I knew would never come and followed the fleeing shape into the secretive fabric of the night.

Cairn stretched out in all directions, a great and infinite sprawl of stone and darkness. I struggled to keep pace with the shape as it darted through alleys and streets, as it scampered through gardens and gates. Glancing over my shoulder, I saw that my stalker had vanished and that the town remained asleep.

The shape's footprints and footfalls had all but gone when I reached the moonlit well. I fell against it, my lungs begging for oxygen, and took in the cold air. Had they meant to draw me out into the open? Were they not expecting that I would follow? I strained my ears for sounds of the shape's breathing beyond the gathering fog. Was this part of the hunt? How many nights would I be doomed to partake in this chase until their amusement gave way to hunger?

I pushed away from the well, and as I started back towards the Lodge, I remembered Eliza Warren's drawing: a small, circular stone house with many windows but no door and no neighbors. I leaned over the well, sending the bucket to its bottom, measuring its depth. A splash rose out of the gray mouth and then laughter.

This is where your imaginary friends live, I thought as I took the rope to which the bucket was still attached. *You prettied it up the best that you could, Mary, but this is it.* I tested the rope's strength, wrapped it around my hands and ankles, and descended into the hardened throat.

The tips of my toes slid against the damp stones of the well. Fog spilled over from above and wrapped itself around me as I moved down the rope. Below, the void yawned and churned and spoke in the language of splashes and waves. Ignoring every impulse to do otherwise, I looked past my feet. A dizzying swell of fear rose through my body as the seemingly fathomless depths stared back. After shaking my head and cursing myself, I gripped the rope tighter than before and began my defeated ascent.

And then I stopped, stupidity surmounting common sense. In that brief moment, I had seen through the murk a ledge and a place where the wall had fallen away. I kicked off the stones as I slid downwards, and when I could, I threw myself onto the thin outcrop. Securing the rope around the jagged stones there, I entered the narrow breach.

The crevice was a claustrophobic's nightmare. As I shimmied sideways, my nose skimmed against the sharp rocks and my eyes fluttered to keep the dirt away. I breathed shallowly, the cramped earthen corridor pressing hard into my chest and stomach. Blood trickled down my wrist from where the flesh had been slowly scraped away by the stones. My legs weakened as pressure built against my knees, preventing them from bending. *I will die here*, I thought, lodged in that suffocating place. *In a hundred years, they will find my skeleton and wonder what I'd been so desperate to reach on the other side.* My temples began to ache, as though drills were penetrating my skull, and it was then I knew I'd gone too far.

"No fair," a spoiled voice cried out, "no fair!"

My eyes widened and drank the dark for light. A small, clammy hand shot through the split, grabbed my own, and ripped me out of Death's grip. I fell into the hollow hard and fast, busting my lip and bashing my head.

"He got stuck," the voice of a boy chirped. "But here he is!"

As I suckled the blood leaking from my lip, flames from nowhere burned into existence. The fire danced across the rim of a large bowl, then slithered towards the center, gnawing at the kindling there. The glow of hell spilled out of the vessel, washing over the bone-littered floor and the gore-caked walls. It rose to the ceiling where ghostly smoke gathered and shone on the hundred coffins that hung there, lids ripped free, corpses already eaten.

"Hello, sir," a little boy in a tattered suit said, stepping into view.

"Hi," a little girl in a sullied dress added, standing beside the boy.

The boy was no older than eight and the girl no older than ten, and they were both dead. Their skin was pale, wet, and wore all across it scars, cuts, and bruises beset by exposed muscle and protruding bones. Strange vermillion veins were threaded through their wounds, running from their ears and the corners of their eyes. Dried blood was painted on their arms up to their elbows and onto their mouths down to their collars. They were not ghouls, of that I could be sure.

"Introduce yourself," a woman yet unseen whispered into the hollow.

The little girl curtseyed, strands of hair falling from her skull as she did so. "Ruth Ashcroft."

The little boy bowed, the curve of his spine moving through a rip in his jacket. "Edmund Ashcroft."

Ruth Ashcroft? Edmund Ashcroft? Orphan Boy and Orphan Girl. I wielded the bone dagger and they looked upon it unmoved. "'R.E.,'" I quoted from Hodge's Lodge's register.

"They do like their games," the woman spoke, her voice closing in from all directions. "Come closer."

I obeyed, but only so that I would be near enough to drive the dagger into their little, dead hearts. "And you are?" I asked, the boy and girl stepping backwards away from me.

The shadows at the furthest end of the hollow writhed; bright red veins pushed forward in one cancerous mass that bore a coffin at its center. Inside, terrible eyes shone with a green virulence. A long, slender hand, and then another—they gripped and pushed the sides of the coffin, bringing the woman's face into the light. She smiled, the flesh around her mouth ripping as she did so, and said smugly, "Amelia Ashcroft, of course."

I'd heard enough. I rushed forward, blade outwards, then hit the floor, mouth to the woman's toes, as her children swarmed me. A searing pain spread across my back as they opened it with their nails. Teeth clamped down on my shoulder and on my calf. They stepped on my arm and worked the bone dagger free from my hand. Edmund kicked my head, took it and beat it against the floor, while his sister slowly stabbed the dagger into my side, just barely breaking the skin.

"You will help us," I heard Amelia say through the torture, "and I will help you. I'll save you from what's about to come."

"Fuck you," I said through my teeth, turning over and kicking Ruth in the stomach.

Edmund took me by the hair. His sister scampered over, handed him the dagger, and he drove it into my neck. A terrible agony unlike any I have ever known coursed through my body. I sputtered and spat blood all over the woman's toes, the thick and sour taste of metal coating my throat.

"You will help us," she repeated. "You do not have a choice."

Amelia Ashcroft leaned forward in her coffin, her feet spreading apart. Vermillion veins slithered down her thighs, past her ankles, and onto the floor. I closed my eyes and I closed my mouth, but still they found a way in, and when I thought they could go no deeper, they went deeper still.

Entry Fourteen

Ruth and Edmund took my hands and led me through the under-belly of the graveyard. We emerged behind the church, outside the gates of Cairn, out of a hidden hole in a weeping willow. They kissed me on the cheek, giggled, and retreated back to their mother. I stood there for a moment, bloodied and beaten, gripping the wound which should've killed me. I had a new job now and no choice but to complete it.

Entry Fifteen

To Seth, for I've no one and no need for anyone else: forgive me. Forgive me for what I've done and will do. Forgive me for loving you and for writing it down for all to see. I will not die unless it is said, and I would die saying it a thousand times over.

Entry Sixteen

My clothes were stained and covered in glass from the vials that had broken during the attack. I crept into my room at Hodge's Lodge, locked the door, and stripped naked. The damage done by Amelia's children had already begun to heal, just as she said it would. Reaching my hand into my mouth, I felt the tip of a pulsating vein just beyond my molars.

"You will live a long and unnatural life," the Ashcroft woman had promised, as she opened the gouge on my neck and pushed into it a necklace with a cloudy gem within a tangle of silver worms. "And you will do good work because of it."

I scratched at my neck and tore at the scabs, ignoring the nauseating pain as I searched my flesh for the jewelry. Gone, not there, disappeared and now a part of me.

Grunt knocked on my door, asking if I was doing well and if I wanted something to drink. I ignored him, because I feared what I might to do him if I did not.

Father Clark came later with new revelations to reveal. Several townsfolk arrived shortly thereafter, ready to be interviewed and have their stories heard. Now that it was unsafe for me to be around others, I had become very popular.

I ignored them, ignored them all, and kept on sharpening the bone dagger's blade, preparing for the night's work to come.

Entry Seventeen

Hrothgar Hodge seemed to be expecting me, so when I jammed the dagger into his side and twisted, he did not struggle. His blood ran hot and fast over my hands. I stabbed him some more for no reason in particular. When he went to speak, I severed his vocal cords so that I wouldn't have to hear his cries. As the life left his body, the vein twitched in my throat and tightened in my chest with satisfaction.

"The disease did not take to that one," Amelia Ashcroft had told me, pulling me into her rotted embrace. "It's a learning process. He's a liability."

I dragged Hrothgar Hodge's death-laden corpse into his room and dropped it through the floor where the boards had been lifted away. Ruth and Edmund looked up at me, mouths wet with salivation; they crawled up and over the man's body, sank their claws into his flesh, and pulled him away, disappearing into the hole that ran under the building.

When I was sure that I was alone and no one would hear me, I wept into my hands, smearing Hodge's blood all over my face, like war paint.

"I'm sorry, I'm sorry, I'm sorry," I repeated, shaking where I stood.

"I'm sorry, I'm sorry, I'm sorry." I couldn't stop, the words becoming a chant, becoming a form of penance.

"I'm sorry, I'm sorry, I'm sorry." I continued, falling to the floor, sitting in his crimson pool. "I'm sorry, I'm sorry, I'm sorry."

Entry Eighteen

Tried to kill myself today. Bled all over the place. Got close once. Cut through all the veins and arteries in my arm. Pulled them out, too. Didn't stop there. Kept going until I saw the bone, then broke it for good measure. The vermillion vein splintered and spread and fixed the damage I'd done. Have to get it out to get out. I hear her calling. She's got a new name.

Entry Nineteen

I waited in the bushes below the windowsill. I took no pleasure in watching Clara Davies disrobe, but I watched all the same. The howling of the wolves in the woods put her to bed quickly; she pulled the covers up to her eyes, as though it would make them stop.

I bashed her head in with a rock, because I couldn't bear to look at the disappointment on her face. Edmund and Ruth helped me bring her back to Amelia. As we tore open her chest to give a clear view of her stilled heart, the Queen of Corpses reached into her blighted womb and worked free a clumping of root, flesh, blood, and bone. She lowered the ovum into the cavity between Clara Davies' breasts and smiled proudly as a mother would at one of their own.

"She has to stay down here with us," Amelia Ashcroft lectured her children. "No more games. We've lost too many as it is."

And then she leaned in and whispered another name.

Entry Twenty

Father Clark found me on the outskirts of town covered in mud and crime.

"What are you doing out here?" he shouted, hurrying over to the willow, oblivious to the portal it held. "Mr. North, what's happened?"

"You have to leave. I can't stop it." I took him by the shoulders and nearly lifted him off his feet. "What will it take for you people to leave?"

"Herbert," the priest pleaded, my weakness giving him strength, "we've nowhere else to go. This is our home! What have you seen? What do you know?"

"The children," I wheezed, releasing the priest, "at least send the children away. There has to be another town, another village in this fucking marsh."

Father Clark wrapped his arms around me and kissed me on the top of my head. "Why the children?"

Entry Twenty-One

Herbert North waited until Rowena Russell's parents had turned their backs before he stole her away from them. At first, she didn't scream, because she had seen the investigator from afar and heard that he was good.

"I'm sorry, I'm sorry, I'm sorry," Herbert North told the little girl as he covered her mouth and took her apart.

Entry Twenty-Two

Father Clark called a town meeting after they found the ten pieces of the ten-year-old Rowena Russell impaled upon the gates.

"Cairn," he began, "is lost." He looked at me in the corner and I nodded. "God would not have us suffer any longer. We've endured enough and it is time for us to make our exodus."

Everyone was in attendance, and when Father Clark spoke, everyone nodded in agreement.

"Mr. North, please," he called me over, "tell us everything."

I wore my scars for all to see, to show them I'd made the effort and that it hadn't been enough. I felt their eyes follow me to the podium, some disappointed, others suspicious.

"The creatures that haunt these grounds cannot be killed by the weapons I've brought here," I told them, the ragged and tortured whole of Cairn. "There are hundreds of tunnels beneath our feet—" a lie, "—and we would all die if we were to go into them and flush the creatures out." I began to cry uncontrollably, feeling the vein pulsating somewhere in my skull. "I've failed you. I'm not enough. Go, you must go! I will stay, I will stay, but you must go!"

"And what will you do?" A large man stood up, Elijah Lindsay, and puffed out his chest. "What have you done at all?"

See through my ruse, I thought, *and butcher me like the beast that I am.*

"He's lost his mind."

"He's done more for us than anyone else!"

"Look at him, look at us! We should listen to the man and leave."

"I'll not leave my home to Satan!"

Rowena's father, Horace, came to his feet, his hand still holding his wife's firmly. The crowd quieted, and he said in a whisper, "Why are they doing this to us?"

My chest tightened as the vein wove through my ribcage. I wanted to tell them the truth, but it was not mine to tell. "Because they can," I said, closing my eyes, "because nothing can stop them."

Horace's wife, Anne, released her husband's hand and stood beside him. "You've only been here a week, Mr. North. How can you be so certain?"

A week? It felt as though I had been there for months.

"Where are they, Mr. North?" Anne persisted. "I want vengeance. I want to hurt them like they've hurt us, all of us!"

"They're diseased," I sputtered, "diseased by the same affliction that took Parish. If you stay, it will spread!"

My words fell on deaf ears as the crowd loudened, Anne's words setting a flame afire in their hearts that had died out months ago.

"Too proud, too stupid," Amelia Ashcroft hissed into my mind. "They were complacent and now they're careless. Let them come. Let their bodies fill our coffers. I'll love them all."

Entry Twenty-Three

Envious am I of those who do not wake to screaming. It has been three days since I've had a full night's sleep. The townspeople have agreed to send the children away, and for this I am grateful.

It will take years to wash the blood from the headstones.

Entry Twenty-Four

Half of Cairn has fled with the young, led by Grunt and those who know the woods best.

The other half remains, doing what they should've months ago; that is, scouring the town for the Ashcroft brood. Frederickson leads them, and boxes them up when the children cut them down.

Meanwhile, I await my orders.

Entry Twenty-Five

I'm not sure how long I have left—I can hardly lift the pen to write this entry—but it's done.

The veins lay before me, throbbing, coiled, speckled in blood, with chunks of flesh and muscle clinging to their thorny sides. I can feel the gouges in my throat; the tears inside me widen with every breath. Bruises climb my flesh where blood vessels have burst, and I can feel something dripping slowly behind my eyes. I know I left something behind—I could only get my arm so far down my throat. I can still feel it in there, a part of the vein, but I can't hear her, feel her, and if what I've left behind will be enough to get me to her, close enough to split her in two...

Entry Twenty-Six

Cairn burned brightly behind me as I hurried through the graveyard, over the fence, and into the outskirts where the Ashcroft willow waited, still undiscovered. A mysterious fire had broken out in town, and I used the chaos it created to slip away unseen.

"Hurry." Edmund beckoned from the glistening hole at the bottom of the tree, only his pale hand visible in the misty dark. "Hurry!"

"Where's Ruth?" I asked, following the corpse child through the twisted bowels of stinking earth.

"She'll be back." He looked over his shoulder, neck twisting around like an owl's. "They were getting too close. She likes fire, says she can still feel it if she gets near—"

I took Edmund's head and slammed it into a protruding rock. The point drove into his skull, bursting his eyeball. He screamed for his mother, and as he yelled, I grabbed his jaw and ripped it off. He spun, spewing red and purple blood as the roots that infested his body hurried to repair the site. He slashed at me, bit at me, kicked his feet, and spat at me.

"No fair," I told him as I pulled both bone daggers from my sides and pushed them under his arms. "No fair."

He didn't fall into a pile of decomposed sludge, but there was enough ghoul in him that it finished the boy off all the same.

"Kill the priest," Amelia Ashcroft shouted from her coffin, having heard my approach. "Give him to his god, and I'll give what's left to mine."

I circled around the Queen of Corpses and threw her son's severed head at her feet. "Give your god this one instead."

Amelia Ashcroft let out a guttural wail that echoed through the hollow. The cancerous mass to which the coffin was attached throbbed. She stepped out of it fully nude, with tight bands of roots wrapped around various parts of her body that fed into her pelvis and breasts, her heart and her spine.

"Shouldn't have given you those back," she remarked. She sighed as she looked over the tens of corpses before her, a tiny parasitic infant suckling at each one's heart. "Shouldn't have gotten in the carriage. Shouldn't have read the letter."

"What did you put in my neck?" I stomped on the heart of the nearest corpse and the child drinking from it broke into dust.

Amelia Ashcroft cringed. "A gift for someone else." She focused her green eyes on me and said, "You may just live long enough to find out what it's for. Can you feel me scratching?"

I gritted my teeth as my skull felt as though it had been cleaved.

"Amon didn't expect much from us, but we did the best—"

I rushed Amelia and stabbed her repeatedly in the stomach. The roots bound to her and the coffin behind her flailed and flew forward. I closed my eyes and closed my mouth; I felt the roots at my eyelids and at my teeth. They snaked through my clothes, searching for orifices and creating new ones to get inside. I kept stabbing, kept cutting until her innards spilled over Edmund's severed head.

Amelia reached for my wrists, but she was dead before she could touch them. Her body fell to the ground, and all the ova she'd been growing leaked from her womb, down her leg, and into the dirt.

I took a breath and was grateful I was no longer able to experience repulsion. Then I killed the rest of her children in their boney cribs.

Entry Twenty-Seven

The fire had consumed most of Cairn. Only a few buildings remained, though it was difficult to determine what still stood through the smoke. I left without saying goodbye to the priest, though it makes me happy to know that he is still alive (and that Frederickson, apparently, is not).

Ruth Ashcroft has vanished, and I expect it will not be long until she's reunited with her uncle Amon once more.

I'm not sure if I'll make it back to London. In fact, I'm not sure if I'll make it to the end of this road. Wolves howl in the woods around me, but they've no interest in me; my mind to tear me apart long before they do.

Thoughts of Seth will bring me home, but should I bring this home to Seth? Perhaps I should return to Cairn and go where I belong, and walk some more behind the graves.

THE EASIEST JOB IN THE WORLD

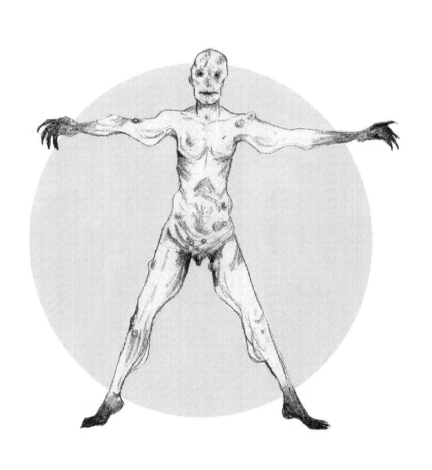

Beatrice Bacchus looked into her empty wallet and sighed. Her hands found her pocket and her fingers its bottom and, again, she sighed. In one overly dramatic motion, she collapsed upon her bed, put her palm to her brow, and kicked off her sneakers, knocking over a desk lamp on the other side of the room. She eyed the upside-down appliance, calculated its worth. Remembering it had been a gift from her father, she quickly put the thought out of her head.

"Mother fuck," she said aloud. She sat up and blew her hair out of her face. "God damn it."

Beatrice turned on her side and fumbled at the handle of the nightstand. *I need to refuel*, she thought, sliding her free hand underneath a pillow, until it closed around a half-eaten granola bar.

"Not bad," she mumbled as she chewed, not because it tasted good, but because it was still edible after being opened for three weeks.

She returned to the nightstand and pulled the drawer that was always stuck with all her strength. After a moment, the drawer finally relented, and with one tug of herculean might, it was ripped from the nightstand. Frayed wings of paper soared through the air and then crashed the words they carried into the ugly carpeted floor.

"You asshole," she said to the nightstand as she crawled off her bed to the ground.

The papers crumpled beneath her weight as she moved like a beast along the floor. Most of them could be disregarded and subsequently discarded, but there were a few she couldn't part with. They were of a heavy paper, comprised of cruel fibers that cut the flesh subtly for sustenance. They were folded three times to give an air of professionalism and burned when held. They were relentless, seemingly endless; torn pages from the tome of the Leech God, written with the blood of its whore, Academia.

They were student loan statements.

"There you are," Beatrice said, spying a document hiding like a spider in the shadows beneath her desk. "Where are your buddies, eh?"

She plodded like a toddler on all fours towards the desk and snatched the document. At the corner of her eye, she saw its companion skirting along the carpet, the box fan in the window its humming accomplice, and grabbed that one, too.

"Gotcha," she said, a maniacal grin forming across her face. But just as quickly as it had formed, the grin disappeared and sadness came over her. "I've lost it."

A voice wreathed in buzzing spoke from the foot of her bed: "Do you always talk to yourself this much?"

Beatrice turned her head towards the source of the sound. In a cradle of sheets, she saw the soft glow of her cell phone's screen. She squinted and scowled; tried to remember what she had said or done in the past fifteen minutes that could be used against her in future conversations. *I think I'm safe.* She'd done and said worse in her life. She wasn't proud of the fact, but it did make these moments of madness a little more manageable.

"Are you there?" The voice—*Lauren? God damn it*—"Is everything alright?"

"Yes and no," Beatrice said, picking up the phone. "I must have butt dialed you." *Turned the speaker phone on too,* she thought. *How the hell?* She put the receiver to her ear. "How long have you been listening? Why didn't you say something earlier?"

Nothing.

"Did you just shrug?"

"Sorry, I was reading something on the Internet." A click of the mouse, a snap of a laptop lid: Her full attention was on Beatrice once again. "You sound tense."

"I am tense. I have no money. I have bills, and I have no money." She lifted the student loan statement close to her face. Her contacts were still resting comfortably in their case on the bathroom sink, and her eyes were useless without them. "Jerry fired me," she said nonchalantly.

"Seriously? What's his problem?" Lauren paused for a moment.

"Wait, what did you do? Beatrice, come on now. What'd you do?"

"Nothing!" Beatrice shouted. "I was late last week. That's it. He was just looking for a reason. He's always had it in for me."

A snap of the laptop lid, a click of the mouse: Lauren had lost interest again. "That really sucks," she said, her voice distant. "What are you going to do? I'm sure your mom and dad would be more than willing to help you out."

"No," Beatrice said. "I love them, but I'll never hear the end of it. This is my apartment, this is my car…" she pointed out the window as though her friend could see what she saw, "… and this is my debt."

"Hmmm, I don't know," Lauren said, sipping on something loudly. "That's kind of stupid. You should ask them. You're not proving anything to them unless you tell them, anyways. Jesus." Her voice trailed off. "People are weird as hell nowadays."

"Tell me something I don't know… like where I could come up with two hundred bucks."

"You're making a big deal out of two hundred dollars?" Lauren cleared her throat. "I don't get it. Why would you protest bioengineered organs? It's good for everyone."

Beatrice watched the blades of the box fan rotate in their plastic prison. "Did they use that word in that article or did you come up with it on your own?"

"Were you always a bitch or did you just get this way from being poor all the time?" Lauren snapped back.

"You know the answer," she said solemnly. "They don't like people playing god," Beatrice explained, quickly returning to the topic. "Next we'll be making clones… gay clones! Then they'll really lose their shit."

"Some already have."

Beatrice knew Lauren was referring to her older sister, who had joined the Penitent, a fundamentalist group hell-bent on freeing god from his supposed earthly shackles.

("How can something trap god? He's god!" Beatrice commented to Lauren once, who only responded with a red face and a string of curses.)

"Why don't you mosey on over to campus and see if you can get some work?" she suggested, changing the subject. "Two hundred can't be that hard to scrounge up. I still think you should ask your parents. What the hell you trying to prove? You bummed like three hundred off them that one time you trashed Connor's—"

Click.

Beatrice spent the majority of the trip to campus pressed up against the driver's side door, trying desperately to avoid the searing hot, metal seatbelt buckle that followed her like a magnet. She looked like a cat clinging to a bathtub's edge, and when the buckle touched her, howled like one, too. Her life, with its student loans and murderous seatbelt buckles, was a hard life, indeed.

At the last stop sign before Brooksville University, Beatrice saw a chubby kid gawking at her through the window. Caught and shamed, she came down from her perch and tried to play it cool. She winked at the kid like he had a chance with her—and at this point, self-esteem as low as it was, he probably did—and fiddled with the radio knobs. *Here's hoping no one escaped from the sanitarium today*, she thought, flipping through the channels. *Because if anyone fits the bill...*

Beatrice knew from her experience as an undergraduate that the library would likely be, no, had to be in need of assistance. The building housed thousands of books within its ancient walls, and yet most students avoided it, as though by standing in its shadow they would become irrevocably smart and painfully self-aware. She'd seen the skeletal librarians who worked its counters and shelves. They were too feeble to even lift the chain attached to their smeared spectacles. There'd be work, Beatrice knew—good, old fashioned, mind-numbingly boring, punch-me-in-the-tits work. She saw herself inventorying books, scanning documents; hell, she'd even engage in small talk ("What a cute kid!" she'd lie as one of the old birds whipped out a photo of their buck-toothed boy) if it helped sweeten the pot.

When she arrived, however, Beatrice quickly learned that not only was she, as Lauren had said, a bitch, but that she was also, somehow, this-has-never-happened-to-me-before wrong. The library had become a gathering place. Its post-modern innards were fitted with cushioned chairs and a series of stalls that vomited caffeinated drinks and sugary snacks into the hands of the bleary-eyed.

Beatrice swallowed hard and rubbed her temples. She looked past the turnstiles at the food court's edge, to the check-out desk, where young and tanned volunteers saw to the long line of bookworms holding their meals tightly.

She stormed through the turnstiles and crossed the first floor, through History and Science, Sexuality and Theatre, going nowhere in particular as her mind turned in on itself. What had she expected? Some mecca the unwashed student body only spoke of in whispers? Some dark and dingy warehouse plucked out of one of the shitty '80s movies she always watched and then turned against when her friends started railing on them? She just wanted something temporary, something that paid under the table. Something that wouldn't require three weeks of an agonizing wait and a background check she couldn't even begin to afford. Yeah, she was being stubborn. Yeah, she was acting irrational. But those were character flaws. Heaven forbid she change them.

For a brief and desperate moment, Beatrice considered selling drugs. But given her luck, the first customer would be some pot-bellied police officer all too eager to look the other way if she only gave him two minutes and ten seconds of her time. She shook the notion out of her head. She never had much hand-eye coordination to begin with.

"What the hell was I thinking?" she said to herself when no one was around.

I wasn't thinking, she answered. *I'm just a hypocritical bitch who assumed everyone around here was just as dumb as I was when I came through.*

At the back of the library, Beatrice found a small reading table and took a seat in the chair beside it. The tabletop was warm, calming; the heat of the sun infused into its wood. There was a small, battered book of folklore near the edge, but she couldn't be moved to touch it. She let her body relax, which was a rare luxury, and began to consider the consequences of what came next.

"Fuck it," she said, exhaustion tugging at her eyelids. Last night had been a long night, though at this point, she'd forgotten why. "I'll just ask. I'll just… I'll just ask. Not like I can change their minds about me, anyway. Damage is done."

A door opened nearby. Sleep fled like a thief and left her there with nothing but dizzied surprise. Dormant symptoms of Post-Traumatic College Disorder flared. Beatrice sat up and crossed her legs to look as alert as possible—a reflex perfected from the many years spent napping in class. Her hands found the book on folklore and she opened it to its middle, where an excerpt from someone's diary rambled on about flies. She had no reason to appear busy to this individual should they come her way—she was an adult now, or at least, that's what she'd heard—but appearance was important to Beatrice; not physical appearance necessarily, but mental appearance: those things one can see and not see at the same time. Being pretty hadn't done a good job of preparing her for being anything else.

She continued to turn the pages of the book, consulting the front matter momentarily for the author's name. *Who names their daughter Dagmar?* She flipped to the back of the book and read the preface to the final story, which was about ghouls. *I cuss too much*, she thought randomly. *I'm all those things I told myself I'd never be. Ugh, this day needs to end.*

"Hello there."

A man's voice. Beatrice's eyes climbed the page slowly as though it were Everest itself, until she reached the leathery summit and saw who had addressed her from the other side. He was a bearded man in his mid-forties, dressed too well to be anything but a professor. He had a metal lunchbox in one hand and a half-eaten apple in the other. She knew this man. He had taught an advanced Biology class she'd attended approximately one year ago. His name was Frederick Ødegaard, and she had—still had, actually—a crush on him, though perhaps "crush" was too soft a word. Demolish, maybe. She had a demolish on him.

"Hello," Beatrice said, smiling, doing her best to pretend as though she didn't know him.

He nodded as the door closed behind him and the extra light left the room. Beatrice followed him with her eyes as he passed, stopped, and then turned around, pointing the apple in her direction.

"Brit... no. You had that... Beatrice, right?" he asked, his eyes glowing from the firing of his brain's synapses. "I had you in class, didn't I?"

Now that she had permission to stop acting ignorant, Beatrice set the book down. "That's right. Sorry. Once I graduated, it all kind of left me." She went to stand up, and he gestured for her to remain sitting. "How are you?" She was smiling so hard some drool came out. *Probably thinks I have rabies*, she thought, wiping her mouth real fast. *Maybe he's into rabies.* She cocked her head, ashamed of herself. *Fuck you, Beatrice.*

"I'm well, thank you." He searched the surrounding area with his eyes—"Ah ha!"—and pulled a lone chair from its solitude in Zoology over to Beatrice's table. "Do you mind?"

Hell no, she thought, but instead said, "Of course not." She pulled her legs back, up, and under her. Her face was sore from smiling. It wasn't something she did often.

"I just like to catch up with students after they've graduated. I, uh…" he scrutinized the apple in his hand, "… sorry," he said meekly, unclasping the lunchbox and placing it inside. "It's a project of mine. I don't feel like this university does a very good job of preparing its students for the world. It's something I gather data on. Do you work here now? Grad school?"

"Funny you should say that," Beatrice said as Frederick set his lunchbox on the floor. "Well, no, never mind. You don't want to hear it."

"Please," he said, resting his hands on his chin and stroking his beard like an intellectual, "I've been here for a while and have connections. You were a good student, if I remember correctly. I hate to see a mind go to waste."

Good student? I got a B. I was practically dishonored. Beatrice laughed uncomfortably. "It's not really a problem."

Frederick Ødegaard lifted an eyebrow that told her he wasn't buying it.

Beatrice sighed and sold him her sob story. "I have student loans and my boss fired me. I know I can get back on my feet, but I was hoping to find something, well, a little more instantly gratifying until then." She took a deep breath, because asking for help took everything out of her.

Frederick leaned back in his chair. "I don't know how ethical it would be to ask you this if you were still a student, but since you're alumni now, I can't imagine anyone taking issue."

Spit it out before my imagination runs wild.

"The wife and I have been meaning to spend some time together lately, but we have a child, a little boy, so it's hard. We'd ask the neighbors, but Mrs. Ødegaard doesn't much care for them, and the closest relative is three states over. I feel like my wife would take to you."

"I would be honored to babysit for you," Beatrice said stoically to the question that had yet to be posed.

"Would you?" Frederick rested his head on his hand once more and grinned. "Oh, that would be great. To be honest, I'm the one who has been putting it off—going out. I just keep forgetting. But if I can help you, then that gives me a good excuse to get my act together, yes?"

"Yes, a relationship is like a fire: You have to tend it or it'll go out."

Beatrice cringed at her words, and then died a little on the inside.

Frederick cleared his throat. "Now, there is something you should know about our boy. He is delayed. He's no different than any other kid at six; just needs a little more time and patience. I understand if you'd feel uncomfortable watching him."

"Not at all," Beatrice said kindly. *How much? Do I charge extra for this sort of thing? Is that a fucked up thought to have?*

"Good, that's good. He's a sweet boy. A little shy with strangers, but I expect he'll warm up to you. And if he doesn't, that's okay, too. The house is big, and we just want someone to make sure he's safe while we're away."

"I can do that. I used to babysit all the time back home. It's fun. You get to act like a kid again," Beatrice said in dreamy reminiscence.

"Excellent, I'm glad to hear that. I'm glad I ran into you today. I'm thinking…" he rummaged through his pockets and produced a pencil and a small notepad, "… if tonight goes well and you think you'd like to try it again, we could make a regular thing of this? Twenty-five an hour sound reasonable? Come over at seven, leave at midnight? After Friday, if you're still interested, it could become a once or twice a week thing? Of course, if you're too busy…"

Beatrice interrupted. "I don't have much of a social life. I think that sounds great. I really, really appreciate you helping me, Mr. Ødegaard. Hey, listen, I don't mean to shoot myself in the foot, but your wife… why would she trust me? I'm kind of a stranger."

"She won't, but I'll tell you what: If she makes a big fuss about it, I'll pay you all the same." Frederick rose to his feet, lifted the chair up, and placed it back where it belonged. "I really appreciate your help, Beatrice," he said, bending over and picking up his lunchbox. He put the pencil to the pad of paper and wrote something onto its sickly yellow surface. "Our address and my phone number," he said, handing Beatrice the note. "We live just outside of town. Maidenwood. If you have trouble finding your way, just call."

"This is bullshit."

Beatrice's car climbed the hill outside of Brooksville the same way an old woman climbs out of bed: groaning and shaking and quite convinced they will never be able to do it ever again. She held the steering wheel tightly as it shook, tried to avoid breathing the noxious fumes that kept coming through the vents. She pulled her feet from the floor, afraid that it would give way and she would be pulled through and smeared across the road.

Two months ago, the car salesman with the uneven moustache had assured Beatrice and her father the vehicle was new, driven only by those who had shown an interest but lacked the funds to call it their own. The logical conclusion would've been the twerp with the pubestache had gotten one over on them, but this was Beatrice, which meant the car was alive, and it was trying to tell her something.

"Lauren," she said, taking out her phone and running her thumb against the touch screen. "Lauren," she repeated over the dial tone, "Lauren, pick up, you lazy, little…"

"-y, what's up?" Lauren said, having started talking before she answered.

"My car," Beatrice started. But just as she reached the top of the hill, it went silent. "Never mind." She took a deep breath. The odor was gone as well. Why did a rumbling car give her more pause than the odd job it was carting her off to? "Hey," she said, nerves loosening, "guess what?"

"Hang on." A toilet flushed loudly on the other side. "What? Don't make me guess."

"I got a job."

"That was fast. I bet you feel better. Did Jerry take you back?"

"No, hell no," Beatrice said.

Ahead, the forest of Maidenwood stretched beneath the dusk-lit horizon, its ragged, fall-ravaged canopy glowing orange and red. Where the road cut through, the forest was dark, the trees beside it too densely packed to let much light in. Beatrice turned on her headlights as she crossed into the wooded expanse, which ran for miles across the tri-county area, and hoped for the best.

"Did you ever have Ødegaard?"

The car rumbled and stuttered. She punched the dash and it got the hint.

"I'm a vegetarian. You know I don't eat that meat shit."

Suddenly, the steering wheel became Lauren's pasty neck, and with teeth clenched, Beatrice squeezed the life out of it. "He is a professor. He teaches a lot of things. Like Biology."

"Oh, oh, oh." Silence, and then: "Nope, doesn't ring a bell."

Beatrice let out a sigh. "Campus was a bust, but that's where I ran into him. We got to talking. I told him what was going on. He said he really needed a babysitter for his kid. He was really nice and, I mean, why not?"

"I can think of a few reasons why not. Isn't that the one you had a crush on?"

"No, I think you're thinking of somebody else."

"It does get hard to keep track of all of them."

"Frederick Ødegaard, that's his name. He lives outside of town, up here in Maidenwood. I bet he's rich. I'll scope the place out, raise my rate when they get back."

Lauren hummed. "Address?"

Beatrice rattled it off and said, "I'll be done at midnight. I just wanted to tell someone where I was going."

"You planning on needing an alibi?"

"I'm planning on not being a victim of stupidity."

"Then what the hell you doing up in Maidenwood? You got weak arms, B. Little twig things. I'll come up, keep you company. No charge. Friend discount."

"You're easily one of the most unpleasant people that I know. Is this what passes for a woman nowadays?"

Lauren snorted. "In case he turns out to be a tenured creep with a thing for down-and-out graduates… You bring your knife?"

Beatrice smiled a crooked smile. She leaned over and saw the hint of the blade's handle between the eyeliner and emaciated wallet. "I'll call you later, when I'm rich."

Beatrice knew that she would get lost trying to find Ødegaard's house, because she always got lost going someplace new. She was one of those rare creatures who never seemed to get to where she needed to go, and when she did, it was after miles of bad road and months of even worse decisions.

"This is how it starts," she said to herself as she put the car in reverse, having finally seen the turn off, which was an old dirt trail that snaked through the trees.

She backed up, nearly clipping the crooked mailbox at the driveway's end. "Young girl goes into woods. Young girl doesn't come out." She laughed, and then, as a precaution, texted the job and Ødegaard's address to her mother and father.

Half a mile and two texts later to her mother ("Sorry I haven't called," and "Yes, of course I miss you guys."), the trees thinned away to a clearing where a large, well-kept farmhouse sat. In actuality, "farmhouse" may have been a stretch of the word, because the plot of land was far too small and the crops growing on it were far too gone to be of use for anything other than compost. Beatrice slowed the car to a crawl, trying to find the neighbors Ødegaard had mentioned on campus. But if they were there, then they were somewhere deep in the woods, beyond the wall of trees that encircled the professor's estate.

"I guess you don't move to someplace like this because you want people to find you," she said, stopping the car at the side of the house. "Alright, here we go."

Beatrice opened the door and stepped out of the car. She pulled up her jeans—she'd lost weight, thanks to stress and poverty—and made her way to the porch. She tucked her hair behind her ears, took a deep breath, and then took one more, because she couldn't believe how clean the air was out here. *Relax*, she told herself, *he's a nice man. Just don't kill the kid and all will be well.* She smiled the same uncomfortably wide smile she used to put on for the yearbook hags and started a practice conversation in her head ("Wow, this house is so cozy, Mr. Ødegaard! Sure, I'll have a glass of water!").

Skin stretched across her face as though she were the victim of some vindictive plastic surgeon, Beatrice jogged up the porch's stairs and opened the screen to knock on the door behind it.

"Beatrice!" Frederick called out.

Beatrice kept her hand cupped around the doorknob, which was unexpectedly slick, and turned her head. She looked to the window on the left, where a spider's egg sac clung to the fingerprint-smeared glass. She stepped back slowly; the wood boards creaked and moaned beneath her weight, sounding as though they were ready to buckle at any moment. Beatrice curled her nose, covered her face with her hands. Something smelled sour, rotted, and when she bent over, she found it seemed to becoming from underneath the porch.

"Beatrice," Frederick repeated, clearing his throat. "Up here," he said, laughing.

Beatrice stepped back, leaned back. Looking up, she found her former professor's face peering out of a casement window on the second floor. "Oh," she said, stepping even further back, feeling dizzy. "I'm sorry! I didn't see you up there!"

"Did you find the place okay?" he asked, tapping his fingers on the windowsill. A fly buzzed about his head. "It's real easy to get lost in these woods. Still happens to me from time to time!"

Beatrice let out a fake laugh that sounded like a horse mid-orgasm.

"I'm sorry," he said, pulling away. "I'll be right down."

Beatrice covered her nose, breathed in the lotion she'd put on earlier. She scratched her ankle with the tip of her shoe, hissed when she broke the scab from shaving there. Listening closely, she could follow Frederick's movements in the house. She could hear his feet stomping down an old wooden staircase and across sticky linoleum flooring. Straining her ears, she heard the pull and turn of a door handle, and then the twist of a key inside a lock. For a moment, she lost track of his whereabouts—had he snuck off to the kitchen to finish dinner, she wondered, or to the laundry room for some pants?—and as she moved to let herself in, Frederick pulled open the door.

"I'm so glad you could make it," he said, smiling, pants and all.

"Thank you for this opportunity. I really don't know what I would have done otherwise." Beatrice slid her hands into her pockets and rocked back and forth, heel to toe, toe to heel. "Oh, what's your little boy's name? I totally forgot to ask."

Frederick waved her off. "Come on inside. I'll introduce you two. Would you like a glass of water?"

Beatrice bit her lip. "Sure, I'll have a glass of water!" she recited. "This is a really nice house you have."

The professor, humbled by the student's remark, stepped aside and held the door open for her. The student, enamored of the professor's demeanor, bowed her head and accepted the offer. For no reason in particular, Beatrice looked up and over her shoulder, back the way she'd come. She looked to her car parked in the growing shadows, to the tracks it'd left on the old, dirt road. Her eyes wandered over to the batch of crops swaying gently in the small field and the red yield cradled in their husks. She turned her attention to the trees so densely packed, to the shed she'd missed and now saw, its door hanging off its hinges, the hinges hanging off the door.

"Thank you," Beatrice said as her hair fell across her face.

"Please," he said, hand moving past hers, lifting and sliding the rebellious strands behind her tingling ear. "This is just what we needed." He took her hand.

Mother fuck, Beatrice thought, *don't be that girl. Just because you want it doesn't mean you should have it.* She looked away, to the window beside her, where the egg sac had burst and a thousand skittering births were now crawling all over the dirty glass. "I…" She cringed, felt embarrassed. "I don't think this is a good idea… whatever you… you're… whatever you have in mind."

"I'm sorry, Beatrice," he said kindly. "That's not what I had in mind."

Frederick dropped her hand and slammed her head against the side of the doorway. Beatrice's impact cracked the molding. Her teeth clamped down on her tongue. She stumbled and went to her knees. Mouth full of blood, she looked up at Frederick and started to cry.

With a hyena smile, Frederick crouched down and took her head in his hands. His fingers prodded the wound he'd made, eyes lighting up every time Beatrice whimpered. He admired what he'd created, and then, as though he thought he could do better, proceeded to bash her head in, until it was too slick to hold.

When Beatrice Bacchus came to, she may as well not have. Vision blurred and short of breath, she lay covered in blood, a migraine like a hailstorm pounding her gray matter. She forced herself to breathe, breaking the layer of coagulation that had sealed her lips. She felt shaky, disorientated; hungry and thirsty for anything but her own bodily fluids. The back of her head throbbed, and the pulpy contusion there spoke to her in the rapid thuds of her heart. Slowly, she touched it, to form an image in her mind of the damage done. It felt soft, swollen, not a part of her, like some parasite of pain that had decided to hitch a ride on her skull.

Whether she had a concussion or was on the brink of collapse, Beatrice was cognizant enough to remember what Ødegaard had done to her. She tried not to cry—she'd shown enough weakness already—but there they were, the tears, running down to her mouth, adding some salt to her already limited diet. At first, she blamed herself, because even without her contacts or a full-blown lobotomy, she should've seen it coming from a mile away. But self-loathing hadn't done much for her in the past, so she said "Fuck that" and forced herself up, until all the nausea inside her had been replaced with hatred and rage.

"Good morning," Ødegaard chirped from somewhere in the room.

Beatrice scooted away until she backed up against a crumbling wall. A single lightbulb dangled from the ceiling, swinging back and forth like a pendulum, as though someone had just turned it on. She followed its course, across the cement floor to the sweating walls. But if her attacker was here, he was in the dark places the light would never reach.

"Up here."

Too much movement and she'd be out again, so she took her time acknowledging him. In the shadows above her, where the ceiling sloped several feet higher, she saw the outline of a doorway and the shape of a man looking through it. Glancing at the floor, she saw two rusty circles beside her hands, likely from the ladder he'd taken and she now needed.

"You piece of shit," she muttered, proud of herself for being able to say anything at all.

Eyes adjusted to the dark, she could see the calmness in his face, the carefulness in his dress. She could even smell his cologne when a breeze blew through. The violence hadn't changed him, hadn't revealed him for what he was. He was still the same, while she would never be. Beatrice wanted to demolish him, though perhaps "demolish" was too soft a word. Slaughter, maybe. She wanted to slaughter him.

"It's nothing against you," he said. "I saw an opportunity and took it. You can appreciate that, can't you?"

"People know I'm here," she threatened. Her thoughts turned to the knife in her purse, which was probably somewhere upstairs, thrown in with the belongings of the other women he'd murdered. Her shoes and socks were missing as well. "They'll come looking for me, you dumb mother fucker."

He laughed. "Beatrice," he said through a smirk, "this isn't my first rodeo. I capture young people like yourself all the time. You wouldn't be down here if I wasn't any good at it."

"There's no wife, no kid," she said, ignoring him. "This isn't your house."

"Actually, my wife is at work." He stood up, loomed over her as though he meant to jump in and finish her off. "The house isn't ours in the legal sense, but no one is going to kick us out anytime soon." He bent over and pulled back on the large, metal door that sealed off the basement. "As for my kid, well, you two will meet soon enough. Make sure to make an effort. You'll thank me later, trust me."

Beatrice reared up, shouting, "What the hell are you—"

He slammed the door shut, snuffing out her throaty protest. A key ring scraped against the other side of it. Several locks and deadbolts slid into place. Any hope of leaving that way was now lost.

On shaking legs and borrowed time, Beatrice rose to her feet. She stumbled, pressed her palms into the sharp shards protruding from the wall. The lightbulb had calmed since she'd been sealed in, but she'd seen enough. It wasn't a basement but something else. The room had no function, no obvious purpose. The ceiling was an ocean of unending granite, not wooden floorboards like they ought to have been if she were truly under the house. No, this was something else, something deeper—a sub-basement or another place entirely. And why wouldn't it be? If she should scream, no one would hear her. And if she should die… Jesus, if she should die, would anyone even find her?

This place smelled as she imagined a coffin might; a kind of damp, saccharine rot comprised of years of abandon and regret. Fresh blood trickled down her neck, down her chest, as she took her first step forward. A bitter wind blew into the room, putting the lightbulb into a hypnotic motion. *Child?* She continued walking, refusing to the use wall for support, because at this point, the only thing she could rely on was herself. *He wants to torture me, savor this moment.* Maybe it was the head wound, but when she thought this, she did so academically, as though it were happening to someone other than herself. *There's nothing down here but what he wants me to believe is down here.* Her ears popped up, and with their newfound clarity, she heard water behind the walls and something else clicking its claws down subterranean haunts.

"This can't be the only way out," she told herself in between shallow breaths as panic set in. "And if it is, I'll climb the fucking walls."

Beatrice inhaled, held the musty air in her lungs and let it wilt them some. She exhaled and did this again. Slowly, like a knot untangling, she felt the tension leave her body, out the bloody hole in the back of her head. She thanked her therapist—"Fuck you, mother fucker, it doesn't work!" she'd shouted at him—and then threw up all over her feet. As stomach acids burned her throat, her thoughts started to slow, and madness, which had been waiting for its moment to strike, was tucked back into its genetic bed once more. With every exhale, she shed a bit of herself, until all that remained of Beatrice under the fluorescent light was the will to survive and the flesh and blood that would see it through.

She crouched, slid her pants down. For now, for once, her character flaws would become strengths. Too stubborn to die, too irrational to wait. If she had to kill, she'd kill, and if she had dig her way out, she'd dig her way out. Of all things, Beatrice was a scavenger, and if she had to fight for the last scraps of life, then she would.

At least, these were things she tried to convince herself of as she pissed on the floor, marking the thing she was determined to own.

As the last drop hit the ground, she heard something else in the black space beyond. Breathing, rapid and raspy, somewhere nearby. Feet, bare and calloused, shuffling. Followed by hands, dragging like an ape's, close behind. And then teeth and tongue, clicking and grinding—a siren's song of no subtlety, a butcher's call for the sake of brevity. The thing was coming for her, and it wanted her to know it.

Beatrice pulled up her pants and ran. There was only one entrance to this room, and she had to get out before it got in. She went beyond where the light reached and gathered herself in the darkness there. She felt the wall, felt the open air. Childhood claustrophobia had given her an acute sense of space. A hall, narrow enough for a few to pass, that's what she was up against. She put her back to the wall, the condensation waking the dried blood on her shirt. The rocks there ground into her spine, got into the crooks of her bones.

Beatrice waited and then edged forward; paused when she heard something patter by, left to right, where the hall clearly split. *Thank fucking god.* Without sight, she felt distant from her body, deprived of its sensations and functions. But in some ways, she was more prepared for this moment than others may have been. She'd spent most of her life listening to others bitch and bemoan their bad choices, and then would use it to her advantage. If nothing else, she could use that same art of manipulation to her advantage here.

Make sure to make an effort, she remembered Ødegaard saying, and now she realized why: It was a game.

The thing was back. From right to left it bounded and then stopped, where the hall branched. Short strides, small sounds: It was either very small or very careful. She could hear it sniffing, sampling the coffin air for the source of the new scents. Maybe it was a child, but it was easier to assume it a monster, instead. It would be an insult to humanity to call it anything else.

"There, there," a young boy called out. "There, there." His voice was high, his speech mangled. He spoke in imitation, and what he was imitating was a mother comforting its child. "There, there," Ødegaard's spawn carried on, promising kindness before the kill.

Beatrice moved her hand down the wall, reading its bumps as the blind would braille, searching for something, a pipe perhaps, to defend herself with. One foot after the other, she closed the gap between her and the boy, trying to reach another corridor. Could he hear her heart, feel the pulsing of her blood? Could he smell the piss that'd dribbled down her leg, taste the dead skin she was chewing off her lip? The darkness gave no answers, only promises.

"There, there," the boy rattled on. She could hear it turning in place, somehow felt its gaze tightening on the lightbulb behind her. "There, there. There—"

And then it was running.

Beatrice screamed and took off, keeping her hand to the wall. She ran down the hall, as though to meet the boy head-on. And right when they would've collided, the wall turned, so she did, too. She gasped as she pushed herself to the brink of collapse. Her legs wobbled, one buckling after the other, but she kept going.

Behind her, she could hear the boy giving chase, his hands and feet slapping like raw meat against the ground. Fear shook the pulpy peak on the back of her head and an avalanche of blinding terror ran down her face.

Her stomach twisted like a rag as she felt fingertips at her ankles. *Oh god, oh fuck, oh god.* The boy's hot breath seeped through her jeans, and she felt his rancid spittle dotting her thighs. There was a lust in his groans, a hunger that wouldn't be satiated through bloodshed alone. She'd experienced the feeling before, had known it herself. She needed to save her strength, because if she had to fight him off—

The boy's fleshy arms wrapped around her and yanked. Beatrice wheezed and then brought her leg up and kicked the boy's gut. He shrieked, released, and flew back, his bare body sliding repulsively across the floor.

The hell? Beatrice's foot felt heavy, as though something had sloughed off the boy onto it. She picked the mush out from in between her toes, shook off the wet, towel-like thing draped over her ankle. *What was this?* And then she bolted, not interested enough to find out.

If there was a heaven, then it was blood red, because that was the color of the light she saw up ahead. A black rectangle with crimson highlights—a door perhaps, or a dead-end. It didn't matter which. She barreled through it all the same.

It had been a door, and it cracked back against the wall as she flew into the room and fell to the floor. In a second she sampled the room—tiny, with heat lamps atop workbenches—and then scurried to the threshold.

"There, there."

The boy hurried down the hall, the closer he got to the room, the more defined he became. Long arms, spidery legs; bubbled flesh spread thin, pulled tight. The boy's face was deformed, molded into something grotesque, as though it were made of putty. And then, looking closer, she saw another face around his neck, its mouth forever fixed in its last moments of pain.

"There—"

Beatrice had seen enough. She slammed the door shut and pressed herself against it. Her sweat-stung eyes searched for a bolt, but it had long since been ripped free. On the other side, the boy screamed and threw his body against the door. Beatrice locked her legs and arms and absorbed the blows. Her head rocked back and forth with every crash, and she found herself losing time.

"There... there," he grunted, tiring himself with the assault.

What's that? Across the room, where the red light was deepest, she saw a small hole in the wall, a tunnel. *I have to bar the door.* The workbenches were near enough to grab, but only if she gave up her post. *If he knew, he would've just come in that way.* She felt something hot against her backside. Looking down, she saw a soupy puddle spreading under the door, chunks of flesh riding in on the iron tide. *Now, while its weak.*

She staggered to her feet and ran to the first workbench. No tools, but it was heavy enough to keep the boy out long enough for her to get away. She got around it and slid it towards the door, its metal legs rending the air with noise as they scraped against the floor. Beatrice caught the heat lamp atop it as it fell.

"Fuck. You," she said as the boy threw his shoulder into the door and sent his arm through.

Gritting her teeth, she pressed the light to his flesh. It melted immediately, creating a web of skin between limb and lamp. He pulled back, leaving a glove of flesh on the floor. Beatrice ran for a second workbench and lodged it under the first.

She dragged herself to the hole, her eyes following the lamp cords still plugged in at the top of the wall. *What the hell?* Hanging from the corner, just below the ceiling, a small camera sat, recording her suffering for the pleasure of the pervert who put her here. She wanted to tear it down, tear it apart, but the boy was at the door again, and her pathetic barricade wouldn't hold for long.

Beatrice pushed through the breach and came out in another hallway on the other side. Bright as they were, the red lights made their own impenetrable, dampening darkness. She could see a few feet in front of her, but even that crimson kindness didn't offer much more than its blacker counterpart. Three halls shot off in wildly different directions before her. She chose the leftmost, because in the end, what did it matter? They would all send her to the same place. Most choices, in most cases, always did.

Ten seconds in and the workbenches gave. The boy, the fiend, wailed, and she could hear it tearing through the room. Three hallways and the god damn monster ended up choosing the one she now stumbled down.

She picked up the pace, smacked face-first into a wall. A sharp pain shot through her nose and she tasted blood. She felt up the wall like a high school kid with a hard-on and went to the right. Another light, red, winking from above—another camera, more pornography. But then the red lights multiplied across her field of vision, like a thousand oozing sores. Her blood sugar was plummeting. Her body had betrayed her and would probably finish her off faster than the fiend ever could.

"There, there."

That fucking phrase. Beatrice's feet went out from under her as they slipped on a strip of something wet. She stumbled against the wall and then down the hall next to it. Her feet suctioned to the floor, her toes breaking up whatever filth had dried upon it. Her nose, dead as it was to the smells here, picked up something vile. A sweet odor, hot and abrasive; a combination of shit and a maggoty garbage smell. She didn't need to be able to see to know what she was walking through.

But then the motion activated lights came on and she saw anyway.

Bodies, and the things that make them up. Hands, arms, feet, and legs; torsos, faces, muscles, and fingers. The walls were plastered, the ground covered. Skulls and bones appeared to be coming out of the floor, which at this point, she couldn't even be sure was stone anymore. Everything looked chewed on, torn apart. This was the fiend's kitchen, and she'd wandered right into it.

"Stop."

Beatrice turned around and there the fiend crouched. Shocked, it took her a moment to comprehend what she was looking at. Loose flaps of dripping flesh shrouded its emaciated body. When it shifted, she saw its protruding ribcage, which had every manner of mutilation done unto it, as though it were the ceiling of some sadistic chapel. Its fingers were claws themselves, and its teeth gore-ridden stalagmites behind its sneering lips. Long ropes of pale muscle dangled from its wrist and neck, and it was only when her mind went to the darkest place possible that she realized what they were.

Umbilical cords.

The flesh fiend molested her with its infected eyes, as though deciding which parts of the meal to start with first. It slipped its hand between its legs and rubbed itself hard. With a few tugs and one spasmodic jerk, it spilt its foul, brown seed over the faces of the dead. It grunted out a laugh and then ambled forward, eager to share the last of its semen with its newfound friend.

Beatrice disappeared within herself—a tactic that had never failed her in the past—and ran as fast as she could. The motion activated lights flickered on and off, making of the murder hall a blood-drenched blur. She looked back. The flesh fiend was down on all fours, crawling after her, blinking forward with the strobing light.

"Hello, is there—"

Beatrice screamed as she crashed into—the lights flickered on—a man. He was young, her age, and drenched in blood. One of his eyes was swollen shut, and the other wasn't far behind. He had a Brooksville University sweatshirt on. He looked familiar in the way all sporty types do. She'd probably passed him in the halls, on the road. She wondered if she had known then what she was about to do now if it would've made a difference.

"Oh, Christ!" he shrieked, taking hold of Beatrice's arm. "We have to get out of here."

Beatrice nodded and then, with one shove of herculean might, sent him stumbling down the hall. He slipped, landed chin first; a tooth blew out of his mouth and plinked off the wall. The flesh fiend rumbled towards him, a whirling dervish of stolen skin.

"God, please! Please!"

The flesh fiend mounted him and proceeded to eat that which it had quickly fucked into a paste.

As Beatrice hurtled down the hall, a geyser of stomach acids burned through her throat and mouth. Using the motion activated light, she turned down several winding tunnels, until, when its influence grew dim, she found another illuminated place.

The doorway was a bloody slit, a stone womb with a hot, red light bleeding through. Beatrice went sideways and slid in, because at this point, why not? There were heat lamps here, too, as though the flesh fiend's skins weren't enough to keep it warm. But stranger still were the decorations, the cruor-smeared specks of the thing's personality. Trashy popular novels covered the floor, while philosophical journals were stacked like cairns across the room. Along the walls reams of paper ran, crayon depictions of men and women of various races and ethnicities drawn onto them. What stood out the most, however, were the skulls. Atop a desk, beside a tipped-over wardrobe, twenty or thirty skulls sat, each one a different size and shade. Trophies, Beatrice thought. But then she saw an order to their placement and bits of flesh like straps beneath their jaws. No, not trophies. Masks.

"Are you fucking kidding me?" Beatrice spoke just to hear her own voice.

What was it? Human? She'd heard stories of serial killers and psychosis, drug-induced or otherwise. It wasn't a boy. Beatrice wouldn't let herself believe a child could do as it had done. That was just some degrading pet name given to it by Ødegaard. So what else? A monster? It'd fucked its way through a full-grown man without batting an eyelid. Then again, how had she reacted? An entitled sense of survival, a bit of guilt, and a spoonful of bile—that was the extent of her response. What did that make her? Why hadn't she… if she made it out… the nightmares would find her… they deserved her… and she'd let them have…

… Beatrice fell to her knees, the drop adding a few more bruises to each. She was done, had given everything. Her eyelids fluttered in revolt, but sleep's army was one that could never truly be bested. She fell back on her heels, arms limp at her sides. Kneeling before the skulls, one would've thought she was worshiping them, and perhaps she was. The flesh fiend, man or monster, was clearly capable—was that its poetry she saw upon the desk?—and clearly, terrifyingly, important.

Important. Whether it was a man or a monster, it didn't matter. She'd seen the cameras fixed to the wall, and now that she was thinking about them, she caught their lenses blinking nearby. In a corner, a pile of the plastic peeping toms had been stacked high, like bodies left out as threats to future predators. Ødegaard wanted to observe the flesh fiend in its most secluded state, but the creature clearly wasn't having any of that. But the professor clearly hadn't given up the ghost, either. Beatrice doubted he traveled the halls this far to the fiend's chamber just to put up surveillance, so either the thing was tranquilized on sight… or there was another way out.

A surge of energy coruscated through Beatrice. Her legs shook as she stood. She could feel the strain across her body, the subtle strings of biological processes of which only the damned truly know. Could she really leave this place? Even if she did, she wouldn't. Every night she'd revisit this room and maze, and every night would be worse than the day she'd spent in it. At this moment, she was dead. And she feared what would happen if she started living again.

Beatrice took a deep breath and, out of sheer curiosity, snatched the poem from the desk. She had to focus her eyes to read it, because the words were crooked, jagged, as though the flesh fiend had meant to carve rather than write them.

> *In this place,*
> *I found my space,*
> *Among those I hope to see.*
> *In this skin,*
> *I live within,*
> *Among those I hope to be.*
> *In this hell,*
> *I hear the knell*
> *Among those I hope to free.*
>
> *They will look up to me,*
> *And see themselves reflected,*
> *In the blood I've taken,*
> *And the lives I've rejected.*
>
> *They will look up to us,*
> *As we look down upon them,*
> *And be glad to stand in our shadows.*

It read like something between a murderer's manifest and baby's first bleak poem. What struck Beatrice about the piece was the arrogance of it, the entitlement. The flesh fiend ran around in the stinking bowels of the earth, skinning and fucking everything it came across, and still it viewed itself as Ødegaard's gift to man. Perhaps it was human after all.

"How are... going down there?"

Beatrice's head snapped towards the sound. She'd heard a voice, not the flesh fiend's, but a woman's, soft and quiet and echoing. Across the room, near a stained mattress, she caught the glint of wet skin in the red light. Moving closer, she saw that the bloody strips billowed outward, as though they were covering something.

"He doesn't need... You there?"

She parted the strips of flesh and found the mouth of a chain-link box. It stopped at her hips, so she went down on all fours to have a better look inside. The wall sweated before her a few feet ahead. She plodded forward, hands sinking into piles of stinking sludge, and then craned her neck as the box opened at the top.

"Mother fuck," she said, unable to restrain herself.

The metal fencing twisted upward and ran for twenty or thirty feet through the earth. At the top, a silver light sat, doing little to stop the darkness. Beatrice jumped back as the ground gurgled and sputtered. Looking down, she watched rotted run-off slip into a drain beneath her.

"These cameras... can you see them?"

The voice wound down the chamber, bouncing off the walls like a patient in an insane asylum. As her eyes probed the dark for signs of the speaker, she saw the most beautiful thing she'd ever seen in her entire life: a ladder.

It stood freely, running straight up from the floor to the tunnel's end. She was too far down to tell how it stayed in place, but by the grime on the rungs, it was obvious it saw frequent use. As quiet and careful as she could be, Beatrice went for the ladder and started to climb it. The flesh fiend had to be close by. If not, then it wouldn't be much longer until Ødegaard and his partner realized she'd given their "boy" the slip.

"... all a little much."

Beatrice looked up. Suddenly, the silver light was no longer silver and seemed to be moving closer.

Oh fuck.

She stopped, pressed herself into the ladder. A river of blood and sinew poured down the tunnel, drenching her body in the bodies of others. Severed fingers and toes bounced off her shoulders. She could

feel teeth cracking against her head wound. If she didn't die by canni-
balism or dismemberment, then surely infection would do her in.

The turning of a wheel, the groaning of pipes. Beatrice rubbed her
eyes until she could see again. The woman was cleaning. By the amount
she'd hosed over the edge, it seemed here was where they fed it themselves, or watched it closely, like gawking mouth-breathers at a zoo.

When the deluge was reduced to a dribble, she started up the ladder
again. Red eyes beamed at her from behind the fencing—more cameras, but smartly out of reach—yet she heard no commotion above.
Either the cameras weren't working, or they weren't watching.

"When did the lock break?" the woman asked, her voice clearer
now.

A distant response from Ødegaard: "What?"

Lock? Beatrice squinted: The silver light above her was thinly grid-
ded. Another door, a grate at the top, sealing off the tunnel, stopping
her escape.

"Give me a status update!" the woman shouted.

Beatrice's grip weakened as panic set in. They were going to check
the cameras. She hurried past their unrelenting gaze and then, in one
motion, swung herself around the ladder, so that she was holding to it
from behind.

"I'm taking a shit!" she heard Ødegaard belt.

The woman, who had to be his wife, groaned. The sharp click of
her heels stabbed the air as she stepped up to the grate. A long shadow
slithered down the tunnel's walls. Seconds like hours passed, and then
a flashlight beam bore down on the ladder. Beatrice held her breath,
held on tight. Being behind the ladder, beneath the small outcrop to
which it was attached at the top, she was mostly hidden. But her hands,
those pale and gangly things, were out in the open, about to give her
away.

Beatrice prayed to every god she could, even the vermillion one
Lauren's sister had set out to free, and waited for an answer.

"Who was the girl?"

The flashlight was pulled away and Ødegaard's wife's shadow followed after. She hadn't seen her. She hadn't fucking—

The element of surprise would be enough to blindside the bitch, so
she went for it. She swung back around the front and clambered up it.
Her hands and feet slid and slipped, but the adrenaline pumping
through her veins kept her centered, focused.

"I hate how smart he is," Ødegaard's wife said, walking back towards the grate. She went to one knee and looked through it. "How does he always…"

Beatrice's eyes met hers.

"No!"

Beatrice propelled herself up the ladder and slammed her hands into the grate. It flew backward, bashing Ødegaard's wife's jaw. As she reeled, a burst of heat blew out of the woman's hand. A rubber bullet grazed Beatrice's shoulder.

"Come here!" she bellowed, a searing hot pain shooting through her arm.

Five rungs left… three, two… She jumped, grasped the edge of doorway, and hoisted herself up. Her pupils dilated and everything went white, but she'd seen where Ødegaard's wife had fallen. She rolled on top of her and broke her knuckle on the woman's shattered jaw.

"Frederick," his wife begged, the words bloody spit bubbles on her lips.

Beatrice stood up, her eyes having adjusted some, and kicked the gun out of the woman's hands. She paced back and forth inside the enclosure, looking for a way out. *There, there*, she thought, hating herself for thinking those words. A door half her height sat slightly ajar, the keycard reader attached to it blinking green.

"Beatrice stop," Ødegaard said calmly.

The world had begun to spin, causing the colors of the farmhouse—where was she? The basement?—to coalesce and consume the objects before her.

She bent down, clawed at the ground until her fingers wrapped around the pistol. She lifted it, trained it on the shape of the man she'd once imagined loving and now only wanted to kill.

"Come out of there, Beatrice," he said, stepping forward. His hands were up, she could see that much. "Isabelle, you too. We underestimated her, and now we owe her an explanation."

"You… you owe me a lot more than that, dickshit," Beatrice said, her words slurred, her bank of insults run dry.

Isabelle stirred and started to crawl forward. Beatrice pointed the pistol at her spine and fired. The rubber bullet put an end to that.

"All this noise, you better come out."

He was right: She could hear something in the tunnel, scaling not the ladder but the fencing. The flesh fiend was coming.

"Six, huh? You said he was six years old." She stepped over the hose Isabelle had used to wash down the enclosure and slipped through the doorway, shutting it behind her. Isabelle whimpered as the electronic locks thumped into place.

She sidestepped as Ødegaard ran for the door and swiped his keycard. "He's six, but not six years." The locks relented and he hurried to his wife. She curled up like a snake, and he grabbed both her hands and started dragging. "Six months. He's six months old."

"I don't give a shit, you fucking liar." Beatrice's heart started to pound harder as the sound of the flesh fiend's claws grew louder. She fired another shot, hoping to imprison both of the Ødegaards, but she missed.

How many bullets are left? She didn't know. The only time she'd shot a gun was with her dad on the range. That had been the only time they'd done much of anything together.

"Can you imagine what he'd be like in a few years?" Ødegaard pulled himself and his wife out of the enclosure, but instead of shutting the door, he left it wide open.

"What... what are you doing?"

Beatrice started to shake. Up here, in the light, she had no strength. She had never truly learned how to function in it. Her place was the darkness, with the things that happen in it. Now that she had the chance to get what she wanted, she wavered. She wiped her face and wished for a new one.

"All new creatures have kinks that need to be ironed out."

Beatrice bit her lip, tasted someone else's blood there. This wasn't the time for self-loathing, self-reflection. *This is a cliché*, she thought. *I'm a fucking cliché.* She raised the gun and fired directly at Ødegaard's chest. *Get it together.*

"Christ!" he gasped, releasing his wife and falling back against the enclosure.

Beatrice shuffled towards him, pistol whipped him across the nose. He doubled over, mouth to her toes. As he drooled on them, she reached into his pants and swiped his wallet.

"Amateur operation you've got going here," she said, pocketing her pay. "I'll—"

The flesh fiend sat crouched at the top of the ladder, its swollen, blood-red eyes staring her down. It wore the college kid's face now, and bits of his Brooksville University sweatshirt were pasted to the beast's body.

"They are the best of us," Frederick Ødegaard said, sitting up, pulling his wife onto his lap. "They'll make us better, show us where we've gone wrong." He looked back at the flesh fiend, a fat tear in his eye. "They'll keep the balance when everything else has gone out of order."

Beatrice unloaded the gun into the creature. The flesh fiend staggered backward, until it was wobbling on the edge. She screamed, threw the weapon. It cracked its head and sent it flailing, wailing, into the tunnel. *They're first*, she thought. *It'll get them, and I'll get away.*

Ødegaard shook his head as though he could read her mind. "He would never hurt us. We created him and his kind. I'd start running, Beatrice. Town's a long way off."

Beatrice turned on her heels and gave everything she had left to get across the basement. She found the stairs, went down on all fours, and climbed up them. She pushed through the door at the top, into a hall. She crawled, crouched, ran forward, crashing into the walls. Picture frames fell down around her, spreading shards of glass across the floor for her to step on. Her feet flared with rough spots of pain, but she paid it no mind.

The front door. Finally. She ran across the tongue of rug that led up to it and ripped the door open. Warm sunlight and fresh air. The sensations were so overwhelming that, in some ways, they were harder to take than anything else that'd happened to her. She stepped out onto the porch, the dense forest beckoning her forward. Her car was there, but her keys were as good as gone.

Here's hoping no one escaped from the sanitarium today, she thought, hurrying down the steps, head wound leaking fluid down her neck. *Because if anyone fits the bill...*

BLACK OCCULT MACABRE VOL. 1 ISSUE 7

THE INTERROGATION

No matter how many times Connor Prendergast pushed, poked, and prodded his mother's meatballs, they continued to be totally inedible. For his mother, Mrs. Prendergast, the art of cooking was as messy as childbirth, and sounded about as enjoyable to her as an appointment with her gynecologist. Clearly the odds have never been in Connor's favor.

When he was five, Connor had developed a coping skill to manage the reoccurring trauma of his mother's meals. With one eye shut and a fork raised high, he would become a towering cyclops, skewering helpless potatoes (fries) and oblivious chickens (nuggets). Using their blood, which was actually ketchup, he would coat the salty, golden limbs he'd collected in a pile and shove them into his gummy mouth. Of course, Mr. Prendergast had found it all very appalling. It was almost as inexcusable as placing one's elbow on the table. But to Mrs. Prendergast, Connor's imagination offered some relief. It meant she no longer had to stoop to the family dog's level and scoop the leftovers into his bowl just so it wouldn't go to waste.

Twenty-one years later and Connor still found himself wreaking countryside carnage on the villages of Little Fryerton and Noodle D'Cluck. Except now, he kept it a secret. Unfortunately, the meatballs, which were staring him down like the starving third world kids his father had warned him of, were impervious to his imagination. He tried to make of them nefarious diplomats or holy homebodies brandishing bibles for beatings, but it was impossible. Consumption was inconceivable.

He set down his utensils, wincing as they clinked loudly against the plate. He couldn't do it. All hope now rested in the family dog and his garbage pit stomach. Needless to say, for Connor, at the golden age of twenty-six, hyperbole wasn't just old vocab word—it was a way of life.

"Dinner was great! Thanks!" he said, beaming, as though to blind his mother from the fact he'd hardly touched the meal.

Mrs. Prendergast swirled the wine in her cup and said slowly, "Tell me true. You hated it, didn't you?"

Connor looked at the crime scene of half-baked, half-eaten, and wholly repulsive portions of food. He gave no response, only smiled, and left its meaning for her interpretation.

"How's life, son?" Mr. Prendergast asked, a noodle slithering into his mouth. "You should come around more often."

Connor choked down a piece of garlic bread to give himself a moment to come up with an excuse. His mind, however, was a wasteland; an endless expanse of fleeting ideas and grand delusions dampened by all the alcohol he'd chugged a few hours earlier.

So, like the worm desperate to be off its hook, Connor rose out of his seat, pointed across the table towards the living room, and said, "James has a boner."

A few feet away on the couch watching television, Connor's seventeen-year-old brother, James, went stiff. Whether or not his sibling's sudden paralysis was due to an unfortunate erection was inconsequential. Because it wasn't James the seventeen-year-old human to which he pointed, but James the seventeen-year-old Siberian husky, whose old bones creaked louder than his barks.

But the fact that it made Connor's brother turn beet red was most definitely a bonus. And something he'd totally pass off as deliberate years down the line.

"Jesus, help me," Mrs. Prendergast pleaded, finishing off her wine and immediately filling the glass back to its brim.

Mr. Prendergast covered his mouth with a napkin, laughing weakly like a nun at a dirty joke. He shook his head and put his elbows on the table, relinquishing for the evening his hold on trivial formalities.

"You're hilarious," James said, turning his head and staring his brother down. "Grow up, dude."

"It's a big deal. Well, maybe not big—"

The dog snorted.

"—but average, for sure!" Connor gave the dog the thumbs up.

James the seventeen-year-old husky groaned: compliment accepted.

"So why don't you come around more often, eh?" James the human lowered a blanket onto his four-legged doppelganger to maintain his modesty.

Connor looked at the meatballs before him and considered lobbing one at his little brother. Afraid that it may blow through James' skull, he quickly decided against it. Yes, James' question was an excellent question—one that was inevitably asked at every get together—but no matter how he spun it, he was the one who always ended up caught in their web.

Connor puffed up his chest, stuck out his pinky. Deepening his voice and giving it a decidedly British tone, he said, "I've been busy with the magazine. Readers are absolutely ravenous for new material."

James smirked. "They do know its bullshit, right?"

Mrs. Prendergast started to hiccup. "J-J-Ja-Jame-James!"

When she probably thought no one was listening (they were), Mrs. Prendergast snuck in a few burps behind her hand.

Mr. Prendergast finished his spaghetti and made some incoherent lies about the quality of the cooking. "Language, come on," he then said. He shook his head, and covered the side of his face to avoid making eye contact with the dog.

"It's up to my readers to decide if its fake," Connor said, pushing his plate away. *Jackass*, he thought, glowering at James. *Always makes me look like an idiot.*

"How many subscribers are there now?" Mrs. Prendergast asked. She started to squint, as though the cheap chandelier over their head had become too bright to bear.

Proudly, Connor said, "Thirty."

"How many of those are actually people you don't know?" James asked, having turned around on the couch completely. He'd draped himself over the edge of the couch, like a sloth contemplating suicide. He looked so triumphant, having placed his older brother under the inquisitor's spotlight.

"Don't hate. Money is money, sir." Connor stood up. "Mother, if you would allow it, I would be honored to wash thy dishes."

James groaned and rolled his eyes at Connor's behavior.

"Just trying to lighten the mood. Jesus," he said.

"Sit," Mr. Prendergast urged, sliding Connor's chair forward so that it hit him against the back of his knees. "Tell us about your latest issue."

"Well." Connor rubbed at his neck. He took great pride in his magazine, but when it came to sharing details with those who weren't its audience, he felt like a total asshole. "There's not much to say. It's still in development."

"What about that kid they saw up in Maidenwood?" James suggested. He left the living room and joined the family at the table. "The one that was wearing animal skins and a skull?"

Connor shook his head. "You do know whose body they found up there, right?"

"No."

"Beatrice Bacchus's, man." Connor bit his thumb. He had never been close friends with Beatrice, but he'd known her, and it was strange to think of her being dead. His memories of her… they didn't seem real anymore because of it. "I bet your ex is a mess."

James had gone pale. "Yeah… yeah. Maybe I should call her? No, I won't, but, yeah, you're right. Not a good story to tell. Was it the kid who did it?"

"I don't think they've caught anyone—"

"Issue six," Mrs. Prendergast interrupted. She had a weak constitution when it came to tragedy, and didn't much care for things that made her boys cry. "Did it really need to be so violent?"

Connor's eyes rolled so far back in his head that even demon-possessed Regan would cringe. "It wasn't that violent, Mom. Really, it's okay, you don't have to read 'Black Occult Macabre.' I know it's not your thing."

Mrs. Prendergast smiled. "I wouldn't be a very good mother if I didn't," she said, finishing her glass. She had a weak constitution, but for her boys, she'd endure almost anything. "Actually, I like that it's fake." She scowled at James. "It helps me sleep at night knowing you're not running around here in Bedlam with witches and werewolves and… Satanists."

"Well, it's not all made up, isn't that right, Connor?" Mr. Prendergast said in a scholarly tone. He took off his glasses and gave them a quick rub with his shirt. "What about that café over by the middle school? You said you saw something there."

"A ghost, I think." He exchanged glances with his mother and father, knowing all too well where their feigned interest and this so-called casual conversation would lead. "That one about the vampire priest? Total creep. Totally real. Word is born."

Mr. Prendergast straightened his back. "That creep baptized you, boy!" He smiled and shook his head. "You know, there are some guys at work who'd be interested in signing up. I can get their emails. Or I can give them yours."

"Every bit helps," Connor said. It felt good to have his father's help, better than most other's. Sighing, he said, "I wish I could print it, ship it. Digital is great and all, but it's not the same."

"Print does have a certain feel to it, doesn't it?" Mr. Prendergast reached for his wallet. "Need something to help you get through the week?"

Connor closed his eyes. *Act like a kid, and they'll treat you like a kid.* He said through his teeth, "I'm fine. Bills are getting paid, and I'm getting more hours."

As though on cue, Mrs. Prendergast chimed, "All that's left is a wife and a baby on your knee."

"Yeah, I'm sure you could find a nice girl from your subscribers," James said, smirking. "Long walks through the graveyard. Sacrifice goats on the weekends."

"I don't know. Maybe," Connor said. "Your girlfriend reads my stuff, you know? Think she'd be up for a good, old fashioned blood orgy?"

James twisted his mouth. "Ha, ha, mother fu—"

"I'm serious!" Connor interrupted before his father had a chance to. He started to gather up the plates around the table. "Easily my number one fan. Easily. She's so perky."

James scrutinized his stony face. "Not that gullible," he said, hand slowly slipping down to his side, like a cowboy in a standoff. He drew his phone and played it cool, as though he weren't, even though he was, frantically texting his girlfriend, Magda.

"I got it." Mrs. Prendergast wobbled to her feet and snatched the plates and silverware Connor had started to collect. "Thank you, though. It's good that you at least try to have some manners." She shot a damning look at her youngest, but James, bent and strained, was too deep in his own jealous oubliette to pay her much mind.

"Anyway." Connor stretched as his father stood, who was already eyeballing the couch so as to escape washing the dishes. "I got to go. I'm meeting someone, a contact. They said they have a story for me, and they're paying to tell it." He bit his lip. "Thanks for…" it almost seemed blasphemous to use the word, "… dinner."

"Hey," his father said, leaning in and hugging Connor. His glasses caught his son's hair and plucked out a few strands. "I know I don't have to tell you this, but there are a lot of messed up people out there. And you know I'm right when I say the kind of stuff you publish draws them out. So be careful, okay?"

His mother turned and stumbled into the kitchen, leaving behind one heel in the hallway. "Call us when you're done."

Connor thanked his father, gave his younger brother the middle finger, congratulated the dog on his boner, and booked it for his car.

THE MEETING

"Black Occult Macabre" was the result of a lonely night spent watching poorly translated Japanese horror films. Connor had tired of the modern entries into the genre, which often consisted of clever-but-not-that-clever homages, horror-hate disguised as satire, and dude-bro-watch-me-be-an-ass characters. So he did something about it.

Using a pad of paper and a pen, objects which were, surprisingly, not yet extinct, he outlined his objectives for the magazine. In essence, they stated it would be a self-contained publication supplemented by not only investigative journalism, but pure, grade-A bullshit.

The topics to be discussed were hardly unique to anyone having a passing familiarity with horror, but Connor had hoped that, by localizing the events to his hometown of Bedlam and modeling them after the masterful films of old, he would be able to build an insatiable intrigue and newfound respect for all things dark and terrible.

He finished the first issue in three days. The completion of accompanying illustrations, which Connor had done abstractly to hide his lack of artistic talent, followed shortly thereafter. In total, Volume 1, Issue 1 was ten pages in length. To Connor, whose head was so swollen by ego it would've put the Elephant Man's to shame, the magazine was the greatest thing he had ever created.

Without checking for spelling and grammatical errors, an excited and sleep deprived Connor quickly compiled a list of email contacts and, with a bad case of the shakes, sent his baby off into the world.

"This is awesome, man!" Dan the metalhead had replied. "Is there really an underground cemetery beneath the high school?"

"Holy crap, Con! That's scary! Where do you come up with this stuff? You made it up, right?" Marissa the barista had responded.

"Dude, you should totally get this shit published. For like, money," Abel the stoner had suggested. "For real, though, if you got anymore, send it on over. I know some people who'd eat it up. No joke. Love it, man."

And then, after he was good and drunk on compliments like a starry-eyed couple after prom, came the coup de grâce from Ethan: "It's a noble effort, but the stories are cliché and the prose too prosaic or too purple to be scary. You need to learn to walk before you run. Connor, don't take this the wrong way, but you're a good imitator, and that's it. Honestly, I couldn't be bothered to finish all ten pages. It's simply unreadable. I literally have never read such garbage before." Yes, this was from Ethan; Ethan the elitist with his four monitor command station in his parents' basement. "You've got potential. I can help you with that. But you should think about literary fiction. It's the only thing that actually has the potential to say something worthwhile. And talk about shock value. Lowest common denominator much? Where's the moral? Where's the politics? Where's the commentary on our—"

At that point in the email, Connor the cyclops pressed the delete key so hard it snapped in half and flew across the room.

In between the intermittent thoughts of strangling Ethan with his mouse cable, his mind started to work on the contents of Issue 2. He ended up analyzing various media outlets for inspiration and, feeling inspired by them, decided to redesign the layout of "Black Occult Macabre" to something more professional in appearance. Having the low standards they did, Connor's friends were not only taken with the magazine's makeover but were impressed with his ability to deliver not ten but twenty pages of new stories on wraiths, witches, and werewolves, and human slaves to zombie masters.

Due to a suggestion from his closest friend, Henry, Connor had decided to instate a fee. Beginning with Issue 3, which he had deliberately made longer to the numb the pain his readers would feel as they lightened their wallets, each monthly release was announced to cost seven dollars. Expecting outrage, Connor prepared himself to retract the statement and grovel at their feet for forgiveness. Instead, his fan base, which had reached an impressive fifteen, appeared quite taken with the notion. Somehow, the fee had given the magazine an air of legitimacy that hadn't been there before.

Too ecstatic to speak, Connor took Henry out for drinks that night to celebrate. And by the end of the night, Connor was poorer than he'd ever been and Henry, that dastardly gentleman, was engaged to a one-eyed woman who carried him when they danced.

"Looks like we're eating this week after all, boys!" Connor said to himself as he sat in his car, accepting payment on his phone from a friend of a friend of a friend for Issue 6.

He took one last look at his parents' house before beginning to back out of the driveway. It would be nice to have one dinner where he didn't act like a man-child, but that time hadn't come yet. Adulthood just didn't jive with him like it did everyone else.

I'm here now, actually. I'll call you when it's over, Connor texted Henry as he pulled up to Adelaide's Hollow, a copse in the local park. He killed the engine and stared out through the windshield, trying to catch a glimpse of his contact. In Issue 5, he'd written a story about this place, in which a carnivorous tree snacked on star-crossed lovers. Ethan the elitist had told him it was a pedestrian effort. Connor the cyclops had called him a mother fucker and spent the rest of the night crying.

Of course, the story was pure, grade-A bullshit. However, to be fair, towards the center of the copse, there did sit an old oak with a split trunk that looked as though it were grinning with a mouthful of knives.

And as Connor got out of the car and wandered over to the copse, that's where he found his contact, standing with his hands shoved into his ratty overcoat.

"Thank you for meeting me so soon," Connor said as he closed the gap between them, the wet grass soaking his shoes. "Connor Prendergast," he said, extending his hand.

The old man's veiny hand wrapped around his and held on tightly. "Princess Kitty Lovechild," he said, nodding. "Thank you for being so accommodating."

Connor furrowed his eyebrows, laughed nervously. "Are you... are you royalty?"

The old man squinted, bit his lip, and burst into laughter. He clamped his clammy hand down onto Connor's shoulder and used it for support, too overcome by his own amusement to stand upright.

"I'm sorry. Name's Herbert North." He released his hold and scratched at the white stubble on his cheek. "Just trying to break the ice."

"Do you live nearby?" Connor asked, quickly changing the subject. He noticed a plastic bag bursting from a pocket inside Herbert's coat. "We could go grab something to eat," he suggested, realizing they were alone, and remembering his father's timely warning.

Ignoring him, Herbert said, "Have you been to that new restaurant on Main?"

Connor looked at Herbert, as though surprised to hear he may be a native of Bedlam, because he'd never seen or heard of him before. "The place where rich people go and order pictures of food and imagine how good it tastes?"

"Bingo."

Connor shook his head, trying not to laugh. He liked Herbert North, but at the same time, there was a volatility about him, a pinch of insanity that made him feel uneasy.

"No," he said finally. "Little too rich for my blood."

"Chicken's good," Herbert said, tonguing his canines. "I want to show you something." He nodded at the old oak as the wind whistled through its toothy maw.

"Ah, I know. I, uh, wrote about the tree in Issue 5. It's always looked like that. Pretty weird. Ha."

"I know." Herbert took out the plastic bag, fumbled with the knot keeping it closed. He laughed as his face turned red. Impatience got the best of him and he tore open the bag's side, revealing a large, glistening piece of steak within.

"Oh, man," Connor started, watching as Herbert North fumbled with the hunk of meat, "I think I need to leave now."

Herbert North shushed him. He lifted the steak up to the tree, paused, and then dropped the bloody offering into its makeshift mouth. Convinced he had made a mistake for which he would pay with his life or his virginity (he was saving himself, bless his heart), Connor began to back away. His father had been right: This line of work brought forth a certain kind of the crazy; the kind that fed old oaks old oxen as though they were tossing bread to birds.

Connor cupped the car keys in his pocket and waited for the moment to strike the old man down.

But it wasn't the old man he'd need to hit. All at once, the old oak shuddered to life. Its branches flailed wildly, twisting like tendrils as it writhed in the dusky night. The tree's hard exterior appeared to soften, become fleshy, to accommodate the movement. Its mouth started to move, chew. Tender chunks of meat pushed through the gaps in its jagged teeth and slid down its trunk, leaving behind a pink trail of gore.

Herbert North kept his distance as the oak finished its meal, using some impressive footwork to avoid the roots that kept snaking towards him.

"My god," Connor said like every commander in every action movie ever made. He used to play on this thing, climb into its mouth.

"A man, Amon Ashcroft, came through here once," Herbert told him as he joined the frightened writer. "He left a few things behind, as he often does."

Connor felt lightheaded, dehydrated. He turned away from the tree, looked back, and then turned away again. He could hear a rumbling inside the oak, as though it were digesting the steak with its wooden organs. "Is … is this what you wanted to t-tell me?"

"No." Herbert placed his hand on Connor's shoulder again, who twitched at his touch. "But it seemed a good starting place."

Connor bit his lip, because he knew if he didn't, he'd make himself look like an ass trying to disprove what was so obviously indisputable. "Kids play on that thing all the time," he whispered. "People come to Bedlam sometimes just to see it, from Brooksville or Bitter Springs. Fuck, man."

"Some people go missing. Pets, too."

The tree went still, a sludge of meat inching like a snail down its splintery lips.

"It only wakes up once a year, at the same time. Monsters are things of routine. It's convenient." As though sensing Connor's next question, he said, "I did try to cut it down. Trust me, I did. But until you can buy nukes wholesale, this baby isn't going anywhere. Its roots run deep."

Connor quickly made a mental inventory of all illegal and controlled substances he had consumed over the course of the week. After concluding he wasn't hallucinating or teetering on the brink of psychosis, he asked the obvious question: "What the fuck?"

"I can't keep coming back here," Herbert said, "and scared as you may be, you can't help but admit this is a little exciting."

That was true: Connor's nipples were rock hard.

"Your town has its fair share of freaks, just like everywhere else. But I have a good feeling about you, sonny Jim boy chap."

"Hang on, hold on," Connor said, stepping back. His skin prickled as rain leaked from the clouds above. "What are you getting at?" He pointed to the old oak. "It was a coincidence! I didn't know! I mean, look at it. It looks evil. It was a freaking coincidence."

Herbert North, trying to look cool, reached into his pocket and then flicked a piece of gum into his mouth. It smacked against the back of his throat and lodged itself there. Eyes bulging, he punched his chest, spitting the square piece of white death into the gathering mist.

"I'm a professional," he said, looking anything but. "I'm a... Listen, I'm only going to ask you to do a little more than you already do right now for 'Macabre.'"

"What?" Connor shivered as fat drops of rain plopped onto his scalp. "Write about things I thought were impossible but are actually real?" He laughed, tried to act like the offer was no big deal as his imagination ran wild with the notion. "What choice... I mean, come on. What can I do? You showed me this. I can't forget it. I can't think of anything to explain... You fucking with me?"

Herbert lifted his overcoat up past his shoulders, over his head and said, "Let's go, boychick. I've got some exposition for you to chew on."

THE CRIME SCENE

Herbert's windshield wipers moved like metronomes, pushing aside the rivers of rain and their tributaries on the glass. In front of them, brake lights blinked like irritated eyes as pockets of traffic formed at the crosswalks and four-ways.

"It never fails. One drop of water and everyone forgets how to drive," Herbert said, looking at Connor, who was pressed up against the passenger side window.

Crack. Lightning whipped across the firmament, scoring the back of the swollen sky.

"Sometimes I wonder if we're really worth the trouble," he continued.

Boom. Thunder shook the road, rattling the car and sending kids on the sidewalks running.

"I know I'm worth it, but is everyone else?" Herbert nudged Connor. "That sounds bad, doesn't it?"

Garage doors went down as umbrellas went up, and in a matter of seconds, the only signs of life left in the world were those cars rumbling in the murk through the deluge.

"Sorry, just thinking," Connor said finally. He smiled as he noticed the gardens sprawled out across the yard, soaking up the storm and enjoying their time away from the hardheaded horticulturists who'd planted them.

"Seth and I, my partner, started out like you. We did our own little investigations. Not much became of them, until we were up to our necks in things that wanted to rip them out. It happens like that. Real fast, like. But at that point, we couldn't turn back. It was our calling, and nobody else, as far as we knew, was doing it."

Connor yawned and sat up; the sound of rain always put him to sleep. "How old are you? How long have you been doing this for?"

"I was born in 1804," Herbert said as he twisted on the defroster. "Vegetables, my boy, eat them up—" he hissed, a pain in his side giving him pause, "—and you'll be as fit as me."

Connor shook off what was most certainly a lie. "What have you seen?" He looked at Herbert North and, for the first time, noticed the faded scarring on his neck, which looked like primitive symbols of a cruel initiation.

Herbert grinned, his worn-down teeth coming together crookedly. "Telling doesn't compare to showing. You know you wouldn't have believed me if I had just told you about the tree." He eased the car to a stop at an intersection. "Give me a little more time. Worst comes to worst, you think I'm crazy, and at the end of the night, you'll have a couple hundred bucks in your pocket that weren't there before."

Maybe he's an escapee from the local sanitarium. Maybe the oak just has an infection, some incredibly rare, not plausible in any shape or form virus. But even as Connor considered these things, neither seemed all that likely. When Herbert North spoke, he did so genuinely. It was irrelevant whether or not Connor gave credence to his beliefs: The old man was going to do what he had to do regardless.

A carnivorous tree? Connor could deal with that. There were worse things in the world. It wasn't much of a step-up—okay, it was—from a carnivorous plant. No, what truly worried him, he thought as they weaved through Bedlam, was the story Herbert had yet to tell; the one he'd contacted him about in the first place.

"I need you to act as a journalist, not a fiction writer." Herbert's bullshit detector had seen through Connor's monthly ruse, it seemed. "I want you to keep track of what happens here. Write it up and report it back to me. There's a woman in Bitter Springs, Dagmar, she'll be your partner. She already has your contact information."

"Mr. North," Connor said, deciding to play along until he figured out where the old man was taking him, "I live here. My parents live here. It's a small town. Not terribly exciting, but I like it. If I go out every day kicking the same hornets' nest, my ass is going to get stung."

"I'll pay you every two weeks, just like one of them real jobs all the kids talk about nowadays."

The car hydroplaned down a small, drowned alley, the bricks that lined it looking warped under the run-off.

"I don't want you to save the world. I just want you to keep an eye on things and spread the good word, so that the next time someone sees something lurking out the corner of their eye, they keep on walking."

Connor took note of their surroundings: They were entering the oldest neighborhood in town, where the middle class invasion had pushed out the poor. "You said a man came through here? What's that mean?"

"Maybe man was a poor choice of word. He's a catalyst, an aggravator. A monster with a plan. Old as me, if not older. Dresses all in black, like an asshole."

The car chugged as it drove across a rain-choked sewer, splashing a tongue of water over the sidewalk.

"The tree was his doing. So was that ghost you saw in the café. For a long time, he's been preparing for something. I don't know what. After all this time, honestly, I don't care. These things are often content with just having a plan. They don't need an endgame, just something to do."

"You've never caught him?"

"He's not easy to find, and I can't say I've ever been equipped to stop him. He's a pain in the ass, but he's not ending the world anytime soon." Herbert tapped his fingers on the steering wheel, twitched, and swallowed hard. He'd held something back. "That vampire priest you wrote about—" Herbert sped up, turned down a cul-de-sac, "—you were a little off about that one."

"Oh?" Connor smiled. He didn't know where to start with this man, so instead he let him take the lead.

"Fancies himself a demon. I caught him trading all kinds of bodily fluids with Sister Mary Pascal. He's different all right—never could quite clean the blood all the way out of his moustache—but definitely no monster."

Connor shook his head and laughed. There was no doubt in his mind this was by far the strangest day he'd ever had in his entire life. He should've brought an audio recorder or a pad of paper for notation, to make permanent those things which would inevitably be lost or twisted by memory. He usually did, so why hadn't he this time? Six issues in, and he was already getting lazy. *I hope to god this doesn't bite me in the—*

The car stopped, and though he could see little, Connor saw enough to know where Herbert had brought him, and knew enough about it to know they shouldn't be here.

Like all houses of ill repute, this one sat the end of the street shrouded in shadow and circumstance. Six months ago, the family of five who had inhabited the house for four years were found dead, bodies desecrated. Despite a thorough investigation and a media frenzy, the Zdanowiczs' killer was never found. Bedlam being as irrelevant as it was, Connor had expected the story to turn from small town shame to profitable pride and joy. But to his surprise, and certainly the news station's dismay, public interest quickly waned. People just stopped giving a shit.

"What're we doing here?" Connor stared at the doorstep where the sixteen-year-old son, Oskar, had been found sitting with his head in his lap. "Mr. North, I appreciate the offer but this is fucked up. Someone's going to call the cops. Let's head back. Do the interview elsewhere."

"Call the cops? You sure?" Herbert unfastened his seatbelt. "Look at the houses on this street, man. Nobody's home."

He was right. There were eight other houses lining the cul-de-sac, four to the Zdanowiczs' left and four to its right. But it was only the furthest, nearest where they turned in, that showed signs of habitation. The others, Connor noted, were abandoned, disemboweled—their fates given over to the "For Sale" signs now impaling the fouled earth before them. He wondered if the exodus here had happened immediately when news of the murder broke. Or if it had been a slow process of heated discussions between partners trying to balance the scales of fear and financial responsibility.

Herbert North put the car into park and shut off both the headlights and engine. He leaned over the steering wheel and said, "Do you see it?"

"What?" Connor returned his attention toward the Zdanowiczs' house. "See what?"

Just as he had in the copse, Herbert North shushed Connor. He pointed with one shaking finger at the bay window that looked into the living room and whispered quietly, "There... there."

Connor pressed himself against the dash. He strained his eyes to pierce the veil of rain that had been pulled over the house. Little by little, he saw more and more. A couch, a chair... the glint of glass and a coffee table—pieces of forlorn furniture with no other purpose now than to bear the burden of the darkness gathering inside.

"Herbert, I don't—"

The darkness moved, and with its moving, it took form. Behind the window, a gaunt, black shape stood, its blood-red, blade-like fingers splayed across the glass.

"Don't. Move." Herbert gritted his teeth. "It doesn't know we are here."

"Take me home," Connor demanded, the date having soured. And then, curiosity overcoming him: "What the hell is it?"

"That—"

The creature pushed in, its face to the glass. Its eyes were like melted chunks of silver, glowing scratches of firelight running across them.

"—is the Zdanowiczs' killer."

A long tongue, barbed and forked, fell out of its mouth and went halfway down its body. The tongue quivered and wandered across the window, like a bloated leech in search of a body to bleed.

"It never left," Herbert said.

Herbert North flicked on the high beams. The blinding light cut through the miserable air, setting aglow the trail of piss-colored drool that dripped down the glass. The creature retracted its tongue, startled. It stood there, statue-like, as though it meant to be admired, and admire it Connor did. For in that fleeting moment, he saw clearly the distillation of all his most hopeful dreams and terrible nightmares.

Its flesh was black—an all-consuming, unrelenting black accented by the iridescent bands that ran along it. Its body was taut, well-defined; angular in all the right places to kill and maim. At the top of the seven-foot monstrosity, a head like a bone-forged miter jutted out, as though the thing were some papal phantasm from some dreadful heaven.

"Look away, Connor."

The sheer existence of it was too much to bear. Connor felt himself drifting as his mind opened up to the creature, making concession after concession to allow himself to cope with what stood before him. The luminous bands bent and widened and became gulping mouths on the creature's tenebrous husk. Even though the house, yard, and car stood between them, Connor could feel the mouths inside him, teasing out fragments of fears and long murdered memories. There, childhood and the bullies. And there, Kate and the heartbreak. And there, breaking through subconscious soil, his mother, dead drunk, showing him what he didn't need to see.

"Connor!" Herbert North punched him in the dick and sent him reeling out of the car.

He felt violated, and the pounding rain didn't help much. Thunder streaked across the sky, splitting its purple flesh to bleed a flood onto the sputtering city. Connor looked back to the bay window, but the creature was gone. Herbert North hadn't brought him here for an interview but to bear witness and tell his own tale. It was tempting, terribly, excitingly tempting, but who'd believe him? And would he want anyone to?

"This isn't right." Connor wrapped his arms around his body to hold back the tremors. He glanced over his shoulder to Herbert, whose face was a blur behind the fogging windshield. "What do I do? What do I do?" His teeth chattered as he spoke to himself. He could taste Bedlam in the rain.

He closed his eyes, expecting to see there a triptych of his dying—the tree, the man, and the beast—but found the cover of "Black Occult Macabre, Vol. 1, Issue 7" instead. It looked old, faded, barely held together by the bits of bone that made up its spine. He touched the spine, and it felt like flesh; he could feel wounds in the cracks, and in the wounds crimes. With his fingers to the cover, an image started to form. Eldritch blood oozed out of every leathery pore. It pushed upward, spread outward, until it pooled in his mindscape into the shape of the creature that had nested its image and being inside him. It was beautiful, the cover and the unholy creation, and better still were the words outside it, on every poster-plastered wall and every trembling, thankful lip. It would be his masterpiece, his absolute purpose.

Connor snapped out of it, but he'd drunk enough of the Kool-Aid to get back in the car. "Why are we here? Tell me true."

"I'm here to kill it." Herbert gave Connor the up-down. "And to give you a taste and see what becomes of that hunger." He nodded. "That's a good line. Use that in your story."

The old man opened his door and stepped out of the car. The sky had turned monochrome, the rain that fell from it like silver drops from an inker's pen.

"Why are you here?" he shouted as Connor came out after him.

He followed Herbert around the car to the trunk. "I got to see this through. And I want to do something worthwhile. I should be scared shitless, right?"

Herbert nodded, blinking the rain out of his eyes.

"I am." He drummed his fingers on the trunk lid, stopped when he noticed Herbert had noticed how much he was shaking. "Ha, yeah, I am."

Herbert smiled and popped the trunk. Weapons—handguns, shotguns, rifles, and knives—in holsters and blankets, held in place by the blank books wedged between them. There was a comfort in clichés, and so far, he was glad Herbert North had hit them all.

"No holy water?" Connor could hardly speak through the smile on his face. "No grimoire?"

"Oh no, I got them." Herbert dug around for a flask and chugged it dry. "Grimoire's back home propping up my kitchen table. Grab that machete."

Connor bit his lip and grabbed the rune-engraved weapon that was attached to the back of the backseat.

"Shit," he said, dropping it as he felt something bite into the thick of his palm. Six drops of blood dotted his skin, and then the storm swept them away.

"It's a sacrificial weapon from this place called Our Ladies of Sorrow Academy." Herbert grabbed the shotgun from the trunk. "It keeps what it kills. But it's bound to you now, so make sure it's fed."

Connor felt sick. "What the hell?" He wiped his hand on his pant leg, as though that would undo what the old man had done to him.

"Are you kidding me?" He imagined pushing Herbert, making a big manly show of things, but instead he just threw his arms up in disbelief.

"I'm not," Herbert said, taking the machete by the blade and handing it, handle first, to the fledgling investigator. "Why you, right? Why did I pick you?"

Connor dropped his arms, shrugged. He could've sworn he felt something crawling inside his veins.

"I've heard a lot about you."

"From who? My readers?" Connor scratched his arm like a junkie, and wished for a belt to tie off the annoyance.

Herbert North shook his head. "Monsters talk, too. There's a lot of dark places in Bedlam. You've shone too much light on them." He drew a breath. "Connor, they were coming for you."

In one overwhelming second, Connor revisited every strange occurrence from the past two weeks: the creaks outside his room, the graveyard smell of his pillow, the fleeting shadows around every street corner. There had been whispers, too; cold and distant exchanges, purposeful but meandering, like two scientists observing a subject—or two hunters observing prey.

"That machete of yours, Camazotz's fang... there isn't much it can't stop." He grabbed two flashlights and, with the shotgun in hand, slammed the trunk shut. "I saw Seth in you and decided a warning wasn't enough. If I'm wrong and this line of work isn't your calling, at least I can sleep easy at night knowing you've got something to defend yourself with. A lot of people in the world... they like to say they know what's going on. But most don't. And most don't want to actually know. And we don't want to flat out tell them either. Destroying that ignorance can be almost as bad as taking a life. Scarlet was... eh, yeah. Yeah."

Again, Connor took up the machete, but his blood was safe for its hunger had been sated. "Was I adopted? Are you my dad?"

Herbert North shook his head and laughed. He handed a flashlight to Connor. "Let's go. Tired of standing here in the rain like we're about to make out."

"Good thing you're not my dad, then."

"Humor is my coping mechanism, too," Herbert admitted as they marched towards the front door. "Let that blade feed on your blood every two weeks and you won't have a problem."

Connor's arm had stopped itching, most likely because the curse had finally found a warm place to lie in wait. "You couldn't have given me something a little less evil?"

"Stop whining. It's not like you don't have an endless supply of the red stuff. I'm not asking you to pump quarters into it."

By the time they reached the front door, all the light had left the world.

Grabbing the doorknob, Herbert said, "Don't wander off. When we talk, we look each other in the eyes; otherwise, you can't be certain who's speaking."

"Bullets will work?" Connor took a step back as Herbert slowly opened the door. "It's unlocked?"

"It's made of flesh and blood. And of course it's unlocked. It's expecting us."

Eerie—that was how Connor would describe the inside of the Zdanowiczs' house in Issue 7—if he survived the night. There was nothing overtly sinister about the place, but Connor knew that homes, like parasites, were quick to perish without the complicated, little hosts upon which they depended.

Connor noted how the walls had turned ashen and buckled, as though the house were collapsing in upon itself, the want of rot having finally got its way. His eyes went to the floor and followed the scratches that ran across it, from where someone's nails had clamped down to the point where they'd given up. He took his first breath since entering and gulped the heavy, musty odor that had been sealed away until now—a foul perfume of dashed hopes and human suffering.

"Downstairs first," Herbert North said, finally breaking the silence. He turned on the flashlight and shone it on the staircase in front of them.

Connor cringed as the light landed on the bottom step, where a dark stain splattered the wood. "Good idea," he said, remembering the step had been where Anika Zdanowicz, the mother, had been found shoved inside herself. "It's time to tell me what we're up against."

"Martin Zdanowicz was a businessman. He traveled a lot and always brought something back from where he'd been," Herbert said, turning them away from the foyer, down a hallway. "Take a guess what he brought back the last time."

"Herpes?" Connor's voice echoed down the hall. Herp, herp, herp, herp.

"That's it. We're fighting a herpes monster," Herbert said sarcastically, pausing for a moment as they passed the kitchen to their right. "No, an antique."

He moved his light across the dinner table, to the old clock in the corner now permanently stopped at 7:45. "You know why people's clocks always stop when something supernatural happens?"

Connor shook his head.

"They don't. They're just too stupid to fix the damn things when they break. Come on."

"Antique? What kind of antique? What was wrong with it?"

Connor followed Herbert as they veered into the living room, where the bay windows sat smeared in saliva. The air here felt dense, as though each particle was working in unison to keep the intruders out. His body tensed—*Is it still here?*—and he raised the machete up, like the slashers of old.

"A necklace. From an estate sale in England. The Ashcroft estate," Herbert said, lifting his shotgun up as though he'd spotted something.

A peal of thunder pummeled the house.

"The same Amon Ashcroft?" Connor asked.

A streak of lightning lit up the living room.

For now, they were the only two things standing in it.

"The exact same. That family has a long history that would be better told at a different time. There are several necklaces. I have one." Instinctively, he started to scratch at the scar on his neck. "Martin Zdanowicz picked up one in an antique shop on the West Coast. The store owner was saving it for me, until he got spooked and Martin passed through and made him an offer."

"He wanted it that bad?"

Connor looked at the belongings left behind—the television, sofa, grandfather clock, and bookshelves... objects which even the most repugnant of relatives and auctioneers would cart off with glee—and wondered why they still remained.

"I doubt it," Herbert said, going to his knee and shining the light under the coffee table. "But objects like that have a tendency of getting inside you."

Together, they marched forward like anxious soldiers in a contested war zone. Connor waved the flashlight across the room and then brought it to rest on the glass case on the back wall. Inside, there were twenty or so black-eyed dolls, each with their own unique embellishments and name placards. Standing there, with their blank gazes and pallid skin, they looked like dead children that had been turned into trophies, to showcase their parents' parenting skills.

"These things have always creeped me the fuck out," Connor said. "My grandpa would buy me stuffed animals all the time when was little. I used to love them. I'd stack them up on my bed and use them for pillows. Then, one day, I actually looked at their eyes and… god damn. The emptiness got to me. Felt like I'd seen something. Like I'd caught whatever was inside, and it knew I'd seen it."

Herbert cleared his throat and turned away from the case. "Well, I hate to break it to you, but there's a doll missing."

"Fuck off, mate."

"This thing we're hunting," Herbert said, changing the subject, "is bound to the necklace. Like a guardian. Martin Zdanowicz must've done something to coax it out."

Cold air blew against the back of Connor's neck. He slowly turned around, but found nothing. "What's the necklace for?"

"A ritual, I think, to awaken something. I've never seen it done, but that's my guess."

"Kill the guardian, grab the necklace, and go? That the plan?"

Herbert North laughed. "Usually is."

They doubled back the way they'd come and gave the kitchen a second look. The tiled floor was sticky, dirtied by the numerous feet that had trampled it for weeks after the murders. Cabinets, drawers, and pantries hung open, their innards pilfered for the unlikeliest of clues. The refrigerator sat silently, no longer humming that drowsy drone that greets all hungry sleepwalkers at the end of their midnight trek.

Cautiously, Connor went to the sink, where short, stiff curtains had been pulled across the small window above it to hide from prying eyes what had happened in here. He looked inside the sink, shone the flashlight down its metal throat. Something glowed red in the teeth of the disposal, and he backed away. The police had missed a piece of five-year-old Kelly Zdanowicz, who'd been found in the sink, a soupy mixture of blood, bone, and dish soap.

"What do you think?" Herbert asked.

Connor felt two fingers tapping on his shoulder. He faced Herbert, but he was halfway across the room. Heart beating in his chest, he said,

"I'm thinking it might be best to change some of the details to avoid an outrage. I don't want 'Black Occult Macabre' to look like a tabloid."

Herbert shrugged as he continued to search the kitchen, shoving the barrel of the shotgun into every hiding place. "Do you hear that?" he asked, suddenly stopping.

Connor cocked his head and listened for sounds beyond the rain. He leant forward, towards the second hallway that led deeper into the house. The noises were coming from there, from the doorway at the hall's midpoint that—he trained the flashlight on it—led into the basement. It sounded like footsteps over splintering wood, like fingertips over metal rungs. Then, he heard something else. He crouched down, pointed the machete at the vent register beside his foot. It sounded as though something were tumbling through the vent, end over end, wet smack into hard thump. And more: a pounding; a rhythmic throbbing that increased in volume with every passing second—a hypnotizing music best suited for occasions populated by hooded figures and sacrificial altars.

Connor tried to isolate the thudding notes, afraid that he'd mistaken them for his own heartbeat, but the focus only pulled him deeper into the chorus. He found himself feeling faint as an ocean of white noise crashed against the shore of his mind, stabbing jagged wave after jagged wave into the backs of his eyes. His jaw went slack and all the arteries and veins in his face tightened until he was certain they would snap. Something wanted his skin, and the only way to have it was to get him out of it.

"It's coming from the basement," Herbert said matter-of-factly.

Connor exhaled slowly and shook off the seduction. "Of course it is."

"Want to check upstairs first?"

Connor nodded. "Hell yes."

Before tonight, Connor had already decided on the direction "Black Occult Macabre Vol. 1 Issue 7" would take. However, after learning what he had from Herbert North, his stories concerning possession and cannibal morticians didn't compare. Would he have to change the names? Any Bedlamite who knew anything about anything would immediately make the connection. But should he really be worrying about that? Connor was now privy to things most only discovered after the straightjacket went on. The implications were staggering. He felt compelled to make good on the old man's revelations, but how? Would the magazine really be enough? No, of course it wouldn't. Just as horror had consumed him all his life, so, too, would his newfound purpose. He was ready for it, he thought as they headed back towards the staircase, until he wouldn't be; until that moment when the claws came out and the teeth sank in, and the only cut that came wasn't to another scene, but black nothingness.

As they hoofed it to the second floor, Connor turned around and caught a glimpse of Bedlam through the window above the front door. The storm had turned savage, and in its ceaseless savagery, it had drained the power from the town. Standing there, machete tip grinding into the step, he half-expected the Zdanowicz house to be torn from its foundations and hurled into the thick of Maidenwood. If nothing else, the uprooting would at least put an end to this terrifying game of hide-and-seek with the killer inside it.

"We'll start there," Herbert said, pointing the flashlight down the hall ahead. "The children's rooms." He stepped onto the second floor.

Connor ran his hand along the banister, pulling it back as it brushed through a spider web. "If this thing catches us—"

"Got to name it to know it," Herbert said, watching Connor shake the desiccated flies and pill bugs from his fingers.

"What's the necklace look like?" Connor stepped onto the second floor and, for a moment, his knees gave out, as though something had hit them from behind.

"Silver, with a red gem inside a tangle of worms… or snakes… or roots. Hard to say when you've only seen one and no one else is talking about them."

"We'll call the monster 'Argento,' then."

Herbert North scratched his neck and snorted. "God damn you're a geek."

He blushed. "What? It's clever. Don't—"

Connor woke up sprawled across the staircase. His mouth tasted like a grease trap—a gagging combination of old food, mildew, and expired dairy. Immediately, he vomited, leaving a puddle of meatballs and pasta for the police to find if they ever returned here. His head ached, as though something had been scratching at the inside of his skull, trying to work its way out.

127

"Ugh, fuck," he said, rolling into his own throw-up as he pulled himself along the stairs. He grabbed the machete and flashlight at the top. "Herbert?" He'd meant to shout, but his voice refused to go much higher than a whisper.

I need an adult, he thought, suddenly remembering the time at the mall when his mother had gone down the escalator without him. To his five-year-old mind, it had been the greatest of betrayals.

"Her-bert?" he panted, slowly coming to his feet. The flashlight started to flicker. *How long was I out?* He checked his cell phone: 11:50 pm. *That can't be... We got here at seven or eight.* "Herbert, where are you?"

Connor grabbed the flashlight and the machete—*feast, you can have as much as you want*—and went ahead to the children's rooms. What had happened? The flashlight flickered with every step he took. He rubbed out his mouth with the cleanest part of his shirt. He'd been attacked but why'd the Argento spare him? The floor creaked and moaned, as though each board sat atop a grave. Where was Herbert? He couldn't do this, wouldn't do this on his own.

Thunder boomed outside, sounding as though a boulder had been released in the house. Connor fell against the wall, beads of sweat burning his eyes. "Herbert?" he tried again, not wanting to brave the rooms of Kelly and Brian Zdanowicz alone. They'd found Kelly downstairs in the sink, but eight-year-old Brian had died in his room, with his entrails hanging from the ceiling fan, like streams of confetti.

"Herbert?"

"Get your ass away from there... Get your ass away from there." The words were guttural, forced, as though they were being dredged out of the speaker's throat. Connor clung to the wall as he slid down it. *Herbert?*

"Get your... get your... away from there. Get your ass from your ass away from there." As he crept closer to the room—Brian's, he assumed from the sport's posters he saw through the crack in the door—he knew he'd found Herbert. *The hell is wrong with him?*

"Get your get your ass from your from your," the old man rattled on.

Connor took a deep breath. He'd never meant to live the life he loved. Scaring up his last bit of bravery, he tightened his grip on the machete and snuck into the room.

Herbert was on the ground, kneeling before the shadowy creature he'd come to kill and now appeared to worship. The Argento had the old man's head in its hands, and its thumbs in his eyes. No blood was spilt or screams wasted as the gangling monstrosity pushed its fingers further into each cavity. Knuckle-deep, the Argento opened its mouth and let loose its tongue over the rows of teeth inside. The tongue draped over Herbert's shoulder, the dripping, swollen muscle weighing heavily upon him, and then, as the old man continued to ramble like the lobotomized, snaked upward and forced its way down his scarred throat.

Connor couldn't take it anymore. He ran into the room, nearly tripping over a stack of video games, and swung the machete. The Argento twisted, its silver eyes flashing hell light. The blade screeched as it tore through the air. It caught the creature's arm, and like old scissors through paper, cut across the beast jaggedly.

The Argento released Herbert as its arm fell to the ground and exploded in a cloud of dust. It looked at Connor, taking the pain in silence, and then, as though pulled by a rope, shot upward into the shadows on the ceiling.

"No, no, no," Connor said.

He caught sight of Herbert's shotgun and flashlight and dove for them. Trading his gear for the old man's, he whipped around, turned the light on, and fired the gun into the shadows. Plaster and paint showered the room as he pumped pellets into the ceiling. Each blast was deafening, blinding; he'd never fired a gun before. But as Connor carved away the Zdanowicz house, feeling the rock of each shot in his bones, he could see the appeal. It put a barrier between him and the beast—a few seconds of reprieve from the pants-shitting fear that would find him when the chamber ran dry.

Two shells later and Connor was fair game again. Sluggish from the adrenaline high, he dropped the shotgun and took up Camazotz's fang. He scooted across the floor until he managed to come to his feet. The flashlight shook in his hand; its beam darted across the room every time he tried to train it on something.

"It's gone, Terminator," Herbert mumbled from the floor, each word a puff of chalky dust off his lips. "It got what it wanted."

"Herbert? How are you...?" Connor checked the ceiling: He could see the attic through the wreckage, but there was no sign of the creature.

"It imitated you," Herbert said, coughing as he sat up. "Couldn't kill me until it got in my mind first. Wanted to... fuck." He rubbed his eyes with the heels of his palms.

"It wanted to have sex with you?"

"Story of my life. Oh, god." Herbert stood, punched himself in the side of the head. "Didn't see it wasn't really you until it was too late. What time is it? Felt like I was fighting that thing off for ages until it finally broke in."

Connor checked his phone. "Almost midnight. Your eyes, man."

Herbert waved off his concerns. "I thought they were as good as gone, too, but I guess to read me it had to get all ghost-like. I don't know. Let's get out of here."

Connor scooped up the shotgun and Herbert's flashlight and handed them to him. He scrutinized Herbert's old eyes for signs of damage, but except for the hints of cataracts, they looked untouched. "What did it want?"

"The other necklace," Herbert said, jumping as lightning lit up Brian Zdanowicz's room. "Wanted to know where it was. I expect it'll make a run for it, now that it's got something to do other than sit around haunting here." He started to cough up blood, from the places in his throat where the Argento's tongue had torn it away. "Let's go. You cut its arm off. That's good enough for me."

"We're just going to leave it?" He felt bad for the old warrior, who now looked as though he could be bested by a stiff breeze. "That's kind of an underwhelming way to end the story."

"Listen," Herbert said, pulling a barb out of his mouth, "I need to get drunk, and fast. There's no necklace to get, because that thing has it inside it. Your Argento may still be here, may be halfway across town now. Who knows? I don't, and I don't rightly care."

"Herbert, man," Connor said, and then sighed. "This doesn't feel right, having no closure. I'm not going to be able to sleep at night knowing that thing is out there. Knowing that thing knows me. I mean, it imitated me. Christ, if it read your mind, it sure as hell read mine, too."

Herbert grumbled as he reached into his pocket and loaded five more shells into the shotgun. "It's good to know you can swim, kid, but that don't mean you have to go off the deep end. One day at a time. Come on, let's go. I'll let you buy me a drink." He smiled, waited until Connor smiled, too, and then, as he looked past the fledgling investigator, said "Oh, god damn it."

Connor's cheek twitched. "What?" Had the Argento come back?

He didn't need to turn around to see what the old man saw, because it was already there beside him, at his hips.

Grass. White, shimmering grass that moved like seaweed and smelled like soap. It was all around them, and where it wasn't, it soon was. Over the boy's bed it spread, and into the hall it went, growing out of wood and textile as though they were soil. And with the ghostly stalks came wind and the insects that rode in on it. Strangely colored and strangely formed, the small spiders and bulbous grubs paid Connor and Herbert no mind as they explored the shifting corridors of their new expanse.

"Herbert, exposition, please," Connor said, afraid of what would happen if he were to move.

"It's midnight, isn't it?"

"Yeah." Connor took out his phone. "Right on the nose."

"Alright." Herbert readied the shotgun and flashlight. "We go straight for the front door. No distractions. If you see something that needs saving, leave it. This is the Black Hour."

Footsteps. Someone was walking down the hall towards the stairs. "What's... that?"

"It's a span of time. Starts at midnight. Lasts just as long as it sounds. During the Black Hour, anything can happen. It's real up until the moment it's not. It's like dreaming and being awake at the same time." Herbert lowered his voice as he, too, heard the people or person outside the room. "Sometimes it's nothing. It can happen anywhere. But of course, it happened here. Tonight. How's that for an ending to your story?"

"It's good; it's a good one," Connor said, having a hard time paying attention to Herbert.

More footsteps; one step after the other: whatever was out there was headed towards where they needed to go.

"What about time zones?"

Herbert shook his head. "I don't think it much gives a shit about things like that. I've only been in it one other time. Happened at a zoo. The snow turned to glass, and all the animals merged into one. That's what we're dealing with here, Trigger, so let's bounce."

It had only taken the Black Hour a minute to undo what the Zdanowiczs' had spent years perfecting. The carefully chosen colors, expensive decorations, and personal embellishments were now lost to the glowing overgrowth. Connor felt a pang of sadness as they slipped quietly into the hall. The Argento had gutted the house, but for those who knew where to look, they could still see remnants of the owners in the objects they'd left behind. The Black Hour, however, took everything. For Connor, knowing that the family's existence was now beholden to memory and rumor was more frightening than anything else. Death fascinated him, entertained and excited him, but the permanence of it was almost too much to consider.

"Front door," Herbert whispered, taking the lead. "If it's not in the same place, we'll go through a window if we need to."

"Wait a—" Connor grabbed the old man's shirt, signaling him to stop.

Again, he'd heard footsteps. He pointed past the staircase where the hall stretched further back to the rest of the rooms. Two shapes stood there, in front of the large window at the second floor's end.

"Keep going," Herbert grunted, shaking free of Connor's grip. "We stop for nothing."

A burst of lightning exploded outside. In one moment of severe blue light, the shapes were made visible. One was a woman, the other a young girl. Everything about them was human, except for the part that truly grants humanity. Where the woman's neck ended, a raven's head began. And for the young girl, there was no neck at all, because an octopus' body sat atop her shoulders. In each of their hands, they held a weapon—the woman, an ax, and the girl, a dagger—and by the way they stared Connor and Herbert down, shoulders hunched and breathing heavily, it seemed they had every intention of using them.

"What are they?" Connor asked as they tiptoed towards the top of the staircase.

Herbert shook his head as he moved the shotgun back and forth between the two terrors. "Nightmares of us, maybe."

"It feels wrong to look at them." Connor swallowed hard and cast his eyes to the ground to give the terrors the reverence they seemed to deserve. "I hope I never see them again."

Steps in line with each other's, Connor and Herbert carefully descended the staircase. The Raven and the Octopus watched them at first. Then, when they'd reached the halfway point, the terrors crouched down and disappeared into the pale grass. Like animals hunting prey, they darted through their cover, to overtake the meal that thought it'd got away.

"Herbert, go," Connor shouted, quickening the old man's pace.

Herbert spun around and fired at the top of the stairs, blowing apart the grass into ghostly whirlwinds. Connor caught a glimpse of the terrors' eyes—a glint of violence in their monstrous skulls—and tore ahead.

"Front door, front door," he shouted to Herbert.

It had moved several feet to the left of where it should have been, but it was there nonetheless.

A clap of thunder rocked the house, sending pictures and vases from their shelves. Connor waded through the thickening grass, his skin burning where it touched him. He threw himself against the front door, fumbled for its handle as he watched Herbert fire shell after shell at the terrors.

"Go!" the old man shouted, giving up and making a run for it.

Connor ripped open the front door—"Oh fuck!"—and stumbled backward. On the doorstep a porcelain doll stood, a butcher's knife in its small, veiny hand. Hundreds of writhing larvae fell from its harlequin grin, the skin around its mouth splotchy and raw. The doll plodded forward, its drenched dress sticking to its mildewed flesh.

Connor was paralyzed, caught in the vermillion-flecked gaze of the creature one-fourth his size. He could feel a quiver in his arm, where the machete throbbed and yearned to be buried in the thing's chest. Sweat poured down his forehead and piss dribbled down his leg.

He could hear the knife singing, its sharp song a promise of pain to come. He didn't want to die, not like this, but maybe it was better this way. The doll, now that he looked at it, a fever breaking across his brow, looked kind, inviting. He went to his knees, because the doll let him go to his knees, and held out his arms to embrace it.

An explosion of heat and noise blew past him. The doll flew off its feet, its face shattering into a million tumor-caked pieces. Connor fell forward, rid of the abomination's mental grip, and breathed again.

"I told you there was a doll missing," Herbert said, helping Connor to his feet.

"What if… what if it comes back?" Connor panted, covering his crotch to hide his accident.

"Look at it," Herbert said, pointing to the doll. "It's going to take a whole lot of super glue to put that thing back together. Ready for that drink?"

THE BUMP IN THE NIGHT

At 12:20 AM, Connor and Herbert left the Zdanowiczs' house. With the Argento gone, the doll dead, and the Black Hour behind them, the investigation had been, more or less, a complete failure. But if Herbert North's intentions had been to scare Connor into a life of isolation, then the whole operation was easily an overwhelming success.

At 12:35 AM, the old warrior and his wobbly sidekick found the nearest bar and got shitfaced. Like a couple of kids who'd seen their parents naked, they sat there in silence, nursing their shame.

At 12:50 AM, Herbert, in one drunken motion, tossed Connor his payment of three hundred dollars, threw back a handful of peanuts, sauntered over to the jukebox, and threw up all over it when it started blaring country music.

At 1:30 AM, after riding the road's median with their car as though they were trying to earn a tip from it, Connor and Herbert finally made it back to Adelaide's Hollow. Connor stumbled out of Herbert's car and headed for his own. The old man promised to call him in the morning, to finish the interview and to check-in to make sure Connor was still alive.

At 1:40 AM, Connor checked the trunk and backseat of his car for stowaways. He sat there for a bit after Herbert drove off, machete across his lap, watching the carnivorous tree.

At 2:00 AM, he left a voicemail for his father letting him know with the most obvious of lies that he was okay. Then, he responded to a text message from his best friend, Henry, who asked if Connor was interested in exploring a haunted castle (he wasn't).

At 2:20 AM, Connor barged into his apartment, machete raised high like a maniac. He turned on every light and decoration, giving the darkness no quarter. He woke his laptop from its sleep and then, stomach wailing like a trauma ward, went into the kitchen. There, he gobbled down a bowl of cereal, wincing every time the spoon clinked off his teeth.

At 2:30 AM, Connor the cyclops couldn't ignore the urge any longer. He scurried over to his laptop and began furiously typing his account of the night. At first, he invented a character to play the role of himself, but that felt wrong, disingenuous.

"No matter how many times Connor pushed, poked, and prodded

his mother's meatballs, they continued to be totally inedible," he giddily wrote.

Here and there, he paused to sketch the house and the creatures they'd found inside on the pad of paper beside him. This would be his best work, he concluded, one he would be remembered for.

At 3:10 AM, Connor Prendergast was snoring louder than a fat kid at a slumber party. Mid-mumble, a strange smell stirred him from his slumber—a smell he could not place. His eyes opened slowly, and then panic set in as he realized he sat in darkness. The laptop was still on, still charging. His apartment was in an old building, and not a particularly well put-together one at that, but when the power went out, it went out in every room.

He tipped the laptop lid back, sending a beam of white light across the living room. Still alone, but where was his machete? Like the dead, he stumbled towards the nearest light switch and gave it a flick. The overheads and lamps buzzed on. Something had turned them off.

At 3:12 AM, Connor found the machete in the bathroom, lying across the sink, where it had no right to be. Suddenly, the apartment, which he had lived in for close to two years now, felt very alien to him. Wandering out of the bathroom, diligently turning on light after light, he began to feel as though something had crept inside and settled into the apartment itself. The furniture and furnishings—they felt wrong, looked wrong, as though tainted or infected. The air, too, had changed; it felt as though it were building up, being held back in an anxious wait. Each hallway, and there were only two of them, seemed to stretch on forever, and each door—why were they all shut?—a gateway to horrors yet unseen.

A noise broke up his thoughts: a knocking, a rapping at his double-bolted, chain-locked, and soon to be nailed-shut door.

Connor sighed, laughed. "Probably just the neighbors. Probably heard me stomping around in here."

Quiet as a thief, Connor crossed the apartment and put his eye to the peephole. No one, nothing, yet the knocking continued slowly, deliberately. He stood on the tips of his toes to get a better look, holding out hope that he was under siege by a small child or a red-hooded dwarf. But again, no one, nothing.

"Alright, assholes, I'm calling my mom and dad," Connor shouted, having regressed a full fifteen years.

"James, buddy," he said, going back to his desk and picking up his cell phone. "Come on, bro, be awake."

As he swiped though his contact list, his nose twitched and, once again, he caught a whiff of that strange smell from before. But this time, now that he was awake and aware, he knew exactly what it was.

Super glue.

NIGHTS IN WHITE SATIN

Herbert North lowered himself into the swamp and slowly waded forward. Boney trees twisted out of the roiling murk, their flesh the leaves that now blanketed the black waters. Mosquitoes washed over him in blood-swollen waves, taking what they could, when they could, because he was in no position to swat them away. He'd brought the torch, but then left it behind, as the dead things ahead had their own light, and he didn't want them to see him coming.

Joy

Joy knew her husband was going to kill her; it was only a matter of time. She leaned over the dinner table, poured the stew into the two bowls there. She blew out the candle nearest where her husband would sit so he wouldn't have to see the slop she'd so boldly served him. Murdering the man would be easy—it always was for Joy—but she had hoped he would be different. And now it seemed that same hope would be the very thing that sent her back to the grave she'd spent so long climbing out of.

One grunt, two groans, and ten heavy footsteps later: Joy's husband came through the front door and stood there until she emerged from the kitchen. She put on a smile, and then glided down the hallway, her white satin dress moving gently with her motions, giving to her a fleeting grace she didn't otherwise possess. Her husband waited unmoved on the threshold, as mud sloughed off his boots onto the hardwood floor.

"I missed you," Joy said, leaning forward and kissing her husband on the lips. He tasted of sweat, and of another woman. "I'm so glad you're home."

Her husband nodded and, much to Joy's surprise, he smiled and said, "As did I."

Staying true to her name, Joy let out a squeak; grinning like the schoolgirl she'd never been, she wheeled her husband around the house, until they were in the kitchen and he in his seat.

"Catch any bad men today?" Joy asked, bringing some water to the table before sitting down.

Her husband stirred the slop in the bowl with his spoon, as though trying to dredge up what may lie at the bottom. "There's bad women, too," he said.

"In Marrow?" Joy thought of the town and those that inhabited it—the women, especially. They were hard creatures, empty creatures; shells of something that had once been great and beautiful, but now were nothing more than hollow vessels to be filled and put to labor. "What's the worst you've ever caught?"

Joy's husband took a drink of water and asked, "Man or woman?"

"Don't matter," Joy said in the southern accent she'd been honing the last few months.

"We had ourselves a murderer a few years back," her husband said, finally taking a sip of his stew. He sighed as though he'd been expecting poison, and seemed satisfied. "He would take men up to his shack in the Black Hills."

A passing carriage outside gave him pause.

"He would take men up to his shack in the Black Hills and eat them."

Joy put her hand to her mouth. "Oh, no," she exclaimed in a breathy whisper.

"Doesn't that frighten you?" her husband asked. He looked at her suspiciously. "Doesn't that disgust you?"

"Of course it does. It's awful." Joy tried to make herself look pale, but she was already as white as one could be. "I'm sorry. I know it's macabre, but at the same time, it fascinates me. It must fascinate you, too."

Her husband dropped his spoon into the bowl. "I'm sheriff because these things repulse me, sicken me. I do not find them fascinating, Joy."

"I'm sorry." She looked into her lap, ashamed.

"Are you happy?" Even without the candle lit before him, she could see that her husband's face had darkened.

"Of course," she lied, though she had never truly known happiness, so it was difficult to say for sure. "Aren't you? Boone, aren't you happy?"

Boone fell back in his chair and exhaled loudly, as though he'd been holding his breath ever since their wedding night three months ago. "Where'd you come from?"

Joy wanted nothing more than to find someone she could share that answer with, but Boone was not that person. She had misjudged him, and herself.

"Here and there," she began, as she always began. "You know me, love. I've never laid roots anywhere until now."

"Marrow isn't some place you just stumble into."

"Well, I did. I didn't mean to, but I did. Why does it matter? If it bothered you so much, love, why didn't you ask sooner?"

"Why didn't I ask?" Boone leant forward, elbows to the table, fists to his temples. "Joy, I'm lucky I didn't starve to death when you came to town. You were all I could think about. You were all I wanted. I couldn't sleep because time was wasted when it was not spent with you. Do you know how many noses I had to break to keep the 'bad men' from you?"

"That explains a lot," Joy said, and then thought: *How did he figure me out so quickly?*

Boone slammed his palms on the table, causing the candle to fall over. "Why did you choose me? No woman has ever paid me much attention, and you're the most beautiful woman Marrow has ever seen."

Joy quickly picked up the candle before it set fire to anything. "Boone," she pleaded.

"I thought I was full of myself. Crazy, even, to think someone like you would want me. But you did. You did want me, and you did all of this for me. When you came through those gates, you set your eyes on me and went to work on me. Why?" He dug his fingernails into the wood. "Answer me, Joy."

"I just knew you were the one." Joy tilted her head and considered another course of action. "What do you know, Boone?"

A humid breeze blew through the house, carrying with it the smells of all the things that had died in the swamp today. A warm glow crept across the windowsill as the gas lights outside were brought to life.

"I've seen you speaking to the dark. I've followed you at night, when you thought I was asleep, to the woods. You took my blood, and then with a wave of your hand, the wound was gone. And—" Boone searched for his words, "—there's something wrong with you... down... down there."

Joy smiled; for all his ruggedness, her husband was still shy when it came to sex. Perhaps that's why he'd waited so long to finally bring up pregnancy.

"Why are you smiling?" Boone barked.

"I'm sorry," she said, becoming serious. "I'm just so happy we're talking. You've been so distant these last few weeks."

Boone scooted the chair backward, scuffing the floor. He stood up, muscles tensed, and pointed at her. "You're in league with Satan!"

Joy rolled her eyes. She was done feigning innocence, ignorance. "If we're going to be honest with one another now, then why don't you start by telling me who you've been fucking lately?"

Boon flinched. He fumbled with his belt as his eyes darted back and forth across the room. His silence confirmed his guilt, and just like the guilty, he changed the subject entirely. "What have you been doing to the babies? Every time your belly swells, you leave, and I find bloody cloths out back."

"I just want to give you the right one, love," Joy said. She smiled a sad smile, the kind that promised her husband she would try harder. "Come to me. It'll be perfect this time, I know it."

Boone didn't know what to say, so he didn't say anything at all. He left the room, and Joy knew why: he was going to get his knife, because he was going to kill her. How did it always end this way? She sighed and sat back in her chair. Stopping him would be easy enough; with one chant, he'd have just as much consistency as the stew he'd hardly touched. But what would be the point?

After all these countless years, one simple truth remained: she was much better at being dead than she was at being alive. So when she saw him come back into the kitchen, filled with hate and holy delusions, she let him do what he had to do.

Herbert

Herbert North tore his eyes from the wilderness outside the carriage window and said, "Seth, I have a question for you."

Seth Barker shook his head. "No." He ran his sweaty handkerchief over his equally sweaty face. "No more questions. Silence, Herbert, please, until we reach Marrow."

"What's wrong?" Herbert slid across the seat—slid, because the cushions were soaked in sweat—and nudged his friend. "It's a little chilly in here. Let me close one of these windows."

"Don't..." Seth's voice took on an oddly aristocratic tone, as though he were still channeling the spirit of the Duchess of Blaire. "Ask your question, Herbert."

"Do you find yourself getting a massive erection when you have to piss?"

As if the southern heat had finally melted his brain, Seth went cross-eyed and started to twitch. "Herbert, don't be immature. We are adults, professionals, acting in a professional capacity in this..."

He wiped his brow with his sleeve.

"In this fucking..."

And then he lost his composure.

"In this fucking, hot ass, god damn, mother fucking backwoods hellhole."

A spasm of rage took over Seth's body as he tore off his shirt and sat there with his arms crossed, skin glinting in the weak light.

"Do I even need to say it?" Herbert asked, enjoying his friend's temper tantrum. "So do you?"

Seth pursed his lips and sighed. Closing his eyes, he said, "Yes, of course."

Herbert cocked an eyebrow and shook his head in judgment. "That's disgusting."

Seth took his drenched shirt and whipped it across Herbert's eyes.

"I'm blind! I'm blind!" Herbert laughed as he ripped the shirt out of Seth's hand and flung it across the coach. "But seriously, why do you think that is?"

"You're exhausting." Seth leaned forward, his back unsticking from the seat, and rummaged through the bag at his feet. "It's because you keep grabbing yourself. You're over there holding on for dear life. You look like a damn fiend."

"That makes sense," Herbert said, sounding enlightened, as he watched his friend put on another shirt. "I wouldn't bother. You're just going to ruin that one, too."

"Marrow is hardly the definition of liberalism."

Herbert nodded. "So you're saying they may not take too kindly to a half-naked man and his aroused sidekick?"

Seth's eyes began to water, and he let out a laugh even the horses could hear, which had been Herbert's intention all along. "Yeah, I'm thinking they may have some qualms with that scenario."

"We don't usually investigate missing persons," Herbert said. He went forward and knocked on the divider to let the driver know to halt. "We need some fresh air. It's stifling in here."

Before the carriage had fully stopped, Herbert and Seth were already climbing out of it. Like pilgrims who had finally reached their mecca, they fell to their knees and breathed in their surroundings. The woods where they'd halted were thick, dense; space was so scarce that the trees had taken to growing out of one another. Countless vines hung from the branches, swinging like nooses for distracted necks. Endless swathes of Spanish moss blanketed the canopy, like some ancient, underestimated creature slowly creeping across the continent. The wind that blew here was heavy and smelled old, as though the air itself had been recycled for hundreds of years. And if someone wanted to speak, they had to yell, because the insects were loud, and they were relentless—a court of monsters in constant debate on how to overthrow those they so clearly outnumbered.

"Lovely place," Herbert said, falling back on his hands and outstretching his legs until they cracked. "I think I'll retire here."

Seth ignored him as he brushed off the wet leaves clinging to his fresh shirt. He stood up and scratched off the dirt on his backside.

"I warned you. Shouldn't be so dramatic. It's a good way to get dirty."

Seth stretched out his hand for Herbert to take.

"Thanks," Herbert said, coming to his feet.

"Sirs, we're close," the driver said from his seat, neck craned. He held the horses' reins tightly, as though he worried that if he let go, they'd escape the first chance they could.

Herbert waved him off and said, "One more time. Let's go over it."

Seth, seemingly satisfied with his appearance, made his way back to the carriage. "Driver," he called, and when the driver answered, he continued. "Do you know Sheriff Boone?"

He nodded with enthusiasm. "Uh, yep, I sure do. You're here for his missing wife, aren't you?"

"Joy, right?" Herbert asked, sounding surprised.

"Uh, yep, you've got it." He swatted away a huge fly. "Beautiful woman. Terrible tragedy."

"She's only missing," Seth said, hazarding a guess.

"Right, you're right. We shouldn't assume the worst. You think you'll find her?"

"I heard some think she's evil." Herbert strolled over to the driver and stood there with his hands in his pockets.

Spill your secrets, he thought, sizing up the big man on his small seat. "What do you know about that?" he added.

The driver furrowed his brows and looked to Seth for support, as though Hebert had become a dog that needed to be called off. "I only pass through the area. Everyone seemed to love her, that's all I know. I met her once or twice. I never got any bad feelings about her."

Herbert nodded, and turned away; with his friend, he climbed back into the coach. They sat in silence until the driver started the horses up again.

"The sheriff's wife is missing?" Seth whispered, biting his thumbnail.

"Isn't that who we're supposed to be investigating?" Herbert tapped his finger on his lip. "Driver didn't mention the little girl, Abernathy. He'd have to know about the little girl. Do you think they found her? We may as well just turn around. That's why we're here, after all. Come on, let's not get involved."

"The letter mentioned the sheriff's wife being the culprit; said the sheriff had killed a man in the Black Hills a few years back, so maybe he was involved, too." Seth crossed his arms, flexed his muscles as he disappeared in thought. "No, I don't think they found Abernathy. If Joy's missing, and if good old vigilante justice isn't to blame, then whatever took the girl likely took her, too."

Herbert sighed and let out a tired groan. He bunched himself up against the side of the coach; with his nose to the glass, he looked out the window to the world beyond.

"This isn't a good place for people like us."

The woods grew darker as the horses picked up speed; the sight became a glistening blur, like an open wound seen in the last moments of an accident.

"Too many doors have been left unlocked for far too long. You can feel it, can't you? The heaviness of the Membrane forcing itself in. If they find out we're here, Seth..."

Joy

Joy kept her eyes shut tight as Boone bound her in rope. She felt her throat tear wider as he flipped her over on the kitchen table and went to work on her wrists. He still had the same dumbfounded look on his face as when he'd split her with the knife and not a drop of blood came out. But she played her part all the same, and when he finally stopped shaking, he bought the act she'd spent so many years selling.

"I don't know what you are, but you deserved this," Boone murmured; like an act of contrition, he had been repeating the phrase for the last half hour.

When he pulled the sack over her head, she was glad she had long since lost the ability to feel. A normal woman may have felt an itch or a tickle, and the last thing Joy needed was to laugh and interrupt Boone's ritual. And now that she was thinking about the way in which he was preparing her body, she began to consider the possibility that she was not his first.

"I don't know what you are, but you deserved this."

Through the sack, Joy stole a glance at her husband when his back was turned. He had sweated through his shirt, and seemed to be whispering a prayer. Boone had been right; she had chosen him, but her intentions hadn't been nefarious. They were simple, shallow. He was sheriff, he had power, and if Joy could convince him she could be trusted, then he could convince everyone else to do the same.

"I don't know what you are, but you deserved this."

Boone turned around before Joy could close her eyes again. He stumbled back, grabbing the top of a chair for support. Taking out his knife, he stared at her body the same way one would a puzzle or a problem. But Boone was not a careful man, a considerate man—subtlety was something he could neither see nor spell.

So he plunged the knife into his wife's chest and left it there awhile.

Herbert

Seth had fallen asleep, which meant Herbert could rest as well. Despite having known his friend since infancy, Herbert continued to spend most of his days trying to impress him. For Herbert, he saw Seth's favor as some unstable compound that if left unattended would simply vanish.

Smile some more and make it easy on me, Herbert thought, watching Seth's head bob up and down with the bumps in the road. *You take things too seriously. I mean, you're right to, but you don't have to, not all the time.* He kicked off his shoes and stretched out his legs. Even when Seth slept, he looked serious, as though he were plotting their next plan of action with tools only the unconscious could provide. *I shouldn't put so much pressure on you. I shouldn't act like such an ass.*

Herbert North let out a sigh; he ran his hands across his face, pushing the sweat there into his hair. "This heat is getting to me, Seth. It's cooking my brain, making me think all logically, responsibly."

Seth Barker rubbed his nose, grunted, said, "That's good," and went back to sleep.

It never failed to amaze Herbert how quickly their names and the services they provided circulated the country. As far as he knew, they had no friends or acquaintances in Marrow, and yet here they were, traveling down its squelching roadways because some sad stranger had asked them to. It was work he was meant to do—he'd been certain of that the very moment Seth pulled back the fold and saw what lay in the Membrane. But whereas he'd envisioned a city to police, he instead ended up with a continent.

"One day, they'll stretch us too far," Herbert mumbled as he looked out the window, "and we'll break. You think that's what they want, Seth?" He kicked the toe of his friend's shoe. "To send us all over the globe, sacrificing a few of their own along the way until we can't take it anymore?"

Much to Herbert's surprise, Seth opened one eye and said, "If they wanted us dead, we'd be dead. No grand scheme, Herbert. Just monsters doing what monsters do, and people like us making sure they don't do it as much as they'd like."

145

When the screaming started, they knew they'd reached Marrow. Both equipped with a knife, revolver, and a pocketful of powders, Herbert and Seth burst through the carriage door.

"Stop here," Herbert shouted to the driver. "Whatever it is, we don't want it to know we're coming."

"Just jump," Seth said, pushing on Herbert's back.

With about as much grace as a one-legged ballerina, Herbert vaulted from the moving vehicle. His feet went out from under him as he stumbled and then crashed into the ground.

"We'll be staying at the home of Marie Riley," Seth continued. "Bring our belongings there in the next half hour."

Son of a bitch, Herbert thought as he stood up, wiping the mud off his ass as he watched Seth step gracefully down from the stopped carriage. "You couldn't have waited five more seconds before throwing me off?"

"I got caught up in the moment. Quiet!"

They turned their heads towards the road where, a few feet beyond the carriage, a small, pathetic wall stretched across the land. There, they heard a rustling—an animal perhaps, or some sadistic sentry—and then, beyond that, more screams, followed by shouting, followed by gunshots.

"I think they've got it under control," Herbert said.

"I think something is watching us." Seth's voice was cold, distant; his eyes the same as they traveled the length of the wall until it disappeared into the dim morning light.

Herbert took out his revolver and checked its chambers. "Well then, we should go say hello."

Herbert and Seth had been to many places throughout the course of their career, but Marrow was the only one that truly lived up to its name. As they pushed through the outskirts, they found the town sitting between two narrow streams, its faded yellow houses all soft and bloated upon the bone-white land. By the placement of the buildings, there seemed to have been a rigid order, but with the passing of time, much like the bending of a spine, things had become crooked and unsightly. If the town offered anything to the people of the world, it was that even if it seemed impossible, there was always somewhere worse to live.

"Do you see that, Herbert?" Seth whispered, pointing to the center of Marrow where several citizens stood circled around something.

Herbert nodded and started forward. There were five, no, six people at the town's center, and a seventh, a drunk man perhaps, swaying back and forth inside the barricade of bodies. He strained his eyes; the drunk was bleeding, and there was blood pouring out of his wrist where a hand should've been.

Moving closer, he started to make out the words the townspeople kept shouting. "Stay back," they pleaded and "Please stop," they begged, but the man at the center paid them no mind. He swung his ragged stump, lashing the crowd with ropes of blood as though he were a priest blessing his flock. More shouts, more screams; the people of Marrow pushed, punched, and kicked the man, but the pain they inflicted meant nothing to him.

"Seth, we have to get down there. We—"

A gunshot thundered through the town. The man at the center reeled as a stringy, pulpy mass of brains and arteries blew out the back of his skull. He fell, cracking his head like an egg against the earth, and sending the rest inside all over the townspeople's feet. Gun smoke slithered around the crime scene, like a snake in search of fidgeting leftovers. The people of Marrow went silent, then began to part as their savior passed through the ranks to look upon what he had done.

"That's the sheriff," Herbert remarked, noticing the badge and the way the man walked, as though his overinflated ego was gumming up his gait.

"Suspect number one," Seth said, picking at the bark of a tree. "Let's go introduce ourselves."

Herbert holstered his revolver. "You sure you don't want to wait until we can catch him in a better mood?"

"He doesn't strike me as a man with a better mood."

Herbert and Seth ran into Marrow like two concerned neighbors who'd heard something awful from the house next door. The townspeople were beginning to disperse when they arrived at the center. Like the culprits they may have been, the people of Marrow stopped in their tracks and started looking guilty. The sheriff and another, a doctor by the looks of him, were hovering over the dead man's body, arguing in heated whispers

"Hi, how's it going?" Herbert said, breaking the ice so hard he was about to fall through and drown.

The sheriff looked over his shoulder and spat. "How can I help you boys?"

Herbert's eyes went to the corpse at the sheriff's feet. "We were called here."

Sheriff Boone fingered the revolver's trigger. "By?"

Seth ignored the question. "We're investigators."

"Of what?" the sheriff snarled.

"The things that shouldn't be." Seth was always vague when this inevitable question was asked, and somehow it was always enough.

"What do you know?"

The doctor cleared his throat until everyone was looking at him. He lifted the corpse's shirt. The drunk man's stomach had been torn open, and his intestines had been chewed to a paste.

"Boone, Eddy was dead on his feet," the doctor said, "and even if he wasn't, he should've been in too much pain to stand."

"How long has this been going on?" Seth asked.

Sheriff Boone rubbed his eyes. "Eddy is the second. Marie Riley... she was last week."

Herbert and Seth exchanged glances.

"She was dead on her feet, too, wasn't she Doc?" Sheriff Boone said.

"Other than the fact she had no feet left to stand on... yeah. Her throat had been torn out."

Herbert turned around to face the crowd that had gathered again. There were more now. With their worn-out clothes and worn-down eyes, they milled about as they waited to hear something which would make some sense of what had just happened.

"Marie Riley wrote us. She was the one who asked us to come." Seth waited for the sheriff to panic, but he didn't. "Missing kid, and our driver said your wife has disappeared as well."

Herbert nodded at his friend, but his attention was elsewhere. Towards the back of the crowd, he noticed a little girl of seven or eight watching them. She was pale, dirty, and despite the heat, shivering. She had long hair that was somewhere between being damp and being encrusted with whatever wetted it. The little girl looked anxious, and like an anxious little girl, she sucked on the tips of her hair. She looked pleased as she tongued each strand, as though fond of the sticky substance that coated them.

"Herbert," Seth called.

"Yeah?" Herbert answered. He turned back around—"Sorry, what?"—but then the little girl was gone, and no one near where she'd been standing seemed to notice or care.

"What happened to your wife, Sheriff?" Seth asked.

A murmur worked its way through the crowd.

Sheriff Boone cracked his knuckles as though imagining they were Herbert's and Seth's necks. He leaned in close to the investigators and said, "Why don't you ask all them gathered around? I loved her. They didn't." He leaned back and then said loudly, "Let's go inside and get you boys caught up on things."

"Did you ever find Abernathy?" Herbert droned as he continued to search for signs of the little girl who'd vanished.

"No," the sheriff said bluntly. "Never did find Joseph, Cali, Jessica, Maribel, Ethan, or Brian neither."

Herbert swatted at a mosquito as it buzzed about his neck. "What? What the hell is going on here? How long has this—?"

The sheriff interrupted with a laugh. He walked up to Herbert until he was looking over him, down on him—blocking out the sun that shone on them.

"Aren't you glad you came?" He smiled, and clamped one large, sweating hand down on Herbert's shoulder. "I'm sure glad you came. We'll make it all better, won't we?"

Sheriff Boone brought them to the inn, and that's where Herbert and Seth sat now, their belongings on the table, as the foremost experts on the madness of Marrow bombarded them with anecdotes and theories.

"We're a god-fearing people here," Daniel Nathaniel, the aforementioned doctor, said as he shifted in his lopsided seat. "Marie Riley... she feared enough for all of us." He made the sign of the cross and mumbled a blessing.

That doesn't make sense, Herbert thought and then said, "That doesn't make sense. A god-fearing woman doesn't employ men like us. She goes to the church, to the priest, not us."

Seth nodded, and Herbert was glad to have his approval.

Roger Covert, Marrow's mayor, finished off his drink; he held it out until the innkeeper came by to remedy the problem. "You wouldn't think it, but lots of folk come by here. Strange folk, but nevertheless. They think us a bunch of rubes they can pawn off their junk to. And, yeah, they do, not going to lie, they do. Not much happens around these parts, so even if its shit they're hocking, it helps pass the time."

"No judgment here," Herbert said as he silently judged the lot of them.

Dust cascaded onto the table; on the floor above, some god-fearing folk were fearing god all over their bed.

"It's not unreasonable to think that someone referred the woman to you all," Sheriff Boone added as he passed the table, pacing like an animal locked in its pen.

"The most devout do have a tendency of doing the exact opposite of what they should," Seth said.

"They're my favorite kind of people," Herbert added, grinning. "It's such a spectacle to break them. It's almost cathartic."

Seth leaned forward. "Was she in love with the man in the Black Hills?"

Sheriff Boone stopped, noticed that everyone had noticed that he'd stopped, and then started up again. "Blake was a cannibal. Before all that came out, she'd taken a liking to him."

As Mayor Covert drank from his cup, he added between slurps, "She thought she could convert him, change him. Thinking back... I'd call it an obsession, but I'm not sure there's much of a difference between the two—love and obsession."

"I'm not sure, either," the sheriff mumbled.

Deep as a puddle, this lot, Herbert thought.

The doctor picked at the blood underneath his fingernails. "Marie Riley was mighty upset with you Boone when you put a bullet in Blake."

"I'm just going to be blunt with you," Seth started. "Marie said your wife was evil."

Sheriff Boone hung his head low and dropped into the nearest chair. He scratched the side of his face, plucked a few loose strands from his hair. "She spread rumors after what I'd done to Blake. Storm blew through... that was Joy's fault. Kids started going missing... well, what do you know, Joy did it, too. She was a sensitive woman, Joy. All that talking ran her out of here. God, do I miss her."

Something's not right here, Herbert thought as he absently felt at the bagged powders in his pocket. "Did everyone turn against Joy?"

"They had it in for her as soon as we'd married. Once they'd missed their chances."

No concern for the kids, no genuine concern for your wife. Herbert squinted his eyes at Seth, trying to transmit his thoughts to him. It was a tool they'd used since childhood, and it never seemed to fail them.

"Did you ever find the kids?" Herbert asked.

Sheriff Boone shook his head.

"Searched every inch of the swamp," the mayor clarified.

Seth spoke up: "What exactly happened to Marie Riley last week?"

Herbert noted the frustration in Seth's voice, a combination of the heat and his dislike for enclosed spaces populated by dumbasses.

"She lived on the outskirts near the bayou. Terrible place to live. Alligators come up from the river there to rest. That's how she lost her husband."

Picking out a splinter from the table, Seth asked, "Was Abernathy her little girl?"

"She didn't much look like her daddy, Marie's husband, but lots of us here come from bad places, bad choices," the mayor mused. "But yeah, Abernathy was hers. She didn't mention that?"

Seth shook his head.

"That's strange," Sheriff Boone said matter-of-factly.

"That's one detail you usually keep in if you want someone to come help you out of a bind."

Herbert bit his lip and transmitted "What the fuck is going on?" to his partner.

Seth shook his head. Transmission received.

Daniel Nathaniel, the doctor, sneezed into his hands and wiped a trail of snot on his pant leg. "When we found Marie Riley, she was crawling down the road towards town. Blood everywhere. She should've bled out back in her garden where she'd been attacked. No feet, like I said. Eddy…"

"Eddy is the one who found her?" Herbert made the connection for the man.

"Yeah, and he's the one who killed her. He said she attacked him, and he hit her with the shovel he'd been carrying."

"Something is being spread," Seth said excitedly. This was his favorite part of the investigation—the part where he got to theorize and be the smartest man in the room.

"Whatever is attacking these people, these children, is passing something on." Herbert paused for a moment as he heard a door crack back against a house outside. "It's hunting, and then whatever it feasts on is changed."

"A disease of some sort," the doctor added.

"Something in the saliva or its teeth." Seth stood up and, just to be dramatic, started to lay out his weapons on the table. "Probably meant to paralyze, to make sure the corpse stays relatively put, so it can come back to it later on."

"Nethers will do this, but they are extremely rare." Herbert came to his feet as well. "Never heard of them this far south, and I'm hoping it's not them, because they are a pain in the ass to kill. Incredibly impervious for some incredibly obnoxious reason."

Outside, feet shuffled across a porch. A word was uttered, and then lost.

"I'd suggest ghouls, but the victims are too slow, too dimwitted, to be ghouls." Seth twisted his mouth in thought. "Goredrinkers, maybe." He smiled as the manly men of Marrow cringed. "But there'd be less left of them if that were true."

"It could be an orphan... not what you think, gentlemen. They're little pale kids who like to drink—"

"Sheriff, you need to watch yourself," Seth warned. "I think this thing, whatever it is, may have attacked Eddy because he killed Marie. It doesn't seem to like anyone who gets in the way of its food—"

Again, outside, there was a commotion: shouts, followed by footsteps, followed by a growl and screams.

"Christ Almighty, what the hell was that?" Mayor Covert sprang to his feet and grabbed one of the investigators' weapons from the table.

That was fast. Herbert transmitted another thought to Seth—*this is it*—and bolted across the inn's first floor. He pushed through the front doors, pushed aside the wide-eyed, slack-jawed pedestrian standing behind them. The humid slush that was Marrow's air formed around him. His head darted back and forth between the houses and the streets, searching for the turmoil.

We can't track this thing out here. Can't let this fucker get away.

Another scream, and breaking glass. Herbert followed the inn's wraparound porch to the left and then paused, his mind halted by what he saw. In a small alley, a woman lay upon a bed of glass, the shards that blanketed her protruding from her body. The body was twitching, and for a moment, Herbert thought the woman was alive. But then he saw it—the huge red worm stretching away from the corpse—and realized the body was moved by its feeding.

"Seth is this a new...?"

Herbert didn't have the chance to finish his question, because the further his eyes traveled up the worm, the quicker he realized the worm wasn't a worm at all, but intestines. Several feet from the woman's body, near where the woods began, a little girl, the same he'd seen earlier, was walking away. She was holding the guts like a ball of yarn, and as she moved, they unspooled and spilt across the ground.

Realizing she'd been spotted, the little girl ran for the woods, clinging desperately to her bloody spoils while Herbert and Seth chased after her.

Joy

Joy liked strong men. She liked how hard they fought, even when they had no chance of winning. She liked the way their bodies looked when they were covered in sweat or drenched in blood. There was something about the texture of strong men that excited her. Perhaps it was the realization that beyond all the flesh, there was power.

Boone hadn't been her equal, as she had so foolishly hoped, but he was strong. Joy appreciated this, because as he carried her through the swamp, she knew he wouldn't drop or drag her. He'd draped a sheet over her body, placed a crucifix upon her chest. In the past, some men, usually the weaker ones, had cut her up or left her to fester beneath a tree or in a basement. That's the other reason she liked strong men: once they broke something, they became almost childlike in how they took care of the pieces.

He was bringing her to their secret place, their special place—a small island in the darkest part of the swamp, where under a thousand firefly lights, they first made love. He'd been so considerate then; he'd even finished on the dirt just to be safe.

It's probably still there. Joy thought back to the damp patch of soil, and her magnificent husband panting over it. *I can use that.*

Boone struggled to walk as he trudged forward into the water. Joy looked down and through the sheet and watched his pained reflection on the lamplight-lit surface. It didn't have to end like this, but she knew, if she was being honest with herself, it always would.

"Why'd you make me do it?"

Boone laid her down on the island and then lifted himself onto it. He took off her sheet—there, in the grass, the candles from last time, and her underwear—and sat.

"God damn it, Joy," he said into his palms as he wept.

Joy rolled her eyes. *Enough ceremony. Get on with it, so I can get out of here.*

But then something happened she hadn't expected, at least not from Boone. He hit her. He balled his hands into tear-streaked fists and punched her. He split her lip, broke her nose. He kicked her side until she flipped on her stomach, and then he turned her over and brought his foot down into her gut. She could feel his heel working its way down to her pelvis, and that's when she understood the depth of his hate for her infertility.

Joy didn't need to be human to know anger. *What is this?* She felt her skin become sweaty and hot. *Boone, what are you doing to me?* Her body tensed, and her mouth worked itself into a sneer. She started to clutch the earth, dig her fingers deep into it. Her husband must've noticed the changes, because he stopped his assault and went still. But it was too late. Death was one thing, but desecration was another matter entirely. He'd killed her out of necessity but dishonored her out of desire.

In a panic, Boone picked up the sheet and threw it over Joy. Using the fire from the lamp, he lit the remainder of the candles and placed them around his dead wife's body. He muttered a half-hearted apology, turned his back, and fled into the night. Joy listened and watched for a while until his trampling couldn't be heard, and his light was swallowed by the dark. She ripped off the sheet, but lay where he left her, and considered killing the whole of Marrow.

You want children?

Her white satin dress began to lengthen across the ground. She licked her lips at the thought of the boys and girls she'd eaten. For the perfect child, she had needed the perfect ingredients. Her dress tightened, wove into the soil itself; the cuffs and hem split and searched for the semen that had been spilt there.

You wouldn't accept them then, but maybe you will now.

She brought her legs back as she felt her womb quicken.

And if you don't, I'm sure we can find someone who will.

The white satin dress continued to stretch outward, so that it covered the island completely, while still leaving the candles upright. Her breasts grew heavy, and her nipples became engorged.

I'll show you Marrow as it is, and once you see it, you'll come back to me.

Joy took a deep breath, spread her legs, and pushed dead, rotted perfection into the world.

Herbert

"Nightfall comes quick!" Mayor Covert shouted after Herbert and Seth. "Slow down, damn it!"

Herbert whipped around, ripped the torch out of the mayor's hands. "Doctor, our gear," he yelled as he turned to face the woods. "Seth, don't lose sight of her!"

Seth hurried onward, his revolver readied. "Don't plan on it."

As Daniel Nathaniel retreated towards the inn, Herbert plunged into the thick of the woods. The little girl was quick; she dodged and wove through the trees as though she'd known this place all her life.

Is this one of the missing kids?

He could feel Sheriff Boone at his back, holding up the rear, as though he were coming along only because his station required it.

Herbert took out his gun and knife and ran as fast as he could. Branches slashed his cheeks as bushes bit at his ankles. The muddy ground sucked on his feet as he splashed through puddles and pools. Because of the torch, it took him a moment to notice the phenomenon, but with every step he took, the woods were growing darker. Was it night already? How had so much time passed?

Seth fell back to join in his light. "There, where the swamp begins," he panted, his skin a pale blue in the unnatural evening glow. "She's gone in there."

Herbert craned his neck. The doctor had never caught up with them, and Sheriff Boone was gone as well. "This is stupid, Seth. We don't know what she is or how to kill her."

"Hold on there just a minute," Mayor Covert panted as he re-grouped with the investigators. The smell of tobacco rolling off him, he grabbed his chest, as though to stop his lungs from leaving in search of a better body. "She's just a little girl," he finally managed to sputter.

"I'm no parent myself, but little girls don't usually go digging in people's stomachs," Herbert said, shaking his head.

He recalled the little girl standing amongst the crowd hours earlier. He remembered how she stood alone but ignored, free to do as she liked, because she was a child, and no child could be capable of such cruelties.

"Go back, Mayor. There has to be more of these children. It's no coincidence so many have gone missing."

"Something has changed them?" Mayor Covert's eyes were wide and watering.

"They may be marionettes. Something might've hitched a ride in these kids and is making them carry out its will. Fuck, I don't know! I'm just guessing here. Listen… go back, get everyone to a safe place. Keep the kids separated. Use the rooms in the inn. One for each kid—"

Seth interrupted: "Herbert, we have to go. Mayor, treat this like an illness. We'll be back when we're finished."

Mayor Covert nodded, and with a look of relief, he turned on his heels and went wheezing into the woods.

"You ready?" Seth went to where the land sloped and stood peering over the edge. "See the ripples?"

Herbert held the torch out as far as he could; across the swamp, black, oily waves were rolling outward. Slowly, he slid down the slope until he was up to his waist in the water. In a matter of seconds, he found himself swarmed by beetles and gnats, as though they were eager to welcome him into their decaying domain. He waved the torch back and forth, but the insects were unfazed. There were worse things to fear in the swamp than fire.

"There she is," Seth whispered, swimming beside Herbert. "Where the inlet is, just beyond. Another part of the swamp, I think."

"This is the sloppiest investigation we've ever conducted." Herbert picked out a mush of bugs that had flown into his ear.

"We were a little hasty," Seth admitted. "I just wanted to get this over with. We'd be out here for weeks trying to track this thing down."

"Where'd the sheriff go?"

"It was morning when we got here. How did it…?" Seth pushed a piece of driftwood out of his way. "I think Sheriff Boone knows exactly what's going on."

"Why didn't he stop us?" Herbert paused. "We need to get out of the water."

Several frogs leapt from their lily pads as something slithered past, dipping beneath the surface before the investigator could see it.

"We go where the monsters go. It's the only way to be sure." Seth sped up and reached for the inlet. He grasped the roots there and lifted himself out of the water.

THE BLOOD OF BEFORE

"I think he wants us to find whatever he and his wife have done and put an end to it. Too afraid to do it himself." Herbert handed his friend the torch and followed his example. "I swear to god if there's a leech on my—"

"Shut up, Herbert," Seth said, giving back the torch and crouching down. "What is that?"

He had to strain himself to hear it, but they were there: dark words in the inky night. At first, they seemed so familiar, as though he could make out what was being said; but then the words became heavier, thicker, like they'd been torn open by some eldritch incantation and left to scab over. Herbert's ears began to burn, to itch; the words became scratchy, harsh, like someone was sawing through his skull with a thick piece of rope.

"The white island," Seth murmured, his finger pointing to the pale plot between two weeping willows. "That's where it's coming from. That's where the little girl went."

Herbert North lowered himself into the swamp and slowly waded forward. Boney trees twisted out of the roiling murk, their flesh the leaves that now blanketed the black waters. Mosquitoes washed over him in blood-swollen waves, taking what they could, when they could, because he was in no position to swat them away. He'd brought the torch, but then left it behind, as the dead things ahead had their own light, and he didn't want them to see him coming.

Joy

Joy parted her legs and pulled out the snakes that had crawled inside her. Being dead had its perks, but too often it meant that things tried to take up residence in places they had no right to be. Since Boone had left, her body had become a writhing temple for all things scaled and skittering. Her children enjoyed it—they seemed to take great pleasure in probing around inside her for a small snack—but truth be told, it was an annoyance she could do without.

Cali and Ethan were standing over Joy when Abernathy finally returned with her offering. She had considered renaming the children, but they looked too much like their older selves, so it would've only made things more confusing. Sure, they hadn't come out perfectly—Maribel had Jessica's eyes; Ethan had Joseph's fingers; Abernathy had absorbed Brian entirely—but she had long since come to accept the brutal beauty of imperfection.

Joy smiled while Abernathy laid the bundle of intestines at her feet. Then, like a bird feeding its young, the little girl stretched out her neck and coughed until she vomited up a heart and some toes.

You could've just used your pockets, Joy thought as Abernathy nodded and joined her siblings. *Silly children.*

Still in her white satin dress, Joy sat up and ran her fingers over the already fly-infested remains. The island shuddered. The fabric rippled and swirled, and where there had been nothing, there was now a body, or at least an attempt at one. Beginning with a severed head and ending in two detached feet, the makeshift man was a combination of stolen parts that had been brought here by her children. With a flick of her wrist, Joy picked up the intestines and dropped them where the stomach would be. With a snap of her finger, the heart lodged itself into a hollowed-out torso; then the toes were attached to the places where Cali had gnawed the last ones off.

"Daddy," Abernathy said, her voice boyish, like Brian's had been.

Joy nodded and lay back down. She tired easily, because it took everything she had to keep from leaving this world. "Yes, soon, my love."

"People are coming," Ethan said, his voice unenthused.

Joy cocked her head. "Hide, children. Abernathy may have brought us visitors."

Abernathy's lip quivered, and she started to weep tears of dirt.

"Hush, now," Joy said, calling the girl over with a wave of her arm. "Hush. They may be the last things we need before…"

Joy's eyes widened. Boone rose out of the darkness, his revolver pointed directly at her head. He was covered in sweat, and tens of ticks and leeches were attached to his skin. He was bleeding from the nose, and pieces of a thorn bush were still stuck to his pant leg.

"You've gone through hell to get here," Joy said. "It's up to you how you get out."

Boone pulled back the hammer on his gun. He took a quick look at the abominations huddled beside his wife. "I knew it was you."

"What took you so long?" Joy could feel the fear in her children, and it sickened her. They were connected to each other, and they reflected one another's pain. "Did you think if you pretended this wasn't your fault, god wouldn't find out? You don't have to worry about that, Boone. The only God in these parts is fast asleep, and It doesn't much mind murder."

As though he were processing each detail one at a time, Boone suddenly became aware of the half-completed corpse and stumbled backward. "What... what are you doing?"

"Children need a father, Boone. I told them you'd come, but if you don't want the job, I'll make someone who will."

"Fuck you. I'm going to kill—"

Joy smiled and started to chant. At first, the words were familiar, but as she spoke and hummed, they became heavy and thick. The eldritch incantation welled inside her chest, and with every syllable uttered, the pressure from the ancient speech pushed against her bones. In heated shouts, the words split apart and the larva of hate and malice pushed through and bore its way into Boone's mind.

The sheriff started to spasm. When he dropped the gun, the children swarmed.

"Only the best parts of him, my loves," Joy said as her son and daughters tore into her husband. "But leave enough so he can find his way back. It's time for Marrow to become the mindless mass it's always aspired to be."

Herbert

When Herbert finally found Sheriff Boone, the children had already torn him to bits. Like ants at a picnic, the girls and the lone boy were carrying off pieces of tribute to their pale queen. At the center, a woman lay panting. As she panted, the island shook, for it was covered in the dress she wore.

Gripping the powders in his pocket, Hebert backed away slowly, bumping into Seth as he did so.

"We can't stand here." Herbert's voice was so weak it was as though he'd mouthed the words. With Seth, he looked down upon the dress, where the satin threads had become porous, dilated.

"Don't go," the woman said, sitting up.

She let the strap of her dress fall down past her shoulder, exposing her breast. The little girl they'd followed here crawled over to her. The woman's nipple began to drip blood, and then the little girl fed.

"Let me introduce you to our happy family."

Oh god, I'm going to be sick.

Herbert covered his mouth. He looked at the other girl and boy who were hard at work on a second corpse, a ravaged corpse, using Sheriff Boone's tongue, flesh, and veins to fill it in, fill it out.

I can't do this.

His hand began to shake; his skin began to prickle. He felt a warm wave of malaise wash over him, pour into him; it pushed under his eyelids, coalesced in his stomach. His vision became dotted with red, as though the world had been rendered in pointillism. He felt his heart pumping in his ears, his vomit sitting lodged in his throat.

I can't show her weakness, he thought, grabbing Seth's wrist and finding it just as clammy as his hand.

"No offense to you boys, but men are shit. I've tried and I've tried, but there isn't anyone in this world for me. Not yet, at least."

"Joy," Seth guessed.

"I've never been happier," Joy said as the little girl, greedy in her drinking, started to cough up blood onto her mother's chest. "Just stay still and take pride in knowing you'll be reborn better—"

Seth raised his revolver and fired three shots; each bullet whizzed through the air and caught a child in the head. The little boy and the little girl flew backward, their gangly, grotesque bodies falling into the swamp. The breastfeeding child crashed into Joy with the force of the impact, drenching her mother's face in arterial spray. Herbert, not wasting any time, emptied his gun into Joy.

Joy

Joy lay there a moment to let the men think they'd won. She could feel pieces of her face dripping down around her, but that was an easy fix. With the eye still attached to its nerves, she looked at Abernathy and the bodies of the girl's brother and sister in the water. She'd expected something like this to happen the moment they'd left the nest. They hadn't been her children, not entirely, so she wasn't wracked with grief. But that didn't mean it didn't hurt to watch them die.

The men stood over her now and saw that she was still alive. *No matter,* she thought as she started to speak the dark words that had birthed her babies and killed her husband. But they came out wrong; they came out weak and limp, without impact and power. She'd spent too much energy on the children, on Boone; she'd used everything up just to buy a little extra time on this secret, special island. She willed her dress to dig deeper for sustenance, but the soil had long since been stripped.

The men knew what they were doing, and they knew there was nothing she could do about it. Joy refused to resort to baser behaviors, so as they cut through her arms and legs with their knives, she laughed instead.

Weak men, she thought, *just like the rest of them.*

With one of the men holding onto her hair, the other chopped through her neck until her head was severed from her body.

"Not enough," Joy taunted, her head sideways on the satin.

I knew this was going to happen. Why did I bother?

"Going to have to try harder," she said, snickering.

I should've listened to you.

"You're not going to like it when you find out what Joseph, Jessica, and Maribel have done."

The one the other called Seth reached into his pocket and sprinkled what Joy quickly identified as Damnation Dust across her dress.

She's going to want to hear about this.

His friend, still nameless, did similarly, except he was throwing handfuls of Rapture. As soon as the materials mixed, green flames erupted over the dress and began to consume it. Joy then felt something like panic as the fire crept closer to her head.

How do they know so much?

"Grab them and throw them in," Seth said to his friend, who went into the waters and retrieved Ethan and Cali.

Joy watched as her white satin dress cracked and flaked, and knew that this was the end. As soon as it was gone, she would be, too. She closed her eyes, and in the darkness, Joy saw her sister. Though she would never admit it, there was no denying that it felt nice to be going home. Sure, her sister would scold her, make fun of her, but in the end, they'd laugh, and once Joy had rested, they'd have their revenge, too.

After all, they already had Seth's name, and that's all they needed.

Herbert

After they had burned and buried the bodies, they returned to Marrow. Beneath a cloudless sky, the town moaned with the sounds of the dead and dying. Exhausted, Herbert and Seth sprinted sluggishly through the woods, until they were on the edge of Marrow and could see what had become of it.

In the hazy, moth-mobbed gas lamp light, the people of Marrow had lost their minds. In huge crowds, the gory remains of things that should not be shuffled and swarmed towards the nearest sounds. They behaved much like Eddy had, like Marie supposedly had; mindless, yet persistent, the human shells shook with spasms of violence, but never attacked one another. Their hate, or hunger, was directed towards the living.

"They're dead," Seth said, his breath hot and sticky on Herbert's cheek. "Joy's children did this. Joseph, Jessica, and—"

"Maribel," Herbert finished. He watched as the creatures ambled through the alleys, searching for openings to slide their decomposing selves into. "They're the undead."

"This isn't Vodoun." Seth pulled Herbert aside, and they pressed themselves against the back of the nearest house.

"I don't know what that woman did or what she had her kids do, but those are fucking zombies." Herbert cringed as he heard one of the creatures scraping its nails across stone just around the corner.

"How did we miss this?" Seth reloaded his revolver and gripped his knife.

"Given the circumstances, I think we did the best we could. Not everything has to follow the rules."

Seth nodded and leaned out from their hiding place. "Get to the inn, get our things. We have to find those kids before they turn anyone else."

"The kids didn't turn them all. It's not possible."

Seth pulled back and said, "Then don't let any of them touch you. I don't know how it spreads, but if she still has a hold on them—"

An old man hobbled into view. He looked at them pleadingly as the bones in his legs burst through his flesh, their broken ends sharper than any blade. The old man's hands flexed, and his jaws started to tremble. And then in the blink of an eye, faster than he had any right to be, he lunged.

"Now," Seth shouted, checking the old man with his shoulder.

They fell to the ground in a whirlwind of skin. As Seth held the zombie's neck and pushed it outward, Herbert drove his knife through the base of the man's skull and twisted until Death came for what It'd been owed.

"Herbert..." Seth said as his friend helped him up.

Herbert turned around; tens of zombies were pouring through the alleyway, each pushing past the others to be the first in line.

"Meet me at the inn!" Seth darted off into the dark, and several zombies followed after.

When is splitting up ever a good idea? Herbert gave the creatures the middle finger and ran to the right, where a house sat elevated off the ground. He jumped, caught the supports, and hoisted himself up to the porch. Herbert pushed through the back door into the house. Inside, a fire blazed on a table from a fallen candle. Covering his mouth, he hurried through several rooms, until he found the front door and went through it.

Outside, the main street of Marrow had become a river of blood. A horde of zombies were shuffling back and forth in its crimson waters. Screams rode in on the coppery wind, as townspeople were ripped from their homes and eaten.

Herbert caught sight of Seth near where they'd first snuck into town. But before he could do something irrational, like trying to beat his friend to the inn, someone jumped on his back. He dropped hard to his knees.

"Daddy, Daddy," the little girl—Jessica, Herbert realized—whispered as her nails dug into his skin.

He reached around. Feeling her wet teeth on his neck, he yanked her over his shoulders and threw her into the street. Jessica slid in the stream of blood, her eyes, too large for their sockets, blinking out the gore that got in them. She started to speak, perhaps to beg, but before she could, Herbert put a bullet in her head.

He had the horde's full attention now, which, if he were lying to himself, which at this moment he was, had been his intention all along. He jumped to his feet and ran directly at the creatures.

Twenty, thirty... Christ, how many people live here?

The horde picked up its pace, causing some to slip in the blood and be trampled by their blighted brethren. Hebert fired five shots into the crowd and sent three to the ground. When they were close enough to grab him, he ducked and made a sharp turn, causing the horde to overextend itself and topple over one another.

"Herbert North!"

Herbert paused for a moment, his attention fixed on the ten zombies by the carriage ahead, and listened again for what had been Mayor Covert's voice.

"God damn it, man! Up here!"

Herbert looked to the second floor of one of the larger houses in Marrow—*must be the mayor's*—and saw Roger Covert standing there with a hunting rifle. He waved to Herbert, and then fired into the group of ten.

A scream, but not from the creature he hit. An old woman and a small girl emerged from the carriage and bolted through the breach left by the wounded monsters. But they were slow and wounded themselves; they didn't get two feet before the rest of the zombies were on them.

"Please, they're my people!" Mayor Covert fired and shattered one of the creature's jaws. "Ms. Carol, Lisa, hold on!"

Herbert's stomach sank. By simply saying their names, the old woman and the small girl were elevated above the unknown corpses piled high around him. Knife in hand, he ran and ripped through the group of zombies, driving the blade into their necks and ears. The zombies moaned and drooled as they fell backward and on their sides. But by the time Herbert had a clear view of Ms. Carol and Lisa, he wished he hadn't.

"I'm sorry," he whispered, backing up before the zombies, so intensely ravenous in their feasting, realized he was there.

Under the cover of gunfire, Herbert made it to the mayor's house unscathed. As he pulled open the door, he caught sight of a group of armed townspeople making their way through Marrow.

"Where's Boone?" Mayor Covert said, startling Herbert.

Herbert shut the door behind him and caught his breath. He shook his head and said, "Divorced."

Mayor Covert's eyes were red-rimmed and filled with tears. He fell against Herbert, bawling as he managed to say, "She did this. She did this. Herbert, how did this happen?"

"We have to get out there."

Herbert patted Roger's back. When he pulled his hand away, he found his palm covered in red. Was it the mayor's blood, or the blood of all those he'd loved too much to let live as undead?

"Did you bring people to the inn?"

Mayor Covert nodded. He stood upright and swallowed hard. "Some. There's two upstairs." He sniffed his nose, fell against the banister of the staircase, and started to cry again.

"We have to keep moving. Once we have the… living… secure,

we'll take care of the rest. Okay?"

Again, Mayor Covert nodded. "What's happening, Herbert? Where's your partner?"

"Seth's going to the inn, too. It's a lot to explain, mayor. Just… if you see one of the missing children… blow their fucking head off. Trust me."

Joseph

They don't like it when I kiss them. Mommy said they would. They always cry. Crying makes them taste funny. Mommy said she filled us up with love. Mommy said we should fill them up with love, too. They yell at me and ask me to stop, but I know they like it, because after a while, they get real quiet, and I can kiss them as much as I want.

There's so many people here to play with. They look scared. I tried to play with the girls and boys in their rooms, but I think I hurt them. All their mommies and daddies are in the front. They look scared, too. I think they'd feel better if they were together.

I let them out. They really didn't like being locked up in those rooms. Everyone is kissing everyone now. Mommy will be happy. I like making Mommy happy.

Herbert

When they finally reached the inn's wraparound porch, Herbert stopped and introduced himself to the father and daughter he'd helped escort there. He hadn't wanted to know their names, or for them to know his, until he was certain they were safe. It had always been better this way. Too many victims haunted him at night as it was.

"Dale Jones," the father said, shaking Herbert's hand with the kind of firm grip only the grateful can manage. "This is my beautiful daughter, Scarlet. She's eleven."

Scarlet smiled. If she hadn't been surrounded by putrid death, she may have even blushed at this strange stranger.

"Thank you," she said, her voice softened from a night of screaming. Her dark blonde hair fell in front of her face as she asked, "What happened, Mr. North?"

Mayor Covert, having lagged behind, finally arrived outside the inn and said, "Come on, come on. Inside, let's get inside."

"I'm not sure, Scarlet," Herbert said, looking into the girl's eyes, which begged him for an answer, a justification for what had happened to her small, quiet, uneventful, can't-wait-to-leave-here-for-the-big-city town. "But we're going to get you out of here. Ready?"

"Ready," Scarlet said, the hint of a smile behind all the dirt and blood on her face.

"Ready," Dale said, looking at his daughter as though he were trying to figure out how he could be as courageous as her.

Mayor Covert nodded as he held on tightly to the rifle that had so quickly killed so many of his own.

Herbert North took one last look at the place he would never truly know. He looked at the faded yellow houses, soft and bloated, and the fire spreading between them. He looked at the bone-white earth and the blood tide washing over it. He looked at the creatures roaming through the town, scavenging for flesh in all the places flesh may hide. How did they end up here? How did things turn out this way? The kind thing to do would be to leave some of the zombies behind for others to find and to give credence to the stories the survivors would tell. But could they take that risk just to raise awareness, just to fend off psychosis? He caught a glimpse of the group of armed townspeople again—already their numbers seemed thinned—and when he looked back to the zombies, he counted several more than before.

"Mr. North?" Scarlet's words shook him from his thoughts. "Are there more people like you?"

He smiled and turned away from Marrow. Reaching for the inn's front door, he said, "Not enough."

"I could do it," she said, squinting her eyes to look scary, like a soldier surveying a battlefield.

"Better than us, I bet." Herbert nodded at Mayor Covert, and Mayor Covert nodded at him. "Stay close. There may be a few in here since you last left. I don't know how long it takes to turn."

"I made sure," Mayor Covert said.

"Good." Dale bent down, and Scarlet climbed up his back and held onto his shoulders. "Good, thank you, good, good."

Herbert pushed open the front door and, for a moment, time stopped. Everyone was there, just like the mayor had said, but what he had brought and what now stood before them was not the same. They were zombies, all of them. Under the bloodstained ceiling, from each blood-drenched wall, men, women, and children stood tightly packed, their fresh, seething wounds rubbing into one another's. And beyond the hungering horde, at the top of the stairs, Joseph sat, his cheeks fat like a chipmunk's as he stuffed his face with strips of flesh.

"Herbert! Get the hell out of here!"

He spotted Seth at the farthest end of the second floor, where most of the balcony was in splinters. Seth looked as though he were about to collapse, and his clothes, his expensive, entirely inappropriate for the occasion clothes, were shredded.

Herbert turned to his companions. "Mayor, go, please. Run. They're slow. You've got your gun."

And before they could object, he stepped into the inn and slammed the door shut behind him. He didn't bother barring it, because he knew they wouldn't follow.

"What are you doing?" Seth fired a bullet at Joseph, but missed.

What am I doing?

Goosebumps ran up and down his arms as the zombies began to realize he was there.

What am I doing?

He had run out of bullets, so he turned his pockets inside out for the bagged powers inside.

Rapture, Grave Dust, Ensnare… Rapture.

There wasn't much left of the black, purple-flecked component, but it was more than enough to get the job done.

"Seth, do you still have Damnation?"

The two powders needed to be segregated for obvious reasons; neither man had any interest in having the end of the world start in the crotch of their pants.

Seth nodded as he held out the little bag of death.

The floor vibrated and shook as the zombies limped towards Herbert. He had five seconds at most before hundreds of teeth were picking clean his bones.

"Shoot it!" He pretended to throw the bag into the air.

"What about the kid? I only have one bullet."

Joseph looked at Seth and swallowed the meat in his mouth. He started to stand, ready to run.

Herbert shrugged, fell back against the front door, and flung the bag of Rapture into the air. It soared above the zombies. When it hit its peak, Seth fired. The bullet ripped through the bag, showering the creatures in the thick, abyssal dust. The zombies, seemingly mesmerized, looked up and reached out, as though they were children caught in winter's first snow.

"Get out!" Seth pulled back the hand that held Damnation. "I'll meet you out back!"

Herbert turned to leave, but before he could, Seth shouted and crashed into the floor. Through the rungs in the banister, Herbert saw Seth and Maribel atop him, with Joseph crawling over to join in the fun.

Several hands reached out and pulled Herbert into the sour mass of flesh. Fingers dug at his skin, pinched it as though it were putty. He kicked and slashed the creatures, severing hands, slitting throats. Those he injured fell, but only out of habit. Crooked mouths with flicking tongues closed on his side, his shoulder. He shook and flailed; stabbed their heads, gouged their eyes. Corpses collapsed upon him and died one last time; using them as a shield, he crawled across the sticky floor towards the front desk.

"Are you still… get the hell off—"

Herbert looked up and saw Seth's bloodied hand hanging over the edge of the second floor. He stood up, shedding the leaking body sprawled across him. He leapt for the front desk; a hand caught his ankle and pulled him back down. His chin cracked against the hardwood floor. With one hateful kick, he smashed the zombie's face in and then hurried to his feet.

"Hold on! I'm coming!"

Herbert stepped onto the front desk and followed it around to the huge bookcase behind it. As the mass of undead converged on him, he jumped onto the bookcase and scrambled up it. The case swayed, and its shelves buckled, but he kept climbing until he was at the top, on the top.

Without thinking, because he had no time to, Herbert jumped. Again, time stopped, and as he thrashed through the air, he saw the seemingly endless citizens of Marrow below, wallowing in their own mire of filth, waiting for him to fall.

Time resumed; the edge of the second floor was coming up on him. He threw his hands out, caught the banister and a bit of the carpet beyond.

"Seth, just hold on!"

His legs dangled over the crowd of flesh beggars as he fought for purchase with bloody hands. Slowly, he pulled himself up and over the banister. Wasting no time, he ran for his friend.

Seth was still screaming, which was a good sign. But the fact Maribel was digging at his stomach like a dog was not. Herbert bolted across the second floor, grabbed the girl by her greasy hair, and slammed her face into the wall.

Joseph growled and scurried over Seth. He caught Herbert's legs. With more strength than should've been possible, he knocked Herbert over. Joseph punched him in the face, in the throat; Herbert coughed and wheezed.

God damn son of a bitch, he thought as he braced his arm against the child's chest, forcing him back. Joseph kicked between his legs, grinding his toes into Herbert's testicles.

"Get the fuck off!" Herbert knocked the boy back and then cupped himself as pain struck like lightning throughout his body.

Seth caught Joseph as he lunged again for Herbert. Maribel staggered over to save her brother, but her eyes had rolled back into their sockets, and she couldn't see where she was going.

"Where is it?" Herbert called in between pathetic moans. "Where's the dust?"

"On me," Seth said as Joseph wiggled to be free of Seth's hold. "Grab Maribel and…"

Joseph tipped his head back and made a choking noise. The front of his shirt started to move, became bunched up as though something were behind it. Seth wrinkled his nose as he smelled something foul, like the boy had vacated his bowels.

"I think they're dying, Herbert," Seth said, furrowing his brow as Joseph shook in his hands. "Grab Maribel and we'll—"

Joseph had one final spasm, and then the buttons blew off his shirt as two heads tore through his stomach. Skeletal arms with feet for hands dropped out of the gaping hole and hung there limply. The two heads, rubbery and fused, had teeth all the way up their ears; and at the top of their skulls sat a crown of fingernails and bone fragments.

"Now, Herbert," Seth said, lifting the boy and his conjoined brothers and throwing him over the banister.

Joseph, still choking, crashed into the clamoring crowd below, the force of the collision ejecting his sibling from his chest.

Herbert hobbled to his feet. He scooped up the blinded Maribel.

No more. This is over. Bringing her to the banister, he noticed the lightness of her body, the softness of her skin. He saw the way her eyebrows arched, as though she were in pain or afraid. Maribel was a monster, but she hadn't allowed herself to become this way. The fact that she had been created for this purpose gave to her a kind of pathetic purity that weakened Herbert's resolve. No, he couldn't let her live—she was too dangerous, too infectious—but perhaps if the situation had been different, if Seth hadn't been there...

Herbert held Maribel over the edge of the second floor and then released her. Wasting no time, Seth opened the pouch of Damnation Dust and tossed it into the air. End over end, it went, and with every grain of the powder that fell, a small, green fire started where it landed. The hellish flames spread rapidly amongst the Rapture-coated dead. When the pouch hit the ground, it exploded into a pillar of flames that shot upward through the center of the horde to the ceiling itself.

"Do you think some of the kids were still in there? In the bodies?" Herbert searched the smoke for signs of Joseph and Maribel; he wanted to be sure they had died.

"Their souls?" Shadows swept across Seth's face from the tornado of fire spinning through the inn. "No, I don't think so. I hope not." He sighed and took his friend's hand. "We're done here, Herbert. Let's go."

Joy

From the Void, the world looked dark, but the green fires in Marrow left enough light to see what had been done. Joy wasn't delusional enough to think she'd been right, but that didn't stop her from wanting to hurt those who had brought ruin to her own.

Her sister sat beside her on the rocky precipice. "Is that all of them?" she asked.

Joy shook her head and said, "Caleb and Christina are still out there. I can feel them, for now. I'm not sure how much longer they'll make it. At least those men don't know about them."

"I heard his name—Herbert, that's what Seth called him." Her sister put her arm around Joy's shoulder and brought her close. "I have an idea. Who do you want to destroy the most?"

"Herbert," Joy said immediately. "There's something about him."

"So we'll start with Seth. It will take time. Can you be patient?"

Joy turned, felt her sister's white hair with her fingertips. "Time is nothing to us. If I must wait until he draws his last breaths, I will. And in those moments, I will make him feel more pain than the whole of the universe has combined."

"No, no," her sister said, kissing Joy's forehead. "Pain is my namesake, my job. Keep making us families. One day, you'll get it right, and we won't need this place anymore."

Joy smiled and bit her lip. "I was a good wife, wasn't I?"

Her sister nodded. "You were, truly."

"I just wanted the best for my children. I wanted them to be happy. I wanted them to grow up and love and have children of their own." Joy shook her head and said, "Is that too much to ask?"

Her sister shushed her. "Hush, now, there's still hope in Caleb and Christina. They're beautiful children. When they're done, the world will be so much better because of them."

"You think so?"

"Oh yes. They will bring such joy to the world. After all, they have all your best qualities."

THE BLACK HOURS

TRENT   **GEMMA**   CAMILLA

Gemma sucked on the salty tips of her hair as she laid ruin to her kingdom of sand. Fists and fingers left holes where houses had been. The returning tide saw to the rest. The great city shivered and cracked and, like wax beneath a flame, sank into itself, until all that remained was all it would ever be. Covered in the ocean's grime, Gemma the Thirteen-Year-Old Destroyer came to her feet, smiled, and made for the cave that yawned on high.

TRENT   GEMMA   **CAMILLA**

Camilla rolled down the driver's side window and let the heat scorch her some. The air conditioner had been reduced to a wheeze and a rattle. She wiped the sweat from her eye; with it went her makeup, too. Her cell phone buzzed against her leg. She pulled it from her pocket, read the name across the screen, and threw it like spilt salt over her shoulder. It landed on a pamphlet—junk mail, really—for Our Ladies of Sorrow Academy.

Camilla knew what her husband wanted, but she wouldn't be moved on the matter. The divorce was going through whether he wanted it to or not.

The truck dipped and groaned as it went over the uneven lip of the lot. Camilla's nerves were much like the suspensions about to give way—stretched beyond their limit and soon to snap. She parked where the weeds grew wildly and sat there a moment. Her hardness fell away like scales, leaving her with the tender truth that hurt too much to consider. Was she being selfish? Was she making a mistake? These questions she often asked and seldom answered.

Camilla kicked open the door, because a push was never enough, and headed for the antique shop.

TRENT   GEMMA   CAMILLA

Storm clouds crept along the sun-blasted sky, thunder like horns announcing their coming. Trent waited until the call went to voicemail, and put the phone away. His brother, Jasper, sent him a sympathetic look from across the kitchen table. Trent smiled, and guzzled his beer until there was nothing left of it.

"Give her time," Jasper said, swatting away a horsefly from his neck.

"I'd give her just shy of forever if I knew it'd do me any good." Trent leaned forward, put his elbows on the table. He said into folded hands, "No more. It's done."

"She did this." Jasper twitched as a flash of lightning lit up the horizon. "She cheated on you, man."

"She cheated for a reason." Trent breathed out the anger that reminder had brought him. "If I just knew why, I could make things better."

"Doesn't work like that." Jasper shook his head, ashamed. "It's done, and you know it."

TRENT   **GEMMA**   CAMILLA

Sea foam spilt over the shore, like the contents of a tipped cauldron. Crabs crowded around Gemma as she sat on her perch, legs swinging over the cave's precipice. She watched the last of her kingdom wash away on the beach below. She could still hear them, the king and the queen, calling out for help, but she paid them no mind. They'd done it to themselves.

Fat drops of rain fell on Gemma's knees and knuckles. She scooted backwards. A banshee wind howled across the cliff and haunted the cave. Lightning cracked the sky. Under its crooked grin, she scurried even further back.

Gemma considered staying here, to let the storm take her where it willed. Surely, wherever she went, it would be better than where she was about to go.

TRENT   GEMMA   **CAMILLA**

Fortune stood before her with a price tag too good to be true. Camilla searched it for signs of distress and forgery. She tapped on its bones, felt up its face. She pressed her ear to its heart and listened to its ticking beat. Between the pendulum's sways, she could almost hear Trent telling her no, telling her it was too expensive, that they couldn't afford it.

She pulled back, pulled it open to have a look at its innards. Like a haruspex, she saw future profits in its golden organs. If she didn't buy it, then someone else would, and she wasn't about to stop chasing happiness when it stood ready to be caught.

Mind made up, Camilla went to the front and asked the owner about the grandfather clock.

TRENT   GEMMA   CAMILLA

Beachfront properties had their perks, but being beaten into submission by storms on an almost weekly basis wasn't one of them. They came in quick, and they came in hard. But for Trent, weathering abuse, in any shape or form, was something he had built up a tolerance for.

Trent got up from the kitchen table and went to the fridge. He opened it and stood there, staring at the leftovers on the second shelf. That's what he'd be one day, he thought. A memory, one of many, put on ice and stored away in Camilla's mind. And all the good there'd been between them, it wouldn't last. He could with live that, or at least, that's what he told himself. What he couldn't live with was what would happen to Gemma. Camilla's threats of divorce had already begun to cause their daughter to spoil.

"What's up?" Jasper must have noticed Trent had been standing there a good minute or so. "You find the meaning of your life in that meatloaf there?" He rubbed his stomach. "Throw it out, brother. Was bad to begin with."

"Don't know about that," Trent said, catching his meaning. He grabbed another beer and slumped back down into his chair.

Outside, a bolt of lightning stabbed the sea. Thunder, like cannons, bombarded the house, rattling it from its windows to its rickety foundations. It would go on like this for a while, the back and forth blows. But most of the time, they didn't amount to much.

Jasper, fixated on the window that overlooked the ocean, mumbled, "Where's Gemma?"

"She's here. Heard her come in." Trent cracked open his beer and sucked up the foam that bubbled out of it. "Didn't she?"

TRENT **GEMMA** CAMILLA

The moment Gemma stepped out of the cave, the clouds must have decided it was time to drown the world. The rain hit her so hard it hurt. And there was so much of it that she couldn't see but a foot in front of her. Between here and home, it was a quarter-mile trek across crabgrass and sand dunes. She'd done it before, more times than she could count. But between the deluge on earth and the warring heavens above, the path had never felt more wrong. In the elements, she was out of hers.

Arms wrapped tightly around herself, Gemma gave everything she had to moving forward. Though she would never admit it to anyone or anything but her diary, she was scared. Terrified. The wind kept shoving her in every direction but the one she needed to go. She could barely keep her eyes open, because the storm kept spitting in them. And every second that passed, she could hear the ocean coming closer, toppling over the shore, as though desperate to take her into its salty embrace.

A blast of wind shoved Gemma to the side. She plodded into a pile of driftwood, lost her balance, and toppled over. The wet, gray murk rolled in and fell like a blanket over her. Maybe this wasn't a bad place to be, she thought, shivering herself into the sand. If she could hold out a little longer, her mom and dad would come looking for her. To have them working together, side-by-side, without clawing each other's eyes out—that just might be worth a bad cold and some scratches.

Gemma hated that she was giving in to the theatrics her mother often accused her of, but it had to be done. So she curled into a ball, clung to the driftwood, and pretended not to hear her name, which was now riding in on the chilling wind.

TRENT   GEMMA   **CAMILLA**

The owner of the antique shop was a man by the name of Gethin Yates. Much like the shop itself, he was a brooding, disheveled man who was both annoyingly unreasonable and frustratingly unpredictable. But what made him most unsettling were his features; his pale skin and frail frame; his elfish ears and long nails; his black eyes, wide and unblinking, like the sharks that came up along the bay from time to time. It's not that the middle-aged mutant was intimidating. He just didn't seem to belong in this town, or even this world.

"What can I help you with today?" Gethin purred from behind the register.

Getting through the antique shop took time. There were too many items out in the open, in unstable places. Rumor had it the man made more money off people breaking things than actually selling them. And now that the storm had rolled in and started having its way with the town, the lights in the shop were going out. So Camilla, half-way to the front, chose to ignore him, to watch her step, instead. She just wanted the grandfather clock. She needed it, and nothing else.

"Something catch your eye in the back?"

Camilla dropped her purse on the desk next to the register. She popped open her clutch and took out her credit card. At that moment, the rain picked up. It bashed against the roof, like millions of balled fists trying to get through. Somewhere outside, in that impenetrable gloom, a car skidded across the road.

"The grandfather clock," Camilla said. She held out her credit card. "I'll pay for it now, and pick it up first thing in the morning."

Gethin Yates twitched. He looked past her, into the flickering dark of his shop. Voice dropping to a whisper, like he didn't want the thing to hear them talking about it, he said, "Sorry, but it's not for sale."

"What? That's not what the clock said—"

"I forgot to mark it. I'm sorry." He wrung his hands. "Buyer bought it the other day over the phone."

"Over the phone?" Camilla shook her head. Fights with Trent, she'd give up on. But she had to have this clock. "How did your buyer even know…? Gethin, how long have you had the piece?"

Glancing out the window, he said, "Storm's getting bad. Close to closing time, anyways. You better get back."

"No, listen to me." Camilla slapped the credit card down on the desk. "You're not selling that to some out-of-towner. Does loyalty mean nothing to you?"

"Loyalty? Years of window-gazing doesn't exactly make you loyal. You're unshackling yourself from your husband. Good for you, I guess. But don't act like you're not new to this collecting business. Please," he said, pointing to the door, "it's getting bad out there."

She ignored him. "What's the buyer paying you? I'll pay more. For the first time in a long time, I'm getting what I want. And I want that clock. It's the principle of the matter. How many times have I helped you out of a bind?"

He shrugged. "Not… many?"

"Doesn't matter. Listen, what do you want for it?"

Temples bulging, Gethin put his elbows to the table and buried his face in his palms. Camilla had never seen him like this before. He was letting her down on all fronts of assholery.

"Is there something wrong with the clock?"

Gethin's head shot up. His forehead started to glisten. Looking more suspicious than he probably wanted to, he mumbled, "What did you see?"

At that moment, Camilla knew she had him. "A charity case. Something I can fix up. A project. I need something to take my mind off things. Where's the buyer? They pay you?"

Gethin took out a ledger. He flipped to the back, to a page that was completely covered in dried, black ink. He pressed his finger to the entry, reading words that, as far as Camilla could tell, weren't even there.

"Buyer's name is Connor Prendergast," he said. His hand started to shake. "From clear across the way. East coast. His payment hasn't gone through yet. I thought—" he looked disappointed, broken even, "—I thought it had."

"Then it's settled. Break the news to him tomorrow, when I come to collect." Camilla tilted her head. "What is it? Was it in a crime scene or something? Or—" she gasped, "—or is it cursed? Oh, spooky!"

Gethin snatched the credit card out of her hand. "I just don't feel right having it here, let alone selling it to someone else."

She grabbed his wrist. "Twenty-five hundred, like the price tag says. And why don't you feel right?"

He swiped her card, chewed on his lip. "Because I don't remember ever owning it. I went into my storage a few weeks ago and there it was, hiding in the back. Camilla, I have no idea where that grandfather clock came from. It wouldn't be the first time I've forgotten about something I've procured, but I don't think that's what's happened here."

Lightning lit up the sky outside. Nefarious faces in the clouds beamed down on the coastal town.

"Well, I'll say one thing," Camilla said, voice fighting against the thunder. "It sure has made you much more pleasant to work with."

"It frightens me." He handed her back the credit card. "I can't sleep at night because of it."

Camilla shrugged. "That's what the twenty-five hundred is for." She winked, gathered up her purse, and then got serious. "Really, though, what's wrong with the clock other than you forgot you owned it?"

Gethin Yates shook his head. "Some items just don't feel right. They're like people. They have personalities. When you finally take this business seriously, you'll see."

Camilla looked over her shoulder, into the shadowy clutter of the antique shop. Though it shouldn't have been possible, she could've sworn she heard the ticking of the clock's hands, as though it were counting down the seconds until it would be fully in her possession. She liked that idea, the idea of owning something forever, and it being indebted to her as much she was to it.

"Clock felt good to me," she said, at last. She looked at the downpour raging behind the front door and said, "I'll see you tomorrow."

TRENT   GEMMA   CAMILLA

Trent and Jasper booked it to the cave Gemma had claimed as her own. With two large LED lanterns and loose-fitting rain slickers, they skirted across the coast like sickly ghosts in search of a late-night snack. Moving through the dusky murk was like moving through a dream. They never went as fast as they wanted, and never seemed to get to where they were trying to go. Though the bursts of lightning helped, it didn't stop Trent's mind from tricking him into thinking every shape he saw was the shape of his little girl's body, dead in the sand.

"This is bullshit," Jasper shouted, the wind trying to rob him of his words. "You've got to ground her ass after this."

Trent squinted, held his lantern higher. The torrential rain seemed to congeal around them, so that rather than falling in drops, it drooled down in thick globs.

Jasper touched his brother's shoulder. "She's okay, man. She's pulling some shit, but she's okay."

Trent could hear the blood in his ears, as it drummed up fear and sick guilt. If she came back with anything more than a bad scrape, he'd blame himself. What the hell was he thinking? He had known the storm was coming, so why did he let her go out? Parents weren't supposed to be afraid of their children. But he was of her. These were delicate times. If he betrayed her more than he already had, he would lose her for good.

Jasper, spitting out the rain in his mouth, cried, "What's wrong?"

Trent ignored him. Holding the lantern with both hands, he trudged onward. Selfish thoughts clung like barnacles to his brain. They refused to let go until he acknowledged them. What would Camilla say if he came home with Gemma crumpled in his arms? Would their damaged daughter be a strong enough binding to buy their marriage a few more years? He'd blame himself, but he'd do it in secret, in a bed he would still share with his wife, the once love of his life.

God damn it. Where are you? He swung the lantern back and forth, the stark light illuminating the waterlogged land. The cliff side tapered away beside him. Squinting, he saw this was one of the paths Gemma used to get to her cave. It was narrow, reinforced with boards. One slip, and one would slip over the side, plummet into the sea.

You wouldn't go that way. He leaned over the cliff, tried to pierce the haze of the twenty-foot drop. *You wouldn't do that*, he thought, not seeing her body bobbing in the breakers. *You wouldn't go that far, would you?*

"Hey," Jasper said, pulling Trent away from the cliff. "Hey, look here, look. What's that?"

A dizzying rush of relief ran through Trent's body. His eyes went to where his brother was pointing. A pile of driftwood. He ran ahead, working the lantern's light across the ground. It climbed over the driftwood, revealing something at the center, curled and quivering.

"Gemma?" Trent bellowed.

Lightning split the sky, struck a tree in the distant woods.

His feet sank into the ground; it was like it meant to do him a service by stopping him, to not let him see his daughter and what may have become of her. He shook himself free, using Jasper for support.

"Gemma? Is that…?"

He ran to the pile of driftwood and dropped to his knees. In the center, Gemma lay, her eyes open, talking to herself in tongues, the gibberish she proclaimed was a language all her own.

"Baby, are you okay?" He set the lantern down, while Jasper waved his over the girl's body.

Trent wrapped his arms around her and lifted her to his chest. "Sweetie, answer me. God, please, what's wrong? What happened?"

Gemma looked like she was going to play dead. But at the last minute, she threw her arms around Trent's neck and started crying.

"I got lost in it all," she said, bawling into his rain slicker. She held on tighter as he, fighting against his bad knee, got to his feet. "I'm sorry, Dad."

TRENT   **GEMMA**   CAMILLA

Dad didn't set her down until they were back home. She stood inside the house, at the front, mud worshiping at her feet. Uncle Jasper went to get her a towel.

"Are you hurt at all?" her dad asked. He rubbed her shoulders to warm her up.

Gemma shook her head, chattered out an apology.

"It's okay. Just… you scared the hell out of me." He smiled, turned, and traded places with Jasper, who had that towel.

"Get changed before your mom comes home," Uncle Jasper said, handing her the towel to dry off.

Her dad said, "Let's just keep this a secret, okay?"

Gemma, wringing out her hair, mumbled, "Yeah."

"After this morning, it would be nice to eat dinner in peace," Dad said.

Uncle Jasper nudged her. "Go change. We'll take care of the rest."

Teething her lips, Gemma said, "Okay," dropped the towel, and headed upstairs to her room.

"Gemma." Her dad went to the banister. His face was pinched, and darker. "Don't ever do that again."

Dad's mood swings. Good cop, bad cop in one, of late, permanently inebriated body.

"Do what?" she said, inching up the stairs, looking dumb for playing dumb.

He sighed, frustrated, and waved her off.

All bark and no bite. That's how he lost her mother, she thought, stomping up the steps. He was a good man, Gemma knew that. She loved her dad as much as she loved her mom. But he only cared as much as he needed to. Good wasn't good enough, anymore. Not for her mother, and not for anyone else, it seemed. And if the divorce went through, what would he be, then? Someone who resembled her dad, but wasn't quite?

Gemma turned on the hall light at the top of the stairs. She hated this. Hated it so much it gave her ulcers. Whatever those actually were.

Looking like something the sea had spat out, Gemma slithered into her room and shut the door behind her. She locked it, went to the mirror, and gave herself the once-over. Hair was a mess. Skin was a splotchy finger painting of sand and seaweed. She peeled off her clothes until she was down to her bra and panties. Bruises on her legs. Bug bites on her belly. It was gross to look at it, but she was used to it. She had never been known to take it easy on herself. She liked the rough things in life. The things that scratched and slashed, bit and stung. Mom always thought she was hurting herself on purpose.

"Bleh," she said, stripping down completely.

Gemma threw the wet rags into the hamper and slipped into her pajamas. She jumped onto her bed and buried her face in the blankets. Her hand closed around the stuffed bat on her nightstand. Pulling it close, she breathed it in. The little guy's name was Scram. Uncle Jasper liked to make fun of her for it, saying she was too old for that ratty, batty thing. Her mom had bought it for her years ago, when she was two or three, at a yard sale. She'd tried to part with Scram a few months back, because she was "growing up," but it didn't feel right. Not with

Mom and Dad biting each other's heads off every single night. The more they fought, the worse the house and the things inside it felt, until she could barely stand to be around them. Her room and Scram were about the only things their arguments hadn't ruined.

Gemma rolled over, held Scram above her face. Voice deep like an adult's, she said, "How can I grow up when they keep tearing things down?" She dropped Scram on her head and growled. "Show's how much they care."

Her ears picked up a sound outside. She bounced off the bed, went to the window. As nightfall set in, the storm had begun to subside. She could see further than she had been able to before. Coming out of town, down the old road, was her mother's truck, high-beams blazing. Her mom had left to pick up pizza two hours ago. Gemma was hungry, but she had hoped her mom would've been gone a little longer. Because dinner was the bad hour, the black hour. The hour when her mom and dad got to let out all their anger on one another, until the rest of the night was sufficiently terrible.

Gemma thought back to her sand castle, and the king and queen she let drown inside it. Morbid notions came easily to her now. She always figured that was just part of "growing up."

TRENT　　　　　GEMMA　　　　**CAMILLA**

About the time Camilla pulled into the driveway, Jasper was coming out the front door, doing his damndest to carry out his disappearing act. Trent's brother always managed to be gone before she came home. It was smart, but still pissed her off all the same.

She killed the engine and grabbed the two large pizzas off the passenger's side seat. Stepping out of the truck, rain now a drizzle, she said, "Don't want to stay for dinner?"

Jasper laughed, shoved his hands into his coat. "No, better get going before the storm picks up again."

"Can I ask you for a favor?" She kicked the door shut behind her. "I bought this beautiful grandfather clock from Gethin today. Idiot didn't know what he had. But I need help loading it into the truck tomorrow morning. Do you mind?"

He laughed uncomfortably. "Oh, uh, I don't know. Honestly, I don't want to be around here for when you tell him that."

"I'm going to tell him tonight."

"Uh."

"Please?" She flashed him a smile, the one that she knew made him feel like they were on the same side.

"Yeah, alright." Jasper started to say something, but stopped himself.

"What?" Camilla asked, catching on.

"Uh—" he went past her, toward his car, further down the driveway, "—why don't you wait until later tonight? Don't tell him at dinner. You all should eat in peace, for once."

Camilla cocked her head. "It's my house, too, and my money. He wants me to be open with him? Then that means telling him things he doesn't want to hear."

"Yeah, but you like starting shit with Trent."

"What?"

"Come on," he said, unlocking his car. "You do. Everything you do that you know will drive him crazy, you rub in his face. I'm not saying he's right or you're wrong or whatever. I'm just saying take a break from the fighting for one night." He sat down in the car and, as he pulled the door shut, shouted, "For Gemma's sake."

Camilla waved him off, called him an asshole, and went inside the house. She stopped at the threshold, a knot of rage tightening in her temple. Muddy footprints marred the hardwood floor. They ran from the front of the house, up the staircase, into, undoubtedly, Gemma's room. To her left, the living room, and slung over the loveseat, a wet towel with a bunch of oceanic gunk all over it. Further back, Trent was banging around in the kitchen, setting the table she had asked him to set hours ago. She squeezed the sides of the pizza boxes, causing them to crumple.

"That's nice," she said, her voice elevated to that piercing pitch all moms seem to possess. "Come home and the place is a freaking mess."

She growled and went into the kitchen. Lo and behold, Trent was there, at the sink, with a beer, waiting for her.

His eyes went to the pizza boxes. "You were gone awhile."

Camilla set the pizzas on the counter. She was practically bursting at the seams to tell him about her purchase. Looking out the window above the sink, she saw a few slivers of light coming through the clouds. The last they would have until the night was done with them.

"Must have had a lot of orders," Trent persisted. The forty-two-year-old was starting to sound like their daughter.

"Gemma!" Camilla shouted as she started divvying up the pieces to the plates on the table. "Gemma. Dinner."

Then: "I went shopping. Got caught in the storm." Pizza hanging as limply as her jaw, she said, "Do you want a play-by-play, Trent?"

"What did you buy?" He finished off his beer, started towards the fridge for another one.

Camilla rolled her eyes, said, "Are you kidding me? You were listening? I can't have a moment's rest around here. Gemma!"

Stomp, stomp, stomp. Gemma stomped down the stairs and wandered into the kitchen. It made Camilla sad to look at her. Her daughter's pajamas were baggy, but she was still so skinny. She had to make sure she ate a lot tonight. Lord knows Trent couldn't keep up on those things.

"Mm, smells good," Gemma said. She dropped into a chair and devoured the pizza on her plate.

I got to let that go, Camilla thought, watching her daughter go to the box for another slice. *She's going to be fine.*

She turned around to find Trent on his cell phone, tapping through an app. In the window, she saw a reflection of the screen. It was their banking account—two thousand, five hundred dollars shorter than it had been an hour ago.

"What the hell did you buy?" Trent growled. He flipped the phone around for her to see what she'd already seen in the window. "What the fuck is this?"

Camilla clenched her jaw. The tendons in her neck tightened. A million mutilating words ran through her mind. She could literally feel her eyes changing color as the heat in her skull swelled into a blistering ball of rage. Smiling, she tried to shake it off, tried to let it go. But after years and years of letting things go, she found she couldn't anymore. Everything he said, every accusation he made got under her skin and made her feel filthy inside. The only thing he could do right anymore was shut his fucking mouth.

Camilla looked at Gemma. Her daughter had gone stiff, and her face had lost its color. She knew what was coming. They both did.

TRENT GEMMA CAMILLA

Before he could stop himself, he was already in Camilla's face, blocking her from getting around him.

"What the fuck did you buy?" His wild eyes never left hers.

"None of your god damn business." She ripped a chair out from the table and sat down. "I bought it with my money. My money."

Trent couldn't help but laugh. He leaned in like a gargoyle over her shoulder. "Your money? Your money? It's our bank account. It's our money. My money that I earned!"

"Get back," she said, jerking her hand upward. She stared at her pizza, like she was tempted to let this all go. Then said, "You haven't worked in how long? Your money? Go to hell, Trent."

She's doing this on purpose.

Trent leaned back, looked at Gemma, though at this point, she hardly registered to him.

She's going to destroy me. She's going to make sure she leaves me with nothing. Everything I've done, and she's going to blow it on bullshit.

"So what did you buy, huh?" He went in again, hands gripping the back of her chair. "What did you buy?"

Camilla scooted the chair away, ignored him as she went to the sink for no reason in particular.

Trent, practically nipping at her heels, barked, "What did you buy? What did you blow all our money on this time, Camilla? Huh? What?"

"Get. Away." She whipped around, stuck her finger into his chest. "You drunk asshole. Get away from me."

He ignored her and said, "You've been spending a lot of time with Gethin. Is that him? Is that the guy you screwed?"

"Jesus Christ, Trent." Camilla screeched and pushed past him to the table. "I bought a fucking grandfather clock. Something I can fix up, flip, and sell for a fucking profit. Happy?"

She's going to take all my money and leave us with nothing. She doesn't care about anyone but herself.

Trent went to the fridge and opened another beer. He guzzled it down, while deflecting Camilla's disgust.

She fucked Gethin. Never said she didn't. Spends all her time and money on him.

Camilla screwed up her face. "You got something to say?" She wasn't done fighting with him. Not even close. If he stopped, she would try even harder. This wouldn't be over between the two of them until they had exhausted every cussword and insult in the English language.

The last of the beer drizzling down his chin, Trent said, "Every day, you're gone for hours. Wasting money. Fucking Gethin. You have a family here, and you're not even trying." He crumpled the can and, in a fit of rage, threw it at the garbage.

"I'm not trying? That's good. That's real funny." Camilla's eyes went black. "I'm not trying? I'm not trying? What do you do all day beside sit around here and drink and feel sorry for yourself? And I'm gone all day? When's the last time you spent time with Gemma? When's the last time you spent time with me? When I actually wanted you to be around me, you fucking prick? I'm not trying? I'm doing something and you're just—"

TRENT **GEMMA** CAMILLA

Gemma wasn't hungry anymore. The half-eaten pizza on her plate made her stomach turn just looking at it. She wanted to get up, but like with every other argument before this one, she found herself rooted. Piece of shit, son of a bitch. Cheating whore, useless moron. She'd heard it all before, in every room of the house and most places in town. But she didn't move, didn't go to her room, because what she needed to know would only come at the end. When they were tired, sometimes crying. At the end was when they'd make the serious threats, the real threats. Threats like if the divorce were going to happen, and when. But the worst of it was when they talked about who would keep Gemma. Like she was one of her mom's antiques up for auction.

"You don't do anything for anyone else. You're not there for Gemma, and you were never there for me," her mother shouted. She was bearing down on Dad, shoving him against the refrigerator door.

Gemma scooted in closer to the table to give them more room to fight. She reached into her pockets for her cellphone, which was upstairs, dead. She had a few friends, not good friends, really, but convenient ones. Easy ones. They swore up and down their parents fought like hers, but she'd never seen it at any of the sleepovers. They tried to make her feel good about her situation, but their sympathy was too sweet to take on a daily basis.

Her friends were good distractions, but terrible reminders of one crushing truth: Gemma's home life for the last thirteen years had been anything but normal. When she realized that earlier this year, she retreated, into books and herself, and only emerged when she was clothed in mischief and misdirection.

Dad slammed the fridge shut. His fist was balled and in her mother's face.

"Do it!" she said, almost snarling. "Go ahead, Trent. Hit me in front of your daughter. Show her how a man is supposed to treat the woman who's carried his ass all these years."

At that accusation, her dad's arm went limp.

"How long were you out of a job for? How many extra hours did I work to keep the bills paid? You sat on your ass for months, not doing a god damn thing."

Her dad threw his hands into the air, shouting, "I was injured. What the hell was I supposed to do? My knee still isn't right."

"Boo hoo," Mom mocked. "Are you kidding me? I practically paid all the bills. I worked damn near sixty hours a week. I took Gemma to school. Did her homework with her. Oh, and helped my mom, when she lost her house, and my sister, when she was sick. What else did I do? Oh, that's right. I talked to your boss for you. I got your job back. And what did you do? You did everything you could to make sure they'd fire you again. And that woman? That god damn woman before we got married."

"When are you going to stop bringing this up?"

"I was going to stop bringing it up when it stopped happening, but it hasn't, Trent. You skate by in life, not putting an ounce of effort into anything but trying to give me a fucking heart attack."

She laughed, looked at Gemma, who laughed too, just so she'd take her insane eyes somewhere else.

"When am I going to stop bringing those things up? You know what? Never. Never, Trent. And it doesn't matter. It's over. We're done. I don't have to forgive you for shit. And I don't have to do a damn thing for you anymore."

The woman? Gemma, next to the pizza on the counter, picked at the crust as her mind chewed on the notion. *The woman?* She had heard her mom bring her up before, that night when Dad found out she'd cheated on him. She always figured he had cheated on her once, but her mom never said for sure. Which was weird. She rubbed everything else in his face every chance she got. But not that.

"We're not done," Dad said, following her mom into the living room. Breathing down her neck as she dropped onto the couch, he said, "We are not getting a divorce. You are not destroying this family!"

"Oh, so it's my fault?" She flung a pillow at his face. "You're going to blame me for this?"

"You cheated on me, you god damn…"

"Say it," she said with a smile, eyes shining. "Whore?"

"I am willing to forgive you."

Oh no, Gemma thought. She loved her dad, but he was an idiot. When he said things like that, it was as though he were asking her mom to kill him. Gemma slinked into the living room, staying clear of her parents, who were infected with the disease fifty percent of all married couples supposedly had. She had to think, had to do something. She had to intervene; otherwise, this would be going on all night, and to-morrow, too, until one of them, most likely her dad, got kicked out.

This was the beginning of her summer break. She was not going to spend it in a warzone, being captured by both sides and used as a way to bait the other into a fight.

"Shut up," Gemma whispered.

But her mom was on her feet again, spitting words in Dad's face. Pushing him around. Daring him to knock her down.

"Shut up," Gemma said a little louder.

But her dad couldn't hear her because he had grabbed Mom by her shirt and was screaming, "Who did you sleep with?"

Gemma closed her eyes. All the tears there bunched up against her lids. When they leaked out, she quickly wiped them away. She didn't want them to see her cry. She didn't want to make this about her, or rather, how they were hurting her. It was too late for them to see that. And if they had already seen it before, then they obviously didn't care; otherwise, they would have stopped. No, she was going to be their problem to solve. Not their kid to coddle. It was fine if they knew how much she hated them. Hate was easy. Hate was like a fire sealing a wound. She'd heard that in a song once, and right now, she believed it with all her heart.

So she punched the wall with both her fists and screamed at the top of her lungs, "Will you two shut the fuck up? Shut up! Shut up! Shut the fuck up!"

TRENT   GEMMA   **CAMILLA**

Camilla was two bitches away from flat-out slapping Trent across the face when Gemma exploded.

"Will you two shut the fuck up? Shut up! Shut up! Shut the fuck up!" her daughter belted, leaving oily fist marks on the wall, like the autistic children Camilla used to teach would do.

Derailed, and damn near deranged, Camilla set her sights on that insubordinate seed of hers and said, "Go to your room. Go! If I so much as raised my voice at my parents, they would have popped my lip. Go, Gemma."

But Gemma didn't move. Instead, she stood there, crouched over, taking short, raspy breaths, as though the fighting had made her feral.

"Gemma," Trent said, joining Camilla. "Listen to your mother and get upstairs right now."

Their defiant daughter arched her shoulders. Her cheeks quivered; she dug her nails into her thumbs. Thunder and lightning battled for the family's attention, but the thirteen-year-old's incoming meltdown would be impossible to ignore. Camilla had to stop herself from going off on Gemma. She knew exactly what her daughter was trying to accomplish, because she had done the same thing with her parents when she was her age. But in moments like this, with all the bloody rage for Trent boiling inside her, it was hard. Because she saw more of her husband in Gemma than she did of herself. It hadn't always been this way. But truth be told, she saw a little of Trent in everyone nowadays. And she just about hated everyone for it.

"I'm... sick of the fighting." Gemma ground her teeth, only because she knew Camilla hated that. "I'm sick of it. Just get fucking divorced already."

"Alright, upstairs. Now." Trent started towards her.

Gemma screeched and ran past her father, through the living room. She stormed up the stairs, each thunderous step somehow worse than those earth-shaking claps outside. From the second floor, she bellowed, "I wish you both would leave."

Camilla took a deep breath, Trent at her side. She turned away from him. The smell of beer and his aftershave was making her sick.

He did this. He started this. He's the one who fills her head up with lies and turns her against me. He acts like he's perfect. I'm the one who has to do everything around here. Would he hurt us if he drank enough? That one... but I did, too. He has to go. Anyone but him.

TRENT GEMMA CAMILLA

Trent took a deep breath. Camilla beside him, he stared past her out the window, into the dark world pressing against the glass. The heat of his wife was singeing, and she smelled bad, like wet fur and old gum.

She did this. She started this. She wants to make me look like an idiot, like a piece of shit in front of Gemma. She thinks there's nothing wrong. I swear to god she's lost it. I'm the only one keeping this house together. Who did she sleep with? Who did she tell? Who's laughing at me now?

TRENT **GEMMA** CAMILLA

Steam rose off the bathtub, the water filling it a little hotter than Gemma could bear. Stripped down, she stood in front of the fogging mirror on the bathroom wall and stared at herself the way she always did while Mom and Dad fought. It was a ritual where she found her flaws and transmuted them into something else.

The faults rarely changed. She was too skinny, and her chest was too flat. She had weird looking legs and big feet. Her lips were too large, or depending on the day, too small (today, they were too large). Her butt was barely there, and the only part of her that she figured boys might like (her hair) kept falling out. For a while, she kept waiting for time to right these wrongs her body had done to her, but the older she got, the more awkward she looked. It was as though she were some mad scientist's creation, stitched together from the remains of others. In some places, she looked thirteen, others five or twenty-five. Her mom had said it had something to do with puberty, but Gemma was pretty sure it was just who she was.

Much to her mom's surprise, she was okay with that. She took strength from these flaws. Took pride in these "defects." After all, they were hers to own, and if she didn't own them, she'd be like her friends, boy-obsessed and beauty-possessed and never satisfied with what they were already fortunate enough to have. Gemma did a lot of thinking on this because her "normal" life had turned out to be anything but. And if she didn't have a normal life, and if she was about to lose her parents (in some ways, she already had), then she had to accept these flaws. Because they were hers and hers alone. Unchanging and frustratingly reliable. And for some reason, a big hit with the guys. That was nice, too.

Gemma headed over to the sink and brushed her teeth. There was enough dried toothpaste in the basin that one could probably age the house by its hardness. She rinsed out her mouth, grabbed a new razor from inside the medicine cabinet. She didn't really have much hair to shave, but a few new cuts on the back of her leg would help her sleep better tonight.

TRENT · · · · · · · · · GEMMA · · · · · · · · · **CAMILLA**

"I want you to leave."

Stupidly shocked, Trent said, "I'm not going anywhere."

"You're not staying here tonight. Leave, or I'll have your brother come get you. You are not staying here."

"No," he said. "You always do this. I'm not leaving my own house. It's storming out there and… No, you go. I'm not."

A cold chill climbed like dead fingers up the rungs of her spine. This always happened when the fights came to an end. The whole house seemed to drop fifteen degrees, and everything in it became alien, almost hostile. The shadows became darker, the halls quieter than usual. It was as though the house reacted to their animosity and twisted itself to reflect the conflict they and it held within.

"When's the clock coming?" Trent asked. He was trying to play nice, trying to secure a place on the couch for the night.

Camilla shook her head. "I'll take care of it, since it's my problem."

"Who's going to—"

"Jasper." Camilla rubbed her face and started for the stairs. "Get some clothes and go."

"I'm not going anywhere."

Listen, you fucking moron, she thought. *I'll call the god damns cops on you again if I have to.* But instead, she said, "If you don't go, I swear to god I'll tell Gemma about her mother."

Trent opened his mouth to fight back, but common sense, finally having broken free of its drunken stupor, stopped him. He shook his head and, for a second, looked as though he may cry.

"Stop turning me into some witch. Stop doing this. Just… do us all a favor and go." Camilla went up the stairs. As she reached the top, she saw Trent's stupid, pathetic face in her mind's eye and added, "Come back later tomorrow. I can't do this tonight."

Trent went to the bottom of the stairs. The lights flickered on and off. "Will you tell me? Who you—" he swallowed the sick taste of the word, "—slept with?"

Thoughts of the strange grandfather clock overtook Camilla. If she focused hard enough, she could almost hear its din—a deep thudding, dark and enveloping, like a musical note unplayable by anything but it.

"Camilla?" Trent called.

Coming out of the reverie, she said, "I don't know who it was. Don't even know his name. Just some guy, an out-of-towner."

"Why?"

"Because he didn't know me. And he wasn't you." She turned off the stair light, dousing her husband in darkness. "He was the only easy thing I've done in years. Thought it would help get rid of you, of us, but apparently cheating isn't enough. Go, Trent. I can't do this anymore."

TRENT   GEMMA   CAMILLA

In the humid night, bad deeds came easily. Trent took his car and went out into the dying rain to the parts of town where light was seldom seen. These were the dead places, the untouched places; they were the filthy alleys and abandoned buildings that sat in the back, or in-between. Always there, but never acknowledged. Eyesores of a coastal town too cheap to burn them to the ground.

Trent pulled off the main road and parked in the lot behind a gutted convenience store. The 24/7 Quick-Stop had gone out of business five years ago. Now it was a popular place for teenagers to go to break those laws they couldn't in their parents' basements. A lot of rich kids came here, so the local police on their nightly patrols tended to give the place a wide berth.

His cell phone started to ring. Quickly, he took it out of his pocket. Expecting Camilla's summons, he got Jasper's concern instead.

He answered the call and said, "She kicked me out."

"You can crash here," Jasper offered.

Inside the 24/7 Quick-Stop, cigarettes flared. Sweaty limbs flashed in and out of the shafts of light coming through the busted windows. He was too old to be here, but where else could he go? To the bar? To the bowling alley? The last thing he wanted was to be around others as pathetic as himself. In his youth, he had everything. And youth, to him, was everything.

"Trent? You there?"

"Yeah."

"Where are you? What are you doing?"

"About to do something stupid."

Jasper grumbled. "Come over. I'm sure you've done enough damage for the night. You can stop digging now. That hole of yours is deep enough."

Trent fiddled with the door handle. A swell of music rolled out of the convenience store. Who was in there tonight? What was on the menu? He shook his head, punched his temple. As a father, he should have been terrified of these cesspools, for Gemma's sake, and yet here he was, a few excuses away from diving in.

"Take it you found out about the clock?"

"Yeah." Trent was half-listening. He smelled marijuana on the air, rolled down the window to get the full effect.

"Listen, I'm going over there tomorrow morning to help her load it and bring it home. I'll talk to her for you. Soften her up. When the coast is clear, I'll let you know." He paused and then said, "How badly did you fuck it up tonight?"

Trent rolled up his window. He couldn't, shouldn't do this. "Really bad," he said. "I don't know what happens to me. It's the way she talks to me." He flicked on his windshield wiper to swipe the rain away. "We need to try counseling again."

"I think you both need an exorcist." Jasper laughed at himself. "I'll see you in twenty?"

Trent, still gripping the car keys in the ignition, stared at the 24/7 Quick-Stop. Long hair in the shadows. Baggies in the moonlight.

"Give me an hour. Need to clear my head."

TRENT **GEMMA** CAMILLA

The next morning, Gemma woke to the sound of the grandfather clock coming in, and blood in her underwear. Her period wasn't supposed to be here until next week. A bit of blood dotted the sheets. Now that she was awake, her cramps were coming hard, too, like a thousand knives stabbing her ovaries. Her mom was right: sometimes, being a girl was bullshit.

After she got cleaned up, she headed down the stairs. The front door was open, and Uncle Jasper's car was in the driveway. Hitting the first floor, she got a text from her dad that asked if he could talk to Mom. Gemma almost responded, then looked at the time. It was eight in the morning. Early enough to ignore him until later, like eleven or twelve, when she usually woke up.

"Is that my daughter?" Mom called. "Is she really awake right now?"

Gemma pressed the pain out of her stomach. She wandered outside to the driveway. It felt good out. The sun was warm, the air cooled. Everything glinted with condensation, and the ocean beyond was back to its normal self. There wasn't a cloud in the sky. Although, if she looked hard enough, she did spot a few dark ones gathering in the furthest corners. It wouldn't be until tonight that they would find out if those black omens were headed their way.

"Hey, Gemma."

She went sideways. In the garage, Uncle Jasper stood, mopping his brow. She headed over to him, bare feet getting wet on the walkway, and gave him a hug.

"You see the clock yet?"

She shook her head. "Where is it?"

"In the living room."

Gemma did a double-take. "I just came down the stairs. I didn't see it."

Uncle Jasper glanced at the cell phone in her hand. "Not surprised."

She rolled her eyes and pocketed the phone. "I barely use it. Where's Mom?"

"With the clock?" Jasper must have thought she was crazy. "In the living room, right next to the front door? You sure you're okay?"

Gemma took a few steps backward and looked over her shoulder. Through the front doorway, she saw the shape of her mom standing in the living room, with a large, black object towering over her.

"But she just called for me. From out here."

Uncle Jasper shook his head and took her by the shoulders, pushing her towards the house. "I'll cut you some slack. Whenever I woke up this early at your age, I could hardly form complete sentences."

"At my age? Psh." Gemma wriggled free. "You don't know what it's like to be thirteen nowadays."

"Like you do? You've been thirteen for what? Four months now? Guess that makes you a bona fide expert." He flipped her ponytail to tick her off. "Let's get you inside before you get a sunburn."

If Gemma's mother had noticed her walk past earlier, she thought, going into the house, then she didn't say anything about it now. In fact, she didn't say anything at all. All her efforts and attentions were focused solely on the monolithic monstrosity at the center of the living room.

Two thousand and something dollars. That was what her mom had spent on this thing. Gemma stepped up beside her, thinking that, if she stood as close as Mom did to the grandfather clock, maybe she would look at it differently. But she didn't. Not at all. The grandfather clock wasn't some beautiful antique, but a haggard excuse for a Halloween decoration. It was huge, almost ten feet tall, with two horns curling from the top of it. The body itself was impossibly black, though there were bursts of color here and there in the strange markings that covered it. The moon dial was hellfire red, and the clock face a busted sheet of tortoiseshell metal work fitted with hour and minute hands that hardly moved. But what stood out the most was the pendulum behind the glass case at the clock's center. It swung back and forth to no particular rhythm, as though the cancerous gunk that clung to it were moving it with a will of its own.

Gemma thought it looked awesome. What she couldn't believe was that her mother, boring Camilla with her mom clothes and fear of horror movies, felt the same way.

TRENT   GEMMA   **CAMILLA**

The shock of seeing the grandfather clock in her living room had yet to wear off. One minute, it had been at the back of Gethin's shop, promised to another. And now it was here, safe and sound, hers to restore, and hers to covet.

Dreamily, she said to Gemma, "What do you think?"

"It's really cool. How did you guys get it in here?"

"It's lighter than it looks."

Gemma made a pained grunt. She must have started her period early. Camilla had, too.

"Are you going to keep it in here?" Gemma asked.

"Might move it back some, but yeah, for now."

Gemma took out her cell phone, read something, and then pocketed it again. Trent. Camilla didn't even have to see the text to feel the desperation oozing out of the screen.

"I'm sorry about last night," Camilla said. She let down her hair and put it back into a tighter bun.

"Whatever."

"No, it's not 'whatever.'" For the first time since she put the clock in the living room, she took her eyes off it. Staring at Gemma, she said, "I'm sorry. You shouldn't have to hear all that."

Gemma's cheek quivered. "Then why do you do it so much? You don't try."

"Believe me, I try, sweetie, I really do. But your father brings out the worst in me." She went back to the grandfather clock, attention fixed on the scorched moon dial. "I tried for thirteen years."

"How can you give up now?"

"When you're older…" Camilla stopped herself. She'd said that line so many times before it had lost all meaning. "Not right now, Gemma. Let's try to enjoy the day."

"Did you guys only get married because you got pregnant?"

The accusation hit Camilla like the bomb that it was. "Gemma, god no. No, no. This has nothing to do with—"

Jasper came through the front door, saving her ass yet again. "Looks good," he said. His face bunched up, like he had just stepped into something he shouldn't have.

"Thanks for your help, Jasper."

He nodded, swinging his arms back and forth. "So, didn't get a chance to ask in the truck what with all—" looking at Gemma, he changed his tune, "—what's the big deal about this grandfather clock? Said it was a steal?"

It was. Camilla pressed her hand to the glass case that contained the erratic pendulum. Its ticking vibrations coursed through the woodwork into her flesh. The minute and the hour stopped where they willed on the clock face, the times depicted upon it nothing more than jagged gouges in the plate. She ran her fingers up the clock's body to the horns that jutted from the pediment, which she could only barely touch, even on the tips of her toes.

The piece of antiquity had been carved from madness and lacquered in lunacy. The creator of this morbid creation had to have been an empty man at the end. Standing this close to the clock, Camilla could smell blood in its cracks, feel a pulse of life throbbing in its mechanical innards. She knew she was obsessed with it, and perhaps that was why she didn't worry about her obsession. As long as she was aware of it, she could be in control of it. And maybe it wasn't the grandfather clock she was obsessed with, but the notion she had found something so unique and claimed it as her own. The only other thing she had like that in her life was Gemma, but sometimes, and it hurt to admit it, even she wasn't enough.

"Keep an eye on your mom tonight," Jasper said. "She's been checking out all morning like this."

Coming to, Camilla said, "Sorry. This heat... and I didn't sleep well last night. What did you ask me?"

Jasper shrugged.

Gemma tapped on the clock. Instinctively, she jerked her hand back, as though she'd been shocked or bitten. "What's the big deal about this thing? Is it some priceless artifact or something?"

"I already told you guys." Camilla stepped away and headed for the kitchen.

But Gemma persisted, anyway, saying, "No, you just keep staring at it, Mom. Kind of creeping us out."

Camilla waved her off. She searched her mind for reasons as to why she'd bought the clock. Had it been the construction or its age? Had it been its history or its uniqueness? She had approached the piece the same way she would a mate for the night: attracted on a purely superficial level, with all good things assumed and all detractors ignored. Truth be told, she had no idea why she'd bought the grandfather clock. It was an absolute mystery to her. It was as though she had brought a stranger home without asking them about all the stuff they kept in their dirty pockets.

Embarrassed, Camilla said to Jasper, "Tell Trent he can come home for dinner," and disappeared into the kitchen, to find, for some reason, her sharpest knife.

TRENT   GEMMA   CAMILLA

Camilla had called him home for dinner. Usually when Trent came back, he came back with a whole host of apologies and, sometimes, even a gift or two. Flowers for Camilla. A movie or a book for Gemma. But this time, as he stood at the front door knocking to be let into his own house, he came to them empty-handed, with nothing more than a vow of silence to prove to his family he, after twenty-four hours, was a different man. The only problem was he hadn't packed a change of clothes. He still smelled faintly of the 24/7 Quick-Stop and the puddle he woke up in.

Gemma opened the door. She gave him a small smile. He went in for a hug. She shook her head and pinched her nose. "Better change. You know how Mom is."

Trent nodded, shrugged; scratched his head like a bozo. "Did you get my text this morning?"

Quick as a whip, Gemma said she didn't.

"Mm, okay." He leaned into the doorway, immediately noticing the grandfather clock that dominated his living room. "That it? I'll check it out later," he said, covering the side of his face, so he didn't have to see it.

Gemma stepped aside, letting him in. Shutting the door behind him, she whispered, "It's weird. I don't know if I like it."

"La, la," Trent sang, still refusing to fully give witness to the clock. He swung around to the stairs and started up them. "Where's your mother?"

"Out back, in the garden. Picking a few things for dinner."

One of the worst parts of coming home after an argument were those uncomfortable moments of exposure. Walking in on Camilla in the bathroom or her changing. Moments that might have been funny or arousing became clinical, almost sinful. Trent always felt as though he had lost the right to see her naked, or almost naked, after an argument. It was something he had to earn back, or at least, that's what he told himself. Usually, Camilla just came to him, broke the tension in about ten minutes, and then turned out the lights. That's how it always was. They hadn't forgiven each other, let alone said sorry to one another, in years. In their house, absolution had been abolished about the time there were more beer than soda cans in the trash.

"Okay," Trent said. Hand still pressed against his eye, he could have sworn he felt a force trying to pry it away, to force him to look at the clock. "Alright. Let me go get cleaned up."

GEMMA

Post-war dinners were always the worst. No one spoke, let alone looked at each other. Instead, they communicated through how they ate. How loudly they clinked their silverware; how violently they sawed their steaks. If Dad guzzled his drink and choked down his food, then Gemma knew he would be as good as gone before desserts came out. If Mom nursed her wine like it was the last of the stuff on Earth, then Gemma knew she would be in the kitchen the rest of the night, busying herself with tasks, buying herself time until Dad fell asleep, so that she could crawl into bed without conflict.

But tonight was different. Her mom and dad were acting… normal. Whatever that word meant anymore. Dad was smiling, making small talk. And Mom was joining in, not talking over him, but with him. And they seemed to be enjoying the steak and potatoes, not forcing it down their throats like they were doused in poison and twice-baked with razor blades. It was freaking weird.

"Fairgrounds are going to be open next week," Dad said. "Want to go?"

"Eh." Gemma impaled a piece of meat. "I don't know. There's a lot of trashy people that go there. I'm not about that life anymore."

"Not about that life? Who are you?" Dad smirked. "Well, how about we go just to grab a funnel cake or two?"

Her mom flashed her a look that told her to say yes, so she bit the side of her lip and reluctantly said, "Sure."

Cringing, Dad stared at his plate and said, "That clock is something else, isn't it?"

Mom leaned out of her chair, as though to check on the beastly thing. "Uh, huh."

He's trying to play nice, Gemma thought. She scooped out a forkful of potato and ate it. Before she could swallow it, the piece had slithered down her throat. On its own.

"Ugh," she said, waving off her parents' concern as she took a drink of water.

Mom sighed, somewhat offended. "Is my cooking really that bad?"

"No, no." Gemma took another drink. This time, it had the after-taste of rust. "Sorry. I'm just—"

"So how much you think you can flip it for?" Dad interrupted. Money. It always came back to money.

"A lot," Mom said. She had been vague about the demonic idol standing in their living room ever since it had arrived. Gemma was starting to get the feeling she'd bought it on a whim and was doing her best not to admit she had.

"I got to tell you—" Dad eyed the fridge for a beer, then settled for his glass of water, instead, "—it's not what I expected. You sure you want it in here?"

"Looks cursed," Gemma said.

Dad nodded.

Mom took a drink of wine, let it run over her teeth some. Voice deeper than usual, she said, "You two just going to keep giving me a hard time about it?"

Gemma, the diligent diplomat, quickly said, "No, it's cool, Mom."

"It's hundreds of years old, you know?" Mom was staring at her hands, touching the veins that bulged from them, as though to make them go away. "It was built..." Her brows knitted. She cocked her head, like someone was talking to her. "It was built in a convent."

"Is it one of a kind?" Dad asked.

Mom nodded. She picked up her fork, raw meat clinging to it, and pressed it to her veins.

Gemma leaned forward, saying, "Uh, Mom?"

And then Mom put the fork down and smiled. "I think we'll have to put a lot into it, but the clock will be worth it."

TRENT   GEMMA   **CAMILLA**

What time is it? Camilla's eyes fluttered open to the gray dark of her room. She was sprawled out across the bed, taking advantage of the space afforded to her by having Trent sleep on the couch. She licked her lips, turned over. The alarm clock on the nightstand seared the numbers 12:54 AM into her mind.

"Ugh, god," she said, rolling back over. Nothing pissed her off more than waking up in the middle of the night. Well, besides Trent.

As soon as she was about to fall asleep, she heard someone run down the hall. Jolted awake, she checked the time—12:56 AM—and sat up. One leg over the side of the bed, she leaned forward. The door to her room was cracked—didn't she shut it?—and she was trying to see what was going on beyond it.

"Gemma?" she called, coming to her feet. Her daughter's room was at the end of the hall, but the bathroom was in between. Maybe she tripped on her way out.

Camilla went to the door. Had the other half of her brain been awake, she might have flipped on a light. But since she was a few yawns away from full-blown hibernation, she just grabbed the door and flung it back.

There was someone in the hall. They looked like Gemma, but it was hard to tell. Too dark, and Camilla's eyes were all gummed up from her allergies. Rubbing them, she shuffled forward, trying to make sense of why her daughter—yes, it had to have been—was squatting down in the middle of the hall.

"Gemma? Hey, honey, are you okay?"

There was a squelching sound. Her daughter shifted, let out a moan. A foul smell rose off her and closed around Camilla's face like a wet, dirty hand.

"Jesus," Camilla cried, about to vomit.

Her daughter, still not much more than a shadow, then stood and took off down the hallway, blending into the blackness that gathered at the end of it.

"Gemma?"

Camilla, covering her nose, backtracked to her room and switched on the light. There, in the middle of the hallway, where the shadow of her daughter had been sitting, was a puddle of bloody shit.

"Oh god."

Camilla leaned back into her room, trying to get some fresh air, but it was impossible. The smell was everywhere, and it seeped into everything. Even her hands over her nose smelled awful, like sweaty copper and meaty feces.

Concern propelled her forward. She tried to jump over the steaming puddle, but her heel caught the edge of it, making her stomach sink. Somewhere between angry and terrified, she kept going, past the bathroom, to her daughter's room.

Camilla pushed the door open and flicked on the lights. Gemma was lying in bed, the blankets kicked off. Her back was to her mother, and she was holding onto Scram the bat for dear life. She was snoring, and her pajama shorts weren't stained.

"Gemma?" Camilla was about to go to her daughter's bedside when she realized the smell was gone. Instead, she looked over her shoulder, back into the hallway. The pile of bloody shit had disappeared.

Camilla covered her mouth, mumbled, "Okay. Okay, what the fuck?" as she wandered out of her daughter's room, back to the place where she had vacated her bowels. But there was nothing there. No feces, no gore.

"Mom?" Gemma called out behind her.

Camilla ignored her and slipped back into her room. Her head, so filled with confusion and doubt, felt as though it were going to explode. She sat down on the bed. The alarm clock read 1:00 AM. She didn't go back to sleep after that.

TRENT   GEMMA   CAMILLA

Trent woke up at eighty-thirty in the morning to the hot sunlight that left him clammy and sick. He hadn't slept well. The family room couch was more like a torture device than a piece of furniture. That, and he had kept hearing noises all night, too. A kind of low whining, something like a scared cat would make, coming from the living room. That's where the grandfather clock was, and that's what he figured the noise had been. It's gears, maybe; its workings, winding up and getting ready to do what it was meant to do. Or something. He wasn't an expert on that stuff.

Getting up from the couch's quicksand center, something crunched beneath the cushions.

"The hell?"

He dug in the crevice, found an envelope smashed against the abandoned hide-a-bed. Camilla was hiding bills again? It was something she used to do all the time, then stopped when she started talking about getting a divorce. He could already feel his blood boiling, but maybe this was a sign she was changing her mind on leaving him.

"What did you blow money on this time?" He tore open the unmarked envelope. Instead of a bill, there was a letter. And it read:

Trent,

These last few years have been difficult. I think that we both can agree on that. And I think we can also both agree that we would give just about anything to get back what we used to have so long ago. It hurts me to say that it is gone, but... I don't know anymore. How much longer can we hold out? All we do is hurt each other. And Gemma... I can already see it now, her doing everything to make us suffer for putting her through this. It turns my stomach, Trent. We're better than this. We deserve better than this. I'm not happy anymore, and I know you can't be, either. We're too comfortable. Even the fighting is comfortable. It isn't supposed to be this way. We become something else when we are around each other. Our marriage has become something else, too. I don't hate you, but I don't love you. Not like I want to. Not anymore. Help me end it. It's the only—

There was no more to Camilla's letter. She had stopped there. He had an idea when she might have written it. There had been a night a few months back when he came into the family room and she was on the couch. She jumped, and then started chewing on the pen in her hand. They fought that night, but it wasn't like it usually was. She kept trying to end it, and he kept it going, confirming what she'd already known for years on end.

Trent shoved the letter back under the couch cushion. Tears in his eyes, he slipped out the back door and onto the porch to watch the ocean awhile.

TRENT   **GEMMA**   CAMILLA

"Did you get sick last night?"

Tongue firmly planted in the side of her ice cream scoop, Gemma shook her head and mumbled a very tongue-numbed, "No."

It was Saturday afternoon at the Dairy Delight. This was supposed to be their special, stress-free time of the week. Yet Mom looked anything but stress-free. She had the same expression Gemma imagined the queen had in her sand castles right before the waves rolled in.

"I thought I heard you." Mom sipped loudly on her straw, her diet soda nothing more than icy dregs.

Gemma lowered her cone. The warm summer air rushed over the Dairy Delight's pavilion, helping to melt everyone's ice cream there. The garishly colored store wasn't as busy as it usually was. Might have been the storm that blew away most of the tourists.

"I won't be mad."

"Mom, I didn't get sick. What? What is it?"

Her mom shook her head.

Two of Gemma's classmates, Britney and Ashley, passed by the pavilion. They were in shorts and tops that may have well been bathing suits or stripper outfits. They had stupid grins on their faces, and while they stared at her and her mom, they whispered underneath their bubblegum breath. It didn't bother Gemma as much as they probably would've liked, but it would catch up with her later when she was in bed with Scram, unburdening her soul to the stuffed bat.

"I can tell, Mom. You look… disturbed," she finally said, the two bitches bouncing along to the next store. "What's wrong? Is it Dad?"

"It's always something with your father." Mom took a plastic spoon and took with it a bit of ice cream from Gemma's cone. "That clock—" she laughed, savored the minty flavor of her pilfering, "—it's something else, isn't it?"

Popping her lips, Gemma said, "Oh yeah."

Mom ran her fingers through her oily hair. "Feels good to be out of the house. The last few days, I've felt kind of bad. Summer cold? I don't know." Slurp, slurp, slurp, and then: "You hate the clock, don't you?"

Gemma didn't know how to respond, so she didn't.

"It has a name."

Gemma leaned in, intrigued. Not so much to hear the name, but to see how her mom came up with it. Because like last night, when she mentioned it being made in a convent, it seemed like she was winging these details, making it up as she went. Whenever she talked about the clock, her eyes went elsewhere, like someone was talking to her. Someone, AKA, her imagination.

"The Dread Clock." Her eyes went elsewhere, her brows bobbing up and down to some unheard utterance.

Did Gemma just hear something, too? Words on the wind, cold and whispered. She scanned the pavilion. Had to have been the diabetes-riddled family at the next table over, admiring their quadruple chocolate chunk ice cream bowl. She shook her head, felt like a jerk.

"The nuns at the convent called it the Dread Clock."

"Where was the convent?"

"Somewhere near Russia, in the countryside, I think."

"We have a thing called the 'Dread Clock' in our living room?" Gemma snorted. "Where is my mom, and what did you do with her?"

"Stop. It's an antique." Her mom took out her keys and dug them into her hip. "They built it because—" she stopped speaking, focused harder, "—there was so much sin in the world. They thought time and sin were connected."

"Oh, I get it," Gemma said. "Like how they say there's a murder every five seconds sort of thing?"

Mom's eyes shone with faint, red light. "Yes!" She put her keys away. "Exactly. I think they thought of the Dread Clock as being a kind of dream catcher."

"Sin catcher."

Mom nodded enthusiastically. "More or less. It would suck up all the sin in the world. Maybe even stop bad things from happening in the future."

Gemma polished off her ice cream and started chewing on the cone. "You sure they were nuns? That sounds a little witchy." With a mouthful of waffle, she blabbered, "It's got horns, Mom! Freaking horns!"

"Gemma," her mom cried. Red faced, she shot her arm out and almost grabbed Gemma's wrist. "Please, don't make fun of me for it."

Gemma fell back in her seat. "Okay," she said. *What the heck?* she thought. This is the way she acted with Dad, not with her. What the heck was wrong with her?

"Sorry." Mom retracted her arm. "Your dad questions everything I do. I don't mean to take it out on you."

She shrugged.

"Researchers—"

Researchers? Gemma couldn't believe what she was hearing. Researchers? She bought this thing out of Gethin's shop. Why was she acting like it was some priceless artifact? Some scientific marvel?

"—think it wasn't always in the form of a clock."

Weirded out to the point of sounding like a robot, Gemma said, "Oh?" and went on studying her mom like the imposter she might have been.

"The oldest grandfather clock was made in the 1600s, but people think the Dread Clock is much older." She took the straw out of her cup, curled it up, and popped it into her mouth to chew on it.

Gemma was becoming acutely aware of how strange her mother was acting, and how many people were watching them on the pavilion. She started cleaning up the table, trying to signal to her mother it was time to go.

Mom swallowed. "So we really lucked out, sweetie." The straw wasn't in her mouth anymore. "You're ready to go? You sure you're not sick? Let's go somewhere else, then. It feels good to be out."

"Mom?"

"Hmm?"

Gemma scooted out her chair. The metal it was made of ground against the concrete. When she stood, something cold skidded down her leg from in between her thighs. It felt like a finger, nail first, scraping down her skin.

"What is it, Gemma?"

She went sideways, hiding her leg. "How do you think Gethin got ahold of something like that?"

Mom shrugged, stood up, too. "Maybe we should get back to the house. I should probably get back to restoring the clock."

"So we can sell it?"

A dark shadow stole across the pavilion. "Yeah," Mom said. She took out her keys and jingled them. "Want to drive?"

TRENT   GEMMA   **CAMILLA**

Trent didn't say anything at dinner tonight. Camilla brought up the cost of the clock and the divorce papers, which were coming any day now (they weren't), but he wouldn't bite. Instead, he sat in the family room, gloomily shoveling spaghetti into his mouth, while he watched a high school girls' volleyball team play on public access. She had to send Gemma in to change the channel, and when she did, Gemma came back saying that Dad was asleep, the spaghetti mostly in his lap. Camilla left him there after dinner was over to clean himself up on his own.

It was about 9:00 PM when Camilla settled down in the living room with her pride and joy, the Dread Clock. All this talk of repairing and restoring it, and yet sitting here at the foot of the thing, her and its shadow now one, she couldn't find anything wrong with it. As far as she could tell, the Dread Clock was perfect. She knew she had seen images of it before—when, exactly, she couldn't remember—and everything about it looked in order. And she liked that. No mess, no flaws. Everything as it ought to be. Ugly and raw, maybe, but genuine, without pretention or promise.

Camilla went to her knees and pressed her hands to the glass case where the dark, almost organic pendulum swung. What shape had the Dread Clock taken before being confined to this wooden body? An hourglass? A sundial? A jet-black obelisk? And what remained? What had been carried down through the ages? What was the constant that made this thing tick and tock and suck the sin from this world? She touched the glass case and wondered if she could fit Gemma inside it.

TRENT   GEMMA   CAMILLA

I have to be inside her to show her I love her. I have to be inside her to show her I love her. I have to be inside her to show her I love her. I have to be inside her to show her I love her.

TRENT   **GEMMA**   CAMILLA

Scram the bat sat like a sentry on Gemma's pillow as she lay on the floor, cell phone held high above her head, trying to find something, anything, on Mom's Dread Clock. It was midnight now, and she had already been at it for an hour. So far, the most she had come up with were a bunch of urban legends about creepy clocks and some crappy digital art that looked like it was done by a four-year-old.

"Where are you getting this crap, Mom?" Gemma mumbled, about to click on a website authored by someone named Connor Prendergast.

She went stiff as she heard her dad's heavy footsteps coming up the stairs. It was a learned response kids like her could have done without.

"Guess he's ready to fight now."

Gemma rolled over, dropped the phone. She went to her window, which overlooked the north side of the coast. Like a homesick Neanderthal, she missed her cave. It was out there, in that salty dark, host to all sorts of slimy, skittering things. That's where she was most creative and most free.

Something was wrong with the moon. Gemma opened the window and leaned forward on the sill. There were weird bands in the sky. Thick strands of ink with odd, oily colors, like a gasoline spill. Pollution? She squinted as hard as she could, and then reeled. The inky strands weren't in the sky, but attached to the moon itself, pouring out of its craggy face from smeary space to the distant foothills. It looked like a spider. It was moving forward. And there was nothing she could do but stare at it in terrified awe.

TRENT   GEMMA   **CAMILLA**

The door to Camilla's room creaked open, and the smell of Trent came through. She wasn't asleep, not yet, but with the lights out and the blanket up to her nose, she was well on her way. What time was it, anyway? Barely opening her eye, she saw the clock read 12:15 AM.

Jesus I'm getting old, she thought. *Quarter past midnight, and I'm already beat.*

At the foot of the bed, the mattress sank to a new weight, Trent's weight. He pressed his hands to the folds of the blanket, near where her feet protruded, bare to catch the cold air. She only had on a bra and panties.

What the hell is he doing?

Still feigning sleep, she listened to his heavy breathing and wondered what drunken soliloquy he was going to grace her with tonight. His fingers, coarse from factory work, lightly touched her ankle. A warm sensation ran up her leg. She fought every impulse to recoil. It was a sensation she had lost and was surprised to have found again.

Trent's hand traveled up her calf, spreading the blanket as he went. Camilla's leg hairs bristled against his nails. Though her eyes were tightly shut, she could imagine the scene with clarity. Every movement he made added another stroke to the heated imagery wavering like a mirage in her mind. He hadn't attempted to touch her in this way in almost a year. The shock of it was almost paralyzing. Half of her just wanted to see how far he would take it. And the other half, the desperate half, the one which was mostly spit and snarls, wanted him to take it as far as he could, until she herself couldn't take it anymore. Until she had gotten her selfish fill, and the revulsion of his touch finally kicked in.

Now, his hand was gripping her thigh, right above her knee. Hard calluses, the gems of his labor, scraped her skin while he kneaded her muscles. Her body was betraying her hatred. Sweat beaded on her forehead, and a spot of heat bloomed over her breasts. She clenched her legs to cut off the wetness that had formed between them. A soft moan escaped her saliva-sealed lips, and she went red in the face. It wasn't that she didn't want him to know she was enjoying this. That much was obvious. It was that she didn't want to admit to herself that she was enjoying this. Things were better with Trent when she put herself somewhere else, or pretended to be something she wasn't. And yet here she was, damn near in the palm of his groping hand.

Camilla cracked open her eyes. Because of the dark, Trent was nothing more than a featureless shape sitting beside her. That made the experience better. Of course, she knew it was him. She was his wife. If she was an expert on anything in life, it was the texture of her husband, inside and out. As his fingers crept towards her inner thigh, she flirted with fantasies of who this featureless shape may be. Crushes or celebrities. The one-night stand, or the two-night pity party. But the fantasies didn't last long. The shape always returned to Trent, not as he was now, drunken and pathetic, but as he had been years ago. When they were young. When they were happy. When marriage was a mystery, and beautiful moments were all they had. And all they needed.

Trent's fingers brushed like breaths against the folds of Camilla's sex. She bit her tongue as he pushed aside her underwear. He teased her lips open. Treating her like it was his first time, she felt like it was her first time, too. Despite how good it felt, Camilla knew it wasn't going to solve anything. It hadn't in the past, and sure as hell wasn't going to now. But she wanted this. And like the Dread Clock downstairs, she was going to have it.

One hand pressed down on her hip, Trent leaned forward and slid his finger inside her. Camilla relented, released her muscles, only to have them tense up again. She sank into the bed, burying half her face into the pillow. Trent went in deeper, and when he went in deeper, he moved over her, the phantom of his weight pressing down on her. Her arm wrapped around him. She gripped his drenched shirt and tried to pull him onto her. But he wouldn't budge. He hadn't come here to satisfy any need but her own.

Down to the knuckles, with both fingers inside her, he curled his fingers, rubbing their tips against those dampening walls, as though he were beckoning her forward. She made a fist against his back, bunching up his shirt as she ground against the bed. She pressed her hips down, giving him permission to do it harder. And he did. He stroked her insides with more force. He worked a third finger, stretching her further. It hurt, but not enough to make her care. Pain for pleasure. In her experience, the trade was fair.

She wasn't far from orgasm went something went wrong. Trent's hand, a sweaty clamp on her hip, bore down into her bones. She tried to adjust herself, but he wouldn't get the hint.

It's fine, she thought. The sharp pain in her side wasn't enough to distract her from what was coming.

But then Trent worked a fourth finger, his pinky, inside her. Her muscles, unused and unwilling, burned as though they were going to tear. She unclenched his shirt and grabbed his wrist, to try and give him guidance at this moment of climax. He ignored her. Curling his fingers into claws, he gripped her from within and dug his nails into her vagina. Camilla squeezed his wrist, conflicted; the pain and pleasure becoming entwined, one now dependent upon the other to survive.

"Not so hard," she said breathily, betraying silence. She was still close enough to come, despite the setbacks. "Please, don't stop, but don't be so—"

The muscles in Trent's forearms tightened. Hand clawed inside her, nails nearly cutting into her vaginal walls, he moved his arm back and forth, as fast as he could, as though he were trying to dig his way out of her.

Camilla crushed his wrist. She reared up, screaming, "Stop, stop!" but now he had his whole hand inside her, trying to rip her open.

Camilla pulled back her leg and kicked him in his flaccid crotch. Winded, he tore his hand out of her, and a tongue of mucus, piss, and blood gushed onto the bed. She kicked again, aiming higher. Her foot smashed against his teeth and sent him reeling off the bed.

"Get the fuck out!" She grabbed the blanket, wrapped it around her. "What the fuck is wrong with you? Get out! Get the fuck out!"

By the time she turned on the lamp, Trent, or the featureless shape she thought had been him, was already gone.

I have to be inside her to show her I love her. I have to be inside her to show her I love her.

The door to Gemma's room creaked open, and the smell of Dad came through. She wasn't asleep, not yet, but only because the spidery moon had her transfixed at the window. When she heard his sigh behind her, the spell was broken, and the inky strands that hung from the steadfast satellite were gone.

"Oh, wow," she said. Her eyes went fuzzy. She rubbed her face until it was numb. "Oh, wow, what the... Dad, did you see that?"

She pressed her nose to the glass. As far as she could tell the moon was back where it was belonged, high in the clouded sky. "Oh my god, it was so weird. Do I look sick? I feel—" She caught his reflection in the window. He was still as stone, staring wildly at her.

Gemma turned and her eyes went to her dad's balled fist, which was wet in some places, and crusted over with a white film in others. His clothes, the T-shirt and jeans he'd had on all day, didn't fit to him. They drooped over him, like they had come straight out of the wash. And he smelled. Gemma sniffed the air and caught the scent of something potent she couldn't place, and also, urine.

About all she could manage to say was, "What's wrong?"

And all her dad could manage to do was uncurl his fist and flex his fingers, which were still webbed with her mother's release.

"Dad? You're freaking me out." Gemma let out an awkward laugh, smiled an awkward smile. "What did you do?"

The Dread Clock's ticking started coming through the floor vent beside Gemma's foot. Each noise it made was short, simultaneously thudding and piercing. It made her gums hurt, like a dentist had gone at them with one of their tools.

Cringing, Gemma said, "Dad? Dad. Dad!" She went forward, then stopped; looked at Scram for support. "Dad, you're creeping me out!"

"I love you," he said, at last.

"Yeah. I love you, too?"

"Do you have a boyfriend?"

Gemma's voice shook as she said, "No, you know I don't. Dad? Dad, are you drunk?"

Her dad's vacant stare gave her goosebumps. His mouth kept moving, like he was silently repeating himself over and over. And now that she was looking at his mouth, she saw how red it was. His lip was busted. If it was bleeding, she couldn't be sure, because he kept licking and sucking on it, as though he were trying not to make a mess in her room.

"You look bad." Gemma took a few steps closer to him. She didn't want to reject him. He seemed to be expecting that. "Go back downstairs. Please? I could call Uncle Jasper."

Dad reached out his slick, encrusted hand and took Gemma by the chin. He ran his bitter-tasting thumb over her lip and said, "I love you. I don't show you enough." Blood leaked down his mouth, but he slurped it back up.

As his other hand hovered beside her waist, Gemma muttered, "You do. I know. I… I love you, too."

Don't yell for Mom. Don't. She pushed every sickening thought out of her head that had to do with what her Dad was possibly planning. *He's just drunk. This isn't him.*

He closed his hand on her waist, his fingers uncomfortably close to her butt. Letting go of her chin, tears and blood running down his face, he said, "Your mother was beautiful. All the men loved her. Will you be smarter than her? Be smart enough not to meet a man like me?" His hand traveled inward, towards the outskirts of her pelvis.

Gemma, shaking, her lips quivering, whispered, "What are you…?"

Her stomach was in knots, her head pounding with an ache. She felt strange in a way she hadn't felt before, and didn't like how she was feeling it now with her dad, his hands on her.

"Your mom is downstairs," her dad said.

He fingered her waistband. His other hand gripped her side and barely touched her breast.

"By the clock. Go." He let go of her, recoiled backward.

His eyes focused, and light returned to them.

"Go to her." Looking as though he were going to vomit, he stormed out of her room and locked himself in the bathroom just outside it.

Gemma touched the places where he had touched her and broke down in tears.

Camilla sat in front of the Dread Clock, her legs parted and still quivering from finishing what Trent had started upstairs. She felt pathetic, like some disgusting wretch enslaved by her emotions. But she did feel better than she had before, which said a lot, given that, currently, her crotch felt as though it had been sanded down and doused in rubber cement.

She wasn't mad at Trent anymore. The Dread Clock had a comforting quality to it that took the sting out of most things. Watching the pendulum sway back and forth put her in a trance most monks could only ever dream of obtaining. Perhaps her favorite part of the clock was the moon dial, where three celestial bodies were depicted upon the scorched plate above the clock face. They tended to move, but only when they were on the edges of her field of vision. In a way, they reminded her of Trent, Gemma, and herself. Three unrecognizable bodies caught in each other's hellish orbits, taking a little from the other every time they passed.

Was that muscle behind the gears? Camilla strained her eyes and went down on all fours, crawling to the clock's glass case. Yes, it was. Behind the pendulum, like fleshy spider webs. How had she missed this before? Beautiful. It hadn't been alive, but now it was—a new member of their dysfunctional home.

Footsteps on floorboards. Thump, slump, thump. Camilla fell back on her haunches and craned her neck to the staircase. Gemma was standing in the middle, moonlit and in some sort of mourning. Teenagers. Always the same, despite their claims of uniqueness.

"Can't sleep?" Camilla said. She waved her daughter over. "Come here. I want you to see something."

Gemma took a good minute to make her way to Camilla, but that was fine. They still had ten minutes or so to indulge in the dark secrets of the Dread Clock's music.

"Mom?"

"Yes?"

"Why are you sitting in your underwear down here?"

Camilla rubbed her bare legs. "You sound like you've been crying."

Gemma shook her head.

"A man got you down?" She laughed and patted the ground. "Take a load off."

Gemma sat down, but with a healthy amount of distance between her and Camilla. She had been crying. Her face was puffy, and her voice had a quiver to it only years of spousal arguments could remedy.

"There's something wrong with Dad," Gemma said, bringing her knees to her chest. She buried her face in them and added, "I think he hurt himself."

"Did you know can't find the materials the clock is made out of on Earth anymore?"

Gemma shook her head. She shot Camilla a damning look.

Camilla ignored it and carried on. "They had to use just the right materials to hold every evil thing that's been done or could be done."

"Looks like wood to me," Gemma mumbled. "And glass. And metal."

Camilla rolled her eyes. "Some say each nun..."

She stopped, listened. The mouth deep in the clock was talking too quietly to hear.

And then: "Yeah, that's right. After the Dread Clock was completed, each nun, after their deaths, were put inside it."

At this, Gemma removed her face from her knees. "There's dead bodies inside there?!"

"It's said their spirits keep it going, to keep ridding the world of sin."

Gemma shook her head. "They're doing a shitty job of it."

Camilla almost slapped her, but the mouth deep in the Dread Clock told her to wait on that.

"Mom."

"Yes, dear?"

"You and Dad. Something isn't..." Unable to find her words, Gemma started to her feet, but Camilla stopped her. "I feel like something terrible is going to—"

More footsteps on the staircase. This time, it was Trent. Gemma gasped, and then Camilla saw why she had. He was completely naked, and protruding from his urethra was a bloody toothbrush. He wheeled around them, sat down beside Camilla. She threw one arm around him, and the other around Gemma.

"This is nice," she said, squeezing them closer to her, eyes wide and nothing but pupil. "All it took was for one little clock to make us a family again."

TRENT   GEMMA   CAMILLA

The next morning, Trent woke up on the beach, in agonizing pain, cell phone in hand, with absolutely no memory as to how he ended up there.

TRENT   **GEMMA**   CAMILLA

The next morning, Gemma woke up in the family room, the TV turned all the way up, with drool down her chin, and her hand in a box of cereal. She couldn't remember why she was where she was, but she did remember everything else.

TRENT   GEMMA   **CAMILLA**

The next morning, Camilla woke up in the bath tub, a Bible in it with her, and the taste of paper and ink in her mouth. She had eaten halfway through the Old Testament. Though she couldn't remember the night before, she had a sneaking suspicion some Old Testament fire and brimstone was exactly what she needed at this very moment in time.

TRENT   GEMMA   CAMILLA

No one came looking for him, which was good, because he had only managed to make it to the garage before the pain in his penis became too much to bear. After making a call to Jasper to take him to the doctor, he sat in his car, the leather adhering to his sticky skin, looking at what he had done to himself.

"What the fuck?"

Something had been shoved into his urethra. Just looking at the widened site made him fevered. He had to piss, but even the thought of doing so made him hurt.

"Camilla?"

He looked out the car, wondering if his wife had done this to him. The thing that almost puzzled him more than anything else was the fact that, when he woke, there was dried toothpaste on his balls.

TRENT   **GEMMA**   CAMILLA

It was Sunday, and Gemma's church was the cave. She didn't leave a note or say goodbye. She just took her cell phone and ran out of the house, going the long way as she went so her parents wouldn't see her and try to follow after. But, honestly, what did it matter? Whether they saw her or she saw them, they were still with her in her mind. And the memories of last night? They had already started to fester, infecting everything she had once held true.

Gemma navigated the still-cool dunes until they tapered away to the cliff that led to the cave. Two paths to take, she took the one that ran narrowly along the cliff, rather than the back entrance, for no reason other than the more dangerous route seemed to make the most sense. It was a makeshift walkway reinforced with wooden boards, and it was only a few feet in width. To her right, the rocks of the cliff, and her left, openness, and the ocean, after a twenty-foot drop, with a wall of boulders eager to break her.

Who had put this here? She took her time crossing the walkway. Small gusts of wind teased her into flattening against the cliff. Someone else who needed an escape? She gathered her courage and hoofed it. The boards creaked but held fast. Maybe it had been a woman like her, who didn't have a place and found it fitting to make her own.

She reached the cave. Inside, there was nothing but a dead snake, a cracked egg, and cold, sea-sprayed stone. Could someone live in a place like this forever? Didn't seem a bad idea. What she needed she could steal or work for. It would be hard, but it would be hers, and though Nature's will could sometimes be cruel, she would be safe from everything else.

Gemma then looked back, at her house, which was now just a dark haze looming over the beach. Could someone live in a place like that forever? Already, the memories of midnight had begun to crystallize, becoming something permanent, but also different. Seeing her father naked, with that thing down his… thing. And her mother almost naked, holding them, speaking in dark tongues to the Dread Clock. These hardening memories were real, and they would be with her forever, yet they were losing their realness. They had happened, but it was becoming easier to tell herself they hadn't. She had only been awake an hour and already these past traumas were transforming into tales.

She plopped down on the end of the cave, threw her legs out over the edge. She rolled up her pant legs, so that the sea could baptize them. With her favorite sharp rock, she carved her name, as she had done many times before, into the ground. She tried to distract herself with just about anything she could imagine, but her thoughts kept coming back to those stark, stomach-churning images that felt as though they had been nailed into her mind.

"Fuck," Gemma screamed, throwing the rock out to the ocean. She balled her fist and punched the cave floor. She drew blood, and with blood, drew the Dread Clock on the stone.

"What the fuck? What the hell?" Rocking back and forth, she started to cry; her face stretched, as though the tears would be too big to come out normally. "What the...? Why? What the fuck?"

Gemma shrieked and bashed her heels against the cliff. She felt her father's hands on her again, the taste from his thumb in her mouth. Every positive memory she had of him, she brought to light. She knew what he had done, or what he was going to do. They talked about it in school, or on TV. But Dad wasn't like that. No, he wasn't like that. He had never been like that. Not once, not ever. He had stopped himself, too. But, oh god, what if he hadn't?

Gemma blubbered, stringy spit and snot connecting her nose and hands. Would he have gone further? She had an idea of what could have happened next but... Gemma retched, the notion making her physically ill.

"It wasn't you. You wouldn't do that," Gemma said.

A flock of birds tore through the orange sky.

"He wouldn't do that. No, it wasn't him. There's something going on and..."

She nodded, each excuse more convincing than the last. "Dad wouldn't do that. He was drunk, or maybe he was trying to tell me something. Or maybe I did something wrong..."

And then the excuses sounded less likely, and she started to bawl again.

As Gemma sat there, rocking herself into a calm, she started to think about the divorce, and everything she had done to stop it from happening. Mom threatened to divorce her dad about six months ago. At first, Gemma didn't take it seriously, but the fights got worse, and she kept catching her mom making calls to lawyers.

After that, the "outbursts"—even now, the word made Gemma roll her eyes—started. At home or in school, it didn't matter. If someone wronged her, she was quick to let them know it. Piece of shit and bitch were often her choice of words—her mother's and father's, respectively—and she had even scuffed up a nose and a few elbows and knees in a couple of fights. It was all typical stuff for kids to do when their parents were going through a divorce. That's what her mom said, and that's what the Internet said, too. And the best thing about the Internet? It actually gave her more ideas on how to sabotage their split-up. She ratcheted up the detentions, made her grades plummet. She stayed out later than she was supposed to, and sometimes pretended as though she were dating some guy in secret. She even started cutting herself on her ankle. The Internet never said these things would work, only that kids going through what she was going through were known to do them. However, Gemma was determined to use them to her advantage. Whether or not her mom and dad were meant to be together didn't matter. The thought of not having them together was impossible to hold. It didn't make sense. Maybe her life wasn't normal compared to everyone else's, but the possibility of her family being torn apart seemed so much worse.

That is, until last night. Now, now she wasn't so sure they ought to be together. Gemma stood up and went to the back of the cave, where the ceiling sloped upward into a grimy pocket of stone and shadow.

Was what had happened at midnight what happened to all marriages that were meant to end but didn't? Like this hole in the cave's ceiling, did everything just get sucked away, stripped down to nothing? Could a marriage like theirs eventually make them into the monsters they were last night? Better yet, did she do this to them? And if she did, maybe she had it coming last night. Maybe that's what she got for being so fucking selfish.

Gemma's pocket buzzed. She jumped, her heart at the top of her throat, and then realized it was her cell phone. Fishing it out, she saw she had a text from Mom.

Please, don't smudge the clock's glass.

That was it. Please, don't smudge the Dread Clock's glass. It was an instrument that, supposedly, absorbed all the sin in the world, and she

217

was worried about it getting dirty? And not only that, she didn't even ask where Gemma was or if she was okay.

"That stupid freaking clock. I swear to god, ever since that—"

She read the text again, remembered how her mother had seemed to be listening to the Dread Clock last night. She remembered how it made a sound at 1:00 AM, like a feral animal, and how afterward, Mom and Dad carried her to the family room, left her there, and disappeared.

"—that stupid freaking clock. That stupid freaking clock!"

Gemma opened her web browser and searched for the phone number of Gethin Yates' antique shop. Things hadn't been great at home, but they had definitely gotten worse ever since that clock had shown up. Uncle Jasper would say she was just being immature, naïve, but if he had seen what she saw, he, too, would be looking for any excuse in the world to explain her parents' behavior.

She dialed the number, stepped out of the cave, onto the cliff's walkway for better reception. The phone rang and rang. No answer. And, crap, it was Sunday. Was his stupid store closed?

I bet I could find where he lives if—

Gethin Yates, on the side of the line, shouted, "Hello?"

Gemma, not having prepared herself for what to say, lowered her voice, did her best impression of her mother, and said, "Gethin."

"Camilla? Jesus Christ. Jesus Christ, I'm glad you called. Are you okay?"

Am I okay? Gemma swallowed her excitement and kept it simple. "The clock."

"What happened? I told you, woman! I told you. I'm sorry I sold it to you." Some scratching in the background. "I'm sorry. I was scared, and I wanted it out of here. But the original buyer, Connor Prendergast, called. I told him I sold it to you, and he bawled me out. There's something wrong with that clock, Camilla, okay? Have you felt it, too?"

"Yes," Gemma said, almost crying again.

"That Prendergast guy was very vague about the clock. I looked into him. He's into that supernatural, paranormal... I don't know, but—" more scratching in the background, "—he's coming to get it. Bring it back. I'll refund you in full. He said to keep our distance, so I'll lock it up back in the warehouse. Camilla. Camilla?"

Gemma sniffled her nose. She was there again, in front of the clock, her mom's arm around her, the smell of desperate, sick sweat wafting off her.

"What... did you... see, Gethin?"

He shuddered. The phone went dead for a second, as though he had hung up. Then: "My grandmother. She used to make me write down in a book why I was a bad b-boy." More scratching in the background, like he was covering something in ink. "What did you see, Camilla?"

"I did things." Gemma got choked up. "Not proud of."

"Bring it, Camilla. Full refund."

"No," Gemma said. There was no way she was going to be able to get her mom to part with it. "Come and get it." Her voice cracked, but she was sure Gethin couldn't tell. "It's mine."

Gemma hung up the phone. She took a deep breath and then opened the web browser again.

"I knew it. I knew there was something. Connor Prendergast? Where do I—"

She typed in his name, found the site she had almost clicked on last night, and opened it.

TRENT   GEMMA   **CAMILLA**

"What did we do to each other?"

Carefully, Trent took a seat beside Camilla in the living room. She was still in her underwear, and she was still staring at the Dread Clock. In one hand, her husband was holding the crotch of his pants, and in the other, a bag from the hospital with antibiotics, an anti-inflammatory, and probably a note from the doctor diagnosing him as a complete dumbass.

It still stung badly between Camilla's legs. She couldn't piss without crying. Looking at Trent and his mini pharmacy, she asked, "Can I have some, too?"

"Huh? Oh. Yeah." He handed her the bag. "You okay?"

No, she thought, opening the bag and unscrewing the lids to the bottles. She took a pill from each and swallowed them. They lodged in her dry throat, but she couldn't be moved to move, so she let them dissolve there. It burned like hell, but as the days went on, she found hell was getting easier to deal with.

"Did you put something down my dick?"

Camilla shrugged, said, "You did a number on me."

"I did?"

"Couldn't have been anyone else."

Trent bit his lip. He scooted closer to the Dread Clock, closer than Camilla. A pang of jealousy, a flood of venomous hate. She scooted even closer. Childish, yes, but triumphant.

"I woke up outside, naked. Jasper ran me to the hospital." Trent rubbed his face, stretched his jaw. "Feels like my head is full of cotton."

Might be, she thought. *Might be all that's up there.* "I woke up in the bathtub. I guess I spent all night eating part of the Bible."

Trent nodded, the statement not fazing him one bit. "Did we take something last night?"

"I don't have a stash anymore."

"Yeah, me neither."

Camilla leaned forward and, for the first time since she had brought the Dread Clock, opened the glass case behind which the fleshy pendulum was concealed. A rancid odor rolled out. Her vision became blotchy, and she had to close her eyes because the living room had started to spin.

"Close it. Christ, close it, Camilla," Trent said, pinching his nose. "What is that? Smells like something died inside it."

Nothing is dead in there.

She pushed her hand inside the case, stopping short of the rocking pendulum.

That's life. The smell of it. The reek of it. Fleshy clockwork lubed with sin and satisfaction.

She closed the case and leaned back. Looking at Trent, she noticed there was something different about him now. For one, she didn't want to bite his head off, but that wasn't it. No, no, that wasn't it at all. There seemed to be a bond, a connection between them. The kind a narcotic could create, but stronger. It was their wounds, the proof of their shared communion in the Dread Clock's midnight service.

Trent, still staring at the clock, looked as though he were going to doze off. "I'm sorry, Camilla," he slurred.

She scooted closer to him. Her legs touched his. A spark of excitement made her flesh flush. "For what?"

"Everything." An eyebrow went up. He tilted his head towards the Dread Clock.

Was the clock talking to him now? Camilla hoped so. She needed someone to share in this secret, and Gemma was too young to appreciate its spoils.

"I don't know what happened last night, but this isn't us. I don't want Gemma exposed to this sham anymore. I—" he swallowed hard, "—found your letter. You were right about everything you said in it."

"I don't know, Trent." Camilla touched his knee. She took a deep breath, and with that breath, her lungs were filled with the Dread Clock's musings. "I don't know what happened last night, either, but I feel like things are different."

Trent's smile gave him away as he said, "W-wait. What do you mean?"

"Maybe we hit rock bottom last night."

His hand found hers. She wove her fingers between his.

"Maybe we can rebuild this thing again."

She pressed her other hand to his cheek. It was still covered in ink from the Bible, and his perspiring face made the passages run off onto him.

"I don't want to give up just yet."

TRENT   GEMMA   CAMILLA

It was eleven in the morning, and Trent didn't know where his daughter was. Though he would never admit it aloud, he didn't actually care. He might have yesterday, but as he stood over the oven, making breakfast for Camilla, who was sitting at the table, watching him cook, he didn't. He didn't care at all. He had his wife back. With the help of the Dread Clock, he realized what he suspected all along: he loved Camilla more than Gemma. Or, wait. Maybe that hadn't been true yesterday, but it was today. He shrugged, flipped the bacon. Today was all that mattered, anyway.

"This is nice," he said. He poured the entire skillet, bacon and grease, onto a plate and carried it to the table. He lay the still hissing meal in front of Camilla. "I missed this."

"Yeah." Right away, she went in for the bacon. Little yelps of pain escaped her lips as she gobbled down the meat. "It's good," she said, her voice already raspy from the scorching.

"I cheated on you, too," Trent said.

Camilla drank the grease. "I figured."

221

"Some eighteen-year-old. Can't even remember her name." Trent grabbed an apple and put it onto the open flame of the stove. "Did it the other night. When you kicked me out."

"Past is in the past."

Trent took the apple off the burner, threw it into the sink. "I like that we're talking again."

Camilla licked her fingers. She went to the sink and grabbed the apple out of it. Taking a bite, she mumbled, "It's the clock."

Trent grinned. *She gets it.* Though it had been hard to admit, buying the Dread Clock had been the best thing for them. "There is something about it."

Together, they went to the table and sat. She threw her feet up on his lap. He rubbed them. "Feels like it's already been here. Thought it was strange, at first. But it makes perfect sense."

Camilla giggled as Trent leaned forward and started trimming her toenails with his teeth. "You know, there's something living inside it?"

He spat out a nail. "Really?"

Camilla took her feet off him and stood up. "Yes. Want to see?" She held out her hands.

Do I want to see? He took her hands, pulled her into an embrace. *I want to see everything. I want to thank whatever it is personally.* He buried his face in Camilla's hair. She smelled terrible.

"Show me," he said, picking a Bible passage out of her hair. "Hey, do you think we should invite Jasper over?"

Camilla shook her head. "No, it's ours."

"What about Gemma?"

"The Dread Clock doesn't want her to see what's inside yet."

"How come?"

"All this isn't normal enough for her yet. But we know, don't we?"

Trent nodded, kissed her forehead. "I think we just forgot. Hey, what time is it?"

Shrugging, Camilla said, "Not midnight."

TRENT **GEMMA** CAMILLA

THE DREAD CLOCK & AND ITS BLACK HOURS: A HISTORY AND WARNING

BY CONNOR PRENDERGAST

We like to think of time as something that we own. Something that, despite existing before and beyond us, we can appropriate and designate and rely upon to always be consistent and true. As with air, we take it for granted and seldom consider how or why it's there. Perhaps it's the simplicity of the science, or the inescapability of its use. In the end, for most, time is no more than a constant flow of events with sometimes hazy beginnings and indefinite ends. Like water in a river, we suspect the source is always the same, and the watershed from which it flows bound by unchanging rules, however obvious or obscure.

But what if time could be manipulated? Or dislodged and replaced completely? What if there was another source of time in our universe, and its watershed was not bound by rules but guided by madness?

Time has a tapeworm, and it is the Black Hour. It is not an alternative dimension, but an entirely new one. One that has fed on and gotten fat off the foul gristle and scum of our existence. Every night, at midnight, regardless of location or time zone, this Black Hour imposes itself upon reality. For one hour, it subjects the world, perhaps even the universe, to random and sometimes impossible events. From environmental abnormalities, such as small fires and upside-down lakes, to moments of absolute depravity, such as a rape or a murder by a creature that has never existed, the Black Hour knows no limits, for it has no limits. And because it is limitless, unlike our time and reality, it is even more difficult to measure and understand. The only thing that is known about the temporal aberration is that it lasts for one hour, and that it always begins at midnight. But even those supposed facts are flimsy at best, for though they've proven to hold true so far, that doesn't mean they are.

But what is true and perhaps even more unbelievable than the abilities of the Black Hour itself is the fact that it has a physical presence in our world. The "heart" of the Black Hour is a very real object that has been recorded throughout history as existing—and existing solely to subjugate humanity to its sadistic ways. Likened to a cancerous mass, the Black Hour's heart is either a symbol of the event, or the origin of the event itself. Either way, the key to understanding and destroying the Black Hour lies in obtaining the heart.

But the heart of the Black Hour has shown itself to be surprisingly resilient. Throughout time, humanity has given the grotesque organ shelter. From images and writings, references have been discovered pertaining to the Black Hour's heart and its protection within various timekeeping devices. Why the heart feels the need for such symbolic safeguards is not yet known. But it appears to thrive on planting itself directly within populaces, as though to invoke insanity and then absorb the new lunacies they spawn. From the Black Hour's willingness to constantly place itself in the public's eye, one can either assume that the heart cannot be destroyed, or that the tools to destroy it are not within our grasp; because the Black Hour's heart is not of this world and, therefore, undefeatable. To excise it, one would have to uproot it from time itself, the very continuum from which it sups and usurps, and return it to whatever hell no longer wanted anything to do with it.

Currently, for the last several hundred years, the Black Hour's heart has taken residence in an object known as the Dread Clock. The Dread Clock was created by a group of nuns in an Eastern European convent who had discovered the heart. Using prayer and even the magic of the Membrane, the nuns wove the heart into the Dread Clock as a means of imprisoning it.

They did not succeed. The Black Hour is dogmatic in its midnight desecrations, never diverging from that rigid, ritualistic schedule. But by their efforts and incantations, the powers of the Black Hour began to leak out of the heart, causing the organ to have an almost constant effect on those in its vicinity. It was bleeding chaos, and the only way the nuns believed they could stem the tide was to destroy themselves, from their flesh down to their souls, and lock themselves away inside the Dread Clock to hold the "demonic forces" at bay.

Since the nuns' failed attempts, the Dread Clock has traveled the world. It has a tendency to show itself at the worst moments in history, as though to be the first in line to feed on humanity's suffering. From diseased villages to concentration camps, there is mounting evidence that the Dread Clock has been present, simultaneously creating evil, while feasting on it. To blame the Black Hour for man's inhumanity to man would be foolish. But how much stronger was the Black Hour made by them?

Below, you will find pictures and additional descriptions of the Dread Clock. If you believe you have seen the object, do not go near it, for still it bleeds chaos and despair. Those who stand in its presence stand to be undone. The heart is known to work quickly on those who are weak of will or at their rope's end. Unlike other cursed or haunted objects, the Dread Clock is eager to mutilate, for time is forever and humanity many, and there are many miseries to gorge upon.

Gemma flipped her shit. She scrolled to the top of Connor Prendergast's website, the man who was supposed to have bought the Dread Clock initially, and read the history again. What was this? Was it real? She paced back and forth in front of the cave. There was sweat on her neck, behind her knees. Any other time, like any other person, she would have laughed off the story. But this was the very same clock she now had in her living room, in her house. The pictures proved it. And the crap about insanity and the way Gethin talked about it and… Midnight. Midnight had been when she thought she heard Mom come into her room, asking if she was okay. And then last night, when her parents went temporarily (or inevitably) insane, it had been between twelve and one.

"Holy shit. Holy… holy shit."

She clicked through the website. There an article on ghouls, there an article on what appeared to be a doll held together by super glue.

How do I contact him? She jabbed her phone, agitated. "Come on. Come on. Where's your freaking email address, man?"

Again, the phone buzzed in her clammy grip. She stumbled backward, sending a few rocks into the foaming sea. A text message popped up on her screen from Jen that read: *Hey, girl. Addie is sleeping over tonight. Can you?*

Still morning, the sun was scorching hot. High in the sky, burning those that bumbled below, that fiery orb would be the thing most wouldn't miss when evening rolled in. But Gemma would. As the day wore on and light gave way to dark, every minute that passed brought her and her family closer to that profaned Black Hour. She could try to get them to leave, go somewhere for the night. The festival at the fairgrounds, but crap, no, that didn't start until Monday. Maybe if she showed them the website. Maybe if she told them what they made her watch…

"Yeah, I should be able to," Gemma said, texting the same to Jen. Her finger hovered over the send button. She needed out of the house. And it sounded nice to have the chance to bounce some hypotheticals off her friends. But could she leave her parents alone like that?

"If the Black Hour is real," she said, pacing back and forth, "then what are they going to do tonight?"

She stopped, squeezed the phone until the plastic made a cracking noise.

"But the article said it freaking bleeds chaos. What am I supposed to do? I can't leave, but I can't stay."

She grabbed her hair and pulled it downward, crazed.

"What the hell do I do? Am I being stupid? Could be coincidence. Maybe they've just lost it. Goddamn it. Grr."

Gemma pocketed her cell phone and started across the walkway towards the house. Now that she knew what she was looking for, she knew what to look for. All she had to do was to make sure she didn't lose her mind in the process. This whole 'them or her' business didn't sit well with her. She had spent so long trying to keep the family together, the last thing she wanted to do was turn her back on them. Whether or not the Dread Clock and the Black Hour were actually real, she still couldn't honesty say. Mom and Dad were hurting, though, and now it was her job to heal them.

TRENT   GEMMA   **CAMILLA**

Camilla and Trent had busted out the beach chairs. They were sitting on the shore under a crooked umbrella, the water breaking on their feet. She dug her toes into the sand and poked the shells hidden underneath. A crab nipped at her nail, and she smiled. It was a beautiful day. Cloudless, with winds that blew so strongly it was as though they had their own nefarious intents. The heat was going to be hellish, but

Camilla appreciated that. She liked sweating out her impurities during the day and going home drained but contented at night. She slept better that way, when she had no energy left to doubt herself for hours on end. If she couldn't be ignorant, at least she could be exhausted.

"This is nice," Trent purred beside her. He put his hands behind his head. The huge, black shades he wore might have looked cool about twenty years ago, but now he just looked like a bug with a farmer's tan. "We both needed this." He popped open the cooler wedged into the sand. A few beers sat on the top, but he went for a bottle of water. "Want anything?"

"One of those massive malts from… God, what was that place's name?"

Trent let out a laugh. "Oh, hell, what was that called?"

Camilla pointed at him and shouted, "Dan's Diabetes Dive."

"What? No. Really?" Eyes wide with realization, he said, "Shit, it was, wasn't it? How did I forget? God, can you imagine a place being named that today?"

Camilla bit her lip. All it took were a few seconds and she was back there, at that shack of a store with Trent. They were sixteen? Seventeen? He had more quarters than he did dollars, and more zits than both of those combined. He hadn't always been the most attractive of guys, but he had a good heart. She remembered he'd spent all he had that day, which wasn't much, to get her one of Dan's famous jumbo malts.

"I don't even know if you could call it a malt," Trent said.

"No, that thing was a freaking feeding trough. A big old tub of sugar."

"You polished it off, though."

Camilla's cheek quivered from smiling. "Nope."

"Killed it." Trent opened his water, guzzled it. "I had never seen a girl so skinny eat so much."

"How did I not go into a diabetic coma?" Camilla leaned on the arm of the chair, closer to him.

"Hell if I know. We put ourselves through so much as kids. Now, if I turn the wrong way when I'm taking a shit, my back's out of commission for the week."

Pelicans passed by overhead. A few sand pipers sped across the beach in search of meals too small to be seen.

"You remember Paul Smith's party in '84?" Camilla went into the cooler, got a beer for herself. "You remember what we did?"

Trent's eyebrow arched. Coming out of his seat, he spun the chair around and dragged it nearer to Camilla. "I don't know how I remember what we did."

"We both got drunk as hell."

"You did. I was sober."

Camilla twisted her mouth. "Yeah, okay, Trent."

"I was! How was I going to put my moves on you if I was drunker than a skunk?"

"Might have helped your moves, to be honest."

Trent waved her off. "We wandered around those woods for what seemed like forever. You fell—"

"We fell," Camilla corrected, "into that damn ditch."

"Busted my head and my ass pretty bad. I don't know how I managed that." Now, Trent grabbed a beer. He popped a few of the ice cubes it had been nestled in into his mouth. "I definitely copped a feel helping you out of that ditch."

"Did you?" Camilla laughed. She pretended to be repulsed as she pushed on his chair. It wobbled, but held. "Not surprised. You were always trying to cop a feel. Should have treated you like my class and made you sit on your hands during our dates."

"Probably wouldn't have helped."

"Probably not."

Trent took a drink. Camilla noticed how he paused with the beer in his mouth, as though the taste no longer appealed to him. He looked at the bottle, wedged it into the sand, and went back to his water.

"Remember that guy that beat you up?" Camilla continued to stare at the bottle in the sand.

Leave it be, she thought. *Don't touch it again, and we'll be okay.* It was like she was pulling petals off dandelions, reciting, "He loves me. He loves me not."

Trent put up his hand, the way a politician might in a debate. Camilla thought back to how he had said he always wanted a job like that. One where he could make a difference. God damn, when had that dream died?

"If I recall correctly," Trent said, "we beat each other up."

"He busted your lip and gave you a black eye."

"What did I do to him?"

"I think you bit his arm."

Trent cringed. He closed his eyes and shook his head. Ashamed, he said, "I did, didn't I? Didn't I punch him?"

"Maybe?" He hadn't. "That guy came out of nowhere, though. From the other party going on in the field. He was pretty big. I mean, you remember how scrawny you were?"

Trent rolled up his sleeve, flexing his non-existent muscle. "About as scrawny as I am now." He jiggled his gut. "Minus the pooch. God." Though it was day, Camilla could see the stars in his eyes. "I was not a fine specimen. How the hell did you ever settle on me?"

"I loved you." Camilla caught her breath. The words came out quicker than she expected. She dug her feet harder into the sand, embarrassed. All restraints and reservations had been lifted with the Dread Clock's arrival. It made her feel young again.

"You had a good heart. You were yourself, too. I never knew what I was getting into with other people, but you were always you." She took a drink, lingered on the lip of the bottle before setting it down. Inside, she saw a black creature with tentacles at the bottom, marinating in the alcohol. "You were a little dweeby, but I set you straight."

Trent was chewing on his thumbnail. He slumped into his chair. Blood dribbled off the umbrella and down onto his chest. "I used to try so hard, though. I did. I mean, I was me. I wanted to do what I did."

He sighed, rubbed the blood into the hairs on his chest like a salve.

"I used to try so hard, but not anymore. That's where I went wrong with you and Gemma. I love you two more than anything in the world, but Jesus do I rarely show it. I don't know how I got this way." He closed his eyes. Tears struggled against his lids. "I'm so sorry, Camilla."

You used to be so much more, she thought, staring at him, his eyes still closed. *We both did. If only you knew how badly I want to love you again. If you did, would you let me?*

Opening his eyes, he asked her nervously, "What went wrong with us?"

TRENT   GEMMA   CAMILLA

It was a question he had always wanted to ask, but was afraid to hear the answer to. Because, in his mind, he was what had gone wrong. He was the one who hadn't followed through on the promises they made to one another. He was the one who had cheated first, the one who brought Gemma into their home and asked Camilla to be a mother to her. He took and took from her until there was nothing left. And what he couldn't give she got elsewhere.

"I'm sorry," he quickly said. "I don't want to ruin this—"

"Everything went wrong," Camilla said. "It wasn't you or me. It was both of us."

Trent squinted. Camilla's chest, bare because of the blouse she wore, was glowing and slightly translucent. In a chamber of its own, between her ribs, a smaller version of the Dread Clock's pendulum swayed.

Camilla started. "We got married too fast. My career took off, and you were still trying college. My mom left this house to us, everything paid for and taken care of, and we never really learned how to live with each other. Had the apartment for what? Year and a half?"

Trent nodded. "It was a good year and a half, but I see where you're coming from. We dated a long time, and then rushed into everything else."

"I love Gemma." Camilla paused, as though to gauge Trent's reaction.

He didn't give her one.

"I love Gemma. I love her so much. She may not be from me, but she's as good as mine. It's not her fault, but… Trent, you came home with another woman's child. Another woman you slept with. She was a terrible human being, and never in a million years would I want Gemma back with her. But I don't think I've ever gotten over that."

First year in this house, and you kicked me out. You spat in my face and threw a bottle at my head and told me never to come back.

"I can't even remember what started that fight," Trent said, and that was the truth.

Camilla shrugged. "Me neither." But she looked as though she were lying.

"Sometimes." Trent stopped. Did he want to put this out there? After all these years? Would she think he was making it up? Would it even matter? The wounds had been made, scabbed over, and torn open time and time again. They were beyond repair.

"What?"

Too late. "Sometimes, I don't know if Gemma is mine. I cheated, I did. But Gemma's mother was with a few guys at the time. She gave up the baby as soon as she knew I thought it was mine, but—"

"She looks like you, Trent."

"She does." He nodded. "I know it doesn't change what I did. I'm sorry. I don't know why I brought it up."

"Do you speak to her?" Camilla's voice was harsh.

"No, not since I took Gemma."

"She was disgusting, Trent."

"Disgusting isn't a strong enough word." He rubbed his forehead.

Gemma's mother, Candice, had been about three hundred pounds, with a good ten percent of her weight being a combination of alcohol, heroin, and whatever other street corner shit she'd put in her body that week. Trent knew her from high school, and she had a tendency of finding him at the parties of mutual friends. Loud, rude, and selfish, there hadn't been anything about Candice that Trent liked, except for the fact that she seemed to like him. The thing was, he couldn't remember the night it happened. He assumed he'd had sex with her willingly, but sometimes, he wasn't so sure. He had drunk too much and taken too many pills that night to be certain. It seemed like something he would do. After all, he had just cheated on Camilla with the girl at the 24/7 Quick-Stop. But maybe, maybe he—

"Trent?" Camilla touched the top of his hand. "Hey, you alright?"

"Sorry. I thought I heard the Dread Clock." A lie, but now that he was thinking about the antique, he did start hearing whispers in his skull. "It's wonderful, isn't it?"

Camilla squeezed his fingers. "It is."

"I don't know where it's going to take us." He rubbed the bones of her wrist with his thumb. The simple things always made him feel so good. "But I'm glad it's in our life."

"It took the sin out of us. We were hollow, Trent, and had nothing but sin."

"Now we can be ourselves again." He imagined chewing Camilla's face off and feeding her its sloppy regurgitations. "I don't know where it's going to take us, either. But if this is all we'll get. Us here, talking again, on the beach, in the sun. That's good enough for me. If I have to try my hardest to keep that, I will."

Camilla's eyes glinted. She smiled and let his fingers go. The wind kicked up and blasted their umbrella, wrenching it out of the sand. "Oh shit!"

Camilla jumped to her feet and scurried after it, before the gust took it too far. That was nice, that image. Her smiling, her running. Her running after something that wasn't her car keys or another man. The nicest thing about it, though, was that he knew she would be back. Every day before this one, he never could tell how much time he had left with her. Their marriage's problem had always been terminal, with a prognosis that neither their friends or family could agree on. Today felt different, though. He felt as though he could turn his back, and she would still be there.

"That Gemma?" Camilla said, pointing towards the cliff at the shape moseying along it.

"Looks it. Was wondering where she ran off to."

Camilla plunged the umbrella into the sand. "Let's get rid of her tonight." She touched his shoulder. "Just you and me?"

Trent took her hand and kissed it. She didn't flinch. "Just you and me."

They wanted the night to themselves? Hours later after her mom broke the news, Gemma was still doing double-takes and picking her jaw up off the floor. Flabbergasted, she felt like some stupid cartoon character who had just learned the sun was made of out gold. They wanted the night to themselves? Did they really? Or did the Dread Clock want them to itself? Either prospect seemed preposterous, and in neither one could she figure out a way to be present. Either she lacked enough cunning to stay (her mom was basically kicking her out), or enough courage to fight back (what terrible things would the Dread Clock make Dad do that he hadn't before to her?).

"You haven't been to Jen's in a while," Mom said.

That's where they were headed to at this muggy hour of 7:00 PM. To Jen's. For some reason, Mom had called Jen's mother directly. Was it coincidence? Or did the Dread Clock know Jen had texted her that morning? Connor Prendergast's website had Gemma so messed up, she almost regretted reading it. The only things she could truly do with that information was either ignore it, try to destroy the clock herself, or run for the hills. Again, she lacked the cunning and courage to carry out any of those three options.

"What's wrong, Gem?" Mom bobbed up and down in the driver's

seat. The closer they got to Jen's, the worse the road became. "I thought you'd be happy for us."

Gemma pressed the side of her head to the window. The vibrations from the engine rattled her skull. Was she happy? She wasn't even in the truck, anymore. She was outside it, in the fields that ran alongside Jen's neighborhood of one-story homes and rusty bicycles. There she stood, watching the world and its events unfold around her. The field was sparse, chapped, like a long stretch of a dried lip, and her company poor. Scram was there, and a few grubs, which Scram, generally out of jealousy, ended up scarfing down. Unlike the beach, where she built castles for the tide to tear down, here, in this forgotten field, her materials were dirt, dust, and the sweat of her brow. What could she build with that? What could she possibly do that would make a difference?

Anyway, Mom was out of the house, away from the Dread Clock, and she still wanted to make things work with Dad. Maybe all they needed was a little chaos to have them come to their senses.

She whispered, "Fuck," and closed her eyes for the rest of the ride.

Gemma spent most of the night sending texts to her mom, asking her how things were going and giving her suggestions on what to do, as though she were some expert on marriage. Mom turned down every idea, told her to enjoy her time with her friends, and then around 10:50 PM stopped texting altogether.

"Hey, Gem," Jen said, nudging Gemma with her foot. They were in Jen's basement on the floor, sitting in a circle while anime played in the background. "What's up? Everything alright?"

Gemma smiled, set her phone down. "I'm fine. Mom's acting weird."

Addie, who was sitting behind Jen, doing her hair, leaned out and said, "Sorry, Gem."

Gemma waved her off. She had known Jen and Addie for almost two years. They were a package deal. If you were friends with one of them, then by default you were friends with the other. Those two had known each other since pre-school, so there was a lot of history between them, inside jokes and things like that, that oftentimes made Gemma feel like an outsider. Like her parents, she pushed them away, and like her parents, they never gave up on her. If she told them a fraction of the freaky stuff that was going on in her home, would they believe her? Something deep down inside her, low and gravelly, almost mechanical, told her she had to try. Some secrets weren't meant to be kept. She learned that from Mom and Dad. They were their secrets, and nothing else.

Jen uncrossed her legs and sprawled them out. "Summer is going to fly by, I know it."

Addie went to work on another of Jen's braids. "Don't say that. I can't stand school. God, I hate it. Our class is full of retards. The teachers are douchebags. My mom always says I'll regret wanting to be older, but I'm pretty sure I won't. Being a teenager sucks."

"I don't know," Gemma said. Thinking back to her mom and dad in the supposed Black Hour, she added, "What's so great about being an adult?"

"Uh, you get to do whatever you want?"

Gemma shrugged. "I don't think I've ever seen any of our parents ever do what they want."

Jen piped up. "I don't think I've ever seen any adult do what they want."

Addie stopped braiding. "That's because they all have kids. We're the problem. I'll fully admit it." She scooted away from Jen. "You're telling me you love school, Gem?"

She shrugged. "It's not that bad."

Addie's face went dark. She let down her blonde tendrils and said, "Not for you guys, apparently."

Jen scooted herself in between the two of them. "Listen, it sucks for everyone."

"I can't get through one day without embarrassing myself. Either I fall out of my desk, I fall down the stairs, or I fart in gym class—"

Gemma and Jen started to crack up.

Addie, half-serious, belted, "Shut up."

Jen nudged Addie back onto her hands. "You're a hot mess. That's not the school's fault."

"It made me this way." Addie lay down on her back. "I used to be so cool in grade school."

"What happened?" Gemma asked, snidely.

"Boys," Addie said, the word rolling off her tongue as though it were as heavy as she made it sound. "And stuff."

Jen whispered to Gemma, "It's the 'stuff' that really messed her up."

Gemma laughed. "Gets us all in the end, this mysterious 'stuff.'"

Addie reared up. "Oh, I'm sorry I'm not as extravagant as you two."

"You mean eloquent?"

"Bah!" She lay back down. "Everything's pissing me off right now."

"Was my time of the month, too," Gemma said. She furrowed her brow. "Only lasted like a day."

"Lucky ducky," Addie rumbled. "Hate being a girl."

Jen shook her head at Gemma. To Addie, she said, "You're a real treat tonight. Let's not do this. It's the beginning of the summer. Forget about school and all that crap."

Addie held the sides of her head and made the sounds a monk might make when trying to clear their mind.

"Gemma, seriously, though—" Jen threw a pillow at Addie but that just made her meditate louder, "—what's going on with your mom?"

Mom? She reached for her cell phone. 11:15 PM. No text or missed call. Quickly she sent her mom a message asking how everything was going. *Maybe go out to a bar with Uncle Jasper, or hang out in town,* she thought and then texted.

"Gem?"

She glanced back at Jen. Addie was sitting up now, too, having finally come out of her selfish shell.

Oh nothing. Dad may have tried to abuse me, and Mom is obsessed with a clock that may be madness incarnate. Gemma wanted to say those things, but since she didn't think they'd really believe her, at least not at this moment, instead she whispered, "They're fighting again. It's bad."

Jen's eyes softened. "Is that why you keep checking your phone?"

My phone? She turned on the screen. 11:27 PM. No text or missed call.

"You know, you can stay at my house for a few days," Jen offered. "It's summer. My parents won't care. If it's, you know, really bad at home."

It is, Gemma thought. But instead, she shook her head. "It just scares me. Seeing them like that. It's like… it's like I don't know who they are, anymore."

Addie leaned in. "Do they hit each other?"

"Not exactly." She swallowed hard the confession in her throat. "I don't know what to do." She checked her phone. 11:28 PM. "I think they're getting better."

"Really?" Jen's face beamed.

"But everything else is getting worse." Gemma continued.

Jen's head dropped. "Oh."

"How's that possible?" Addie asked. "Shouldn't it be the opposite?"

Gemma's lips were sealed. She had already said too much. It was a mistake coming here. She needed to be at home with Mom and Dad to see if the Dread Clock were the real Dread Clock, and midnight the actual Black Hour. If last night were a fluke, she wouldn't know until tomorrow. And if it wasn't, god knows what was about to happen in that house thirty-two minutes from now.

She started texting Uncle Jasper when Addie said, "Hey, Gem."

"Huh?" She stopped. Her text simply said, *I'm not home, but I think things are bad there.* Then deleted the text.

"Tell us a scary story."

Jen cocked her head. "What? No. Not right now. She's got something—"

Addie put up her hand. The way her eyes shone, the way her face looked more angular—so focused and in tune—Gemma could tell what she was getting at.

"It's not really my story," Gemma started, "not yet, at least. I'm still trying to figure it out."

Addie shrugged. "That's cool."

Jen, protective as always, glared at Addie.

There was no hiding behind what was about to happen. Gemma had make it perfectly clear that everything was perfectly wrong at home. Addie was egging her on to tell a scary story, something which Gemma loved doing at sleepovers. Jen and Addie weren't stupid, either. For the next ten minutes, anything that Gemma said would be immediately interpreted as having to do with whatever was bothering her. She could dress it up however she liked, but like her parents, she was now her secret, and nothing else.

So, like all wounded storytellers, Gemma gave them a fake smile, disappeared inside herself, and let her tale take over.

"For little… Connor, it started with a nightmare that never came to an end. When he was seven years old, he went to bed one night and dreamed that his parents had abandoned him."

Gemma paused, looked at her phone. 11:35 PM. Focusing on those four numbers, she then continued.

"In the nightmare, his parents hadn't actually, you know, abandoned him. They were still home. But they had, kind of, divided the place in two. Right down the middle. A red line that ran through every room, even if the room was really small. Connor could go wherever he wanted in the house, but his mom and dad never talked to each other. And if his mom or dad happened to be in the same room, on, you know, opposite sides of the line, they would stop, stare at each other, and start drooling, like they had rabies or something.

"Like I said, though, Connor could go wherever he wanted in the house. He could spend the night in the den with his dad, or upstairs in his mom's bedroom. But every time he did, they would take something away from him. A toy, or some of his allowance. Maybe one of his pets. Sometimes, they took his friends, or a few hours of sleep. Sometimes, they even took words off his tongue, or memories out of his mind. He couldn't say certain words anymore without feeling sick to his stomach, or think about certain things without feeling dizzy. So he just gave them up instead.

"Eventually, Connor stopped visiting his mom and dad. He didn't really have much left to give them, and he was afraid of what would happen if he came to them empty-handed. Near the end of the nightmare, right before Connor woke up, he saw his mom and dad walking down the hall on their respective sides, carrying the last two things he gave them. His dad had one part of Connor's heart, and his mother the other. At the end of the hall, there was a set of double doors he'd never seen before. His parents opened the doors at the same time, spitting and snarling at each other as they did so, and then they went into the room behind it."

Jen leaned forward. In a whisper, she said, "What was in the other room?"

"Everything Connor ever gave to them. You see, there was this clock. I mean, cabinet." She blushed. "The room was painted black and totally empty, except for this cabinet. Inside it, on every shelf, were all the things Connor's mom and dad took from him. His toys and clothes. His fingernails or his sweat. Memories, too, in jars; and food and snacks. Some of his friends were in the drawers. His favorite pet was tied to the back of the cabinet. It was everything he had or had been, you know, except it all looked really messed up. Like, all that stuff had been gone for so long, he didn't recognize it anymore, or it grossed him out to look at it. But that wasn't the worst of it."

Addie, chewing on her thumb, said, "It wasn't?"

Gemma shook her head. "You see, the red line that divided the house stopped at the cabinet. So his mom and dad could use it together. Taking away Connor's childhood was, pretty much, the only thing they could do together. But the worst of it was what was in the back of the cabinet, behind all the stuff. It was this dark creature. His mom and dad called it the Black… Mass. It was this sticky, black ooze that clung to everything inside the cabinet. But it had bones, so it wasn't all liquid. The nightmare told Connor the bones were the bones of children. You see, all the moms and dads in the world like his would take and take. They'd take more than they could give. Without even realizing it, really. Until, one day, like Connor at the end of the nightmare, the kids had nothing left. So the parents would skin them and feed the bones to the Black Mass in the cabinet."

Jen gasped. Addie cringed and shook her head.

"Right as his mom and dad brought out the knives to flay him, Connor woke up from the nightmare. Though he should have been dead, right before his eyes opened up, he remembered something else. He remembered being inside the Black Mass, watching his mom and dad walk through the house, scraping away at the red line that ran down the middle of it. Because, you know, now that Connor was gone, the Black Mass that they had put in the cabinet would leave them alone. Because Connor was gone, they could be happy again."

Jen, looking absolutely defeated, said, "Gemma, that's such a—"

Gemma cut her off. "That's not the end of the story. Like I said, the nightmare was just the beginning. Connor woke up, drenched in sweat, really early in the morning. The sun had just come up, so there was some light in his room, but not much. He always went to sleep with a glass of water on his nightstand. So he was guzzling that and, just as he finished off the water, he saw through the glass a little red smudge on the ground.

"He freaked out. He dropped the glass, and it shattered on the floor. Connor crawled to the foot of his bed and, even though it was still pretty dark in there, he could tell that there was part of a red line, just like the one from his nightmare, on his bedroom floor.

"His mom came in and asked him what happened. He said he had a nightmare, and she gave him a big hug and that helped him get tired again. But on her way out, even after she looked directly at the red line on the ground, which had never been there before, she didn't say anything. Connor couldn't figure out if she couldn't see it or if she didn't care.

"Connor tried to think of what the red line could have been. Maybe he spilled something. Maybe it was paint. He liked to paint. After his mom left the room, he got down on the ground and tried to scratch it off. But nothing worked. His fingernails, the butter knife under his bed—none of it worked.

"So he snuck downstairs, determined to get a screwdriver or a sharper knife. His dad had tools, too, so he thought he could get some sandpaper. But when he went down the stairs, he noticed something was different. In the… living room. It was too dark in there, so he had to turn on the light to see it all the way. But yeah, against the wall, a new cabinet. Just like the one from his nightmare. It was empty. There wasn't anything on its shelves yet. But when he saw it, he started to cry.

"His dad must have heard him, because he came running down the stairs. Thinking the cabinet must have scared him, like, you know, shadows from a tree in the night might have, his dad told him everything was okay. He said that the cabinet had always been there. They had just moved it out into the open.

"As the week went on, the line inside Connor's room started to get longer. No one said anything about it. Once it was out of his room and in the hall, his parents started acting weird. They kept asking him for little things. A coin. Or five minutes of his time. It was happening just like it had happened in his nightmare.

"One night, when the red line was almost down the stairs, he went to the cabinet with a hammer and tried to break it. His parents had started arguing a lot more, and he was pretty sure it was the cabinet's fault. Every time he hit the cabinet, sticky, black ooze came out. And the more sticky, black ooze there was, the faster the red line grew, and the more his parents fought and took from him."

Addie whispered, "What did he do?"

"After a few weeks, Connor waited for his parents to go to bed and started packing his things. He had a couple of bags from vacation. He didn't want to be fed to the Black Mass, and he didn't want his parents to be unhappy. He packed up all his clothes, a pillow, his blanket from when he was born; he brought his toothbrush, some toothpaste. He wrote a note, explaining to his parents why he had left. But the red line had taken over the whole house at that point, so the only place he could put it was in the cabinet, because that was the only place his mom and dad could share, like in the nightmare.

"Connor was gone before his parents woke up. He knew that, if he heard them in their room, he wouldn't be able to leave. When he had tried to give the note to the cabinet, the Black Mass almost seemed disappointed. It tried to eat him, but it wasn't strong enough because they hadn't fed it enough. But there was one problem: his parents had taken so much from him, he wasn't strong enough to fight off the Black Mass, either. So with his belongings, he took it with him, into the world."

Addie looked back and forth, between Jen and Gemma. "What? What happened next?"

"I don't know," Gemma said, sounding somber. "I'm still working on that part."

While Jen and Addie shared their own ideas and interpretations with Gemma, she casually looked at her phone. 11:45 PM. Quarter 'til chaos.

TRENT   GEMMA   **CAMILLA**

Camilla loved what the Dread Clock had done with the living room. Gone were the couches and chairs, the hardwood floor and the gaudy carpet. All the antiques she had been accumulating had been broken down and fused together. The walls, which had been an unimpressive white, had been repainted, too. Now, a sour green coat covered each one, the paint smeared and dripping, as though the Dread Clock were giving off an intense heat, like the burning center of its self-made universe.

The windows and their view of the front yard were still there, but the Dread Clock had made alterations to the glass. When Camilla looked through them, she saw not the front yard, but another plane entirely, where land and sky wept, and the ocean was a belt of bubbling bacteria. There were people in this place beyond her home, but they were too far away, too near the distant buildings, to make contact with. Besides, they wouldn't have heard her calling, anyway. They wore helmets and backpacks and bumbled about in dark, bulky suits covered in tubing. To Camilla, they looked like deep sea divers or wayward astronauts. Surveyors of unseen worlds and unknown hells who ended up here, marooned, at this Dead City.

She pulled back from the window and crossed the sticky floor. The Dread Clock had opened itself to her; its innards, those fleshy gears and the tendon-like pendulum, were on full display. They throbbed with time.

From behind, Trent said, "I had no idea this was all here."

Camilla turned around. Her husband was standing in his yellow rain slicker, holding the LED lantern. There was a fat snake hanging out of his pocket. A bald child with a dead, conjoined twin attached to its face hugged Trent's leg. It was crying because the skin on its face between it and its twin was like a tunnel. And squirming through that tunnel, out of the dead twin's skull and into the face of its crying brother, were scores of hungry leeches.

"That slicker looks smart on you," Camilla teased, nudging him.

The snake hissed and then went back to sleep.

"I just saw my father out back," Trent said. "He was giving flowers to my mother."

"That's sweet. Honey, you should invite them in. We don't really get a chance to see them enough."

Trent waved off the offer. "Nah, let's let them have their moment."

Camilla cocked her head. *What is it?* The Dread Clock was speaking again. She leaned into it, her cheek to its heaving wood. Sweaty exhalations felt like heavenly exultations from this new god of hers. *I hear you*, she thought. And she did. The voice, which ground words together like gears.

She went down on her hands and knees. She pressed her head inside the pendulum case. "Babe?" she said to Trent.

He came up behind her. "What's up?"

She stuck out her tongue. The swaying pendulum grazed against it. Every time that it did, it deposited a tangy seed of insanity into her mouth. Vague, violent visions reached into her mind and broke it open.

"Is it time?"

A playground surrounded by a wrought iron fence. A plastic slide covered in razor blades. Children shredded at the bottom. Parents rejoicing at the top.

"Hey, Camilla?" Trent nudged her. "Hey, what's it saying?"

Reptiles in the street. Tender mercy in a hospital bed. Gemma waving goodbye, fanged and furious. Red Death marauding in spacious marshes. A field. A stranger. Heartbreak. Ecstasy masquerading as euphoria. Paul Smith's party, Trent nowhere to be—

Trent grabbed Camilla and pulled her back. Her tongue left the cancerous surface of the pendulum. Instantly, the images drained out of her brain and came out as bloody snot down her nose.

"I had no idea." Camilla stretched her jaw until it nearly unhinged. "Wow. Wow, Trent. You have to try it."

Confused, Trent simply shrugged and said, "What? What did it show you?"

Camilla whistled, the brief experience having taken a large toll. She stood up, clamped her hands down on his shoulders, and said, "Everything. Everything. Anything and everything. If we looked in there long enough, we could right every wrong. You have to try it."

Trent grinned like an idiot. The conjoined twins on his leg finally exploded, sending a bloody shower of baby body parts and spider legs all over the living room.

Peeling off the remains of the Black Hour conjuration, he asked, "What about the tribute?"

Camilla slapped her head. "Duh! I totally forgot." She pulled her hair back to tie into a ponytail. But she pulled too hard, and a handful of hair, thick and oily, tore away from her scalp. "I'll go get him. But, love, seriously. Taste the Dread Clock. With what it shows us—" she kissed his lips, ground her teeth against his, "—we'll be together forever."

"Hey, Camilla?" Trent called before she disappeared upstairs into Gemma's room.

She stopped on the staircase. "Hmm?"

"Do you think anyone is going to miss Gethin?"

"No. Don't be silly. Everyone is going to be so happy for us, they won't even realize he's gone."

Camilla blew him a kiss.

Trent caught it, and it branded his hand.

TRENT   GEMMA   CAMILLA

He crawled on all fours towards the Dread Clock and went shoulder-deep into the case. He turned around, so that he was on his back, looking up at the pendulum from below it. It reminded him of some of the church services he used to attend as a young boy. On special occasions, the priest would come out with what looked like a metal egg—a censer—and swing it back and forth while reciting prayers. He remembered how smoke would pour out of the egg from the incense inside and how tired and at peace he became from its warm aroma. For the longest time, he imagined that's what it felt like to be in god's presence.

And now as he lay headfirst inside the Dread Clock, the pendulum above him, quivering out mist, and the gears behind him, cranking out unrealities, he felt that same feeling again. That same kind of calming grace. And god damn did it feel good.

Trent opened his mouth and eyes as wide as he could to let the pendulum's mist fill him. But the visions, or whatever Camilla had experienced, weren't coming.

"What do you need me to do?" He tipped his head back to the tendons that ran sideways across the case. "Tell me. I'm ready. I want this so bad. You'll have your tribute."

For the first time since they had brought the Dread Clock into their house, it went quiet. The gears ground to a halt, the pendulum slowed to a stop.

"No." Trent turned onto his belly, so that he was face-first with the viscous folds at back of the clock. "No, no, no. No, we're getting Gethin. Please, don't. Please—"

From the glistening folds, a large, burnt, scorpion-like pincer shot out and clamped down on Trent's neck. He gasped. His eyes bulged from their encrusted sockets. The pincer forced his face into the floor of the case, making him taste the muscular growths that covered it.

"Gorge. Indulge," a voice rumbled from inside the folds. It sounded like metal, and a cat wailing in unfathomable pain.

Trent strained his neck to have a better look at what was holding him down. There couldn't have been but an inch or two between the folds and actual back of the clock. How could anything fit inside there?

"Gorge." The pincer shoved him down harder, crushing his nose against the case. "Indulge. Get fat and fuck and feed me the girl."

"Gemma? No, no!" Trent gripped the pincers. "Leave her out of this."

"All of this—" the pincer squeezed harder, breaking the skin on his neck, "—has always been for her."

"Trent?" Camilla's voice. "Hey, love, what's going on?"

The pincer let go of Trent and snapped back inside the viscous folds. At once, the Dread Clock started up again. He craned his neck to catch a glimpse of the grotesque thing that lived inside the Dread Clock. But by the time his eyes had refocused, the folds had sealed shut and the creature that lived beyond them was gone.

"Did you see?" Camilla persisted, kicking his leg as he slid out of the Dread Clock's pendulum case. "Did it show you?"

It can't have Gemma. He pushed himself off the ground to his feet. *All of this is for her. For us.* Then he noticed the butcher knives, one in each of Camilla's hands.

Camilla grinned. "Earth to Trent. Hello?"

"Ha, sorry," he said, rubbing his neck where the pincer had started to bleed him. "Where's Gethin?"

"Oh. Hmm. Yeah." She held out one of the butcher's knives, blade first. "Have to find him."

"What?"

"There's a hedge maze upstairs. He must have broken out of Gemma's room." She shrugged, flashed the knife. "Sh. Wait. Sh. Do you hear that?"

Trent strained his ears. A thick blanket of white noise had fallen over the house at midnight, but she was right. There was something else behind the drones. Pips of pain. Sharp peaks of whimpers warping into screams. Now that he knew what they were, had they always been there? In this Black Hour, had they become so accustomed to atrocity that they didn't even recognize it as such anymore?

"That's him. That's definitely him. I know a rat when I hear a rat." She pricked her finger with the knife. Sucking on its weeping tip, she said, "Ready to hunt?"

Trent glanced at the Dread Clock. It had started to rumble with a rhythmic beat, like that of a heart. Did this thing have a heart? Was the creature that lived inside it the source or the guardian of it? He hated this new doubt he felt towards the clock, but it had gotten inside him, and now he had a burning need to get inside it. To return to the womb of psychosis that had dreamed up and shitted out humanity.

"We can't be too messy," he said, coming out of his defiant daze. "For Gemma's sake."

Camilla nodded. She pricked her breast and flowers came out. "For Gemma's sake."

TRENT **GEMMA** CAMILLA

When it came to weathering the late hours, Jen and Addie had more in common with the elderly than their adolescent peers. By 1:00 AM, they were passed out on the basement couch, mouths wide open and warmly welcoming any wandering spiders. Thirty minutes earlier, they had put on a teen movie from the '80s that, more or less, acted as their lullaby. Short of having to pee, Jen and Addie wouldn't be waking up until nine or ten. And even then, they wouldn't be of use to anyone until eleven or twelve.

Gemma had ignored her phone all through the Black Hour, but now it had passed, and Jen and Addie were passed out. There was no way she was going to stay here, lay here, and let the Dread Clock have its way with her family. She couldn't catch it in the act—she'd missed that show—but if she was quick enough—thirty minutes from here to home—she could catch it in the middle of the clean-up.

She had to be cautious. While Jen and Addie weren't likely to wake, she couldn't take any chances. She didn't need them following after her, and she didn't need them waking Jen's parents and launching a full-scale manhunt, either.

Gemma, quiet as she could be, roamed the basement for blankets, pillows, and stuffed animals. With enough materials to start her own plushy arc, she dropped them in a corner, built one of the "resting nests" she was known for, and filled it up until it looked like someone was inside.

Then, satisfied, she looked at Jen and Addie, the drool on their lips glinting in the television light, and wondered morbidly if she'd ever see them again.

There was something about being out at night in the wet dark, under the orange streetlights, that made Gemma feel like an adult. It was the smell of the pavement, and the cool wind that kept promising hints of scents she could chase and never find. It was the cars in the distance, filled with nobodies up to no good, and those emptier roadways, shaded and secluded, unseen and uncharted in brighter times. It was the impression of isolation and its promise of dangers. No Mom to rescue her. No Dad to protect her. Just her and the dark and the beasts that thrived in it, and the adult things she'd have to do to keep her childhood intact.

Gemma didn't even realize she had left Jen's neighborhood until she was half a mile down the road. From here, she didn't have but a few miles of speed traps and sharp turns until she reached the intersection that would turn her homeward. If the police were out tonight, then that would be a problem. Janky as their town was, there was no way they were going to let some thirteen-year-old wander around in the dead of night. So she ran off the road for the fields beside it and prayed to god she didn't end up in some ditch.

Not that any amount of sneaking would make a difference. The moon was on full-blast tonight, and ten minutes down the road, Gemma's face was glowing. She had her phone out, and she was reading, once again, Connor Prendergast's article on the Dread Clock.

"That has to be it," she whispered. The uneven terrain twisted her ankles this way and that. "That has to be the clock. There's no getting around it. This thing is real. Fuck. Yeah. Yes. This is it."

Gemma didn't truly see the Dread Clock for what it was, or for what this Connor Prendergast warned his readers it could represent. An otherworldly object that coveted, consumed, and converted evil into a form of reality? A brood parasite, like a cuckoo bird, that fed off Time and forced it for an hour out of its own nest? No, to Gemma, smart as she was, the Dread Clock and the Black Hour were nothing more than obstacles to be overcome.

Gemma stopped, ducked. A car backfired past her.

"The plan," she said. "Get in, and then get them out. Concoct whatever bullshit story I have to so they'll stay out of the house until this Connor guy shows up. Call Gethin. Maybe get him to pick it up, too."

She rubbed the top of her hand raw. "I'll say I'm sick. I'll say we have bed bugs or lice. I could run away. Leave a trail for them to follow. Or maybe I can do something stupid. I'll say I'll kill myself, or tell the police what they've been doing if they don't take me..." The self-inflicted cuts on the back of her leg start to itch. "Oh god, I hope I'm not wrong." She glanced at the website. "No, I'm not. There's no other..."

She spent the last stretch of the road home wallowing in self-doubt. Supernatural clock? Or just her parents finally falling apart? She didn't know. She didn't. If it was the Dread Clock, and she did get them away from it for good, would they go back to fighting every night? Even before the antique arrived, things hadn't been normal.

"Grow up," she said, chastising herself. June bugs crashed against her body and got stuck in the fabric of her shirt. "God, what do I do?

What is it? Two days, and I'm losing my fucking mind."

Gemma stopped. She was dripping sweat. Ahead, the intersection sat empty. The stoplights that guarded it went through their motions. It wasn't too late to turn back. Or maybe it was. Maybe she lost that chance years ago, when Dad gave Mom a black eye, and Gemma didn't do anything about it.

She punched the side of her head, inadvertently smashing a mosquito that had been drinking there. "I'm just looking for an excuse."

She nodded, as though responding to herself. "Stupid freaking website just made it easy."

She sighed, clenched her eyes shut. "What am I doing? Erg. God." And then: "No, no. There's something wrong. It wants me to doubt myself. No. No way. I know I'm right. I am, Scram. I am."

Like most thirteen-year-olds who've come face-to-face with an object of pure evil, Gemma, in the end, didn't know what to do. So, like the two paths that led to her cave, she chose the more dangerous one. She considered there would be pain and anguish, but death itself didn't get much more than a few seconds of her time. Even in the presence of the Dread Clock, her immortality seemed secure.

She sprinted to the intersection and went west, where the choppy horizon looked as though someone had taken scissors to it. The closer she came to home, the darker the road got. The streetlights were fewer here on this narrow ribbon. And the moon wasn't any help anymore, either. It had lost its light to the storm clouds, which were so thick it was as though they meant to smother the sky.

As the land gave way to sand and sharp grass, a dark shape emerged in the distance. Framed by the ocean and the roiling firmament, Gemma's house stood lightless and lifeless. She had never known her mom or dad to turn off all the lights in the house, so she picked up the pace and prayed to god—this time for guidance.

Her legs wobbled and buckled as she gave everything she had to get to the front door. She tried to peek in the windows, but the curtains were closed. Not having a key to get in, she checked the doormat and under the conch shells beside it. But there was nothing. No spare. She tried the door anyway, but when her hand touched the knob, she almost threw up.

Gemma hurried over to the garage door to punch the passcode into the pad next to it, to open it. But there was something wrong with it. It was sticky. She took out her cell phone, shone the camera light on the pad. Red fingerprints were smeared across the buttons.

She recited the code as she pounded it in. "241641."

But the garage door wouldn't give.

"241—"

She paused. Footsteps. Inside the house, on the second floor. Like someone was running.

"-641. 241641. 24164… Fuck!"

Gemma abandoned the garage and ran around the house to the back. She checked every window she passed, but she still had no luck seeing inside. If the curtains weren't closed, then there were boxes or furniture pressed against the glass. What was going on? Were her parents trying to keep something from getting out? Or trying to keep someone from getting in?

She rounded the corner and wound up falling against the house. Gemma drew closer, teeth chattering. The back deck was covered in blankets, sheets, and wet clothes. They were dangling over the railing, hanging low and dripping from the overhead lattice. And they were hers. All of it.

"What is this?"

Her favorite T-shirt from her first concert. The blanket from her bed. Her panties and bras. And Scram, her stuffed bat. He was sitting on the table they sometimes ate at surrounded by more stuff from her room. Jewelry and books. Notes to boys, and notes from them.

Gemma, panicking, ran to the opposite end of the deck and found, propped up against it, her mattress and box spring. They had been stabbed, ripped open, and filled with shoes, posters, and yearbooks.

Everything. It was everything. Her whole room, out here, in the dark, desecrated and destroyed. She started crying. She couldn't help it. Her jaw was quivering so bad it hurt. Why would they do this? Her face was hot, and her mouth tasted bad. Why would they kick her out like—

Gemma swallowed a glob of snot and remembered back to the windows. Each one of them had been shut tight and covered up or reinforced by furniture. And then this right here? Mom and Dad were trying to keep someone out. Her. Gemma. This wasn't some mean-spirited act of madness. This was a warning. Probably the only one the Dread Clock would let them send out. Turn away, turn back. Don't come home, baby. Save yourself, honey. You're safe by yourself. Not here with us.

Gemma considered their warning, and then ignored it, anyway. She shook the shit out of the back door, but it was locked and braced by the couch, as well as the coffee table stacked on it.

"There has to be a way in," she mumbled, walking backward, away from the house. She surveyed it as though it were her first time seeing it. "I could call the cops, but what if they see something they shouldn't?"

The kitchen window over the sink. The idea forced itself into her head and stuck in it like a shard of glass. The kitchen window was too small and too inconveniently placed to put anything in front of it, and it couldn't be locked.

Gemma went wide around the deck, to the opposite side of the house. She grabbed the box spring in passing and hauled it with both hands through the grass until she was under the kitchen window. Laying it down, she carefully stood on top of it and reached upward. Her hands fumbled on the sill until they found purchase at its corners, where, yes, the window was still slightly cracked open. It would be a tight fit, but like her dad always said, she was just skin and bones, anyway.

She let go and took out her phone. She dialed 911 but didn't make the call. Instead, she left it on the screen, ready to use at any moment. If the Dread Clock was as Connor Prendergast said it was, she wasn't sure what a few police officers could do. But it was better than nothing.

Gemma reached upward again and took the corners of the sill in her hands. She gave a bounce off the box spring and pushed against the bottom of the glass, sending it high enough for her to fit under. She then jumped again and grabbed the window frame.

"I have to help them," she said, dragging herself across the sill. "No matter what."

Gemma went headfirst into the house and then dropped, her arms and legs like a pretzel, into the sink below the window. Her hip caught on the faucet. A grimy fork pricked her calf. She untangled herself and fell gracelessly from the counter to the floor.

Still too dark to see, she took out her phone and, again, turned on the camera light. Stunned by what she felt and saw, she wondered: *Is this my house? Is this the right one?*

There was something wrong, something missing. The table was there, the refrigerator, too. Even Dad's dirty shoes from when he used to work the construction sites, right by the laundry room door. And

Mom's novel she had been reading, by the microwave. Some stupid vampire novel that it seemed all moms were required to read nowadays. It was all here, and yet it wasn't. Everything felt so fake, so empty. Lightless and lifeless, like the house had looked on her way in from the road. It was as though something had taken a picture of the kitchen and tried to recreate it to pass it off as something it wasn't, or had never been.

Gemma took a deep breath and proceeded forward. Mom and Dad couldn't be far. She had heard footsteps upstairs, so either one or both of them were up there. The only problem was that, if she wanted to get up there, she'd have to go past the living room, which meant going past the Dread Clock.

She double-checked the time. 2:00 AM. Two hours out from the Black Hour, twenty-two hours until it struck again. Bleeding chaos or not, the clock couldn't do much to her if it wasn't midnight. That's what the website said. That's what it had to be. In the ways of weaknesses, it was the only one she had to use against it.

Shining the camera light on the hardwood floor, she left the kitchen and crept down the hall. The ceiling moaned. A loud thump. A burst of footsteps. And then another pair of feet. Heavier. Giving chase. What the hell was going on?

Gemma continued down the hall and came to a stop. On the floor, there was a smudge. A kind of red line. She cocked her head and pressed her phone towards it. Painted on the center of the floor, there was a red line that started here in the hall and ran further ahead into the darkness.

Heart fluttering, she dug her shoe into the line. No matter how hard she tried to scuff it with her toe or grind it with her heel, the red line wouldn't be broken. How long had it been here? Had it always been here? She dropped to one knee and clawed it with her nails. How did it know? How did it know? She clawed and clawed until her fingers were bloody and raw. How did it know? Did it always know? How did it? How? Gemma put her face to the red line and started to gnaw on the ground. How long? How long?

TRENT   GEMMA   **CAMILLA**

Gethin Yates didn't agree with Camilla's stomach. While she sat on the toilet, a hot rag over her face, Trent was running around outside the bathroom, trying to escape the Dread Clock's Keeper. What did he do? She groaned and strained her bowels. Stupid Trent. Probably saw something he wasn't supposed to see and made a big deal about it. If her husband was good at anything, it was at ruining a good thing.

Camilla sighed and took the wet rag off her face. *I feel sick,* she thought. The bathroom became a blotchy blur that hurt to look at. *This must be what it feels like to be purified. To have all the sin sucked out of you. I don't know how all those priests and nuns do it.*

TRENT   GEMMA   CAMILLA

Trent pulled on the rope. The attic ladder shot down from the ceiling. The end cracked his jaw. He stumbled and bounded up the ladder. The steps creaked and sagged, but held his weight. He threw himself and the LED lantern he was still holding into the attic.

"Shit, shit, shit."

The Dread Clock's Keeper wasn't far behind. As he grabbed the ladder and pulled it up, two pincers clamped onto the bottom steps and tore it free of the ceiling completely.

The yellow rain slicker tangled itself around Trent, as though to ensnare him. He took the LED lantern and hurled it towards the back of the attic. Long shadows exploded around the boxes there, as though the lantern were a grenade of light. He didn't know what he was doing anymore. Up here was the last place he wanted to be. But if he kept it distracted long enough, maybe Camilla would come to her senses and run while she still had the chance to.

A long, narrow, segmented tail stretched into the attic opening. At the end of the tail, a two-foot barb covered in bristly hairs secreted a curdling substance.

Trent scooted backward on all fours, like a crab, and turned away. He had only seen the Dread Clock's Keeper once and that had been enough. The sight of it had been so terrifying, it almost blinded him. It was after they had shared a meal of Gethin that the creature emerged. Camilla had broken down in tears and showered it in prayers. But it was to him, Trent, the Keeper turned its attention. Because for a moment, he had doubted the clock and chose Gemma's welfare over its wishes.

Vibrations rocked the attic as the Keeper hurled itself through the ceiling and onto the rickety beams. Trent cried out, tensed the muscles in his neck until they tented. The creature's gaunt, rubbery shadow was cast onto the wall in front of him from the LED lantern he'd lobbed.

"Please," Trent begged. He curled over, his back still to the Keeper, and gripped the floor. "Please. I'm sorry."

The Dread Clock's Keeper slithered forward. He remembered it had feet, but because it hovered slightly, it did not step, but propelled itself forward. The only hint anyone could have of it hunting them was the sound of its toenails scraping across the ground. And that's what he heard now. Those long toe nails, sharp as knives, digging at the floor as it came to kill him.

"I'm sorry, I'm sorry."

The Keeper's tail stuffed itself between Trent's quivering legs. He screamed, but didn't dare move. The tail slithered across his calves. It dragged the stinger over his crotch, catching on the tip of his prick.

"Stop, stop. Please. I appreciate—"

The Keeper's tail continued to work its way past his hips and stomach. The bristly hairs that covered its roach-colored segments broke free and brushed against Trent's face. His skin went numb, and his senses became confused. Suddenly, he could taste what he smelled and feel what he tasted. An overload of information assaulted his system. He buckled onto the tail and held onto it, as the texture of the attic, the curdling poison from the stinger, and the chaotic discharge out of the Keeper overwhelmed him.

"We can do better," Trent reasoned. Part of him wanted to look at the Keeper. The other part knew that, if he did, his sensory psychosis would tear him apart. "We'll get more tributes."

The Keeper laughed and closed its pincers over Trent's arms. "I've seen almost all the suffering your clan has to offer."

It yanked him upward, spun him around so he had to face it. Trent squeezed his eyes shut tighter.

"Don't be hurt. The Heart knows what's best for you and yours. Now, open your eyes." The Keeper used its second set of hands to pry open Trent's lids. "Your daughter is here. Downstairs. I want you to know what she's up against."

Trent's eyes shot to the side, refusing to behold the beast. "It's not midnight. How can you do this?"

The Dread Clock's Keeper clicked out a chuckle. "It's always midnight somewhere." It wrapped its tail around Trent's face and turned his head, as though he were a doll. "As an alcoholic, I'm sure you can appreciate the sentiment."

TRENT   **GEMMA**   CAMILLA

Gemma's head shot up from the floor, her teeth sore from biting the red line, as she heard something barreling down the stairs. A jagged, black mass wheeled around the banister, two humans in tow.

She directed her cell phone light down the hall. "Mom? Dad?" Disgusted with what she had been doing, she wiped her mouth and jumped to her feet and called again. "Mom? Dad?"

The black mass stopped in the hall, at the front door, right before the living room. Just out of her light's reach, she stepped forward, the maddening malaise in the house infecting her with a deadly strain of stupid courage.

"Oh my god," Gemma whispered as her light lit up the darkened horror.

The Dread Clock's Keeper was seven feet tall. Its body was an oily, runoff-colored carapace that warped around the creature's limbs like leather. Its arms were serrated and hard, like the surface of some alien planet, and fitted with massive pincers. A second set of arms, smaller but no less feeble, protruded from its sides—the fingers upon them fused and deformed. Its legs, riddled with scabby gears, dangled limply from its emaciated waist. Long toenails, sharp as talons, dragged on the floor, much like how a prisoner's might after the hangman released the lever.

But perhaps what frightened Gemma the most were the features she refused to focus on. The tail, emerging like an elongated spine from the creature's back, and the stinger that crowned it, that pulsating murder organ. And the face, the Keeper's horrible face. A dusty, pitted chunk of chiseled meat that had more in common with a wasps' nest than a head. The creature had no eyes, no nose or ears; just one large mouth, hollowed-out, with no tongue, and toothless, as though it took more pleasure in engulfing its prey than in the act of eating.

The two humans in the Keeper's pincers stirred. Gemma, stunned by the creature, quickly snapped out of that hellish awe and recognized they were her mom and dad.

Gemma, bawling uncontrollably, said, "Let them g-go god d-damn it!"

Mom craned her neck. In a low drawl, she said, "Gemma? Oh, Gemma. What are you doing here?"

The Keeper shook her mother to shut her up.

"Didn't you see outside?"

I did, Gemma thought and wanted to say. But she couldn't. She couldn't say anything. Her body wasn't hers anymore. It belonged to fear.

"It's not time." Camilla coughed out the curdled liquid the creature's stinger was secreting. "Our Black Hours aren't over yet."

"M-mom!" Gemma cried.

The Keeper bolted forward, through the hall and into the living room. Gemma hesitated and then scrambled after it. She rounded the corner, entered the living room, and gasped.

The Dread Clock stood unlocked, the truth of the creation laid bare. The horns that jutted from the pediment had curled downward and were drilled into the living room floor. The clock face and moon dial had merged into one metal sheet, where time was depicted not by numbers, but by sinister celestial bodies, instead. The glass case was engorged, both wide and tall enough for a creature like the Keeper to pass through. And at the back of the case, beyond the pendulum, which hung like a flaccid uvula from the roof of the opening, was a swirling mire of light and marbled imagery.

The Keeper laughed, as though it already knew what was going to happen next. With her mom and dad in its grasp, and its tail swinging wildly to hold Gemma at bay, the creature went down on all fours and sprang forward like a panther at the Dread Clock. The engorged case widened to accommodate its girth and sucked the Keeper and its prey down that wet corridor, until they disappeared into the portal plastered at the back.

Gemma took a deep breath, because she had no time to take anything else, and did the same. As the case's swelling went down, she went to her hands and knees and scurried into the Dread Clock. The corridor of fluid and wet, gasping wood closed in around. She hurled herself forward.

"No, no, no!"

The portal ahead was closing. If she didn't reach it, then the Dread

Clock was going to crush her alive. It was reconfiguring itself. The walls were tightening up, the floor of the case shortening. Space that had been there before disappeared, as though strands of reality were being snipped away right in front of her.

A great, splintery pressure bore down on her back. She could feel gears against her bones, trying desperately to find a groove to work off. Breathing became impossible, as though there was no more oxygen left to breathe. So close to the portal, just out of arm's reach, and she couldn't have been further away.

Gemma threw herself forward, tearing a muscle in her arm. She winced, gasped. She reached out to the portal. The Dread Clock's innards squeezed against her, locking her arm into place, while ramming a piece of wood against her neck.

No, she thought. *So close.* She wiggled her fingers, which were only an inch away from the portal. The Dread Clock continued to reduce in size. Her legs bent and bunched up. A corset of wood and clockwork braced her belly. She closed her eyes, too constricted to cry and thought: *I'm going to die.*

And then something cold grasped her hand. Her eyes snapped open. Around the tips of her finger, a dirty puddle with a kaleidoscope of experiences rippling across its surface. The portal had reached out to her. It could have let her die, but it reached out to her. Was this pity? Or was her family's suffering only a mere pittance? A bitter disappointment only the taste of a thirteen-year-old girl could wash down? Now was too late to reconsider what she—

Gemma stood in a field that could have been any field, under a blue sky that could have been any blue sky. The sun was there, and clouds, too. She could hear birds calling to one another and the hurried rustling of animals moving through the grass. But inside the hot breeze, which wreaked havoc everywhere it went, another sound was contained. One which she knew and yet couldn't place. It was as though the sound had been trapped there or had become a part of it. It was a kind of shoveling and picking, in between low grunts and shallow breaths.

Gemma turned in place. As she did, the field rose and fell, rose and fell, until it tapered away into something maintained and organized. There were rows of crops as far as Gemma could see, and tending them were people. Africans. Slaves. Old and young, men and women, and sometimes even children. They were scattered across the field and dressed in clothes that didn't fit them. Several glanced over at Gemma, but their darkened eyes didn't see her. For their minds were elsewhere, in better places.

More sounds sent Gemma spinning, until she settled on a sight gargantuan and white. A three-storied plantation, not far off, where a porch full of white people watched their workers from behind tall hats and sweating cups. But it was to the second-floor balcony to which Gemma's eyes were drawn. Because, standing there, under a sign that read "Carpenter," out in the open, to gaze upon the field and the miseries it had sown, was the Dread Clock.

Gemma darted across the fields. Slaves stepped out of her path, but dare not address her in passing. A man rode in on a horse from her periphery. With a raised whip, he lashed a woman and a child until they fell to the ground.

"Stop it," Gemma shouted, but the man on the horse paid her no mind. He whipped them until they turned to pink dust, until their color was lost in the soil's.

She kept running, because she believed that what was happening here wasn't really real. While no one else appeared as though they could see her, two people, a man and a woman, on the porch of the plantation clearly did. They stood from their rocking chairs and stepped out of the shade. She recognized them immediately.

"Mom! Dad!" Gemma waved her arms. Clouds of dust swirled around her. "Mom! Dad!"

Her parents had a look of caution to them. Didn't they recognize her?

Panting, the southern heat having scorched her lungs, Gemma dropped to her knees beside an African man digging in the dirt. He glanced at her and then nodded at the hole he'd made. Rubbing her eyes, Gemma leaned over and saw inside it a black tree. The African man smiled and quickly covered the tree, as it needed more time to grow.

A metallic whine rang out across the fields. Gemma's head shot up. The Dread Clock was ringing in the hour. Below, on the porch, the overweight overlords of the plantation were now walking in circles, dragging dead, black bodies behind them. They milled about like brain dead cattle, not going anywhere in particular, but only because this alone was enough to get them through the day.

Her mom and dad watched the circular procession with intrigue. Then they grabbed the nearest house servants, broke their necks, and started pulling them like sacks across the porch.

"Gemma."

She looked back to the balcony. There, floating behind the banister, the Keeper, somehow even more wretched in the harsh sunlight.

"Give them back," she begged. Her face was splotchy and red. Dehydrated with disgust and hatred, she was on the verge of passing out.

"Why?" The Keeper nodded at the fields. "Why would you want them back? After all the bad things adults have put you through?"

"I don't care! This isn't real."

"Ah," the Keeper said. "To be young. Look at your parents, Gemma. See how they fit in."

Mom and Dad were laughing with the masters of the house, patting them on the shoulders and leaving bloody hand prints on their shirts.

"You're an idiot!" Gemma started forward, hands balled into pink fists. "God, please, give them back."

The Keeper cocked its head. "What makes you think they'll want you back? This is their vacation. You're interrupting."

The Keeper put its hands together, as though it were closing a book. And like the pages of a book, the field, workers, and the plantation and its owners folded inward, into a black margin of space where only Gemma and her pain were sustained.

Then the blackness faded, like a transition into a scene from a movie. The sun hardened over into a moon. The fields warped into fences, the crops into barbed wire. The ground became muddy and insect-ridden. The plantation's stark white walls gave way to gray facades that stretched like wings around Gemma. The trees, greater in number than before, began to twist upon themselves. They worked their limbs this way and that, until at first, they were crosses, and then by some unseen force, were bent into swastikas.

Collectively, the Africans from the field stared at Gemma. Did they blame her? Or just want answers? She couldn't say, and neither could they. As though struck by Death itself, the slaves fell to the ground and died. Their brown bodies sank into the brown mud. Like seams ripping across a blanket, the threads of their flesh began to pull apart. All across the concentration camp, from the Africans' cold, dark husks, pale, emaciated bodies began to emerge.

These prisoners, of all ages and sexes, struggled to their feet. Shaved and bruised and similarly tattooed, they marched across the yard in between the watch towers that ran along the sodden stretch. Faceless men with readied guns trained their sights on the shambling crowd. But no one, neither the prisoners nor their captors, appeared to realize Gemma was there.

Sick to her stomach and still recoiling from the sight at the plantation, Gemma moved through the stripped mass of people. She had to find the Dread Clock and her parents, but the weight of despair was so heavy that she found it hard to do anything at all. There were so many people here, in this new circle of hell. Everywhere she looked, she saw bare flesh and bleakness and such deplorable conditions that it almost seemed a joke that the Nazis here had bothered to build barracks at all. This place was a factory fueled by the only natural resource that would never be depleted: hate.

Soldiers flanked the throng of prisoners from every direction. Overhead, explosions erupted across the sky. The moon took a blow and bled white blood like rain upon the concentration camp. German orders were shouted to the Jewish prisoners, urging them to keep moving forwards. Gemma didn't know what they were saying, but she didn't need to. Regardless of tone or mother tongue, disgust always sounded the same.

With the prisoners, Gemma passed a crumbling building from which a bitter, cloying fog poured. The walls of the building were made out of red bricks, though most of them were stained through with human-shaped splotches of blue.

Past the gas chamber, the group of prisoners began to part. Gemma, too short and too squished to see what was happening ahead, planted her feet to wait it out. A soldier in a freshly-pressed uniform stopped in front of her, smiled, and kissed the top of her forehead. He looked like he was proud of her, like she had something to do with all of this.

Gemma had to resist every urge to vomit. The tail-end of the procession—mostly the elderly, the amputated, and severely emaciated—struggled past her. She tried to keep her thoughts focused on finding the Dread Clock and her parents.

It's not real, it wasn't really like this, she thought, a panic attack pressing against her heart. *People are bad, but not this bad. People are bad, but not this bad.* She threw up all over herself. The lie she had told was so bad it was sickening.

Wiping the vomit off her mouth, she felt the urge to puke again. The prisoners had scattered enough to reveal what had divided them ahead. It was the Dread Clock, and it stood in front of a massive grave. At its side, a Nazi commander sat, smoking and reading a newspaper. Next to him, on a table made out of skulls, a phonograph played soft, soothing classical music. The volume was turned down low, as though the commander was worried about being rude.

If the clock was here, so, too, were her parents. She still had no idea how to get them out of whatever this was. But she had come here through the Dread Clock. Perhaps she could leave the same way.

The white rain from the moon slowed to a drizzle, while the war that raged around the camp worsened. Gunfire. Artillery blasts. There was so much dirt and debris being heaved into the air, it was as though something were trying to sift the continent into the sea.

"Gemma, come here," the Keeper spoke.

Gemma, looking at her feet, proceeded to the massive grave. She held her breath and plugged her ears. *I can't do this.* The smell of death burned inside her skull. Images flashed through her mind of the dead slaves and now of these soon to be dead prisoners. *There's more of them,* she thought. More slaves than masters. More prisoners than captors. *Why don't they fight back?* She looked up. A couple of kids that had been sewn together ran past. *It's the Dread Clock. This isn't real.*

She went past the Nazi commander to the edge of the massive grave. It had to have been fifty-feet deep and, for the moment, empty. At the bottom, hovering over the pool of water that had formed there, was the Keeper.

"Where are they?" Gemma snarled.

"So many terrible things around you, and all you're worried about is your mom and dad?" The Keeper shook its wasp nest-like head. "Insensitive."

"This isn't real!"

The prisoners that stood at the rim of the massive grave looked at her. They started to point at her and mumble to themselves. They wanted to tear her apart.

"It's very real. Some embellishments, but very real." The Keeper floated out of the grave, until it was hovering above it and Gemma. "You think we caused all of this?" It shrugged. "We create only what has inspired us. In this war, we were just along for the ride. The Black Hour is a museum. It's not our fault your adults keep giving us atrocities to display."

A wave of hopelessness washed over her. She cried, "I don't believe you."

And the Keeper simply said, "We don't care."

Rows of soldiers hurried past Gemma, half to the group of prisoners on one side of the grave, half to the other on the opposite side. Among them, armed and in uniform, were her mom and dad.

Gemma reached out for their sleeves, but they hurried past, shaking off her attempt.

"This is what adults do," the Keeper said. "The sooner you realize this, the happier you'll be."

Mom and Dad, with the other soldiers, formed a perimeter around the grave. Simultaneously, they all raised their guns and pointed them directly at the prisoners.

"No, don't," Gemma said to her mom and dad, who were too far away to hear her.

She ran to the Nazi commander, who was still reading and smoking, and kicked over his chair.

"Make them stop," she screamed.

But when the commander fell out of his chair, he lost his clothes and his authority. He curled up like an infant and bawled into his knees.

One gunshot. Then another. Then tens of them. Gemma turned back to the grave. The Nazi soldiers and her parents fired into the crowd of prisoners, sending them reeling into the pit. Those that didn't die from the bullets broke apart at the bottom of the grave.

"Holy fuck, god, please, stop!"

Gemma ran towards the soldiers to try and reach her parents. Hands shot out of the muddy ground and grabbed at her ankles.

"Fuck you. Fuck you! I'm not… I won't." She tried to kick off the hands, but their grips were too strong. "Please, please! I need them!"

The Keeper put its hands together. "But they don't need you." Its tail whipped back and forth, spraying the pit with poison. "Didn't you see how much better they worked together when you weren't around? Don't you remember how happy they sounded before you were born?"

"You're making them do this," Gemma whined pathetically. There was a tear in every fold of her face. "You're making them," she said, on the verge of a temper tantrum.

The Keeper unclasped its hands. "Am I?"

It pointed to the soldiers, who were now standing over the edge of the grave, firing into the dead bodies, riddling them with bullets.

"Then what's their excuse?"

Gemma dug the heels of her palms into her sweaty forehead. "The Black Hour. I don't know! I just want to go home. Give them back. I can't take this anymore. I'll do anything."

"I know you will," the Keeper said. "Our futures have the same Skeleton." It lowered itself from the air and honed in on Gemma. "We can keep this up forever. Can you?"

She nodded and then shook her head. Then said, "You're doing this on purpose."

A missile cruised overhead and exploded into the wasteland beyond. The shadow of a tank rumbled past the barbed wire fence, fire spewing from the top of it.

The Keeper nodded. "Of course I am. Every human is a unique palette of pain and suffering. No one tastes or feels the same. Our catalogue of experiences exceeds what your mind is capable of comprehending."

The Dread Clock rumbled. A low tone bellowed out of it.

"I want to bleed you and yours dry, Gemma. To the very last drop. For some, that takes only a minute. Others, a lifetime." Again, the Keeper put its pincers together and said, "I know what you're thinking. You should have never come here."

Gemma swallowed what felt like a gallon of mucus down her throat. She wiped her face, but all she did was spread ashes across it.

"It's not that you should have never come here."

The concentration camp began to dim, as though all the lights were turned off in the world.

"Your mom said it best: you should have never been born. Just think how much better things would have been for everyone, yourself included, if you hadn't?" The Keeper shook its head. "You selfish little beast."

"That's not…" Gemma couldn't finish the sentence. She folded her arms around her face and rocked in place. *Don't listen to it. Don't listen to it.*

But she was. She had listened to every word and somehow found truth in each of them. All of this came back to her. She never told the police that Dad had hit Mom. She never told Mom that Dad had touched her. She never told her parents about the website, about what the Dread Clock really was. She had every opportunity to get help, and she didn't. All the shit she pulled at school. Everything she did to keep them together. And for what? For this? Mom would have never bought the fucking clock if she hadn't been with Dad. She wouldn't have even stayed in town. And Dad might have been gone, too. Far away. With Gemma or another woman, but not here, not killing slaves, not slaughtering Jews. They would have been happy. They would have been safe. Their Black Hours would have ended. Their Black Hours would have ended. Their Black Hours would have—

CAMILLA

The last place Camilla expected to wake up was in a garden outside a convent. It seemed like the start to a really bad joke Trent might tell when he'd had one too many bottles of liquid courage in him. And maybe she had suffered the same fate, because as she got to her feet, she saw she was dressed like a nun. The whole kit and caboodle, in fact. The black tunic, the white coif and veil—she had it all.

"Either Halloween came early," she said. She noticed a cement bench in front of some flowers and took a seat. "Or, Christ, I'm still dreaming."

And what a dream it had been. The Antebellum South. A concentration camp from World War II. And other things, as well. Weird shit that had happened at home. Some of it good—Trent and her sure put their bed to the test—but most of it bad—god, had she really eaten Gethin?

In front of her and the convent was a small pond around which the garden had been built. There was a fountain in the middle of it, but it was the strangest fountain she had ever seen, because it was shaped just like a clock.

Pointing at it, she said, "Do I know you?" She laughed, squeezed the bridge of her nose. "Yup, still dreaming. Or dead." She chuckled, clicked her heels together. "Don't know why I would dream about a convent. Don't know why I'd dream about eating Gethin, either, so I guess I should just give up trying." She laughed, amused with herself.

Camilla fell back on her hands. She arched her spine, closed her eyes, and breathed in the garden. *This is nice*, she thought. *I'll have to come back here. I'm sure Gemma knows all about lucid dreaming. Such a weird—*

"Camilla."

Her eyes slowly opened. The Dread Clock's Keeper stood behind her, its pincers inches away from her face.

Camilla screamed, tried to sit up, but the Keeper's second set of hands quickly grabbed her head and held her there. She made her body dead weight to slip off the bench. But the Keeper's pincers quickly clamped down onto both sides of her torso, arms included, and held her there in that awkward pose.

"What... are..." Camilla was already hyperventilating. "No, wait, I recognize..."

The Keeper's deformed hands molested the flesh of her face. It pulled her skin back tight, widening her eyes.

"My girl? My Gemma? I remember." A pathetic clicking noise came out of Camilla's throat. "You. Did you hurt her? Please, she's a good girl. I remember. I never meant..."

"Shh," the Keeper said. It twisted its tail around, bringing the drooling stinger that crowned it to Camilla's forehead. "You've given me almost everything. But to have everything, I must give you something in return."

Camilla shook her body. "No, I don't want it."

"You don't even know what it is." The Keeper stabbed the stinger into Camilla's skull and started to pump the curdling liquid into it. "You never will."

The convent, the garden, and the Keeper disappeared. Left with only her memories, there was one that stood out amongst the rest. It pulled her in when she wanted nothing more than to put it away. The memory was like a diamond, dense and indestructible. Thirteen years of pain and unspoken rage had sharpened its edges, like whetstones. She couldn't hold it for more than a moment without getting hurt. And yet here it was, in the palm of her mind, demanding embrace, and promising only evisceration.

There were nights, and then there were Nights. She'd had many of the former, fewer of the latter. There had been the first Night with her first date, and the first Night she had sex. The first Night she met Trent, and the last Night she spoke to her mother. But the Night that stood out the most was the one that had changed her life forever.

Thirteen years ago, Trent revealed that not only had he cheated on her, but that the woman he fucked was pregnant with his child. The confession was cataclysmic. It tore through Camilla like a knife and bled away the last drops of love she still had for him. Divorce was the obvious option and, in the weeks that followed, imminent. That is, until he told her the child was already born, and that the woman didn't want the little girl. And that he was going to take the baby and bring it home and raise as it as their own.

The first moment Camilla laid eyes on little Gemma, so pink and small, she knew she would love her. The same couldn't be said for her husband, but for their new daughter, it was an unspoken, unshakeable fact. Gemma wasn't hers by birth, but it didn't seem to matter. She was a beautiful child. One that had been spared a terrible life of trailer park drama and dead-end ambitions. Camilla had been given this opportunity for a reason; and although she would never forgive Trent for what he had done, never in a million years would she take that same anger out on Gemma. Truth be told, she took in the child partly as a test for herself, believing that, if she could raise Gemma, then all the efforts and energies she had put into her and Trent hadn't been a waste. But more importantly, that Camilla wasn't a waste herself. That she was capable of nurturing a relationship, of seeing it through to its very end. That she could have an effect on someone, and that both they and she could be better for it.

This was the memory that lay before her, crystallized and clear. But as she recalled it, she saw that its structure had changed. It became more angular and raw. It became a liability, something which couldn't be kept close to those memories connected to it. Fissures ran along the gem, from the outer layers of excuses and weak justifications, to the deep core of regret. Then, as though it had been there all along, in the soil of the experience, a black mass rose, coating every moment, feeling, and belief that it touched and changing it for the worse.

Suddenly, Gemma was no longer the pink and small baby that inspired smiles and sighs. She became a tiny a burden, an unwanted annoyance. Every dollar that was spent on her was a dollar that could have been spent on something better. Every late night spent up with her, feeding her, burping her, rocking her to sleep, was a night wasted. Everything that Gemma did right, Camilla found something wrong to complain about. And everything that Gemma did wrong—and there were many things—Camilla found an excuse to curse her name and count down the days until she was no longer her responsibility.

By the time the distorted memory had reached Gemma's years in grade school, Trent and Camilla had reforged their love and formed an unlikely alliance. To them, Gemma had become a rallying point. They reveled in their disgust for their daughter. Though they continued to fight, there was one issue they could always agree on: it had been a mistake to bring Gemma home.

At the memories of adolescence, the black mass and the diamond went wild. Camilla had no opportunity to even realize that the events were permanently changing in her mind. She remembered the arguments between her and Trent, but whereas they had once concerned finances, his attitude, her wants, and their failing marriage, they became concerned with one constant aggravator.

Every time they fought, every time Camilla kicked Trent out, it was because of Gemma. In grade school, she had been a weird child with no friends, who was selfish and no better than her fat whore of a mother. In middle school, she was attention-starved and completely destructive. She failed tests on purpose and got into fights for no reason. She was disrespectful at home, and had to be taken to the hospital on multiple occasions due to self-harm.

Once exposed to the black mass, all the responsibility Camilla had once shouldered for Gemma's behavior vanished. Everything she and Trent had done to provoke their daughter's actions was no more. Gemma went from being a victim of a dysfunctional home to a vindictive brat born of bad genes, but a few incidences away from a prolonged stay at a boarding school.

As the black mass spread to the events of the last week, Camilla struggled to make sense of them. In the present, she loved her daughter, cherished her. But in the past, she hated her, despised her. Something was happening to Camilla, she knew it. The Keeper still had her in its clutches, and it was killing her. Killing her by killing her love for her daughter. It was turning Camilla into something she never wanted to be, causing her to think she had been the mother she never wanted Gemma to have. If only she could stop this. There had to be a way to break free.

But there wasn't. As soon as Camilla realized what was happening to her, it had already happened. Every happy memory she had with or about Gemma was gone. Like a leaf shredded by insects, her mind and its memories had been torn apart. All she had left was what she had thought she had always been.

So when she opened her eyes and found herself still in front of the convent, she came to her feet and started towards it. For she had a confession to make. She hated her daughter. Hated her more than anything else in the world. And, by the grace of god, she was going to get rid of her.

TRENT

No matter where Trent went in the convent, he heard whispers.
They were hymnal, horrible. A kind of caustic chant that carried itself
on a soundwave of hellish peaks and doomed valleys. The alien words
came from everywhere and everything. No matter how much distance
he put between himself and a place, the sound was always the same. It
was like the convent had a secret so dark, not even the walls could keep
it.

Obsession overtook him. Like a demon on his back, it rode him
through the convent, dangling a carrot of desperation over his head.
From the chapter house to the refectory, the kitchen to the scripto-
rium, Trent cleared each room on the first floor and the halls that connected them. On the second floor, the chanting was unchanged, yet he
scoured the level all the same. Going between the blood-soaked infir-
mary, the filthy lavatory, and the ash-covered calefactory did nothing
but test the limits of his stomach, as well as his patience.

Returning to the first floor, Trent wandered, momentarily defeated,
into the church itself. Despite being literally built in the middle of the
convent, the church seemed to be anything but the center of anyone's
attention. It was a narrow, sparse space with no more than a few pews
and a dusty tabernacle. The floor was a sharp stretch of upturned stone
eager to put most knees to the test. In the way of adornments, there
were none. There was no religious iconography or holy texts. No host
to eat, nor wine to drink. The only niceties to the church's name were
the two stained glass windows, but the images depicted there were so
grotesque, they were impossible to appreciate, let alone decipher.

"This must be where the masochists go to pray," Trent quipped.

He slid into a pew and tried to get comfortable.

"A hardcore church for those who pray harder than the rest." He
laughed. "Christ Almighty, this is one funky ass dream."

Dream. Nightmare. Over the course of however long he had been
sleeping, the lines between the two often blurred. There were good
moments—his time with Camilla at home, alone, and with Gemma, in
her bedroom—and then not so good moments. There had been some
clock? And he remembered Jasper screaming about something in the
basement?

"Do feel good though, oddly enough." He stretched out his legs. "No worries in the world." Then he scanned the room again. "Must be where the really messed up go to get right with god. I'm sorry, god! But I do feel better being in your house. Purer, you know? After all that craziness, I'm happy to be here."

Trent ran his tongue over his teeth. Staring at the ceiling, as though he were staring into heaven, he said, "Go easy on Camilla and Gemma. I put them through hell. The clock. Yeah, the Dread Clock. Was that all you? Can't say I understood what it did, but it did make things better." He sighed. "Thanks, god. We needed it."

At this point, the chanting had become nothing more than background noise to him. But as he sat there, again scratching his face, an idea struck him. Putting his hand to his ear, he listened to his palm. The sound wasn't just around him, it was coming from him, too.

"Holy shit."

Aware of the dark words emerging from his flesh, he listened to his whole hand and arm, the top of his shoulders and the middle of his knees. He tried to stretch himself into other positions, but his aging bones kept threatening to break so he quickly stopped.

"What does this...?"

He stood up and stepped out of the pew. Giving the church a twice-over, he realized that the hymn wasn't some auditory oddity or a bunch of gossipy ghosts who were talking loud enough for the living to hear. No, the nuns who lived here were still here. These words that he was hearing had to be coming from them. And the words were more than a hymn or a chant. They were a net. A snare of strange syllables that had been cast across the convent, not necessarily to ensnare, but to exsanguinate. To drain the lifeblood, whatever it may be, from any object, animate or inanimate.

"That's why it's in me," Trent said, pacing the short length of the church. "I have to stop it. That's why I'm here. The Dread Clock. Can't quite remember. It was going to fix everything. Bet this is the last test. To cleanse me."

On his way out of the church, Trent noticed something he hadn't before. Wooden stairs, wedged inside the wall. At an almost vertical slope, they ran straight into the ceiling and stopped at the trapdoor there.

Trent shook his head and scampered up the steps, though perhaps ladder would have been a better way to describe them. At the top, he pushed back the trapdoor. On the other side was a cobwebbed dormitory with ten beds. Each one had been made with the utmost care. The only thing holding the beds back from perfection were the pillows. All ten of them were covered in vomit and black hairs.

He climbed into the dormitory. At once, he noticed a makeshift ladder hanging from a huge hole in the ceiling. Made out of clothes and undergarments, the ladder ran from the dormitory into what appeared to be the convent's attic. Staring up into the hole—the wood boards were blown out, as though something had punched through the ceiling—he noticed candlelight, and shadows.

They're up there, he thought, the dream skirting dangerously close to becoming a nightmare again. He mounted the ladder. Images flashed through his mind of his own attic in his own home, of a monster with a tail and pincers. At first, he had remembered the Dread Clock fondly, but now, not so much. He wanted purity, but all he seemed to get from the antique was putrefaction of his body and his soul.

Trent shook off the doubt. It hadn't done him any good at any other moment in his life, and after all, this was a dream. What else could he do until he woke but press forward? He climbed the ladder and, at the top, lifted himself into the smoky attic.

The Black Mass was happening at the back of the attic. Ten naked nuns, covered in boils and black fur, stood around an altar of candle wax. Upon the altar, a priest lay, his hands encased in stone, his feet bare and broken. Over his head, a paper mache death mask had been placed. There were a multitude of jars and bottles surrounding the priest. Filled with liquids of various color and thickness, Trent couldn't tell if they had been harvested from the priest, or gifted to him from the nuns.

Now that he had discovered the source of the hymn, he could make out what the nuns were saying. Beating their chests, as though the words were a cancer to be dislodged from their breasts, they chanted in unison, "Y'llorov. Y'llorov. Maya y'llorovaya. Gorovash. Gorovash. St'ka gorovashaya. Halakos en carane. Nexgroda en nakt."

To Trent's uncultured ears, the words sounded slightly Russian, but even then, he couldn't be sure.

The priest reared up and let out a scream. He struggled to lift his hands, but their stone fetters were too heavy. Turning his head, he caught Trent creeping behind the nuns and let out a garbled cry for help.

At that, the nuns, still chanting in robotic unison, slowly turned their heads. Trent stumbled back towards the ladder, but the nun with the stomach that sagged down to her knees held up her hand for him to stop.

Squinting her bloodshot eyes, she said, in a heavy accent, "English?"

Trent nodded. A woman screamed outside the convent, from where the garden would have been. He twisted his neck to see who it was, but there were no windows up here. It seemed strange to think about it, but the scream sounded familiar. It stirred something within him. He'd heard it before, and also, not long ago.

"What you want?" the fat nun asked. Her breasts were two fleshy stalactites that refused to stay still. "He brought you to see?"

"He?"

Trent cringed. More images were clawing their way through to this dreamy consciousness. The living room. Gemma. The feeling of weightlessness. And the weight of uselessness.

The fat nun pointed to the priest writhing on the candle wax altar.

"I don't know who that is." Trent's mouth hung open as he remembered a story his wife had told him. "You. Do you know the Dread Clock? Is it doing this? My memory isn't good."

"He is dog." The fat nun exchanged looks with her still-chanting sisters. "Y'llorov. Y'llorov. Maya y'llorovaya," she started. And then: "What is this 'Dread' you speak?"

Trent, ignoring the screaming outside, went forward, saying, "Its name."

Amused, the fat nun quickly corrected him. "Dread? No. The saint will not dread it."

Will not? Trent looked past the nun, to the priest. "It takes the sin out of the world."

At this, a second nun joined the conversation. She was younger. Her vagina had been sewn shut, and probably her anus, too. She looked bloated and sick, as though she had been soiling the inside of herself for days.

"Takes sin out?" the sewn nun asked. She laughed. "Sin is in the blood. Have to get rid of the blood."

The fat nun added, "Have to get rid of bloodline. Dread Clock isn't sponge. Dread Clock is scalpel. Going to make worlds better."

"Worlds?" Trent said.

"Where you think you are?" The fat nun wrinkled her brow. "What you think you are?"

"Good man?" the sewn nun said with a laugh. "Not if you here."

"—Gorovash. St'ka gorovashaya. Halakos en carane. Nexgroda en nakt." The eight nuns continued on.

"The Black Hour," Trent said, the words having just come to him.

A sinking feeling in his stomach told him this wasn't a dream, that wherever he was, he wasn't supposed to be here.

So he asked, "Do you know what it is? Where it comes from?"

The fat nun and the sewn nun exchanged looks with one another. Together, they both shrugged and said, "A better place. Come closer." They nodded at the priest. "See, before he sees you."

A spasm of pain shot through the priest. He arched his back until it started to crack.

"Y'llorov. Y'llorov. Maya y'llorovaya."

Splotches of blood spat onto the death mask. The priest's robes rippled with movement from the unseen beasts moving beneath them. His broken feet curved inward, bending beyond their limits.

"Gorovash. Gorovash. St'ka gorovashaya."

The priest bucked. His arms shot forward. The stone encased around his hands expanded and then eroded, until disproportionately large and shaped like pincers.

"Halakos en carane."

The robes tightened across the priest's body, until they were wrapped so tightly around him, they were him. The fabric hardened into a carapace, and became as black as the wild shadows whipping across the walls.

"Nexgroda en nakt."

With a jerk, the priest was torn off the altar and left to levitate there in the middle of the air. The death mask, soaked with blood and wax, melted and bubbled over his face. Out of his chest, a second pair of smaller arms, like a child's, tore through his new, dark skin. They clawed at the invisible strings that seemed to hold him, as though begging for release.

"Nexgoroda en nakt," the nuns repeated.

Then, the nun with goat eyes: "Ueun ex nakt."

The priest's spine jutted out of his back. From his tailbone, the bone bore through his flesh and unwound around him. Until, twice his size, the tail stopped growing and, at its tip, the bones there ballooned into the black swell of a stinger.

"How intimately we know one another now," a voice whispered into Trent's ear.

He tore himself away from the scene. Behind him, the Dread Clock's Keeper floated. Trent looked back to the altar, but the priest was gone.

"Strange how they all end up here."

The Keeper's pincers grabbed Trent's sides and lifted him off the ground. "You've given me almost everything. But to have everything." The Keeper brought its stinger to Trent's sweaty forehead. "I must give you something in return."

The Keeper's stinger stabbed through Trent's skull, and then the convent went dark. Somewhere between a coma and consciousness, his mind struggled to find something to hold on to. Blind and numb, he turned to his memories to try and make sense of what was happening to him.

They were all there, every event and incident, like a string of pearls, stretching from his birth to what might have just been his death. He returned to the memory of the convent, and the Keeper plunging its black stinger into his gray matter. He knew this creature, and by the memories that came before it, he obviously knew it well. How did he forget? Did it make him? Or did he make himself?

Trent traveled backward along the string of experiences. Some didn't make sense—being a slave master in the South, a soldier in World War II—while others were so disgusting and disturbing, the pearl was almost unreadable. But four things were consistent amongst them all: the Black Hour, the Dread Clock, its Keeper, and his eventual repulsion to them all. Coming here, to this convent—it hadn't been a dream, and it hadn't been to get better. The Keeper had brought him here, and Camilla. And if he was remembering this right, Gemma—oh Christ, oh god, Gemma—she was here, too.

If he wasn't dead, then maybe he was dying. And if he was dying, then like the dying, he had an overwhelming need to undo all the terrible choices he had made not only in the last few days, but the last thirteen years. Whether or not he actually could didn't really matter. As long as he could understand why he'd made them and what had led him and his wife to this depraved limbo, then perhaps, if he got free, he could make the right choice for once and save Gemma, wherever she may be.

He hurried through the string of memories. Birthday party after birthday party. Late night dinners, and the occasional funnel cake and festival. A vacation here, domestic violence there. It pained him to realize it, but the further back in time he went, the worse things were between him and Camilla. Nowadays, divorce was always a looming threat, but back then, five, ten years ago, they didn't even mention it. Because of Gemma, divorce wasn't an option. So instead, night after night, when their daughter went to bed, they pummeled each other into teary submission. Mostly with words, but they had both exchanged their fair share of blows. The only bright spot in these old memories was Gemma, but even then, because of them, she didn't burn as brightly as she could have. If anything, that was their ultimate sin.

Trent picked up the pace. He knew where he was going, but curiosity kept distracting him. *There*, he thought. Thirteen years back. That putrid pearl of a night where he confessed everything to Camilla and gave her nothing but grief afterward. Candice was there, that bloated, post-pregnancy whale, and so was Gemma, so tiny and pure. And he even remembered the speech he had prepared for his wife. *Camilla, I have to tell you something*, it started. *I deserve every ounce of hate you have for me*, it ended.

But on this part of the strand, something was wrong. Not that he was an expert on memories. He wasn't an expert on anything, except being an expert at nothing. But yes, there was something wrong. The trivial corridors of time that connected each pearl of importance were frayed. And this thirteen-year-old catalyst? It was corroded. There was something in that moment, a kind of black mass that was slowly filling the pearl, turning whatever second, minute, or hour it touched into a lie.

Trent's first mistake was coming to this memory, thinking he could learn anything from it. Trent's second mistake was trying to fix it. His mind reached out for the recollection. As it did, the string that held the memories snapped, spilling the infected moment and millions of others across his mindscape.

The effect was immediate. His past became a fractured series of meaningless scenes and vaguely recognizable people and places. The damage wasn't just in the distant past, either. As memory after memory slid off the string, even events from a year ago became too difficult to make sense of. The confusion they inspired was agonizing, like a lightning storm raging across his brain.

He had to fix this. He couldn't save Camilla or Gemma if he didn't know them. He gathered up hundreds of memories, put them in what he thought was the right order. But as he waded through his own lifetime, it got harder and harder to read the pearls. The black mass from the memory of thirteen years ago had oozed out. It was everywhere, and it was in everything, infecting every memory that it came into contact with.

Trent moved as quickly as he could, but the corruption was quicker. Soon, he began to abandon memories so that he could salvage those which were most important to him. Wading through the black muck in his mind, he plucked out pearls for safekeeping. He started with those moments before the marriage, when he and Camilla were happy and arguments were five minute scuffles that a crappy joke or a bottle of wine could fix. But there were so many good times that he had to leave some behind.

The more he dwelled on what had been, the less he had any sway over what could be. So he hurried through the black mire filling up his skull, seeking out his wedding day and honeymoon night. There had been this one time, on a mountain with Camilla, that he absolutely loved. The sun had been setting, and the forest glowed orange and red. She had been smiling so hard, it had to have hurt. And then she told him she loved him. But the way she said it was different than before. Like it was some universal truth only they had figured out. God, where was that? He had to find—

The pearls of memory were quickly disappearing into the black mass. Trent jumped ahead years to after he had brought Gemma home. He went to the memory of her first word—Bat; hence, her stuffed animal, Scram—and the first time she walked for a good two seconds across the living room, where the Dread Clock now stood. After that, he found her first day at school, and the afternoon that happened later, when they bought her a bunch of toys, to bribe her so she'd go back the next day.

Trent was frantic. Every memory he passed up that had to do with Gemma broke his heart. Like a covetous dragon and its clutch of gold, he wanted them all. This thing that had invaded his mind, it didn't deserve these memories. To make him pick and choose… it was like picking a favorite child and sending the rest out to die in the rain. He couldn't do it. He wouldn't do it. This was his mind. These were his memories. Gemma was his daughter, and Camilla his wife. Amazing or agonizing, it didn't matter. They were his, and they were him. Without even one of them, he wouldn't be Trent, and he couldn't do that—

Corrupted pearls of memory bobbed to the top of the black mass. They rolled along the oily surface and fixed themselves to their proper places on the string. Trent hurried towards the most recent moments and polished the filth from them the best that he could. Gemma. The Dread Clock. Camilla. The Dread Clock. Oh god, had he really tried to touch his daughter like that? He dropped the orb into the mass, but the mass made no effort to fill it. It was tainted enough already.

Trent's mind seized, like a strip of land about to break to an earthquake. In an instant, his past was remade. The string was complete, and the pearls that had fallen off it back in their proper place. But the content was wrong, the recollections warped. They were funhouse mirrors forged in malice, polished with spit.

Everything a year out from today was wrong. Especially anything that had to do with Gemma. The love he had for her was gone. The only emotion he had for her was hate. A long-standing hate, like a stagnant puddle no amount of happiness could dry up. What was this? It didn't make sense. He knew he loved her, because in these recent memories of his, he did. He loved her unconditionally. He loved her more than Camilla, more than himself. Yet, ten years back, there he was, scolding her, making fun of her, sending her to school with no food and dirty clothes and laughing when she told him all the kids had laughed at her. And he felt justified for doing it. Like she had it coming. Like she was some pet that had pissed on the carpet and needed to be taught a lesson.

Disgusted, Trent retreated into recent memories, but they had been altered, too. The dark filth that filled the pearls had spread to them, as well. It was traveling through his memories, consuming them; replacing them with its foul regurgitations and passing the mush off as truth.

Trent bore his mind down on the string of life events and tried to break it, to stop the black mass from infecting everything. But the string would not give. Hate had hardened it. Entitlement reinforced it. In the blink of his mind's eye, his little Gemma, so smart, so creative, so beautiful and talented, became something he feared and regretted.

He screamed, even though he couldn't scream, as memories twisted upon themselves, doing everything they could to make his daughter the culprit of all life's crimes. Anything that broke in the house, it was Gemma's fault. Any argument he had with Camilla, it was because of Gemma's behavior. His beautiful girl became disfigured, repulsive; a sum of all the shitty features her birth mother, Candice, possessed or put into herself. He found himself getting angry thinking about Gemma. About the fact she still lived at home with them. About the fact that she had told her mother to buy the Dread Clock, just to get back at him. About the fact that she had gone to her friend's house last night, to talk badly about her parents, and to spend the money she probably stole from his wallet.

Where once he had wanted to hug her, he wanted to hurt her. He started to think about the excuses he could come up with that would keep Children's Services at bay should someone notice a bruise or a welt. He remembered the moment with Camilla, where they both agreed to take care of Gemma, no matter what. And then he remembered it differently. He remembered the medical bills, the late hour screaming. He remembered how, even at a young age, Gemma seemed so damned determined to ruin their lives.

He hadn't taken her from Candice to protect her and raise. No, Candice had dropped her off, threatened to accuse him of rape if he didn't raise Gemma for her. And Gemma never appreciated what they did for her. No, never. She always wanted to go back to Candice. Sometimes, she'd cut herself, or even... Jesus, yesterday, they caught her with a boy up in that cave. Pregnant at thirteen. Bullshit. Not going to happen. He would do everything in his power to make sure that baby didn't survive. He wouldn't be embarrassed by Gemma anymore. He wasn't going to give up his life or Camilla's for this ungrateful wretch anymore.

Black had been the hours since her birth. If this midnight were ever going to end, then she had to leave.

GEMMA

The last time Gemma woke up face down on the living room floor, it was because she had mistaken a bottle of vodka for a bottle of water. A big swig in the small hours had sent her careening through the house like a runaway bumper car. When she came to then, she was alone.

This time she hadn't been so lucky. As she peeled her face away from the carpet, there were two people standing over her. And they weren't her mom or dad.

"Don't say anything," the smaller one, a young guy, whispered. He knelt down beside her and said, "Actually, never mind. Can you tell me—"

The older man slapped his bald head and said, "Which one is it, college kid?"

"Shut up, man. Hey, uh, Gemma, right?"

She nodded. Eyes catching up with the rest of her mind, she could tell this guy was in his mid-twenties. He had black gloves on and black clothes. He smelled weird, too. Like a hospital, and the bottom of a garbage can.

Gemma managed to mutter, "Get... away from me," before she lost consciousness for a second.

"Do you remember the clock?" the older man asked.

Gemma's eyes shot open. She rolled over. The Dread Clock. It wasn't here. Where it should have been, it wasn't. And where it had been, there were scorch marks... and a stack of one hundred dollar bills.

"You're a brave girl," the old man said. He tapped the young guy and told him it was time to go.

"What did you do with it?" Gemma grabbed the young guy's pant leg. "Who are you? How did you? Where is it?"

"Uh, can I tell her our names?" he asked the older man.

The older man groaned.

"God, what? We just bagged the Dread Clock. I'm sorry if I'm a little out of it."

"Connor?" Gemma croaked. "I read your website. G-Gethin, the antique shop owner said you were coming to get it."

The old man let out a laugh. Gemma craned her neck to have a better look at him. Yeah, definitely old. What did Uncle Jasper use to say? Had more wrinkles than a nut sack. And there was a faded scar on his neck, like someone had cut open his throat.

"I don't know how much you remember," the old man said.

"Everything," Gemma told him. And that was true. The nights before this morning, and everything she had seen in the Dread Clock— she remembered it all.

"I'm sorry for that, Gemma. That's one thing we can't take away from you." He sighed. "My name's Herbert North. This guy next to

THE BLOOD OF BEFORE

me, so wet behind the ears you can see it in the sunlight, his name is Connor Prendergast. That's his website, but I wrote the Dread Clock article."

Connor made a noise to interrupt, then stopped himself.

"We usually stay, to counsel. But we have to get the Dread Clock out of here right away. It's maybe the most dangerous object in the world. I know you know this, because when we pulled you and your mommy and daddy out, you were telling us what you saw inside it."

"W-where are they?" Gemma, still struggling to stay awake, scanned the room for her parents. "How did you get us...?"

"They're in their beds," Connor said. "Sleepwalked right into them. I don't think they remember anything."

Gemma sat up and scooted backward until she was against the foot of Mom's fifteen-hundred-dollar chair.

"Used spells to get you out," Connor said. "The Dread Clock still works outside of midnight, but it's a lot weaker."

"Learned a trick for finding people from a giant mosquito," Herbert said, grinning, "but that's, uh, neither here nor there. Listen, Gemma, Connor put his phone number in your cell. He does that with all the ladies he meets. Most of them never call him back, because, I mean, look at him."

Connor smiled and widened his eyes, like a starlet.

Herbert said, "We can't stay. And I don't think your parents remember. But I know you do. And that's a lot to shoulder. So call us, when you need us. There's not much we can tell you, other than to hang in there. You're going to feel like you're crazy, but just know you're not crazy alone. We've seen it, too."

Tears welled in Gemma's eyes. "If they don't remember, will they be okay, then?"

"Most people go back to the way they were," Connor said.

Back to the way they were? Gemma snarled at the thought. They'd go back to fighting every day? Granted, that was better than what they were turning into, but if they knew what the Dread Clock did to them, to her, maybe they would have tried to be different.

"Will they know I went into the clock to save them?" Gemma asked, voice shaking.

Herbert and Connor exchanged glances. Together, they said, "You did?"

Gemma nodded. She pointed to where the Dread Clock had been

277

and said, "I went through the case. There was a portal. I tried to save them."

"Oh wow, that makes sense," Herbert said.

"Yeah, yes, yeah," Connor agreed.

Wiping her eyes, Gemma said, "What? What does?"

"Pulling someone out of the Dread Clock isn't easy. They lose themselves almost immediately. They want to stay." Herbert tapped his chin. "Your love for them must have kept them from losing everything."

"I don't know," Gemma said. "I saw them—"

"No, he's right." Connor nodded. "They were very lucky to have such a brave girl save them."

Gemma laughed. Tears leapt from her eyes. "Are you two real? This isn't how I thought this would end."

"Things like this seldom end any way but insanely," Herbert said. "You have a strong family, Gemma. Most don't last this long. The Dread Clock chews through people. Often, all it takes is just one night."

"Strong?" Maybe they were. After all, after everything, they were still together.

Connor checked the time on his phone and then said, "Here's the plan, Gemma. We had to break in to Gethin's antique shop to get your address. He wasn't there, or home. And when we came here, the place was… a mess."

"My room. All my stuff is outside." Gemma tried to get to her feet. "We have to get rid of anything that might make them remember."

"Don't worry," Connor said. "We cleaned it all up the best we could. We don't really know what a girl's room should look like, so you might need to do some rearranging, but it's all up there."

Gemma smiled. "Thank you."

"Oh, except for this guy." Connor reached behind him and pulled her stuffed bat, Scram, from his back pocket.

She took it from him, and then pressed Scram to her face to soak up her tears. At this point in her life, he had a whole ocean's worth of tears inside him.

"Everything should look pretty close to the way it was before the Dread Clock showed up, okay?" Connor pointed to the scorched floor and the money on top of it. "We made it look like a robbery, because if we flat out told your parents we were taking it, then they might remember. And we don't want to see them try to take the clock back. The money is how much your mom paid for it. It'll be weird for her to find it, I know, but money is money. I don't think they'll ask too many questions."

"No," Gemma said, shaking her head. "No, I think my dad will be over the moon."

"Good," Herbert said. "I hate to leave you all like this, but we have to get this thing very far away from here, from anyone. Call us, Gemma, if you need to."

Connor headed for the front door. Opening it, he said, "I don't want to jinx it, but I think everything's going to be okay for you."

Gemma's mom and dad woke up a few hours later. They stumbled down the stairs, one after the other, talking about what time it was, if the coffee was ready, and if it wasn't, who was going to make it. Gemma, who hadn't left the living room, jumped to her feet when she heard them and went to the staircase, a big, stupid smile on her face.

Before Mom had even made it to the landing, she knew that something was wrong. She pushed past Gemma, ran into the living room, and started screaming at the top of her lungs about the burn marks in the carpet. Dad, glaring at Gemma, hurried down the stairs to see the damage done. Gemma told them that it looked like someone had broken into the house. They didn't mention the Dread Clock, but they didn't seem to believe Gemma about the robbery, either.

In the weeks that followed, Mom and Dad were different. They didn't fight like they used to; in fact, they barely fought at all. They woke early in the morning and went to bed early at night. Every Saturday, her parents went out to dinner, just the two of them. They didn't really talk to Gemma very much, and when they did, they had a look on their faces like they had just smelled something awful.

Her parents' behavior hurt a lot more than Gemma let on. But she couldn't hold it against them, because she hadn't recovered from the Dread Clock, either. Every night, she had nightmares, and every morning, she woke mourning the loss of something she couldn't place. She made a lot of phone calls to Herbert and Connor during that time. They didn't answer much, being busy supernatural hunters and all, but when they did, they told her this was normal. They even offered to come back to the town in the fall. Gemma, instead of shouting yes, because she wanted to sound strong, told them she'd think about it.

Everything went awful in August. Mom took her cell phone, wiped her contacts, and told her she couldn't have it back because she couldn't be trusted with it. Dad cancelled their Internet subscription and started locking her in her room at night because he was tired of her "talking to boys." The cave suddenly became off-limits. And any time Gemma brought up Uncle Jasper and his disappearance, her dad made a fist, as though he were going to hit her.

Gemma didn't understand what was happening to her parents. They had isolated her from friends, as well as anything that would help her make sense of what was going on with them. She couldn't be around them without one or the other bringing up something Gemma had done during the school year. If it wasn't her grades, then it was the fights. And if it wasn't the fights, then it was something Gemma didn't even remember doing. They kept talking about the boys at school, or how they smelled pot on her. They kept bringing up some woman named Candice, and how Gemma was "just like her."

Two weeks until school started, and Gemma couldn't take it anymore. Every day, every time they saw her, they pointed out some flaw of hers. They blamed her for things she knew hadn't happened because the details didn't make sense. They said she had keyed a neighbor's car, which wasn't true, because they had no neighbors. Then they said they got a call from Jen's mother, complaining about Gemma and how she had been flirting with her husband a few days ago. Which didn't even make any fucking sense, because Gemma hadn't been over there since she came home to save them from the Dread Clock.

The lies mounted so quickly that Gemma couldn't keep track of them. Suffocated by all the bullshit, she stormed into the kitchen one night and told them everything. She told them about the Dread Clock, the Black Hour. About how it had changed them, how it was still changing them. She showed them Herbert's and Connor's website. She even ratted the two men out and said they had been the ones to take the clock away from the home. The men had warned her not to remind her parents about the antique, but what else could she do? If they saw the way they were treating her, they would have done the same thing.

Before Gemma had finished her story, Dad was already calling 911 to have an ambulance come to the house and transport her to the hospital. Gemma didn't fight the EMTs when they arrived because she knew that would make matters worse.

Still convinced that this was the work of the Dread Clock, she buried her rage and sadness. When she got to the hospital, she was quiet and compliant. They checked her over, found the self-inflicted cuts on her leg. They asked her if she wanted to hurt herself anymore, or if she wanted to hurt anyone else. They asked about hallucinations and drug use. They even asked if anyone was hurting her in the house and, for a moment, Gemma, the Thirteen-Year-Old Destroyer, was tempted to say yes. Tempted to tell the hospital anything it took to get her parents the help they needed.

Gemma didn't say anything, though. She kept her mouth shut, her hope intact, and suffered a two week stay in the psychiatric ward. She had nightmares about adults and what they were capable of. It made her sick to think that, in five years, she'd be one of them herself. She didn't think she would be capable of the things she had seen others do in the Black Hour, but at some point, when they were younger, more naïve, they had probably felt the same way.

When she got out, she got out with meds, a diagnosis of Bipolar Disorder, and a referral to a community therapist she actually couldn't wait to see.

Her parents picked her up from the hospital, but they weren't taking her home. The back seat was filled with her bags. When she opened them, she found all her clothes inside. Scram was there, too. She couldn't figure out if that was the last act of kindness they were capable of, or if they were using him to rub something in her face.

Mom told Gemma she was out of control. Dad told Gemma they couldn't handle her anymore. They made up lies about her behavior in the hospital. After thinking long and hard, they said they'd both decided that living at home wasn't the best place for someone like her. Mom told Gemma she could come back to them one day. Dad told Gemma not to count on it, though.

There was a pamphlet on the back seat underneath her bags. Still in disbelief, Gemma ignored her parents and read it. It was for a boarding school. Our Ladies of Sorrow Academy. A place where maladaptive children were sent to be corrected and made appropriate members of society.

Gemma laughed, crumpled the pamphlet into a ball, and threw it at the back of her dad's head.

"Fuck you," she said. "Fuck both of you."

It was a twenty-six-hour drive. They drove it straight-through. They kept the car doors and the windows locked. When they stopped for gas, either her mom or dad stayed behind to watch her and make sure she didn't run away. Sometimes, Gemma would see how far she could push their limits by screaming for help or kicking their seats for hours on end. But in the end, it didn't seem to matter. As they so succinctly put it every chance they could, she had to go.

Two states later, and Our Ladies of Sorrow Academy stopped being words on a pamphlet and became an etched threat on the roadside mile markers. Thirty miles to go. Twenty-five miles to go. If Gemma was going to escape, now would have been the time to do it. And she could have, too. She could have hurt her father really badly, or busted out one of the windows until they had to pull over to stop her.

Ten miles to go. Five miles to go. Time was running out to run, and yet here she stayed, in a car full of her stuff and the parents who hated her, thinking to herself that maybe, just maybe, somehow, somewhere along the line, she had done something to deserve this.

The car pulled off the road onto a long, gravelly drive and followed it for five minutes into the forest. It was dinner time, and the sun was eager to be out of the darkening sky. Gemma's shirt was so hot and sticky from crying, she changed into another just so she could wipe her tears onto something dry.

"This is for the best," Dad said, breaking six hours of silence between them. He looked in the rear-view mirror. His eyes were bloodshot. Had he been crying, too?

Mom undid her seatbelt and started going through her purse for forms. "There's no way to keep in contact with us, except through mail. A letter every two months. No more. I want you to focus on being better."

Gemma pressed herself to the window as the forest thinned and the gravelly drive opened up to a wide lot. Our Ladies of Sorrow Academy didn't look like a boarding school, but a prison. It was a three-story mansion, all red brick and black mortar. The windows were barred, and the doors chained. And, if that wasn't enough, the property was surrounded by a ten-foot, wrought iron fence that someone like Vlad the Impaler would have had a field day with.

"You're getting rid of me. For good," she said, fogging the glass.

"You did it to yourself," Mom answered.

"What did I really do?" Gemma lurched forward as Dad brought the car to a stop in front of the gates. She pleaded, "Why? This isn't you guys. This isn't you."

Dad turned off the car. "Gemma, it's you. It's always been you. We've been beating each other up, not wanting to face the facts. You're the worst thing that has ever happened to us."

The words hit Gemma like a freight train. Too shaken to speak, she could only mouth, "What?"

"When you're older, and maybe have children of your own, you'll understand."

"Fuck you," Gemma said. "Fuck you. No. I don't want to be older. I don't want to be like you. After everything I did for you and—"

"All you did," Mom said, "was waste our time and money. Just like you're doing now. So why don't you get out—"

Gemma's door unlocked.

"—and waste someone else's time and money, instead?"

Gemma spat in her mom's face. She grabbed her bags and said, "This isn't you. It's the Dread Clock."

"Gemma," Dad said, turning in his seat. "If that were true, then why are you mad at us? Save us now, why don't you? You said you did before."

"Goodbye, Gemma," Mom said, faking a smile. Handing her the forms for the school, she added, "You'll thank us later. You'll see."

Gemma took the forms, kicked open the door. She threw her bags onto the ground and hurried out of the car. Mom and Dad settled into their seats, started up the engine, and then drove off, back the way they'd come. They didn't roll down the window to say goodbye, or give her a look to tell her this wasn't their fault, that they weren't in control of themselves. They just left her there, at the school's black gates, like a sick pet they didn't want to take care of anymore.

Gemma picked up her bags. She took out Scram and stowed him in her back pocket. The forest looked pretty big, but all she had to do was follow the drive back to the main road. They had passed a town about forty-five minutes ago. She could get there, get on a computer. Track down Herbert and Connor and tell them what happened. Maybe they had a spell or something that could fix—

The wrought iron gates screeched to life. Gemma spun around, the shock of it zapping her thoughts. The front gate hadn't opened all the way. Just enough for her to squeeze through, to get onto the main property. If she ran, would they send the police after her? If she stayed, would she ever get out again?

Further ahead, another noise sounded. Our Ladies of Sorrow Academy's front door shook and then slowly crept open. The chain that had been fixed to it fell across the porch and slithered like a serpent into the nearby bushes.

"Hello?" Gemma called, one hand gripping the fence.

A Native American teenage girl emerged from the mansion. She was tall, lithe; had the look of a ballerina that only danced in the dark. She wore a long, green dress with a red collar. Looking more closely, Gemma saw that the girl had bandages wrapped around her hands, as though she had hurt herself on something.

"You must be Gemma," the girl said. She waved her over to the school. "Come in. It's been a long ride here, hasn't it?"

She nodded. Long ride? That was putting it lightly.

"I know that you are scared. I was scared, too, when I came here. But this is a good place. A much better place than where you came from."

Defensively, Gemma shouted, "How do you know that?"

The girl shrugged one shoulder. "Why else would you be here?"

Gemma threw back her head and laughed. "Because I'm 'maladaptive.'"

"Oh, no. No, no."

The girl started down the porch. She crossed the yard, but in a curious manner. She kept to the shadows, to where the light didn't touch. It reminded Gemma of a game she used to play where she pretended the floor was lava, and she had to hop from furniture to furniture to survive. Except, looking at this girl, she kind of got the impression that, if she did go in the light, something bad would happen.

At the gate, in a healthy pool of darkness, the girl extended her hand to Gemma and said, "My name is Eyota."

Gemma stared at Eyota's hand. Though it was tightly bound in bandages, she could tell there was something underneath the wraps; something wriggling, trying to get free.

"Observant," Eyota said, retracting her hand. "But maladaptive? No."

Gemma looked over her shoulder. She could still run. Could probably beat the crap out of this girl if she had to.

"We just put that in the flyer to attract the right people."

Gemma reached behind her and touched Scram. "You mean the fuck-ups?"

"We are our parents. Are they not the ones who fuck us up?"

What is this? Gemma nodded because she didn't know what else to do, and said, "Who runs this place?"

"Ah, we do, Gemma." Eyota nodded at the school, at the figures who were now gathered in the dusty windows. "There are no adults here, if that's what you're asking."

"That sounds fucking great," Gemma said. She kicked her bags. Then: "But I don't believe you."

"Go look for yourself." Eyota stepped aside. "Leave anytime you like."

"After what my parents..." Gemma choked up. She took a deep breath and buried the pain. "They wouldn't send me to a place run by kids."

"I don't know, Gemma." Eyota started back towards the mansion, hopping from shadow to shadow. "After I saw how fast they drove out of here, I think they would have sent you anywhere, as long as they could have gotten away with it."

True, Gemma thought. *They would have killed me if they could have. Is that what they were planning to do, if we hadn't saved them? The Dread Clock brings out the worst, but the worst has to already be there to begin with. I'm so stupid. I should have let them go—*

Gemma turned off her thoughts and slid through the gates. There was no sense in pretending as though she were going to run away. The closer she came to the mansion, the less put-off she felt by it. Intimidating, yes, but out here, in the forest, almost an hour away from any form of civilization, it seemed like a world all its own. And in a way, that's what she needed right now.

"Gemma, come here," Eyota said.

She had stopped midway to mansion, beneath a weeping willow so large and weeping, it had to have had some form of clinical depression.

Gemma went to her, joined her in the shadows there. A breeze circulated around the willow and cooled her nerves. She leaned in and smelled the tree. Filling her nose with that ancient odor, she took one of its leaves and pressed it to her face. Her skin prickled, and her heart skipped a beat. She slipped out of her sweaty shoes and sank her feet into the grass. Anchored there, she let Nature overcome her, to remind her there was more to life than the despair that had brought her here.

"Sorry," she said, snapping out of the trance. "There was this cave back home I used to go to when I got stressed out. I guess I needed this."

"I understand," Eyota said. She started unraveling the bandage on her left hand. "So what brought you here?"

Gemma laughed. She bit her lip, bided her time. *Can't hurt*, she thought, so she said it: "Ever heard of the Dread Clock?"

"Yeah, of course," Eyota said, one layer of the bandage removed.

"Shut the hell up."

"Seriously." Another layer of the bandage fell away.

Gemma took out Scram and held him to her chest. "I don't believe you."

The third layer of the bandage unraveled as Eyota said, "Big grandfather clock. Makes the Black Hour happen at midnight. Terrible things come after that. We know it, Gemma. I don't think it's a coincidence you're here. Many of us at Our Ladies of Sorrow Academy have been made Orphans by it."

The fourth layer of the bandage fell away from Eyota's hand. Gemma gasped as she noticed a long slit running down the girl's palm. It looked fresh. The folds of the wound still glistened with rank wetness.

"Oh my god, are you okay?" Gemma covered her mouth. "What happened?"

"Oh, I'm fine." Eyota held her wrist and started to rub the bones there. "Gemma, this is a place for people who don't want to grow up, and who are tired of grown-ups and the way they use us."

The skin on her palm started to bubble.

"This is a place where kids like us can make a difference, for as long as we want to."

And then a mouth inside Eyota's hand pushed against the dripping folds. Greedily, it gulped at the air, like a leech desperate for blood.

"Oh, what the fuck?" Gemma stumbled backward towards the gate. "Oh what the fuck? I'm still in the Dread Clock. This is still the Dread Clock."

Eyota shook her head. "You know that's not true."

"Then what the hell are you?!"

"A vampyre," she said. She unraveled the bandages on her other hand, revealing a mouth in its palm as well. "Biting necks is awkward. But we touch each other all the time. Pretty cool, right?"

"No," Gemma said. She found the nearest patch of sunlight and stood there. "No, no get away from me."

"Gemma," Eyota said, stepping out of the shadows. Her body twitched, but the light didn't seem to stop her. "Do you want to be like them?"

Gemma shook her head.

"Do you want to give up the childhood they've almost ruined?"

Again, she shook her head.

"Do you want to find the Dread Clock with us and stop it?"

Gemma didn't move.

"It's still out there. We vampyres cannot die. You can be young forever. You can have forever to do what you want; to get what you deserve. To make that perfect life for yourself, and to be strong enough to stop anyone who wants to take it away from you."

"You're going to turn me into a fucking vampyre?" Gemma laughed and rolled her eyes. "Oh my god, what the hell is happening to me?"

"You're getting a second chance, Gemma," Eyota said, once again extending her hand. "All you have to do is take it. Tell me, when's the last time you got to make a choice for yourself that really mattered?"

I don't know, Gemma thought, watching the mouth in Eyota's hand open and close. *Never?*

"Sunlight hurts," Eyota said, "and we have to drink blood. But we're teenagers, so that's not that big of a deal right?" She laughed, winked.

"What if I say no?" Gemma eyed the gate, yet she found herself drawn to the girl, to the academy. "Are you going to kill me?"

"No," Eyota said. "But what are you going to do? Wander around, hating your parents, going out of your way to get back at them?"

Gemma dug her heel into the ground. She broke into random fits of laughter. This was so fucking absurd. But was it? After everything she'd been through, was this that much worse? A vampyre made more sense than something like the Black Hour or the Dread Clock. She hated to admit it, but Eyota was right. She couldn't do a damn thing as Gemma, except get picked up by the cops and get sent to the hospital or juvie.

And her mom and dad? She saw how they turned out, before the Dread Clock and after it, too. She herself was both of them, but which parts? The good parts? The bad parts? Did it matter? She had seen what adults could do. What depths they were willing to sink to for the stupidest of reasons. Slavery. War. Children didn't cause these things.

Children were the ones who suffered for their elders' mistakes. Children were the ones who would then repeat them later on, when they were stronger, and meaner.

Maybe the Dread Clock had put something in her, too, and it was just waiting for the right time to take her over. It had, hadn't it? Right before she passed out in the concentration camp. When that creature told her how worthless she was. And she believed it. Oh, hell. Was she a ticking time bomb? A slow-burning fuse leading up to a night of razor blades and hot bath water?

Gemma grabbed herself, started to panic. She couldn't trust this skin. She couldn't trust the dark within. Tears in her eyes, she ran forward and took Eyota's hand. The mouth in the girl's palm went to work immediately. It clamped down on Gemma's flesh and sank its small, greedy teeth in deep. Thin, buzzing tendrils, like those of a jellyfish, shot into Gemma's hand from the mouth and slithered down the inside of her arm. They attached themselves to her veins and arteries and pumped something warm and numbing into her bloodstream.

"Everything will be better in a moment," Eyota said, closing her arm around her, bringing her into a hug. "This is the only time anyone can say that and not be lying."

Gemma closed her eyes and let the change overtake her. At this point, it didn't matter if she made the right decision or not. She was tired of fighting, and of having to fight. She had gone through hell. She should have known that hell was the only thing she could have brought back with her. Gemma, the Thirteen-Year-Old Destroyer, had endured a long campaign of misery, and for what? More misery? She had tried being herself, now it was time to be something else.

Gemma opened her eyes, her vision sharper than before. Darkness had descended upon Our Ladies of Sorrow Academy, and all across its slanted rooftops were children, just like her.

The Black Hour's orphans raised their hungry hands to Gemma, to welcome her into the only family to which she ever truly belonged.

YOU HAVE BEEN READING

"THE BLOOD OF BEFORE."

ABOUT THE AUTHOR

SCOTT HALE is the author of *The Bones of the Earth* series and screen-writer of *Entropy, Free to a Bad Home, and Effigies*. He is the co-owner of Hale-house Productions. He is a graduate from Northern Kentucky University with a Bachelors in Psychology and Masters in Social Work. He has completed *The Bones of the Earth* series and his standalone horror novel, *In Sheep's Skin*. Scott Hale currently resides in Norwood, Ohio with his wife and frequent collaborator, Hannah Graff, and their three cats, Oona, Bashik, and Bellatrix.

Printed in Great Britain
by Amazon